GOOD AS IT GETS

OTHER BOOKS BY SAMANTHA BEAL

The Directory Series

The Cleaner

The Mover

The Keeper

Standalones

Good As It Gets

Good As It Gets

Samantha Beal

All characters and events in this publication are fictitious. Any resemblance to real persons, living or dead, is coincidental.

ISBN: 979-8-993-78031-3

First paperback edition: March 2026

Cover and interior design and layout by Samantha Beal.
Author photo by Elizabeth Beal.

Visit Samm at www.samanthabeal.com.

Disclaimer: Once upon a time, Sheetz sold Krispy Kremes. It no longer does. For the sake of Mollie's sanity, I took some creative liberties.

To the Store 21911 Chapter of the
Samm Beal Hate Club:
Love you guys!!
XXOO,
S.

LITTLE DROP RUN
(#4 on Top 10 Most Humiliating Incidents list)
BISHOP FURNACE
PITCHETTE POST OFFICE
TUCKER'S HARDWARE
PAINT AVENUE
RUN ROAD
FOUNDATIONS FITNESS
GINO'S BARBERSHOP
SAL'S DINER
PITCHETTE VFD
FIREMAN'S LANE
MAN STREET
IGA
PITCHETTE PUBLIC LIBRARY
JOHNSON STREET
CART AVENUE
SOUTH STREET
RISEN HILL CEMETERY
(#2 on Top 10 Most Humiliating Incidents list)
Welcome to
PITCHETTE
pop. 1,200

Mollie's 'No Fs Left' Playlist

"Bad Reputation" by Joan Jett & the Blackhearts

"Trouble" by P!NK

"Fighter" by Christina Aguilera

"Sk8er Boi" by Avril Lavigne

"Teenage Dirtbag" by Wheatus

"Take Me Away" by Christina Vidal Mitchell

ONE

The navigation app on your phone might not say you've crossed the border into Pennsylvania, but there will be signs.

I don't mean the giant blue signs installed by the Pennsylvania Department of Transportation. I mean Biblical signs. Roadkill being at the top of the list. Unmanned construction sites being at the bottom. And in between, potholes that literally swallow whole vehicles and Ohio drivers pretending the interstate is the Indy 500.

Hard to believe this is the land of Philly cheesesteaks and *Mister Rogers' Neighborhood*, right? I mean, who the heck looks at a half-width construction site for raveling asphalt on Interstate 76 and thinks stuff like, *'Taylor Swift grew up just north of here.'* NO ONE. NO ONE thinks stuff like that.

Actually, that's not true. *I* think stuff like that.

Of course, I've been on the road for over three hours after spending the last three days cramming my life into boxes and figuring out if there's a way I can break my Michigan Avenue loft lease without paying three more months of rent. News flash: there isn't. Apparently.

Damn D.C. property management companies.

So yeah. I have my Honda Passport on cruise control and my mind on Taylor Swift.

Honestly, when it comes right down to it, there's only one difference between Taylor and me. She's not Mollie Maris. I am.

Okay. Maybe if I put a little effort into it, I can come up with a half-way decent analogy here. Something about Taylor's Captain of the Cheer Squad look versus my Medusa Had a *Really* Bad Hair Day image.

Or maybe that when Taylor cries in public, she warms hearts. When I cry in public, I warm faces.

Or that as a thirty-something, she owns eight houses. As a thirty-something, I own eight hair ties.

The point is, if I wasn't burned out and strung out, I'd be full of zingers right now. Some really great, jaw-dropping, knock-you-on-your-ass one-liners.

Okay, maybe half-liners.

The truth is, I recently scuttled the last of my creativity writing a letter of resignation to the top-tier marketing firm I worked for in D.C. for the last eight years.

I mean, geez. You don't just *not* put effort into your two-weeks' notice when you work for a top-tier marketing firm. Writing a two weeks' notice is like picking out a revenge dress. You have to let them see what they're missing out on.

Or in my case, let them see that leaving was *my* choice. Not theirs.

An incoming call interrupts my playlist, so I punch to accept it. The bubbly voice of Jess Johnson, entrepreneurial badass and my best friend since we cracked our heads diving for a volleyball in fourth grade, erupts over my earbud.

"BABE!" Geez, she's loud even with like one hundred miles between us. "Where are you? Are you here yet?"

"Not yet. Still on 76." I glance in my mirror. "Just passed

Breezewood."

"Wow, you sound *so* excited to be coming home."

Ha. This isn't me *coming* home. This is me *crawling* home. "Of course I'm excited. Pitchette is exactly where I saw myself in my thirties."

"What happened to all that enthusiasm you had last week when you called to tell me you were getting a new start?"

"It burned up on re-entry."

She chuckles. "Well, call me when you actually roll in. I want to make sure you're here in one piece."

Mom used to say that, too. "Okay. Love ya."

"Love ya! Drive safe."

She hangs up and my playlist comes back on.

Taylor Swift. Of course. GAH!

This is *fine.* This is *normal.* I mean, just because I'm returning to my hometown for an as-yet determined period of time doesn't mean I have to be happy about it. This rock in my stomach is *totally* unnecessary. Pitchette isn't the end. It's just the transition. Between my life in D.C. and my life...wherever.

Right, God?

What I need to do is tune everything down the road out. Focus only on what I'm doing *now.* Break this trip down into bite-sized pieces. Work out a little at a time.

I must get too caught up singing to Avril Lavigne. Because somehow I end up idling at a stop sign next to unsigned state route 6001—just off *actual* PA Route 28—staring at a borough marker.

The aluminum sign has six bullet-shaped holes, and no, I'm not exaggerating. People actually shoot road signs around here. Mostly stop signs, to be honest. Whoever hit this one up arranged the holes to look like a cock-eyed smiley face.

The sign for Pitchette is smiling at me.

"You're not in D.C. anymore, Dorothy," I mutter.

Here's the thing. If you pull out a map of Pennsylvania, you'll see all these towns and cities with cute-looking names. If you're from out-of-state and participated in your third grade spelling bee, you'll assume the names sound exactly like they're spelled. *Reading,* as in Rainbow. *Lancaster,* as in Burt. *Wilkes-Barre,* as in Ballet. *Bethlehem,* as in Of Judea.

But get out of your car and talk to a real Pennsylvanian, and you'll feel like an idiot. It's actually *Redding* and *Lankustir* and *Wilkes-Barry* and *Bethlum*. Because don't tell us how to say things, damn it! We come from generations of hard-working, steely-eyed, plain-speaking immigrants. We're descendants of Italians and Poles and Irish and Germans and Ukrainians. All the folks who left the Old Country, came to America, forged west from New York, and ran out of money crossing Northern Appalachia.

Or most of us are, anyway.

I'm not. My mom came from undisclosed Mediterranean stock that settled in South Jersey. She got knocked-up by her high school boyfriend three months before graduation and kicked out of her parents' house until she 'solved' her problem.

The solution was to get in her Camry and drive west. Obviously.

She ran of money crossing Northern Appalachia. They call that 'irony.'

It sounds super romantic and charming and *Gilmore Girls.* But life isn't Stars Hollow. Life is Pitchette, as in In The Trash. Mom didn't get lucky and find a job at some quaint bed and breakfast. She got lucky and found a job at an IGA that was hiring overnight cleaning staff and didn't care enough about OSHA guidelines to stop her from wearing a baby sling once I was born.

Truthfully, I don't know what I inherited from my biological father. If I hadn't watched that reproductive film in my ninth grade health class, I would've happily lived my life assuming I was the byproduct of a divine encounter. Most of me is Mom. I have black curly hair and mostly hazel eyes and a skin tone a Clinique lady at Ulta once described as "probably olive if you weren't so pale."

I'd like to say that didn't make me stand out growing up, but Pitchette isn't what you'd call a diverse community. I one time wore a kerchief to paint sets after school for the senior high musical and Tara Basher told me she never realized I was Jewish. Whatever the hell that means.

The only thing—aside from zero money—that kept me from lightening my hair and caking on neutral foundation growing up was knowing there was someone else in Pitchette who looked exactly like me: Mom.

It's still hard to look in the mirror and not see her.

Okay.

I take a deep breath and pull onto 6001. It runs right through the heart of the borough and takes me across town to the neighborhood-type cluster of homes just inside the borough limit. The majority of the houses around here were built in the 1970s in response to the jobs created by new strip mining outfits established in this part of the state. Mostly, they look the same. Two-story. Plastic siding. Fake shutters. With the general aura of despair left by the folks who originally bought them before the jobs dried up and took away their dreams.

Geez, nothing's changed around here. There's that tree that got struck by lightning when I was little. There's that mailbox the borough plow took out my senior year of high school. And look, there's Terry Bauer bringing his trash to the curb.

Like he's done every Tuesday night since God created light.

Oh lord.

Is this it? Is this where my life ends? In a no-stoplight town in Western PA, surrounded by people I've known all my life?

Am I back? In *Pitchette?* For *real?*

I am, aren't I? Back. In Pitchette. For real.

Damn it.

TWO

I park in the spot outside Mom's garage, get out, walk around the front of the house, and retrieve the spare key from under the porch. Mine is buried somewhere in my purse, which is buried somewhere in my Honda. Mom's house has a front door, but the key only fits the side door. We've never had a key for the front. Not that it matters anymore. Mom actually painted the door shut years ago when she changed the color from brown to yellow.

Walking in from the side door leaves you in the tiny mudroom and makes your first impression of the house the living room.

Before I was born, Mom started renting a single-wide trailer in the trailer park just outside of Pitchette. It wasn't in good condition, but it fit her IGA paycheck and had a deadbolt on the front door. Most of her neighbors were elderly working class folks and long-term disability collectors. They weren't great company, but they also weren't meth addicts. When she wasn't working at the store, some of them paid her to get groceries or do yard work or wash their little shit dogs. The gig jobs helped buy my diapers and formula.

We moved out of the trailer when I was in third grade. Mom had been working for the bathware manufacturer in town for about three years by then, and she got approved for a loan to buy a foursquare house with a garage and five acres just inside the borough limit on the north end of town. The mortgage ruptured her paycheck most months, but we made the necessary sacrifices to make it work. I didn't mind living in the trailer. Okay, I *did* mind. It was old and sad and not a place my classmates' parents let them visit. But getting our own house was so much more important to Mom. Like she was finally making progress. Or maybe like she finally had a home.

I close my eyes and breathe the house in. Mostly the air is stale and dusty. But underneath, I smell *her.* The conditioner she used. Her laundry detergent. The last time she baked brownies. Like she isn't really gone at all.

Oops.

So I accidentally created a mausoleum by keeping the house closed up.

Mom would *hate* that.

I roll my eyes toward the ceiling. "It's not my fault, okay? I've been in D.C.!"

Yeah. Like she'd buy that.

I sigh. "Alright, fine. I *could* have come up here a lot sooner. Or had Jess open the place up for a few days." I walk into the living room and hoist the double-hung window. "But you know Jess. She totally would've taken over the whole house if I told her where to find the key."

It's true. Jess isn't good about *not* taking charge.

I open all the downstairs windows and let the fresh air filter through. The splashy floral curtains Mom bought last year flicker gently in the breeze.

"I can't believe you decided to go Boho on those," I tell

her. "This house is clearly supposed to be Modern Farmhouse."

That's a lie. Mom's house is clearly supposed to be Eclectic. She preferred things to find her instead of the other way around, which means a lot of her décor came from thrift stores and garage sales and sides of the road. Mismatched patterns for the couch and chairs. Pastel paint on the walls and bold colors on the furniture. The kitchen has a powder blue fridge and a chrome stove. Her bedroom has carpet and the rest of the house is hardwood or vinyl. The only room that makes sense is *mine.* And that's because in high school, I painted the walls Dainty Lace, slapped a pretty terracotta linen set on my bed, thrifted a Degas print, and called it Chic.

Okay, yes. I recognize it's not Chic. That's why I pitched the Degas print.

"I know you want me to move in," I say to the ceiling. "But my stuff doesn't go with your stuff."

Also, unpacking feels really permanent. And permanent feels...*permanent.*

Gah!

Alright. Can't worry about that now. All my crap from D.C. is boxed up, so I can just move it all into the garage. It will take up most of the parking bay. I'll have to keep my Honda outside, but who cares? This is *Pitchette.* Mowing your grass into the road is what classifies as a street crime.

My phone buzzes. I dig it out of my back pocket. Jess.

Oh boy. "Hey."

"Babe!" Her excitement seems particularly amplified. "Are you in town?"

"Just pulled in." Sort of. "I'm just doing a walk-through of the house."

"How's it look? I can't imagine how dusty it is, it's been closed up forever."

More like two months. "Oh, it's a crypt. I'm probably developing asthma just standing here."

"Ooh. Daphne would *so* chew your ass if she saw that."

"I know." It's true. Mom would chew my ass. "Want to come over and help clean?"

"Omg, hell yes!"

"Really?" I'm not above using and abusing my best friend when it comes to death cleaning.

"Totally. I just finished my last cardio class, so I'm already really gross. Might as well get some extra mileage out of these sweaty clothes."

I smile. "I freaking love you, babe."

"*But* I want you to come out with me after."

Gah! I *knew* it was too good to be true. "On second thought, I'll be fine. I think there's a shop vac in the garage somewhere." If not, Terry Bauer across the street definitely has one. And no problem wanting to teach me all about it.

"Oh, come on. You just got back to town. Let's do something."

"Jess, I'm not really in a social place right now. You know, because my mom died and everything."

"Mollie Maris. Daphne would be *appalled* that you're using her death as an excuse not to do things."

Damn it. That's true. Mom was the first person to tell me not to cry too long after she died. Which I told her was a stupid thing to tell your daughter.

Although by the time she got done shoving thirty-three years of *and I did all this for you so don't waste it* down my throat, I was about ready to slam the lid on her coffin myself.

I groan. "I don't wanna."

"Tough. You gotta."

"Gah! You know, I totally forgot you're one of the reasons I moved to D.C."

"Liar!"

I am. I am a liar. "Fine. But *please* nothing big, okay? I've had a long day and I want to be showered and sleeping by eleven."

"Deal."

Um. "That was too easy."

"What? I said 'deal.'"

"*Yeah,* but you said it like you have a lot of fine print you're trying to sneak past me."

"You're crazy."

Bullshit. "Jess—"

"See you in ten!"

Gah.

No way I'm going to be showered and sleeping by eleven, right?

"This is it?" This doesn't seem like It. This seems like a place Jess wants to stop at on the way to It.

She rolls her eyes. "Omg. Stop looking like I'm getting ready to waterboard you. It's a bar. We go in and drink. That's it."

"Uh-huh." Doubtful. Knowing Jess, she's probably signed us up for karaoke or body shots.

She sees my face. "This is Jerry's, babe. In Pitchette. There's no karaoke."

It sucks having someone who knows you so well. "Yeah, but what about the body shots?"

She hesitates. "I don't think those are on Tuesday nights."

GREAT.

Jess pushes through the door and I follow out of habit.

Damn it! I meant to turn and bolt back to the car.

Okay, so I probably could've walked uptown to Jerry's, but I was exhausted from opening up and cleaning Mom's house.

Still. Bet I could be home before Jess even realizes I'm missing.

A few folks holler out to Jess as we move through the crowd toward some empty bar stools and a high table. She laughs like she comes here every night. Maybe she does.

Hell, I probably will. If Pitchette ends up being my permanent place of residence.

Yay. Something to look forward to.

Okay. Yes, I spent the last twelve years living in the nation's capital. Four of them job hopping and then eight at the same company. But deep down, I'm still Mollie Maris. Raised by a single mom on a single income in a single town with a single grocery store. I work hard and save money and I don't do typical young adult things, like party on weekdays or take off for the beach Friday after work and get home Monday before work. I'm...what's that word? Right. BORING.

Which I guess is probably why I love Jess so much.

"Want food?" she asks when we claim our table. Positioned smack-freaking-dab in the middle of the crowd. "The soft pretzel bites are good."

"Works for me." Anything works for me right now. I haven't eaten since I found that Tootsie Roll in my purse on the drive up from D.C. And who knows how long *that's* been in there, because I never buy Tootsie Rolls. Ever.

"Cool. Usual?"

"Yep."

She disappears toward the bar and I edge my ass into the bar chair. I should probably know most of the folks in here. I'm sure if I look, I'll see familiar faces.

Too bad my eyes are squeezed shut like a little kid pretending not to see the monster in her closet.

Freaking Jess. Also, who thought it was a good idea for

social butterflies and recluses to hang out?

My phone buzzes on the table and I angle it to see the number through the privacy screen. Area code 202. Hm. That's D.C. No name, just the generic regional identification. Probably an offer to extend my vehicle warranty.

Jess returns, four bottles of IC Light dangling by their necks from her hands. "Drink up, babe!"

I smile. "You still got it, I see."

In college, Jess did this weird thing where she'd wrap her fingers around the necks of beer bottles and swig from five bottles at once. Like she was a moonshiner in some old black-and-white film who drank from the jug by slinging it over his shoulder. 'Jessing,' she called it. I never understood the physics or appeal behind it. It was wasteful and sticky and honestly dumb. It ruined a lot of her shirts. But it helped her get into a lot of guys' pants, so I guess she considered that coming out on top. Ha. No pun intended.

"Oof." She hauls herself up onto a barstool. "Barely. Between all the fitness classes I'm doing at the studio, my fingers these days are too sore for Jessing."

"Wow." I take a bottle. "That's probably the saddest thing I've heard since getting back. Are we old?"

"Don't know. I've stricken that word from my lexicon."

"You got rid of 'old' but you kept 'lexicon'?"

She rolls her eyes. "Omg, you are *such* a nerd."

I am. I am such a nerd.

"Mmm!" Jess flaps her hand and swallows her mouthful of beer. "Guess who's tending tonight?"

"Tending?"

"The bar, silly!"

"Oh." I glance over her shoulder, but there are too many people too see. "Who?"

"Liam Taggert."

Of course, because why not?

Liam Taggert was a year ahead of us in school and a year-around athlete. You could turn your calendar based on Liam Taggert's schedule. If it was football, it was fall. If it was wrestling, it was winter. If it was baseball, it was spring. If it was two-a-days, it was summer. He was hot and popular and I secretly hope he's turned out to be one of those guys who starts balding in his thirties.

Although my luck, he's probably hotter bald than with hair.

Not that I have to worry about running into him, honestly. His popularity launched him so far above me in high school he was basically Horton and I was basically a Who down in Whoville.

"That's interesting," I say.

"*Interesting?*" Jess' eyes bug. "Babe, you had such a crush on him."

"So did everyone." It's true. So did everyone. Even a couple teachers.

Which is really disturbing, now that I'm thinking about it with a fully developed prefrontal cortex.

Jess sighs. "You're right. It's too bad that skank Tara Basher got him wrapped around her finger in high school."

Yeah. It was too bad. Mostly because no one deserves being wrapped around Tara Basher's finger.

I shudder. "I can't believe I'm back here again."

"Hey, *I'm* here. No need to sound so nauseated."

I laugh. "You're right. Sorry."

"I forgive you." She sighs and takes a swig. "Honestly, I get it. I thought once I graduated, I'd be out of here. I didn't even make it to thirty-five and I came skulking back."

"You did not come skulking back. You came back with a degree and a plan and started your own business."

"Yeah, in a building four miles from where I grew up." Her blonde hair swishes when she shakes her head. "I feel like I'm in the same place I was fifteen years ago."

"You're not. But you know who is? Liam." Okay, maybe it isn't fair for me to say that. Bartending is a time-honored and noble profession. Bartenders are therapists who were smart enough not to spend hundreds of thousands of dollars on degrees. "Reliving the glory days? Pouring booze for the same people every night at the local watering hole? That has to be *so* boring." At least, I hope it is.

Is that wrong of me?

I can't help it. I'm a petty bitch when I'm feeling sorry for myself.

Jess tilts her head. "You know he enlisted after he graduated, right? I'm pretty sure he got stationed in Germany or Korea or something like that for a few years. Or maybe it was in a conflict zone. I can't remember. There was something about a Silver Star, maybe? He rescued some people or helped allied soldiers or something. I think. Maybe that was a show I streamed." She shrugs. "Anyway. Now he's in the Army Reserve."

"What?" Of *course.* Of *course* Liam Taggert turned out to be a freaking world traveler slash war hero.

GAH.

"Okay, no more high school talk." I set down my beer and sit up. "We are so not *those* girls." We are. We are totally *those* girl.

"You're right." Jess *clinks* her bottle to mine. "We're liberated women of independent means. We're interesting. We're funny. We can do what we want, when we want."

"Just so long as it's within budget."

"And not the night before my Sunrise Seniors class. Those old people are nuts. I need a full eight hours of sleep before

I instruct them."

"Oh yeah, we are *definitely* a couple of badasses."

"Hey! We *are.*" Jess eyes our table. "You know, one more bottle and I'd have a full game of Jessing—"

"*No.* Two of these are mine, and I'm drinking every drop. Besides, you said that shirt was expensive."

"You're right." She props her chin in her hand and lets out a massive sigh. "This is it, isn't it? This is as good as life gets in Pitchette."

"Well, babe." I give her a mock salute. "The ship might be going down, but at least we have each other."

We both drink to that like it isn't the end of the world.

THREE

FOUR.

FOUR FREAKING BEERS.

That's all it takes to give me a raging hangover? Come on, God! I mean, I didn't even really do anything *fun* last night to earn a hangover! Literally just sat in a bar with Jess and listened to her tell me about her plans for her fitness studio! And how exactly did I get home if I got so—

I left my car parked outside Jerry's. DAMN IT. That means I have to haul my ass up town to get it. Which is a *worse* walk of shame than an *actual* walk of shame, because it's not like I get anything fun out of the experience.

And it makes me look like a freaking lightweight.

The Pitchette party line has probably already spread the news half-way across the county.

Great. Just great. Off to a wonderful start on this whole next-chapter thing.

GAAAAH!

Alright. I need water. And whatever over-the-counter solutions Mom has in her fridge that aren't expired. I have ibuprofen somewhere, but the cost of trying to find it is just going to be too high. I can tell.

I pull on a pair of baggy shorts and an old tank top I definitely wouldn't have worn in the city, then take four minutes inching down the stairs while I pull my knotted hair up into a clip. Mom's place is pretty well insulated, but like a lot of the houses around here built in the 1970s, it doesn't have central air. I cower from the light streaming through the downstairs windows and feel around the walls for the ceiling fan switches. Once I have some pain relief in my veins, I'll go around and close the curtains to mitigate the heat.

But for now: Advil.

And water. Need to hydrate. BADLY.

And what the heck is that earsplitting *noise?* Like bullets *plinking* off metal. Oh good lord, is someone freaking *shooting* some—

No, that isn't it. It's coming from *inside* the house. From the kitchen.

For Pete's sake. The freaking sink faucet is dripping? Geez, does it have to be so *loud?*

Or is my hearing just very, *very* acute after four beers?

I tear off a paper towel from the roll on the counter and stuff it under the drip to muffle the noise. There. Better. Not a long-term solution, but I'll worry about that later. After my headache disappears. And I find my car. And where the heck are my shoes?

I jump when my phone rings because *that* cacophony is ten times worse on my head than the dripping sink. Who the heck is calling me at eight o'clock on a Wednesday morning?

Jess. Of course.

"Hello?"

"Whoa, babe. You sound horrible." Jess sounds perfectly fine, in case anyone wonders.

"Been a while since I drank on a weekday." Or any day. "I'm sort of dragging this morning." The damn sink drip has worked its way through the paper towel already. My ears are starting to bleed again.

"I wish I'd known. I'd have brought you a hangover sandwich from Sal's."

Yeah, greasy bacon, eggs, and cheese stuffed onto a croissant is the last thing I need in my stomach right now.

I grab another paper towel, fold it to make it thicker, and stick it under the drip. "How are you so chipper?"

"My morning run always gears me up for the day."

"Geez, you *ran* this morning? We're not the same species, right?"

She laughs. "Did you get your car yet?"

"No."

"Did you get coffee yet?"

"What am I, Wonder Woman?"

"Omg, you're so dramatic." She's probably rolling her eyes right now. "Well, *after* you get your car and your coffee, what are you up to?"

"Figuring out how to stop Niagara Falls from flooding Mom's kitchen sink."

"What?"

"The stupid faucet is dripping and it's driving me nuts." I tilt my head. "Do you think I can duct tape over the spout?" That probably won't work, right? Yeah, that probably won't work. I mean the water still has to go *somewhere.*

"The sink's leaking? That's not good. How long has it been doing that?" She gasps. "Oh! Let's go to the hardware store!"

Um. Okay. "Why are you making that sound like a girls' trip?"

"What? I'm not." She pauses. "I mean, there *is* this really cute guy who works—"

"For Pete's sake, Jess. I think all your morning runs and

fitness classes are making your libido *stronger*." God help us if that's true.

She laughs. "I have some questions for him about sealants, actually. I think the studio might need some weatherproofing."

Uh-huh. "You're talking about Hank Tucker's store, right? Down the hill from the post office?" Oh crap. "*Please* tell me Hank Tucker isn't the cute guy you're talking about." Hank is sweet and all, but he's married and has kids we went to school with.

"Of course I'm not talking about Hank. I'm not talking about anyone." She's *definitely* lying. "But I *do* need sealant, probably. So I will totally go with you whenever you go. I mean, if you're planning on going."

I wasn't. But now I sort of want to meet this hardware guy.

Geez, I need coffee. Badly.

I sigh. "Alright. I have to go retrieve my car from Jerry's, so I'll swing by and pick you up at your place." Everything's within walking distance in the borough. But the heat index already hit supernova, so why walk when you can ride in air conditioning?

"Actually, I'm at the studio," she says. "But I'll meet you at Jerry's. I'll grab us coffee from Sal's. And food, since it sounds like you need it."

Oof. Even thinking about food makes me want to barf right now.

"Yay! This will be fun." Okay, she's *way* too excited about this guy.

I mean, this is *Pitchette*. It's not like we have Chris Hemsworth-types walking around, working at hardware stores.

"I'm not going to have to spray you with a hose, right?" I've seen that work on dogs and I'm not above using it on

Jess.

Although, right now getting sprayed by a hose sounds more refreshing than threatening.

"Mollz, I'm *totally* capable of controlling myself."

Yeah, that's what I'm worried about.

FOUR

So, definitely not a Chris Hemsworth type. More like a Chris O'Dowd type.

And for the record, watching Jess manipulate the guy behind the hardware counter is kind of scary.

I mean, I know she's an evil sex goddess disguised as a chipper blonde entrepreneur. *That* isn't the scary part. The scary part is how easily this guy slips into puppet mode. How *all* the guys she works slip into puppet mode. These dudes comprise a large percentage of the voting population in Westmoreland County, and most of them actively participate in the Second Amendment. What if Jess decides to use her powers for evil instead of selfishness? She'll be county commissioner in no time. From there, it's one short skip to the governor's mansion and then onto Supreme Leader of the Known Universe.

In some ways, D.C. is a lot safer than Pitchette.

The guy behind the counter is tall and slender and on the geeky side of dork.

And right now, he's saying something about her choices in sealants. "For something like this, you'll want to have concrete caulk."

For Pete's sake, guy. Come on. Can you make it any easier for her?

"Oh, Andy, I am *very* interested in having concrete caulk," Jess pounces. "In your experience, how hard does concrete caulk get? And is it smooth or sort of lumpy? I don't mind a little texture."

Geez. I'm developing a terminal case of second-hand embarrassment.

So much for *my* plumbing needs.

The obnoxious ringtone I forgot to reset on my phone makes my heart jump.

Seriously? Who the heck is calling me? I don't want to talk to anyone. Everyone I communicate with regularly is standing in this store right now.

I jerk my phone out of my back pocket.

Area code 202.

Except this time, it doesn't pop up as a random D.C. number. This time, it pops up as a name.

Darrin Schwartz.

As in Schwartz Marketing and Media.

As in my old boss.

As in the guy I turned my two weeks' notice in to.

Calling me. On my cell phone.

Um, *why?*

My fingers shake as I accept the call.

"Hi, this is Mollie!" Wow, that does *not* sound like me. And it definitely doesn't sound like someone still fighting a hangover headache.

"Hi, Mollie. This is Darrin Schwartz."

"Darrin! Hi!" Okay, tone it down. No need to give myself an aneurysm. "Um, how are you?"

"I wanted to reach out regarding your resignation letter."

Straight to the point, like always. "Sure. Do you need something else from me? An exit interview or something?"

"No." He pauses. "Actually, yes. I do have a few exit interview questions for you."

"Okay."

Strange that Darrin Schwartz wants to ask me questions personally. This is usually something that goes through human resources. Maybe that department is short-staffed at the moment. That would explain why it took so long for Schwartz to follow up. The company takes operational feedback *very* seriously. Allegedly.

"Do you want to schedule a virtual meeting?" Hopefully, because I'm *not* driving back to D.C. just to answer some dumb questions.

"Do you have a few moments now?"

"Um...." I glance at Jess, flirting away with the guy behind the counter. "Sure."

"What made you decide to leave Schwartz?"

Geez. Okay. Jumping right into the fire with that one. "I felt like I'd reached my capacity in my position there. I left to find a new challenge."

It isn't *untrue*. But it feels weird to be standing in the middle of Pitchette, talking like I'm still in D.C.

"What did you most enjoy about your position at Schwartz?"

Before Mom died, that was a pretty long list. These last six months, though, my excitement for most of my work there has faded. "I guess the collaboration was what I enjoyed most."

"Can you elaborate on that?"

"Um." I think for a few seconds. "Okay, as an example. One of the first major projects I participated in was an educational scholarship campaign for the Smithsonian Institution."

"The Grass is Greener project. I'm familiar with it."

"Right." Of course he is. He's freaking Darrin Schwartz. "Part of that campaign involved working directly with middle school students in D.C. public schools. We went to the D.C. State Board of Education meetings and presented the mission of the Grass is Greener scholarship in-person alongside representatives from the Smithsonian. Then we coordinated with teachers in specific classrooms to reach students who were eligible to apply for the program."

Just thinking about the Grass is Greener program makes me smile. Smithsonian funded the project exclusively to help students participate in summer programming that focused on outdoor curriculum.

"And you found that collaboration particularly rewarding?"

"Yes."

Maybe I liked it so much because I grew up in Pitchette. Or maybe it was that I got to sit down with the kids after the program ended to figure out what worked and what didn't. Whatever it was, it impacted me. I chased that high for eight years.

Geez. Eight years of my life. Washed down the drain just like that. Twelve, if you count the four years I hopped around *before* Schwartz. What do I have to show for it?

"What did you least enjoy about your position at Schwartz?"

Oh boy. What a loaded question. I wouldn't mind answering it honestly if it was asked by some faceless guy in HR. But this is Darrin Schwartz. Son of the man who built the Schwartz brand. Whatever I say sort of reflects on him directly. Just because you're a professional doesn't mean you're immune to criticism.

On the other hand, I don't work for the company

anymore. What could he do, double fire me? Worst case I won't get a character reference. But the bathware factory probably doesn't ask for character references, so who cares?

"One area in which I think Schwartz can improve is company policies for employees."

Darrin hesitates. "Employee policies?"

"Yes. I feel several of them are outdated."

"Excuse me?"

See? Not immune to criticism. "After my mom died—"

"I'm sorry. Your mother died?"

"Um. Yes." Seriously? HR should have a record of that. The process of applying for bereavement leave basically required me to pass the bar exam.

"When was this?"

"January."

There's noise in the background on Darrin's end. Like papers getting shuffled.

"I apologize," he says. "I'm not seeing anything about that in your employee file."

"Are you kidding?" Heat rises in my chest. "The paperwork took forever to process. And because I took bereavement leave for Mom's funeral in January, HR told me I wasn't eligible to take it for her burial in March. I had to take unpaid leave, instead."

"Why was she buried in March?"

"That's when the ground thawed."

"I don't understand."

People don't have to think about stuff like this in the city, where every funeral home has an arsenal of equipment to break up frozen earth. If you die during the frozen months in Pitchette, you usually end up in a funeral home or cemetery holding crypt until the ground softens enough to dig a grave.

I do *not* want to get into *that* discussion in the middle of a hardware store, so I push through the door and stand outside to give him the CliffsNotes.

"The ground was frozen solid here in Pennsylvania when Mom died in January, so the funeral home couldn't bury her," I tell him. "We had to wait until March. I tried explaining that to HR, but the employee handbook doesn't have anything regarding bereavement leave for *burials,* just *funerals.* So HR told me I couldn't get paid for taking two days off to lay my mom to rest. Fine. Whatever. The paycheck didn't freaking matter because this is *my mom* we're talking about. *Then* when I told my supervisor I was taking two unpaid damn days off to get in my car, drive to Pennsylvania, and watch my mom get planted in the ground, my supervisor took me off a major project I'd been working on for four months because she said I was 'not fully focused' and she needed someone who was 'here 100 percent.' Which meant when performance bonuses were handed out at the end of the quarter for that particular project, I was excluded from the list. So yeah. I guess *that* is what I least enjoyed about my position at Schwartz."

Huh. Guess I've been holding onto that for a while.

Darrin doesn't answer right away.

Works for me. Pretty sure I have rapid onset tachycardia.

"I'm sorry to hear that, Mollie. I wasn't aware of our policy on this particular matter. Or of any of that situation occurring." He clears his throat and becomes all business. "I'm making a note about this. Our HR department will conduct a full review of all our paid time off policies. And I will be speaking with our supervisors regarding team input and compensation."

Progress, I guess. Doesn't really do me any good. But at least things will be better for future employees.

"I see you never officially took vacation time in the eight years you were with us?"

Geez. How pathetic is that? "That's correct." I mean, at least it will be paid out in my last paycheck.

"Do you have another job lined up, Mollie?"

"Um. Yes." Sort of. I mean, I haven't actually applied to the bathware manufacturer. But it's not like that place turns down a lot of applications.

"In marketing?"

Okay. That's probably a standard question, but I feel a little attacked. "Marketing-adjacent." Geez. That sounds so fake. "More emphasis on product than promotion." *That* is true.

"Is it in Pennsylvania?"

Why does that matter? "Yes."

"So you have no plans to return to D.C.?"

"I mean. Maybe to visit." Where the heck is this going? "If you're asking if the cost of living in the city was one of the factors in my decision to leave—"

"I'm not. I'm ascertaining whether you'd be suitable for a new role in the company."

"I—what?" I'm having a stroke, right?

Because Darrin Schwartz isn't calling me to personally ask if I want my job back.

"Schwartz is looking to expand into new markets, specifically in educational funding." He's talking to me like I'm sitting in a boardroom, watching his Canva presentation. "With the recent acceleration of government funding to public and private schools, organizations are more inclined than ever before to invest in marketing campaigns aimed at recruitment and retention."

It's been a couple weeks since I used corporate double-speak, but I'm still fluent.

"There's a lot of money to be made off schools right now," I translate. "And you're looking to put someone in charge of collecting it."

"I see there was no artificial intelligence involved with drafting your resignation letter."

"Excuse me?"

"We've been circulating it among our junior associates as an example of our standard of copywriting."

Holy crap. The teacher is using my paper in class? Gah!

I mean, part of me is flattered.

The other part is sort of pissed off. What are the rules again on compensating intellectual property? Shouldn't I be getting royalties or credits or dental or something? *Schwartz* didn't teach me how to write a kick-ass persuasive essay. My college advisor Jim Beam did.

I'm getting screwed by The Man all over again. And not in a way that's leaving me smiling and wanting more.

"There are plenty of good writers at Schwartz," I tell him. "My letter isn't anything special."

"I disagree. It was witty, relatable, and authentic. Sly without being overbearing. Accessible without being dumbed down. Marketing at its best."

What, does he have a thesaurus pulled up on his phone? A word-a-day calendar on his desk?

"I wasn't selling anything." I was just trying to save face. To prove that I wasn't leaving because I couldn't hack it.

Okay, maybe I was showing off. Just a little.

"Regardless, you sold me."

"On what?"

"On the idea of having you come back to work for us."

I've had this dream before. It usually ends with me showing up to the office ten minutes late wearing nothing but a pair of earrings.

I kick some grass clippings off the curb and sit. "I was serious when I said I felt like I reached my capacity in the role I was in."

"I understand that. You also indicated you're looking for a new challenge. Schwartz is currently building a team to take over all projects that fall into the academic marketing category. If you joined this team, you'd be working exclusively with educational organizations at all levels in the D.C. area."

"In sales or content development?" My background's primarily development. The only sales pitching I've ever done was trying to get projects okayed by a supervisor. That didn't involve a commissioned salary, thankfully.

"Either," Darrin says. "I think you have the capacity to be effective in both."

Do I? I can't see myself successfully selling a marketing package to a preschool.

I can't see myself successfully doing anything these days.

"This comes with a sizeable salary increase," he adds. "In the area of twenty percent. In case that's a concern."

Um, it *wasn't*. But that is certainly good to know.

I mean, I've never been someone who's particularly motivated by money alone. I've always placed a higher value on emotional drive. On whether I can give back or make a difference for other people. Maybe that isn't cool for a former marketing associate to admit, but it's the truth. My Schwartz paycheck was great, don't get me wrong. But knowing that I helped folks build their brand and get their message out had always been just as important to me as making next month's rent.

Of course, that was easy to say when I didn't have to worry about next month's rent.

Now that I no longer have a paycheck, I'm sure I'll be falling off my high horse any day now.

Okay. Tough truth time. "I'll be honest, Darrin. I don't know what to say to any of this right now."

"That's understandable. I'm sure you didn't expect this

phone call."

Sure I did. Right after they opened Hell up for the ski season.

"Here's my proposal, Mollie. Let's hold off on processing your letter of resignation."

Um. No. "No offense, Darrin, but I'm certainly not moving back to D.C. right now."

"I'm not suggesting you do. I'm suggesting that instead of terminating you, we process you for a leave of absence. A *paid* leave of absence."

What? "Are you serious?"

"Yes. It's the least we can do, considering the circumstances."

I don't know what to say. "I don't know what to say."

"You don't have to say anything."

"So you're telling me that I'll get paid to stay in Pennsylvania, doing nothing for Schwartz?"

"Not doing nothing. Resting. Reflecting. Considering my proposition." His tone shifts. "Everyone burns out, Mollie. Everyone needs time to re-energize."

That's an enlightened perspective from the manager of a company with handbook policies predating Stonehenge.

I didn't realize it until right now, but I'm craving a new beginning. And agreeing to an LOA from Schwartz feels a lot like stepping backward into the conflicted feelings that sent me scurrying for Pitchette.

Still. The money *would* be good to have. The cushion would give me breathing room. It would give me time to figure out what I want to do. Plus I wouldn't have to worry about developing lung cancer from toxic factory fumes. Yet.

"How long would this leave be?" Just out of curiosity.

"A month."

"A *month?*"

"I'm afraid I can't offer you longer."

Holy crap, a *month?* That's 160 hours of paid time off. I could paint Mom's house. Hang out with Jess. Go fishing. Buy groceries. Write more resignation letters.

Okay, so I'm sort of a boring person. But with 160 hours of paid time off, I could find a hobby. Or at least develop an interesting personality disorder.

"Are you sure you have the authority to do this?"

"Yes." He sounds amused. As amused as Darrin Schwartz can sound. "As my name is on the building."

"What happens if I agree to the LOA and then turn down your job offer?" Not because I'm considering doing that or anything.

"Then I'd at least feel Schwartz compensated you for any emotional distress you may have incurred over the last few months of your employment here."

Everything Darrin says sounds like it was prepared by a lawyer. Maybe it was. Schwartz is a top-tier marketing firm in one of the highest cost-of-living cities in the U.S. It can certainly afford to keep a legal team on retainer.

I guess it can spare a little change to cover a month's salary. "Okay. I accept."

"Which part?"

"The paid-to-stay-home-and-consider-my-options part." Obviously.

"Excellent." Darrin apparently doesn't mind candor. Or maybe he's already gearing up for his next conference call. "I'll have HR start processing the paperwork ASAP. You should receive a paycheck for the next pay cycle."

Geez. Those have to be the sexiest words in the English language.

"I'll be in touch, Mollie."

"Th—"

He ends the call.

"—ank you."

The Supreme Leader of the Known Universe comes out with a bulky hardware store bag to find me staring at my phone.

She joins me on the curb and pulls out an unsweetened iced tea. "What was that about, babe?"

"I think my old boss just sort of gave me a promotion."

"The guy you just sent your resignation letter to?"

"Yeah."

"Wow." She sips her tea. "Is this good or bad?"

"Um."

"Got it. What do you want to do now?"

Honestly, logging onto my online bank account and watching for a Schwartz paycheck to hit is at the top of my list. "Take me to your studio. I want to see Jess Johnson's business empire."

"Oh, babe." She grins. "Hell yes."

FIVE

Pitchette has a main street. Technically. But it's one of those main streets that's really a state route running through the heart of town. Route 6001, which is just a little spur that juts off PA 28 into Westmoreland County.

Like a lot of towns in the U.S., Pitchette renamed its portion of 6001 as 'Main Street' for aesthetic purposes. Personally, I think Pitchette would've been better off with 'Route 6001.' When I was in elementary school, some joker went around and painted over all the 'I's on the street signs with matching green paint. Which, of course, made everything 'Man Street.' Because Pitchette is Pitchette, the borough council decided it wasn't worth spending money on new signs while the vandal was still at large. And before you ask, *no*. It was *not* an indication of the town's economic depression. It was the principle of the thing.

The council's official position was that until the culprit was caught and fined in accordance with Chapter 165 of the borough code, the defaced signs stayed.

And here we are, twenty-three years later. In the middle of Man Street.

Jess' fitness studio is the last storefront on the west end of Man Street, right next to Gino's Barbershop. Gino's is owned by a guy named Bill Dabrokowski who believes no one in their right mind will pay for a shave and a haircut from a Polish barber. Bill is older than Yoda and for as long as I've known him, he's dyed his pencil mustache Cozy Sable to match his toupee. In public, he answers to 'Bill.' In the barbershop, he answers to 'Gino.' There's no rational way to explain how this practice became so widely accepted. Other than Bill/Gino is Pitchette's collective hallucination.

Foundations Fitness manages to both stand out and fit in on Man Street. Jess has it painted an energetic blue, and she installed a giant sign over the front door with her studio name in bold, sleek black lettering. The windows are covered with adhesive screens that provide privacy but let sunlight into the building. A cheerful bell *tinks* when she unlocks the door and ushers me inside.

I take two steps and stop. "Whoa. We're still in Pitchette, right?"

Jess laughs. "I know. I could *not* believe how big this place was when I first walked in here."

Yeah, 'big' isn't the right term. 'Palatial,' maybe. Or 'commodious.' I mean, she has *three* separate studio rooms. And that doesn't count the unisex bathroom and the giant entryway where she has her front desk.

My jaw scrapes the floor as I do a slow turn. "Wasn't this place a plumbing store before?"

"Yeah." Jess drops her bag on the desk. "Marvin's. When the guy who owned it retired, he sold his inventory to the hardware store. It took a while to clean everything out. Then to *clean* everything." She looks around. "But what a pay-off, huh? Who knew the building was so beautiful underneath all those pipes and faucets?"

Who knew. I step into one of the studio rooms and flip the light. "Holy crap. You have *wall mirrors* in here!" And *yikes,* is that me? Yeah, let's just turn off the lights.

"I use that room for Pilates and yoga," Jess hollers through the door. "I'd love to start offering some form of dance classes, but I'm tapped at the moment."

I peek into the other rooms. One has fitness equipment. The other looks like some sort of rumpus room for kids.

Jess peers over my shoulder. "I haven't really gotten it off the ground yet, but I'm hoping this can be kind of like a family fitness room. You know, for parents who have little kids who need to burn off energy but aren't old enough for school sports."

There's a call for something like that in Pitchette? "I would've thought a lot of kids burn off that energy running around their yard or working on their family's farm." Beyond borough limits is mostly farmland around here, now that the strip mining outfits are defunct. And farming is an all-hands-on-deck vocation.

Jess nods. "Right? I thought that, too. Then I had several young moms tell me they'd love to use the studio, but they have no one to babysit their kids."

That makes more sense. Pitchette doesn't have a daycare and most people around here work blue collar jobs. A babysitting service is as farfetched as a rideshare.

I pick up a mini basketball and chuck it at the short hoop across the room. Miss. "Are there a lot of young families in Pitchette right now?"

"More than you'd think. A lot of the parents are people our age."

"Yikes. You mean people we went to school with?"

"Yeah. Actually, several of my clients are our former classmates. Including Tara Basher."

"My condolences."

She grins. "It's not so bad. I have a lot of power over her as class instructor."

"I'll bet."

We flip off the lights and go back to the main room. The sunlight angles through the front windows, catching photo frames on the far wall.

I go over to look at them. "What are these?"

"Oh." She smiles at the display. Lovingly. Like it's her kid or something. "I call it my Wall of Winners. That's everyone who's ever joined one of my classes. Even if they don't come back, I want to celebrate them for trying something new. And for helping me get this far."

"Aw. That's sweet, Jess."

"Yeah." She studies the photos. "And you know what? I only see a couple people here who've never come back. I mean, some of these people tried a class once and then switched to another. But only…what. Three? Yep, three of these guys have never come back at all."

"Holy crap." I squint. "Is that Bob Wolfe in Downward-Facing Dog?"

"Yeah. And believe me, it was *not* easy to get him out of it. You'd think having a hip replacement would make you more flexible."

"Not the case?"

"I was worried I was going to have to call the fire department for a lift assist."

"Jess, this is amazing." I lean closer to study the images. Geez. There are *dozens.* "I had no idea you'd done all this. Why didn't you send me photos or videos or anything?" I dig out my phone. "And where the heck is the studio's social media page?"

"In my head?"

"What?" I open my platforms and check. "Babe, *you're* on

social media. Why the hell don't you have a page or an account or anything for your business?"

"Because I'm old and tired and don't know what I'm doing."

"So is everyone! And *their* businesses still have an online presence."

She sighs. "I know. I had all these ideas when I started out, but I just never found the time to do any of them."

Holy crap. She doesn't even have a *Facebook* page for the studio. "For Pete's sake, Jessica, how are you getting people through the freaking door?"

"I don't know. Most of the people around here know me or my family." She shrugs. "I guess word-of-mouth is my biggest drive."

"And your customer base is growing that way? Through word-of-mouth?"

"I guess. I mean, I don't have a ton of new folks signing up for classes. But, you know. The schedule I have is manageable. It's just me instructing, besides the occasional certified volunteer. I'm stretched pretty thin, so I can't have a lot of clients."

"If you had more clients, you could bring in more instructors. And you could actually pay them. Which would give this place even more credibility."

"That's the dream, some day. I'd love to see the studio grow." She perches on the stool behind the front counter. "Pitchette's too small for a YMCA and the closest fitness centers are in New Kensington. The membership costs are sort of expensive for folks around here, though. Which sucks, because folks here *need* some sort of organized exercise. Pitchette has very high instances of conditions like Type 2 diabetes and heart disease and rare cancers."

"Really?"

"Oh, yeah." She wakes up her computer. "I mean, all

those things are pretty common in Western PA, anyway. But the rate of occurrences in Pitchette is above state average. Like, way above. If we were more populated, the government would probably provide funding for a regional study."

But because Pitchette is a speed bump on the way to everywhere, the state probably isn't even aware of the statistics.

"Where did you learn about this?" Because I've never heard about any of it before.

"It's not something I knew about until I started making plans for the studio." Jess angles the keyboard closer and starts typing. "I attended a couple wellness conferences and started meeting healthcare professionals, and that's where I first heard about it. Then I started reading more about this area and found some crazy reports. I got *super* deep at one point." She frowns around the studio. "There's a file, somewhere. Not that there's anything I can do with it. I mean, I'm just a fitness instructor. Not a doctor or scientist or anything."

I assumed Mom's cancer was an isolated incident. I mean sure, maybe part of me thinks she developed cancer from working for the bathware manufacturer. Her oncologist said at one point that something like only eight percent of lung cancer cases are a result of a genetic predisposition. The other ninety-two percent originate through environmental or lifestyle factors. But it wasn't like she was a factory worker. It wasn't like she was on the line directly. She worked in an *office,* for Pete's sake! And she only worked there for twenty-sixish years. I mean, you know. Not 'only.' Twenty-six years is a long freaking time to work anywhere. But other folks have worked for her company a lot longer. Most of them haven't developed lung cancer.

Some have.

What if Mom's one of the people Jess is talking about? What if she's a statistic?

What can I do about it if she is?

"Jess, *this* is the sort of thing people connect with." I wave my arm at her wall of photos. "These people want a better quality of life, and you're helping them get it. You need to get this story out there. *Pitchette's* story. You need to share your mission."

She laughs. "Babe, I'm running a business. For profit. Or at least I will be, once I break even." She shakes her head. "I can't claim this place is a 'mission.'"

"I'm not saying to fob it off as a non-profit or something like that. I'm saying get your message across. *Tell* people why you're doing this."

A wry smile pulls at her lips. "Yeah, I'm not sure folks will care *why* I opened the studio so much as what it costs to use it."

See, *this* is what frustrates me most about marketing. Alright, maybe not *most.* But a lot. "Jessica Johnson, you have something special here. Something different and powerful."

"Aw. Thanks, babe."

"And it's worth shit if you don't tell people about it."

"Yeesh. Harsh."

"Yeah. You bet it's harsh. And it's going to get a lot harsher if you don't listen to me."

She raises her eyebrows and looks around the studio. "Ma'am, I am so sorry. I didn't even see you come in. I was just talking to my quirky best friend Mollie, but she seems to have disappeared."

I roll my eyes. "I'm serious, Jess."

"Mollz, I know you're trying to help me. But all of *this?*" She gestures vaguely in my direction. "It's just not my thing, okay? I suck at selling stuff. Always have. And even if I don't grow out of this teensy tiny little space that's four freaking miles from where I grew up, at least my business won't be one of those things advertised on Instagram that people just scroll past on their way to better content."

Oh boy. This is going to take a while.

I roll a yoga ball toward her desk and sit on it. Ooh. Comfy. Should I get one for the house?

Okay, okay, focus. "I'm not talking about selling stuff, Jess. I'm not even talking about *selling*." I am. Technically. But Jess makes business decisions based on emotional investment, not cold hard facts. That's not the message she's going to connect with. "I'm talking about *telling*."

Her eyes narrow. "Telling what?"

"Everything. Your story. Pitchette's story. Why you wanted to open this place. What you learned when you started to make plans. What people come to you for. Why they show up every day. What they're doing. How they're growing. What you want for them. What they want for themselves. Just *everything*." I bounce a little on the ball. My brain is churning. "You've got to frame the narrative."

"That sounds familiar. Didn't we learn about that in junior lit?"

Oh crap. Really? I *swear* it's a marketing thing.

Geez, am I actually terrible at marketing? Hm. Maybe I should lock down Darrin's offer before he finds out.

"The point is, if you think about promoting your studio as telling a story instead of selling a service, people are going to listen. You won't just be another social media ad someone scrolls past. You'll be a face and a voice attached to a place. You'll be something real and human and accessible."

Jess leans back from the computer. "Wow. I did not know you were a motivational speaker."

"I practice a lot on myself." And it hardly ever works, so

there's that.

She sighs and tilts her head back until she's staring at the ceiling. "Where would I even start with something like this?"

I roll my hips on the yoga ball. Wow. Who the heck knew you can do gentle stretching on this thing? "You need to create social media platforms specifically for the studio. You need to do this, like, yesterday."

She makes a noise that is not an affirmation.

My brain doesn't have time for her negativity. "Then, we need to start finding ways for you to get your studio name out there. Community events, festivals, stuff like that. We need to start generating traffic to your social media, which means tons of photos and reels. We want your face out there and we want the studio behind you. We need engaging content. But not just generic fitness instructor content. The internet is full of health gurus. We want this to be personal and real and Pitchette."

"About half the state doesn't even know Pitchette exists. How the heck do we get people who aren't even from here to care?"

"They're not going to follow you because of the town, Jess. They're going to follow you because of the story."

She covers her face with her hands and groans. "This is a lot."

"It's easy enough to build your foundation. I can help." Not like I have anything else to do.

"Babe, I barely have enough time to create a class schedule each week."

"So let me do the social media stuff for you. I can get everything off the ground, and then I can work with you to maintain it."

"You know I can't pay you, right?"

"Um, you know I consider ice cream and pizza legitimate forms of payment, right?"

She snorts. "Okay, if I'm going to be paying you in calories, I'm also throwing in free fitness classes."

UM. "What? Why am I in trouble? I didn't even *do* anything!"

Her laugh ricochets off the walls. "Babe, I love you the way you are."

"Funny. Sounds like there's a 'but' coming."

"*But* we're in our thirties. Our *thirties!*"

Like I'm not reminded every time I look in the mirror. "So?"

"So we need to put in more effort to stay healthy now."

Um, is she under the impression I put in effort *before?* I mean, hello! Ice cream and pizza! "Is this prefacing a murder-suicide pact?"

"This is prefacing me telling you we need to eat better and exercise more."

Oh no. "I'm busy!"

"With what?"

Shit, she fact-checked me. "Lots of stuff. Cleaning Mom's house. Painting it." I mean, maybe. "Oh! Mowing the yard. That takes a while."

"You have five acres to mow. Tops. And didn't Daphne get a riding mower last year?"

"Yeah, but I have to figure out how it works. *That's* going to take a while." Probably days.

"You can still find an hour a day to exercise."

"An *hour?*" I scowl. "That sounds like a big commitment, Jess."

"Babe." Her mouth turns up. "It's easy enough to build your foundation. I'll help you."

Low blow. Twisting my words like that. "I hate you."

"I'll get over it." She moves her mouse and clicks something on the screen. "I'm guessing with the move and everything, it's been a few weeks since you exercised."

Yeah. As in months of weeks. "Something like that."

"We'll ease you into it."

I bite my lip. "Like how?"

"Like we'll start with basics. Cardio."

"That's the one that gives you a heart attack, right?"

"We'll go for a run in the morning. We can meet at the high school track."

The track. I *hate* the track. It's boring and ridiculous. And who the heck came up with the brilliant idea to create a dedicated space for well-functioning people to run in giant freaking circles? I mean, if you took the track out of the equation and saw someone running in giant circles for miles at time, you'd call 9-1-1 to report a psychiatric emergency. Am I wrong? I DON'T THINK SO.

Hope isn't lost yet. "Can we be on school property?"

"Sure, since school's out for the summer."

Crap. "I thought they were renovating the football field?"

"Yeah. Years ago."

I need an excuse. *Anything*. "What if it rains?"

"I hope it does. We need it." She types something into the computer. "Also, you're not made of sugar. So you won't melt."

"Please, Jess! I'm weak and pathetic and I don't wanna run!"

"Babe, those are the *exact reasons* why we're doing this."

GAH! Curse Jess Johnson and her diabolical intellect! "You can't make me." Right? She can't, can she?

"I got Bob Wolfe into and out of Downward-Facing Dog." Her intense eyes cut to me. "Tying a rope to your ankles to haul your ass out of bed and dragging you behind my car to the track will be a piece of cake."

I bit my lip. "You put some thought into this, huh?"

She smiles.

Whoa. When the heck did she get so *scary?*
I slump on my yoga ball. "What time?"

SIX

Thank God I'm highly susceptible to peer pressure. Otherwise, I'd do some really dumb things. Like sleep until seven o'clock instead of hauling my butt out of bed at the asscrack of dawn to meet Jess at the high school track and run two miles.

Sorry, that's misleading. *She* ran two miles. I ran a quarter-mile lap and limped the last seven.

"How you feel?" she asks on the way back to our vehicles.

"Dead, mostly. And kind of pissed-off."

"At what?"

"At everything." I tip my sunflower Stanley upside down and nothing comes out. "Did you drink my water?"

"I don't think so. You carried it with you the whole time."

Damn it. "I'm getting gas and going home to sleep. And I don't want to hear from you for at least twelve hours!"

She grins. "That's the base building burn talking. Get something to boost your glycogen levels and you'll realize you still love me."

"Doubtful." What the heck are glycogen levels?

"I think we should make this a daily thing."

"No."

"That way we can get our run in before it gets too hot."

"No!"

"Otherwise, we'll have to do it in the evenings when the heat index is super high and there are lots of other folks using the track."

"Okay. It's official." I unlock my car. "We have beef and we're for-real feuding. Do not contact me."

She thinks I'm joking, which is why she laughs when I slam the door of my Honda and peel out of the parking lot.

If you're from Appalachia, you can appreciate a good feud. The Hatfields versus the McCoys. Pitt versus WVU. Hoagies versus subs. Sheetz versus Wawa.

PA is a battleground state on multiple fronts. The Sheetz-Wawa feud brings out the worst in us. Is it ridiculous to care about where you pump your gas? Yes. If you aren't from PA.

What makes the Sheetz-Wawa dispute so vicious is they're *both* Pennsylvanian companies. Sheetz started as a convenience store in Altoona in the 1950s. Wawa started as a food market in Folsom in the 1960s. Then came the gas pumps. They both have terrific marketing and tasty food and a hell of a fanbase. Big enough that their influences are creeping down the East Coast and spreading west. In five years, they'll probably be major sponsors of NASCAR. If they aren't already.

There isn't any point in getting into the whole Sheetz-Wawa argument on this side of the state. Choosing a side is as much of a choice as choosing which professional sports teams to back. You don't *choose*. Choice is an illusion. Sure, our professional sports teams suck most seasons. But even though the Steelers are meh and the Pens are hit or miss and the Pirates are a lost cause, you can't live in Western PA and *not* back them up. Same deal with filling stations. Pitchette bleeds Black and Gold and Gas Station Red. Always has. Always will.

And just to be clear, you don't *really* go to Sheetz for the gas. You go for the experience. It's fossil fuel dependency and fine dining rolled into 24-7 convenience. The perfect one-two punch of American consumerism, with its infamous Beer Cave tucked up the sleeve for the knock-out blow. If you don't have time to run to the beer distributor or the state liquor store, you high-tail it to the nearest Sheetz and grab a couple Krispy Kremes on your way out.

Hm. A cake donut would hit the spot right now.

I pull up to the first available pump at the Pitchette Sheetz, gave the card reader my social security number and blood type, and lean against my Honda as the pump does its thing. I'm probably leaving a giant sweaty ass print in the artfully curated dust wrap I've acquired driving down dirt roads. Oh well.

I cross my arms and avoid eye contact with the guy in coveralls and a trucker cap on the other side. Lots of nice folks like chatting it up at the pump. So do a lot of *Dateline* contenders. My luck makes it more likely for me to meet Ted Bundy than Ted Turner.

"Respectfully, ma'am. You got a nice pair."

Oh, c'mon, God. Seriously? I don't have enough going on? You need to add a freaking Sheetz-pumping weirdo to the mix?

I check my fuel count and don't respond.

Which the guy across from me takes as encouragement. "They look real soft, but firm."

"Don't make it weird, dude."

For the record, it's already *way* past weird. I just don't want to have to spray him with Unleaded Regular. Seems like an expensive way to shut down a jagoff. And why the heck should *I* have to incur the cost? That's not the sort of financial freedom my foremothers fought for.

"I bet they're warm, too." He sends a stream of chew juice onto my side of the concrete. "Real soft and firm and wa—"

I hang up the pump and jump into my car without grabbing the receipt. A smart woman would drive off, but I *really* want a Krispy Kreme. And damn it, my feminist ancestors didn't starve in prison or burn their bras just so a middle-aged letch with half his teeth can stop me from getting one!

I pull into a parking spot facing the convenience store and get out.

Ted Bundy pulls in next to me.

"How much?" he hollers through the open window of his rusty Ford pickup.

"What?"

"How much you want?"

"What the hell are you talking about?"

"I could just buy one."

"*Excuse* me?"

"Both would be great," he says, "but I'd take just the one. Looks real soft and fuzzy."

"*Fuzzy?*" Okay. I do *not* want some rando offering to pay to see my freaking tits. But I also do not want some rando thinking my tits are freaking *fuzzy*.

"Nylon-polyester blend with a little elastane. Right?"

"I—what?" What the heck is that? Some sort of sexual code I'm too square to know about? Geez, what happened to Pitchette while I was away?

"The socks."

Um. "What socks?"

"*Your* socks. What do you think I've been talking about?" His eyebrows bunch together like I'm nuts.

Maybe I am, because now a small, stupid, non-bra-burning part of me is sort of offended. "You're not offering to pay to see my tits?"

He reddens. "No, ma'am. I would never offer something like that, ma'am. Not unless you was in that business, specifically."

Let me get this straight. "You want to *buy* my socks?"

"Yes, ma'am." He clears his throat, suddenly looking anywhere but at me. "They look real warm and fuzzy. I'm sort of a collector, you see."

Holy crap. Pitchette is a lot more like D.C. than I realized.

"What's your name?" I ask.

"Twister, ma'am."

I slam my door. "They're not for sale, Twister."

"I'd give you twenty bucks!"

Geez. That's the going rate for a pair of used socks? "No."

I dig in the pocket of my yoga pants for my credit card as I walk into Sheetz and bee-line for the donut case.

Except I don't have my freaking credit card. It's sitting in my cup holder. Gah!

Twister is leaning against his truck when I go back to my vehicle.

Okay, here's the thing. I'm not a business-minded person. My skills fall firmly in the right-brained category. I'm imaginative and intuitive and for the most part, sort of creative. Maybe even artistically inclined.

But that does not mean I can't recognize a business opportunity when it's staring at me from behind a tobacco-stained beard and smudged glasses. Twenty bucks for a four-dollar pair of socks is a profit percentage of 400 percent. My savings account is earning .01 percent interest, so that return-on-investment looks pretty damn good.

Plus, twenty bucks would buy like ten donuts. And I won't need to explain that many donuts showing up on my card statement to Future Mollie. Future Mollie is Little Miss Perfect and kind of a judgmental jagoff.

I cross my arms and lean against my car, facing Twister.

"Why do you collect socks?" I don't *really* want to know. I just feel like I need to have all the facts before I cut a deal.

"I like the way they look and feel, mostly."

Not exactly the mind-bending explanation I expected. "So you buy them off folks to wear?"

He shakes his head. "I don't wear 'em. Ruins the value if you wear 'em."

"It does?" We're talking about socks, right?

"Yep. They're investments, you see." There isn't a speck of dishonesty in his eyes. "It's like buying an antique. You don't buy it to use every day. You buy it because you like looking at it."

I'm standing in a Sheetz parking lot, talking to some guy in a trucker cap about his sock addiction. I mean, collection.

What the literal heck is happening right now?

It doesn't matter. I want a damn donut. I mean, I have low glycogen levels and everything!

Twister holds up his hand. "Now, ma'am, don't be thinking I just buy any old pair of socks. I got discerning taste. I only make offers on the unique ones. And I only do it with folks who can spare to part with 'em."

"So they're ethically sourced. Sort of." Weird, but admirable. I guess.

I don't know. Part of me thinks the whole thing is bizarrely funny. The other part just assumes my socks are heading for an unsavory experience with Mr. Twister.

Mostly, I'm thinking about donuts.

Damn it. Should've eaten breakfast.

I sigh. "Show me the money."

He pulls out his wallet and extracts a crisp Andrew

Jackson. What does he do, walk around with stacks of twenties just in case he crosses a pair of socks?

I blow out a long breath. Weigh the options. Donuts. Self-respect. Donuts. Self-respect.

Donuts. You can't eat self-respect.

"Fine."

Twister lights up. "Really?"

"Yep. Let's do this quick." Before anyone I know drives by.

I kick off my sneakers. The asphalt burns through the nylon-polyester-elastane blend on my feet, so I stand on the tops of my shoes and lean my backside against the fender of my Honda for balance. Sweat runs down my face and chest as I drag off my gross socks, one at a time.

"Do you have a bag or something? I just went for a long walk, so they're pretty wet and gross." And smelly, but that probably doesn't bother a sockophile.

Twister reaches into the cab of his truck and pulls out a leather-palm work glove.

"Don't have a bag, but that's okay." He tugs the glove onto his right hand. "I work on a dairy farm. This ain't bad at all."

Whatever the hell that means.

I pinch both socks with the tips of my fingers and reach for the twenty as I hand them over.

"Mollie Maris?"

The masculine voice pulls my attention away from Twister's money toward the store sidewalk. A man is looking at me from under the bill of a Pirates ballcap that's well past its glory days. He's in work boots, jeans, and a gray three-button t-shirt that would probably tell me exactly what he bench presses, if it could talk.

If I could hear it over the collective gasp my ovaries give at the burnished-blonde-hair-to-blue-eyes-to-sexy-scruff ratio he has going on.

His physique is somewhere between Superhero and Pro Athlete. His tan is somewhere between *Baywatch* and *Miami Vice*. One large hand clutches an XL Sheetz coffee. The other clutches car keys. Probably to the mud-splatted F-150 parked three spots down that's screaming virility.

If this wasn't Pitchette and I wasn't Mollie Maris, I might have to do something really embarrassing right now. Like ask this hot dude who the heck he is or pretend to have a heart attack.

Thank goodness I'm blessed with a decent memory and non-killer genes. Otherwise I might be totally humiliating myself right now in front of LIAM FREAKING TAGGERT.

Seriously, God? Are you *kidding* me?

"Mollie?" Liam repeats.

"Um." GAH!

"Hey, Coach," Twister says. "Ready for a run at that PIAA championship?"

"Uh. Yep." Liam blinks and locks onto the sweaty socks swinging in the air between us.

"The boys are doing great things this season," Twister prattles. "Finally nice to see some real ball players coming out of Pitchette High. Think we finally have a real shot at that title."

"That's what we've been working toward." Liam's eyes drift from the socks to the twenty.

"IT'S LIKE BUYING ANTIQUES!" Oh. My. LORD! Did I really just blurt that out? Did I really just try to convince Liam Taggert my old, sweaty socks are antiquities? IN THE MIDDLE OF A SHEETZ PARKING LOT? "I mean, he's a *collector*." GREAT. FIXED IT.

Liam's mouth hangs open. Probably from total confusion. Or abject horror. Could be abject horror.

"Sorry to rush you, ma'am, but I need to get back to work." Twister pushes the twenty toward me and takes the socks. "Huh. They are pretty wet. Don't worry about it, ma'am. I'll leave 'em on the dash and they'll dry out in no time."

Heat scorches me from hair roots to chest.

"Good luck with the game Wednesday, Coach. Go Coyotes!" Twister gets in his truck and waves my hideous socks at me through the window. "Pleasure doing business, ma'am!"

His truck leaves behind a cloud of noxious fumes. I breathe as much of it in as possible. Asphyxiation can happen pretty quickly, right? And the chances of being brought back to life from it are low, aren't they?

"You should stop doing that, Mollie," Liam says. "You're going to hyperventilate."

Gah! Hyperventilating is useless. It has all the embarrassment of dying without the reprieve.

Besides, the diesel fumes are dissipating. And there's too much fresh air, since we're outside. I'm just making myself look *more* like an IDIOT.

I clear my throat. "Okay, so there were these donuts."

"Donuts?"

"I mean, not just *any* donuts. Krispy Kremes." That's *important*. I feel like that's important.

Liam lifts an eyebrow. "You just sold that guy your socks so you could buy donuts?"

Well, *that* makes me sound just plain pathetic. "I just got done exercising and I didn't have breakfast!"

The corners of Liam's mouth flicker up. "You just exercised and you're eating donuts for breakfast?"

Oh, I get it. I'm dead. I'm actually dead and this is actually Hell. This is my personal, one-of-a-kind, custom-designed Hell. Right, God?

"To replenish my glycogen," I lie through clenched teeth. "*You're* the sports guy. *You* should know that."

He smiles. I get the feeling it's at my expense.

I scowl. "It was a *business* transaction. They were for his *collection.* Twister's basically a curator. He explained his whole acquisition process to me."

"I'll bet he did."

"He doesn't just buy anyone's socks! He's *discerning.*"

That stupid smile is growing up into a stupid grin.

"Are you *laughing* at me right now?"

"I'm sorry." Liam shakes his head. "You're right. Fetishes are no laughing matter."

"*It was not a fetish thing!*" For Pete's sake. I wish I sounded more convinced when I hollered *that* in public.

He ducks his head so I can't see his face under the bill of his hat. That's alright. His shaking shoulders get the message across loud and clear.

"Liam Taggert, quit laughing!"

His blue eyes glisten when he looks up. I'd punch him, except I'd probably break my fist on his beautiful face. And also, I sort of have it on good authority that I smell a little like a dairy cow right now.

I huff. "You know what? I hope your team *doesn't* play well Wednesday."

Liam clutches his chest. "Oof. That's harsh."

Okay, that's fair. I went too far. I mean, they're freaking *kids.*

It's not their fault they have a giant jagoff for a coach.

I sigh. "I didn't mean that. I'm sorry. I hope the boys play well Wednesday and I hope they win."

Liam's eyes crinkle. "I'll pass that along."

"I *also* hope their coach gets ejected."

Liam grins. Again. DAMN IT!

"I'll try my best." He *beeps* his truck lock. "Welcome home, Mollie Maris."

He swaggers away. Actually *swaggers.* Like I need any more of an incentive to check out his freaking ass.

DAMN IT.

GAAAH!

So Liam Taggert is *not* one of those guys who starts balding in his thirties. He's one of those guys who looks fine as hell until the day he dies. Which will probably be centuries from now, seeing as he clearly eats nothing but vitamins and uses a placenta-based skincare regimen. And judging by his twisted sense of humor and the quick back-and-forth, he doesn't seem to be in any mental decline. For Pete's sake, he even remembered my freaking name.

Also, Liam Taggert remembers me? *The* Liam Taggert? I haven't seen him in probably five years. And before that, I maybe talked to him directly four or five times. *Maybe.*

Wow. Now I know how those Whos down in Whoville felt when Horton finally heard them.

Jess is going to freak out when I tell her. And then she's going to pretend we never met. Sure, she's fierce and kind of a local badass. But even her rep can't withstand a best friend who sold her socks to some dude at a Sheetz. In front of Liam Taggert. I totally get it. I love her too much to drag her down with me. We had a good run.

Guess this means I might as well go back to D.C.

And damn it, the whole experience totally ruined my donut plans! Plus the crisp twenty in my hand now feels sort of dirty. I didn't even *do* anything wrong!

I scowl down at Andrew Jackson.

I should probably give it to charity, right?

Great. Glad I humiliated myself for *no reward whatsoever.*

Stupid Liam Taggert. This is all his stupid fault.

I swear loudly, climb barefoot into my car, then reach

down and scoop my shoes up from the ground. They *thunk* against the back seat when I toss them over my shoulder.

So much for exercise improving my quality of life.

SEVEN

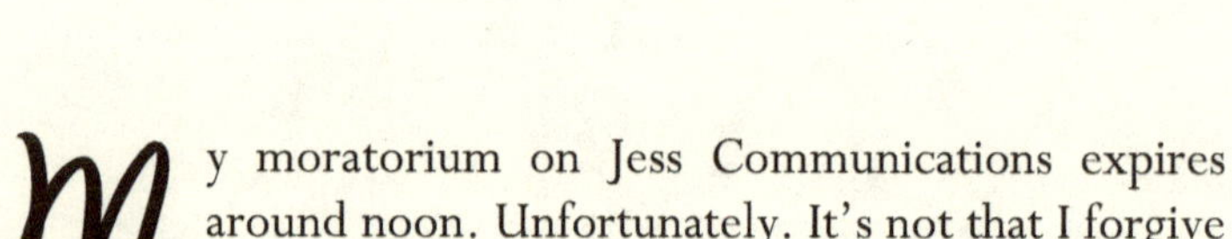

My moratorium on Jess Communications expires around noon. Unfortunately. It's not that I forgive her for the whole running-to-the-brink-of-death thing. I don't. The Liam Taggert encounter just solidified my anger.

Stupid Liam Freaking Taggert.

BUT I promised I'd help Jess establish a social media presence. And that's sort of hard to do without pictures.

"I need you to send me image files for your studio logo," I tell her on the phone.

Silence.

"Jess?"

"I'm thinking."

"What do you mean, you're thinking?" Holy crap. "Jessica Johnson. *Please* tell me you have a logo for Foundations Fitness."

"It's on my list, if that helps."

"It's on your—" Phew. Okay. Deep breath. "Are you freaking *kidding* me?" Okay, so the deep breaths didn't help.

"Mollie." She says it like she's reasoning with a toddler.

"Logos are *expensive.* I can't afford to pay someone to create a logo for me right now."

It's fine. This is fine. I mean, it's not like she knows a *freaking marketing specialist or anything!*

I pick up a pen and write 'LOGO' on the top of my Jess To-Do List.

Freaking Jessica.

"Alright. *I'm* going to take care of the logo."

"You are?"

"Yes. In the meantime, send me a photo of the studio."

"Okay."

"A *nice* photo. That's cute."

"Okay."

"I don't want it to look like a real estate listing."

"Okay."

"Or the set shot for a true crime documentary."

"Omg, *okay* already! I get it! Instagramable."

"Exactly." I pull up the web browser on my computer. "Also, I need a professional headshot of you. Please tell me you have one of those."

She scoffs. "I'm not totally useless."

Good to know. "Do you have a bio you can send? Or if not, you can send me info about your education and certifications. I can cobble one together for you."

"Yeah, I can send you stuff."

"Perfect. And email all this to me. That will be easier than getting a bunch of texts." Three items down. A zillion to go. "I can spin all this stuff together on my own, but I will need to sit down with you to put together your narrative."

"My narrative?"

"About the studio. Why you opened it, et cetera. You know, what we talked about."

Jess sighs. "Alright."

"Babe, we're trying to market your business, not sign you up to be a marrow donor."

"I know, but I just get nervous about stuff like this."

"Why?" Jess is probably the most self-assured person I know.

Other than Liam Freaking Taggert.

"I don't know!" she wails. "What if I make the studio seem stupid and I drive away all my clients and I have to declare bankruptcy and then I have to move back in with my parents?"

Oh boy. "Okay, first of all: you live down the street from your parents *now.* Having to crash in your childhood bedroom for a few months is hardly the end of the world."

She sobs.

Okay, maybe that's sort of a jerkish thing to say. "Plus, you could always stay at Mom's house."

"Really?"

"Yes." Of course, there's the slight chance being roommates will effectively end our friendship. But no point in worrying about that bridge until it's built. "Secondly, where the heck is all this self-doubt coming from?"

"I don't know," she mumbles.

"You believe in what you're doing, right?"

"Yes."

"You believe in Foundations, right?"

She sighs. "Yes."

"Your community? Your clients? All that?"

"Of course!"

"So why are you freaking out like you did when you had to present your senior project to the school board before graduation?"

She answers so quietly, I have to turn up the volume on my phone.

"What if it's a flop, Mollz?"

"The marketing?"

"The *idea.*"

Oh. Yeah, that question is a lot more existential than I'm probably certified to answer.

You know. Considering the whole just-walked-out-on-my-career-and-have-no-idea-what-I'm-doing-with-my-life situation.

My cheeks puff when I blow out a big breath. "Jess, is there anything else in the world you would rather be doing right now than getting Foundations off the ground?"

"No." No hesitation. No second-guessing. She just knows.

Wow. What the heck would it be like to just *know* something like that? So sincerely that it's just a gut reaction, that it's built into your DNA?

"Then it doesn't matter if this idea flops," I tell her. "Because for better or worse, this is what you want to be doing right now. Right?"

"Yes. But just so you know, that's not exactly a peptalk."

"Well, what do you expect from a woman who washed out in her early thirties?"

She laughs. "Fair."

"Um, *excuse* me? *I* can say that. *You* can't say that." I'm joking, of course. Sort of.

"My bad, babe." Perky Peppy Jess is back. "How about we meet up tonight and start hammering some of this 'narrative' stuff out?"

"What time?" Not that I have any plans for the next twenty years or so.

"My last class ends at three today. So let's say four-ish."

"Meet at your place?"

"Let's do the studio. My place is a bomb right now. Too busy to clean."

Ha. Right. Jess is *always* too busy to clean.

"Studio is better," I say. "That way, I can grab any other photos we might need." Although, it would be good to get some shots of people using the space.

A task for another day.

"Cool," Jess says. "I'll run home to shower after class and then we can spend the evening going over social media plans."

"What about dinner?" Not that I'm obsessed with food or anything.

"I can either pick something up or we can go to Sal's, since it's just down the street."

"Dealer's choice."

"Okay. Love ya."

I drop my phone on the desk and rub my eyes. Geez, is it really only noon? *How?* I'd take a nap, but that just seems like the super sad icing on top of the already sad box-mix cake that's turning out to be my life.

Gah.

Alright. Enough of this pity party. Jess needs my help, and that's what matters right now.

Right after I find some cake. I mean, it's freaking lunch time.

And it's not like I had donuts this morning.

When I was a little girl, I believed that I'd grow up and all my insecurities would magically disappear.

Which is *obviously* why I spend an hour getting ready to sit with my best friend in her office while we bullshit over food and work.

Okay, maybe insecurity isn't the real reason. Maybe I miss my D.C. Business Formal clothes just a little. I mean, this skirt is WHBM. This blouse is Ann Taylor. And where the heck am I going to wear my Nine West slingbacks if not to an informal business dinner on the floor of a fitness studio on Man Street in Pitchette?

"Hot damn, babe." Jess eyes me when I walk in. "I think you may have gotten the wrong impression about tonight."

"You wanted a marketing professional." I hold out my arms. "Meet me, two weeks ago."

"Wow. That got sort of depressing there at the end."

Tell me about it.

I haul my computer satchel to her front desk and set it down with a *thunk,* then retrieve a stool sitting near her Wall of Winners.

"The pizza smells good." I drop the stool in place and sit. "Is that from Fox's?"

"Please. Like I had time to run over to New Kensington." She flips open the pizza box lid and slaps a slice of veggie on a paper plate. "Sal's started making hand-tossed pies at the diner."

"No kidding?" Sal Shafer is as German as a cook can be.

"I think Bill Dabrokowski may have talked her into it," Jess says around a mouthful of crust.

"When?"

"When he was Gino."

Good grief. The hallucinations continue. Much more of this and the health department is probably going to investigate us for an ergot poisoning outbreak.

I claim a slice, take a bite, and almost choke. "Um. Is there cabbage on this pizza?"

"Yeah." Jess sips her tea. "Sal hasn't quite gotten the hang of Sicilian flavors yet. But she's unintentionally nailing a fusion vibe. Her house special has sauerkraut and bratwurst."

Hm. That actually sounds interesting. "Is the sauce tomato?" It changes things if so.

Jess shakes her head, swallowing another bite. "Beer

cheese dip."

Yes, please. "Okay, we're trying that one next time."

"Just as long as I don't have yoga the next day." She whirls her finger in the air. "This place doesn't exactly have the best ventilation."

Gross. "Moving on." I set aside the pizza and pull open my laptop. "I've started three different platforms for you, based on age demographics of your target audience. I figured Foundations is going to have three main age groups: seniors, midlifers, and early adults." Yes, the terms are dumb. I just don't have a cooler alternative at the moment. "I'm guessing young adults—as in, teens to college-aged kids—are not who you're trying to pull in. Right?"

"Not at the moment. I'm seeing that a lot of teens are already active in a school sport. And there aren't a lot of college kids around here."

Yeah. They still have a few years before they inevitably end up back home. See also: me.

I open my web browser and pull up Foundations' newly created socials. "Based on demographic statistics, I've started Foundations on platforms that are image and reel-heavy."

Jess picks cabbage off her pizza. "Where did you get these statistics?"

"Pew Research Center, mostly." I pull a printed chart out of my bag and hand it over. "Just in case you want a visual. Basically, you're looking to engage people across all age groups with splashes of color and audio. That chart breaks down the minutia, but that's the bottom line. Consumers are generally easy to please. The less work they have to do when engaging with a message, the better."

"Geez. That makes them sound super lazy."

I shrug. "Maybe it's laziness. I think it's also fatigue. We're bombarded with marketing all day, every day, everywhere. Online, in person, at the gas pump. We're all on overload, so when we sit down to engage with content in our free time, we don't want to have to work at it. We want to be able to see a pretty picture or listen to someone talk and not have to worry about scrolling through paragraphs of text or Googling sources."

Jess has a frown on her face that doesn't bode well. "You're making me feel like getting Foundations on social media is going to contribute to the moral deterioration of society."

I mean. That probably isn't *un*true. In a distant, circuitous, social-media-ruins-everything sort of way.

Now isn't the time to get into all of that. "The reality is having a social media presence for your business isn't optional. Folks need to be able to find you and engage with you. This is how they do it. That may change. But right now, this is it." Until the next big platform emerges, anyway.

"So to improve other people's quality of life, I need to sell my soul."

"Aw, babe. Yep. Pretty much."

She sighs. "Great."

Uh-oh. Her enthusiasm is draining faster than I can bolster it.

I move my laptop aside. "Babe, doing this doesn't mean you're selling out. Yes, you're going to be promoting Foundations. But *you* get to choose how. *You* get to decide the sort of message you send out. What you're putting in front of people."

"Even if what I want to put out doesn't attract a lot of followers?"

Oh boy. "I mean. We don't *actively* want to discourage followers. That's sort of the opposite of our goal."

Her forehead creases. Uh-oh. The panic is starting to take control again.

"But, yes. Even if what you're posting doesn't attract lots of followers." Gah! Saying that goes against everything in my shriveled up marketing soul.

I guess Jess is the first person I've ever worked with who isn't ready to trade anonymity for fame and business expansion. Not a great quality in an entrepreneur.

A *priceless* quality in a best friend.

"Why are you smiling at me like that?" Jess asks before shoving more pizza into her mouth.

"I just forgot how much I love you."

She snorts. "We'll see about that tomorrow morning. When you're dragging your ass around the track, four laps behind me."

"Those *would* be fighting words." I return to my laptop. "If I was planning to do any of that."

After this morning's social suicide at Sheetz, I won't be leaving the house in anything less than Business Formal ever again.

"We don't have to run. We could go for a hike."

What, does she think that's a compromise? "I don't have hiking boots." Thank God.

"You can get boots at Sonny's."

Sonny's is a locally-owned sporting goods store just outside the borough. If your shopping list includes kayaks and 12 gauge shotgun shells, it's the place to go. I'm all for buying local, but I'm not exactly the target consumer for Sonny's.

"I think I've been in that place like twice," I say. "And once was to use the bathroom."

"We can go there tomorrow!" Jess has that shopaholic spark in her eye. "You do really need a pair of good boots, babe. This is Pitchette."

True. Never know when you're going to break down on a dirt road somewhere. These slingbacks are freaking adorable, but in an emergency I might as well take them off and walk home barefoot.

Gah!

Wait a minute. I'm looking at this wrong. There's an opportunity here.

"Alright." I look at Jess. "I'll make a deal. *If* we get through all the Foundations social media stuff and your narrative tonight, and *if* I don't have to wake up and go to the track in the morning, you can take me to Sonny's tomorrow."

When you want something from Jess, you have to make her feel like she's controlling the ask.

She grins. "Omg, yes! Eek! We haven't been shoe shopping in forever!"

Do hiking boots count as shoes? I mean, I guess. Technically.

"When's the last time you did something besides think about the studio?" I ask her. "Because you are *way* too excited for this."

"I am not," she declares. "We're going *shopping*."

Are we? Really? "Jess, it's just Sonny's."

"Mollz," she says. "It's just Pitchette."

Damn. That is so true.

EIGHT

We throw in the towel around eight o'clock. Which, honestly, is a lot later than I expected us to be working. I mean, the pizza and tea ran out around five and our bladders have been empty since six. It's a miracle we made it through everything we needed to.

Jess moves off her seat and onto the floor, going through a series of stretches that are only possible because she's in leggings and a tank top and happens to be superhuman.

"Let's celebrate," she says with her head hovering over her knees.

"With what? We already ate that mini Twix bar you found in your desk drawer."

"We can walk over to Jerry's."

"Alcohol? Now?" Again? I shove our dinner debris into an empty trash bag and tie it off.

"Why not?"

"I want to say 'because it's late,' but I know you're going to make fun of me."

"Fair." She stands and rolls out her neck. "How about just one drink? A nightcap?"

Is it a bad sign that I find that idea terrible? "Jess—"

"Oh, come on. You're already dressed up."

"Um, these are *work* clothes. For an *office*." Not a bar in Pitchette Proper.

"We both know that 'fit classifies as Sunday Best around here."

That's true. And I *did* make the effort to dig these clothes out of my moving boxes. And do my makeup. Gah!

I sigh. "One drink. Because I still have to drive home." And also, because I don't want *any* drink.

"Yay!"

I walk the trash to the shared dumpster behind the businesses on this end of Man Street while Jess grabs our bags and locks the studio. We follow a couple locals I semi-recognize down the sidewalk to Jerry's. I'm hoping to slip into the crowd under the cover of the jukebox music, but I'm walking next to Ms. Social Freaking Butterfly.

"Oh my goodness, that's Nikki Marchand!" Jess sticks her hand up and waves. "She was just asking me if I do personal training. I'm going to run over there for a sec and talk to her."

Aaand just like that, I'm standing alone. Geez.

Alright. Okay. No need to panic. I mean, this is Pitchette. I have to know like eighty-five percent of the folks in here. Oh hey! That's Laney Dupont working the bar, isn't it? Or wait, she's Laney Kibbler now. Right. She married Max Kibbler, who was a year behind us in school. Wonder if she remembers me?

Only one awkward way to find out.

"Laney!" Okay, that's *way* too personable. I mean, I haven't seen the woman in about ten years.

Laney looks up from the register, hesitates, then smiles. "Mollie Maris. I didn't even know you were back in town, girl."

"Yes. At the moment." And probably the rest of my life. "How have you been?"

"Busy." She steps back from the bar counter and displays a solid baby bump. "In more ways than one, as you can see."

"Oh my goodness! Congratulations!" Man, she does *not* look pregnant at all anywhere else. "Is this your first?"

"Third."

"Whoa." Holy crap. Three kids? Already? I can't even commit to a cat. "That's...incredible. Wow."

Okay, I know everyone has their own journey and life isn't one-size-fits all and blah blah blah, but I'm falling behind, right? Yeah, I'm falling behind. I'm in my thirties and not even thinking about kids, so obviously *something* isn't wired right.

"What can I get you, hon?" Laney asks.

Crap. Right. I'm making the pregnant lady with two little kids stand here and wait on me. And it's definitely past both of our bedtimes. Probably.

"IC Light," I blurt, because that's my safety drink.

"Sure. Bottle or tap?"

"Bottle, please." Bottle tastes better, I swear. "If you, um, have it." Dummy. Of course they have it. They just had it here Tuesday night, didn't they?

"I just ran out in my fridge up here," Laney tells me. "Gotta get one of the guys in the back to bring some up. Be right back."

"Sure."

I turn and lean my elbows against the bar. Jess is chatting with a couple that looks vaguely familiar. Don and Dani Weber? Geez. When did they get so gray? Wonder if they're still running the addiction recovery center over in Harwick.

Kind of crazy how busy Jerry's is on a Thursday night. Don't these folks have jobs to get to in the morning?

Dumb question. Of course they have jobs. Those jobs are probably why they're in a bar on a Thursday night.

"Mollie Maris," a guy behind me says. "I'm guessing this is yours."

Oh, of *course.* Because I can't just walk into a bar in my hometown and *not* relive the most humiliating experience of my life. Right, God? GAH!

Okay. At least I'm not selling some guy my socks. At least I'm wearing a skirt. At least my hair is done-ish. At least I don't smell like a dairy cow.

I pretend all that makes a difference when I turn and meet Liam Taggert's eyes across the bar counter. He isn't in a ballcap, but he has on jeans and another shirt that makes his muscles pop. Blue this time. And just in case anyone's wondering, *yes.* The exact same gorgeous blue as his gorgeous freaking eyes.

He uncaps the chilled IC Light in his hand and pushes the bottle across the bar to me.

I grip the cold neck and try not to crack the glass. "Um. Hey." Wow. *Brilliant* opening. The whole college thing is *totally* paying off.

He smiles lazily.

Oh, come *on!* I didn't even *do* anything!

"I haven't seen you in here before." He retrieves a microfiber towel from under the bar and starts polishing shot glasses. "I didn't know Jerry's was your stop."

"And I didn't know *you* worked here." Geez! Could I have sounded more like a middle schooler?

"I don't, technically." The muscles in his forearms are *super* distracting right now. "My cousin owns the place. I help cover shifts sometimes."

"Right. Makes sense." Everyone is related around here. "Do you, um, like working here?" IDIOT! What do I care if he likes working here? What am I doing, job shadowing?

"It's a hassle, most of the time." He looks up from the glass, his eyes catching in the ambient lighting. "Sometimes it's fun."

Yeah. Seems like it.

"So. First Sheetz. Now Jerry's. This is turning out to be quite a homecoming for you." He flips the glass upside down on a clean tray and selects another. "How long you in town?"

Great. Exactly what I want to talk about right now. "I'm, um, not really sure. I left my job in D.C. and I'm sort of between things right now." Which is grown-up code for *I have no direction in my life.*

"Are you looking for something in particular?"

"Depends. Is the Army hiring?"

"Always." Liam smiles. "But I have a feeling it wouldn't be a good fit."

"What, you don't think I have what it takes?" I mean. I *don't.* I just don't like other people thinking that.

And by other people I mean Liam Taggert.

"Oh, I'm not worried about you." He flips over the glass. "I'm worried about the Army."

"Excuse me?"

"I get the feeling sending you through Basic Combat Training would test the limits of 'Army Strong.'"

"What the hell does *that* mean?" My face and chest are hot, and it isn't because of alcohol. Unfortunately.

"It means whoever came up with that slogan never watched you fleece some creepy guy by convincing him to take your socks in exchange for donuts."

"His name's Twister and he's a *collector!*" There's a small chance I'm yelling, but the blood pounding in my ears makes it sort of hard to hear. "And I wasn't *fleecing* anybody. I was closing on a legitimate *business deal!*"

"Trading your socks for donuts?"

"I traded my socks for *money* to *spend* on donuts."

"My bad." He doesn't look like it's his bad. "I'm sure that distinction is important. Somehow."

That dumb grin on his dumb face is going to haunt my nightmares.

I fist my hands on top of the bar. "I would think the Army would *want* someone smart enough to cut a deal in the middle of a Sheetz parking lot that resulted in a 400 percent profit." Not to brag or anything.

"You're overestimating what Uncle Sam wants in a soldier."

"Are you saying Uncle Sam doesn't want soldiers with brains?"

"Not soldiers with *your* brains."

The nerve! "Um, *I* got a scholarship to Penn. *I* worked in D.C. There's *nothing* wrong with my brain." Aside from the embarrassing Hot Guy freakout thing it occasionally does.

Which I thankfully seem to be getting over, if this interaction is anything to go by. Because I'm definitely not seeing Liam Taggert as a sex god right now. I'm seeing him as a punching bag.

Liam's eyes crinkle at the corners, like this whole thing is a joke and not a fast way to get his face slammed off the bar. "I'm not saying there's anything wrong with your brain, Mollie."

"What *are* you saying?"

"That your brain shouldn't be wasted on the Army. It's meant for bigger and better things. Like world domination." He eyes a spot on my forehead. "You're clearly walking around with a weapon of mass destruction on your shoulders."

Okay, here's the thing. Part of me REALLY wants to take that as a compliment.

The other part is almost completely sure that it's misogynistic.

I narrow my eyes. "I can't tell if I should be offended or not."

Liam flips the towel over his shoulder and crosses his arms. He's still smiling, but it doesn't seem so arrogant now. "I know a lot of tough guys, Mollie. And I don't think any of them would want to stand between you and donuts."

Hm, yeah, okay. So the answer is YES, I should be offended.

There's enough heat running through me to warm my IC Light. "You know, just because you're Mr. Perfect and a war hero and have blue eyes and all doesn't mean you can make me feel bad about wanting donuts."

"What's blue eyes got to do with anything?"

"Blue eyes are a status symbol. Everyone wants blue eyes."

"They do?"

"Yes." Okay, I. I am 'everyone.'

"Well, *everyone* shouldn't. Blue eyes are overrated." Liam plants his hands on the bar and leans toward me. "Brown eyes are a lot prettier."

Brown eyes?

Wait. *I* have brown eyes.

Holy crap. Is Liam complimenting my eyes? Did he just say my eyes are pretty?

UM.

Quick! Say something, Brain! "My eyes are mostly hazel." Wow. Well done, dummy. Nailed it. IDIOT.

Liam lifts an eyebrow. "What's 'mostly hazel?'"

"It's when your eyes are actually brown, but you wish they weren't."

He smiles lazily.

"What?"

He shakes his head. "You're a nut, Mollie Maris."

"Wow. You *really* know how to give a woman compliments."

He snaps his towel and reaches for another glass. "For the record, I wasn't trying to make you feel bad about the donuts."

"You weren't?"

"Of course not. You exercised and then used your incredible business acumen to sell your workout socks to a stranger." He shrugs. "If anyone deserved donuts, it's you."

"Oh, *great.* You couldn't have said that before I got all guilty and decided to give my 400 percent profit earnings to charity?"

"You did?"

"Well, I haven't *yet.* But I'm going to." Honest. The twenty is still in my purse. It's either going to the county humane society or Pitchette Public Library. "The point is, I didn't get the donuts."

"Why?"

'Why?' What the heck does he mean, 'why?' "Geez, I don't know. Maybe because *someone* made some comments that sort of tainted the whole experience." Gah. PATHETIC. I'm PATHETIC.

"Coward."

"*Excuse* me?"

"Help one guy with a foot fetish one time, and you get all squeamish about taking a little smut money."

"For Pete's sake, he's not—it wasn't—I am *not* squeamish!" I am. I am squeamish. But that is *so* not the point. "A legitimate businessman approached me with a legitimate offer for my socks, so I made a legitimate sale. *Some* people might find it shady or weird or gross." It was, of course. "*I* happen to find it inspiring."

"Because?"

"Because if I can sell some random guy a disgusting pair of socks, I can sell anyone anything." Hm. I meant for that to come out like a 'suck it,' but it stayed real.

And now I'm secretly impressed with my own capabilities. I mean, I wasn't even trying to sell my socks and I ended up with twenty bucks. Imagine if I'd tried?

Maybe I *should* take Darrin's offer.

Liam's eyes narrow. "You're patting yourself on the back right now, aren't you?"

"*No.*" Yes. Damn it.

I snatch my beer off the bar and claim my exit, taking an extra-long swig, just to look cool.

"Yo Mark Cuban," Liam calls after me. "You're forgetting something."

I swallow my beer and turn. "What?"

"That's four bucks."

Oh. Right. No such thing as a free beer.

I pull the cash out of my purse. "Where's your tip jar, Sam Malone?"

Liam lifts an eyebrow. "Tip jar?"

"Yeah. You know. For money?"

"Mollie, I don't even work here. You don't have to tip me."

"I do." I hold up the twenty. "Remember? *Charity.*"

Liam blinks as I slap the bill onto the bar.

"Buy yourself some donuts."

I smile like sweat isn't dripping down my neck, toss my almost-incredible hair over my shoulder, and swagger blindly into the crowd, looking for Jess. Ha! That should show the arrogant pri—

Wait a minute. Did Liam Freaking Taggert just make a 400 percent profit off of me?

He did. He did do that. Without even trying. Because I'm

an IDIOT!

DAMN IT.

GAH!

NINE

I do a good job of sleeping until seven o'clock Friday morning.

Until my freaking phone rings.

Really, God? What is this? Cosmic punishment for pimping out my socks yesterday? Or for not getting out of bed this morning to exercise? Gah!

I *would* ignore it. You know, like a normal person.

Except normal people don't get calls at Dawn's Early Light from Darrin Schwartz.

And okay, so I don't *really* need to accept a call from him. But I'm accepting a paycheck from him. It probably isn't right not to answer. Right?

Great.

I clear my throat a few times, sit up, and take the call. "Hello?"

"Mollie." Darrin sounds like he just shotgunned a twelve-hour energy drink. "Good morning."

"Is it?" It's not. It's not a good morning.

"Ah, yes. I'm seeing what time it is there. It's eleven o'clock in London."

"Gee, that's a fun fact." False.

"I'm working out of our London office for a few days."

"Hm." Okay. Whatever.

"I'd call you back later, but I'm in meetings the rest of the day. So let me just ask. Have you thought about coming back to work with us?"

Seriously? That's what he needs to know, right this second? Isn't the whole point of paying me for a month of leave to give me space to think about things?

Okay, yes. FINE. I should be grateful that I'm getting paid to sit on my ass and think about work. The least I can do is answer his freaking question.

I rub my eyes. "Yes, I've thought about it."

"And?"

"And I'm still thinking. You know. Per the one-month's-salary agreement." I mean, come on. I can't be expected to be professional this time of day. Especially if I'm getting called up out of the blue.

"Of course. As long as you *are* thinking."

Does he think I'm lying?

"I have a conference call I need to hop on, Mollie. We'll talk soon."

We will? "I—"

He's gone.

Um.

What? What just happened? That was weird, right? Or, I don't know. Maybe I'm just not awake enough to understand? Or maybe this is a dream?

I toss my phone onto my night stand. It misses and *clunks* on the floor.

Okay. Not a dream.

Darrin's neurotic. That's it. Understandable. I mean, he probably has to be to run Schwartz so well. Especially across two continents.

I sigh and collapse back, bouncing lightly on my mattress.

A responsible adult would just get up and start the day.

Good thing I'm not one of those.

My phone rings again when there's a little more sunlight streaming through my window, but not enough to be classified as 'daytime.'

For Pete's sake! What's *wrong* with these people?

"What's wrong with you?" I demand once I find my phone and answer Jess' call.

"Good morning, babe!"

"No, it isn't."

"Yikes. I'd have thought getting that extra two hours of sleep would've improved your mood, not made it worse."

Oh for— "What do you want, Jess?"

"What time are we going to Sonny's?"

"What?"

"I just want to make sure I have enough time between classes."

Geez. I'm not getting *any* sleep this morning, am I?

I kick off my sheets toddler-style. "Whatever time you want to go. You're the one with the nine-to-five."

"More like seven-to-whenever. Hold on a sec." Her voice gets all muffled for thirty seconds. "Sorry. My Sunrise Seniors like to turn off their hearing aids during cool down."

"Why?" Not that I care too much.

"So they can tune me out and nap during *shavasana*."

Nap. Geez. That sounds nice. But you have to be ASLEEP FIRST and WAKE UP before you can officially take a nap. "Can we skip to the part where you just tell me what time you want to go to Sonny's?"

"How about around eleven-thirty? I take some time for lunch between classes."

"Great. See ya." I hang up.

Shadows dance across my ceiling as I sigh. A gentle morning breeze disturbs the curtains, and the lace sends dappled patterns through my room. One of the benefits of having an east-facing window.

This would all be very soothing and peaceful if Terry Bauer across the street wasn't hollering at his dog to stop crapping in the road.

Freaking Pitchette. I had more peace and quiet in my Michigan Avenue loft in D.C.

The only thing capable of propelling me into clothes and down the stairs into the kitchen is coffee, so I—

Damn it! *That's* what I forgot to buy yesterday! Gah!

I slam Mom's mug cabinet closed. I can go without. Ha. Not really. I can run to the IGA and grab a bag. I mean, it wouldn't be anything fancy. And I'm not really in any condition to talk to other humans before my first cup. Or if I can distract myself for a few hours, I can get into town a little early and grab a cup from Sal's before walking down to Foundations.

I mean, I have plenty to distract me. Like unpacking. It doesn't make sense to unpack everything, now that my future with Schwartz is up for grabs. But I can't keep living out of boxes. My brain doesn't work that way. And my clothes don't deserve a wrinkled existence.

I grab a spotty banana from the kitchen, my Bluetooth speaker from the living room, and a box just marked 'Clothes' from the mudroom. My stomach rumbles as I navigate the stairs, so I scarf the banana before I put on my 'No Fs Left' playlist and start filling in my bedroom closet.

I blink and it's filled. And the box isn't empty.

Huh. Guess I officially outgrew my childhood bedroom.

That's going to be an issue if I stay here for an extended period of time. I'll probably have to grow up and switch bedrooms with Mom.

Okay, fine. I can admit it: I'm *not* prepared for the emotional and mental consequences of stepping into Mom's place. I mean, it's one thing to live in her house and sleep in my bedroom. It's another thing to live in her house and sleep in *her* bedroom. Even though she's probably watching me right now, yelling across the cosmos that I'm being an idiot and just take the damn space already!

"For Pete's sake, Mom!" I roll my eyes at the ceiling. "I'm still trying to catch my breath. Give me a break, okay?" Geez!

I don't want to leave my nicer clothes that don't fit in the closet boxed, so I pull off my sleeping shorts and tank top and step into a swirly black skirt and a sleeveless white top with tiny black polka dots. Totally inappropriate for Sonny's Sporting Goods. But cute and breezy and I just don't give a damn, anyway. I *do* give a damn about my footwear. Considering the whole point is to get hiking boots. So even though it looks a little silly, I tug on a pair of ankle socks and sneakers.

Wow. My life is SO *Working Girl.*

I'm not sure exactly how the time disappears, but I end up rushing through my makeup and hair just to get out the door. My brain has started to realize I'm tricking it into not thinking about caffeine and it won't be long before I have a Level 7 Nuclear Meltdown. My life might be borderline pathetic, but I'm *not* going to end up crying in the middle of a sporting good's store. Especially not in the town I grew up in. *That's* the surest way for Jess to ask me to surrender my Best Friend Card. The only reason she didn't ask for it back following the Sheetz incident is because she doesn't *know* about the Sheetz incident.

Sal's is hopping by the time I wedge my Honda into the last spot on Man Street. Looks like the late breakfasters are heading out and the early lunch crowd is heading in. I weave my way through the sidewalk crowd, saying 'Hey!' to the familiar faces. I recognize a lot of them, but not in a way that makes me feel the need to stop and talk. A cluster of guys older than me goes by. One of them is Jess' uncle Jimmy Spencer. And there seems to be a lot of teenage boys coming out of Sal's. Hm. Do they work here or do they—

Oh crap.

Liam steps out of the diner after the boys. His eyebrows lift in surprise when he sees me, but settle as soon as he glances over my outfit. At my shoes.

Or more likely, *my freaking socks.*

Gah! Of *course* Liam Freaking Taggert is the person I run into before I've had coffee. And of *course* he has to look like that, with the joggers and the ball cap and the white shirt with the red sleeves straining over his muscles. Like he just got done with a *Sports Illustrated* photo shoot or something. Why, God? WHY.

"Mollie Maris," he drawls. Why does he already look like he's laughing at me? "You're everywhere these days, aren't you?"

"*No.*" Great! I sound like a complete grouch. How far is it to the nearest cup of coffee? Because I have a feeling I'm going to NEED IT ASAP.

Apparently, Liam takes scowling as an invitation to engage. "Meeting someone?"

"Getting coffee." Hopefully this millennium.

He smiles. "Well, you have good timing. Sal just started a fresh pot."

"Great." Geez. Can I sound any less enthusiastic? I mean, hello, Brain! There's *caffeine* six feet away!

The problem is Liam Taggert is *two* feet away. Standing between Brain and said caffeine.

"Hey, Coach." One of the gawkier boys slides up next to

us, a wide grin taking over his dirt-smudged face. "Who's your friend?"

"We're not friends," I say.

"Ouch, Maris." Liam's eyes crinkle at the corners. "Way to make me look bad in front of my team and coaching staff."

I roll my eyes to cover up my immediate embarrassment. "I'm sure you'll get over it." Obviously. Since he's Mr. Popularity around here and I'm that girl who left years ago, then came back and moved into her dead mom's house.

"I'm Baxley." Baxley sticks his hand out, oblivious to my discomfort. "Call me Bax. You're pretty. You like ball players, Maris?"

Oh geez. This kid is way too confident for his age.

But correcting that is *not* on me.

It's on the enlarged boyfriend of the wrong girl Baxley is inevitably going to hit on.

"Hey, Baxley." I shake his hand, refusing to wince at the clamminess. "I'm Mollie."

"And she definitely doesn't like ball players." Liam's eyes glitter when I meet his look. "Right, Maris?"

Okay. If my brain was operating under the proper influence of coffee instead of sleep deprivation and raging estrogen, I might be able to figure out if Liam is making fun of me or not. The best I can do right now is recognize the lazy smile on his face.

I narrow my eyes at him. "Depends on the player."

"You need my stats before you can make an informed decision about what I have to offer." Baxley's sonovabitch grin is going to get him into BIG trouble. "Understood. Well, Mollie, I'm a first string first baseman—"

"And a senior in high school," Liam concludes. He nods toward the other coaches and Baxley's teammates, glued to their phones halfway down the sidewalk. "Go tell the guys to get in the van."

"Dang, Coach. Don't be all salty." Baxley wags his eyebrows at me. "I was just making a new friend."

"Bet he's headed for some interesting lawsuits," I say as we watch Baxley saunter off.

"I keep telling myself 'one more year.'"

"Good luck." I smile at Liam. And it isn't nice. "He gives off some real returning-after-graduation-to-assistant-coach vibes."

Liam's beautiful eyes widen.

So does my smile. "Well, Coach, see ya!"

I walk into Sal's before he can respond. By the time I get done chatting with Sal and paying for the coffee and impulse muffins, Man Street is Liam-free. Good. I scoot down to Foundations and slip inside as Jess is winding down some sort of Pilates class. She only has about five people, but they take forever to grab their stuff and leave. I almost eat Jess' muffin while I listen to them gossip. Something about something someone posted somewhere in a community Facebook group. Titillating stuff.

"Ooh! Is that for me?" Jess peeks inside the paper bag once the last of her clients leave.

"It's cranberry."

"Thanks, babe! I'm starved." She breaks off a piece of muffin top and pops it in her mouth. "Those ladies just retired, so they have all this energy and nowhere to channel it. It's awesome, because I actually get a workout running their class."

I yawn and pull on my coffee. "I don't know how you have all this energy. I'm basically doing nothing with my life and I can barely function." I'd say it's depression, but that feels like an easy out. More likely it's just my incredible laziness. And the fact I don't have any clear direction in my life.

Jess must sense the mood change. "Well, babe, you're in

Pitchette now. So we're going to get you some kick-ass boots. Then we're going to put them to use."

Yay. Sounds fun. "Want me to drive or do you want to?"

"I will!" She finishes her muffin and grabs her keys. "Dad told me to check out some tackle stuff for him the next time I'm in Sonny's. Don't let me forget."

"Sure."

We climb into her Subaru and head out of town.

Do not be fooled. The fact Pitchette has a sporting goods store doesn't make it an Appalachian metropolis. An outsider might think a town with four churches, a Sheetz, a hardware store, a diner, a bar, and a burgeoning fitness studio is on the up-and-up. Not true. Those things are just the substructure for most towns in Western PA because they accommodate everyday necessities in people's lives. Everyone needs to worship. Everyone needs to eat. Everyone needs a drink. Everyone needs a place to buy firearms.

Okay, so Jess' studio isn't necessarily something you'll find in the small towns around here. Which, as she said, is probably part of the reason so many folks in this region have chronic health conditions. That's why it's so important for Foundations to thrive. Current market research says about twenty percent of small businesses fail within the first year of operation. Fifty percent don't make it past five years. Combine that with the economic and social demographics of Pitchette, and Foundations is already starting behind the line of scrimmage. Or whatever the applicable athletic term is.

Part of me wants to tell Jess she should consider opening her studio in a more urban area. Somewhere east, maybe. Because Western PA and Eastern PA were two different PAs. You can divide Pennsylvania through State College, slap down a new border, and not many people will object. I mean, State College might object. Penn State grads are sort of rabid when it comes to identity.

My first major culture shock was moving to Philadelphia to attend Penn. It sounds ridiculous, but until that point in my life I didn't realize there are Pennsylvanians who never attended Youth Field Days growing up or participated in hunter safety programs in school. I mean, don't get me wrong. I'm *way* more Anne Hathaway than Annie Oakley. But even *I* know the difference between a shotgun and a rifle. Mostly.

Jess pulls off and parks in the gravel lot that belongs to Sonny's. The building is plain and sided with stained wood. The only thing identifying it is the sign over the door. It doesn't matter. Locals know where it is and tourists wouldn't dream of stopping.

Inside smells exactly as I expect. Fifty percent leather and dirt, fifty percent burned coffee. The coffee is from the help-yourself carafe sitting on a folding table next to the minnow tank right when you walk in. I prefer my coffee not burned, but I'm not exactly in a position to be picky, considering what I got from Sal's is long gone. I'd happily help myself, except there aren't any cups. Probably the regulars know that and bring their own thermoses. Damn it! Left my Stanley at home.

I'd been in Sonny's a couple times growing up. Not enough to know where everything is. Which is why I follow Jess toward a corner of the store dedicated to outdoor footwear. It isn't a big section, but it has the basics: hiking boots, trail shoes, water shoes, those sandals outdoorsy people like to wear. Honestly, none of it is really my style. But around here it's prudent to have boots to keep in your car. There's no one I'd rather buy them with than Jess.

"Hm. Not a lot of choices." She pulls a box off the shelf and checks out the chunky dark green things inside. "Try these."

"Yes, ma'am." I wrangle out of my sneakers and into the boots. "Oof. These things are like those weighted boots divers used to wear."

"How do they feel?"

"Clunky."

She rolls her eyes. "Beyond that."

"Sort of snug. Too snug. And the arch is weird." I'm not being difficult. It's true.

And I *really* need more coffee.

"Okay. Try the brown and blue ones."

I trade her boxes and tug them on with as much enthusiasm as I can muster post-Liam-Taggert-sock-fiasco. Seriously, how the heck am I supposed to get into shoe shopping with *that* humiliation hanging over my head? Gah!

Jess eyes me as I tug at the laces. "Are they comfortable?"

"I don't know." I straighten and take a few steps. They aren't *terrible.*

Honestly, I'm just finding it difficult to get into this whole thing.

"Well, do they *feel* comfortable?"

"Jess, I don't *know.* Walking around in here isn't exactly the same as hiking through the woods." Though to be fair, I'm probably way more likely to wear hiking boots inside than outside. Since, you know. I'm not really planning to take up hiking. "I mean, they're roomy. I guess."

"I wasn't paying attention when you took off your shoes. What socks do you have on right now?"

My cheeks get a little hot. For Pete's sake. Am I destined to spend the rest of my life blushing at the term 'socks?'

"Standard," I mutter.

"Omg, 'standard?'" Jess laughs. "What the heck are 'standard' socks?"

Investments, according to Twister. "I don't know, Jess! They're just normal athletic socks. Why does it matter?"

"Well, you'd probably be hiking in socks that are thicker than that. So those boots might be roomy now, but they won't be if you're wearing the proper socks."

Great. "So what now?"

"Um." She glances around the aisle. "Hang on." Then she disappears.

Seriously, what am I even doing here? Dropping money on hiking boots? I mean, they'll be good to have, of course. I'll use them around Pitchette. But is there much point in buying them if I'm not going to be here long-term?

Not that I'm going back to Schwartz. Necessarily. I mean, I'm still weighing my options! It's just the chances of me staying in Pitchette for the rest of my life seem slim. Besides Jess, what exactly do I have here?

She pops back into the aisle. "Okay, put these on."

A pair of wool hiking socks. Still in the package. "Jess, I can't just open this package and put these on!"

"You can if you buy them."

Okay, God. There's a subliminal message here, right? Because no way all these sock situations are coincidental. I mean, do the socks represent something? Like my life? Or my future?

"Yikes," Jess says when I snatch the package from her. "Sorry. Didn't know you felt this strongly about socks."

"I didn't until yesterday."

"Why? What happened yesterday?"

"I had an awkward conversation at Sheetz." Spoiler alert! IT WASN'T WITH TWISTER.

"I know I'm missing something here, but you're kind of intense right now and I'm not sure I want to know."

"You don't." *I* don't.

"Cool. How do the boots feel now?"

Mm. "Actually kind of tight. You were right. The socks

do make a difference."

"Let's try a half-size up." She hands over another box.

I kick off the boots. "That was fast. Have you done this before?"

"Babe, you know I worked for that shoe store in college."

"Oh yeah." I sigh. "You got me so many discounts."

"Yeah." She sighs, too. "I sort of miss it."

Half a size up feels okay with the socks. The boots don't have a price on them, so I check with the cashier while Jess disappears to check out something fishing-related for her dad.

The guy behind the counter—Sonny himself—barely glances at the boot box. "One-forty."

Geez! One hundred and forty dollars for a pair of hiking boots? "That seems expensive." For Pitchette.

Sonny shrugs.

I blow out a breath. Alright. Whatever. I have the money, so it doesn't really matter. This is probably why I don't have any boots to begin with, though. Because they require you to dip into your 401(k).

Jess reappears as I'm finishing up a one-way interaction with Sonny. For a second I think it might turn into a two-way interaction when I ask for a receipt. But then he just glowers and hands it over without a word.

"Yikes," Jess mutters as we leave. "What the heck did you do to Sonny?"

"Asked him how his day was going."

"Ah. That's where you went wrong." She opens her car door. "This is Pitchette, babe. Every day's the same."

Yeah. That's what I'm afraid of.

I don't know how Friday slips by.

Actually, that's not true. A significant part of the day

post-shopping is getting photos of Jess and some of her more willing clients who think the fame outweighs the burden of being featured on social media. It's a special kind of challenge, trying to get action shots of mostly-senior citizens without accidentally turning them into ads for blood pressure medication. Thank God they're so enthusiastic. Really takes the sting out of the fact that I only get about eight decent photos out of the seventy-one I take.

Photography is not my thing, okay? Jess is going to need to find someone to do it for her long-term. A high schooler, maybe. Someone who's artistic. And free. And comfortable working with reels, since that's where all social media is headed. *I* want to be Jess' everything, but let's be honest: I'm a generation behind on what's cool. Yes, Foundations is pitching to an older audience. But young people drive social media trends.

Geez. 'Young people.' What am I, eighty?

I get out of Jess' hair around four o'clock and go home to work on updating her socials. Most of my life is still in boxes, but I've carved out an office-ish spot at the kitchen table where my laptop floats in a growing puddle of notes for Jess. My system is a little scattered. Probably because I didn't return to Pitchette prepared to help my best friend run her business. I'll get organized at some point. Eventually. Once I run out of sticky notes. Despite appearances, my work brain doesn't function in chaos.

That's strictly reserved for my private life.

Engagement is up across all of the Foundations' social media accounts. That's a good sign. The trick now is to get those engagements translated into customers. As happens with social media, a lot of the people interacting with our posts aren't local. So while it's great to see Foundations getting traction, we need to be focusing on attracting people in and around Pitchette. You know. Who can make a difference in whether or not Jess can keep the lights on.

Hm. Wonder what other community groups are around here. Foundations should connect with them to start building a local following. I'll have to talk to Jess about that. See if there are any specific groups she wants to collaborate with. Looking online, it seems like most of them are school- or church-based. No doubt she'll have a better feeling for which ones are more active and effective than others.

My phone buzzes somewhere in the distance. Damn! How is it already eight o'clock? No wonder I'm freaking hungry. My diet today consisted of a muffin, coffee, and half of a pepperoni roll I stole from Jess at the studio when she wasn't looking.

And crap! I forgot to get groceries. AGAIN.

Alright. Phone first. It's probably Jess. Which is good, because I could—

Oh. A text. From Darrin Schwartz.

For Pete's sake, Darrin Schwartz is *texting* me now? Seriously? Two communications in the last fourteen hours? When we aren't even on the same continent?

And he clearly doesn't even really have anything to say. *Just checking in* isn't a good enough excuse for disrupting my dive down the small business Pinterest rabbit hole.

Even though he's paying me a lot of money to dive down the small business Pinterest rabbit hole.

Gah!

Fine. Whatever. I don't need to engage, I just need to acknowledge. A succinct message updating him on the status of my considerations. Which hasn't changed since he called me less than twenty-four hours ago.

Thumbs up. He gave it a thumbs up. What the heck am I supposed to do with that?

Okay, not going to worry about it. I mean, there

definitely isn't any reason to. I have weeks to think things over. The whole point of this leave of absence is to distance myself from work, to get perspective.

Hard to do that when my former slash semi-current boss pops up on my phone every day, wanting to know where I stand. He never paid this much attention to me when I worked down the freaking hall from his office.

So no. I'm not going to let him get into my head. I'm going to step back from all this and not worry about any of it until I have Jess' social media running smoothly. Right now, helping her is my priority. Darrin Schwartz can suck it.

Respectfully.

TEN

Fine. *Yes.* Easier said than done, not worrying about Darrin or his dumb texts or whether I should return to D.C. I mean, come on, God! Can't I just get *one night* of complete sleep? Without daybreak workouts or phone calls or nightmares about my leave of absence being up and Darrin sending federal agents to arrest me in Pitchette because I forget to tell him whether or not I'm coming back? GAH!

Today doesn't feel like a *Working Girl* kind of day, so I make do with a pair of cropped yoga pants, a loose V-neck tee, and sandals. My grumpiness dissipates until I get downstairs and reach for the coffee that isn't there.

DAMN IT! This isn't *Working Girl*. This is freaking *Groundhog Day*.

Oh. Oh crap. That's *exactly* what life in Pitchette is like. I should've seen it sooner. I mean, the real-life Punxsutawney is only about an hour and a half away!

Alright. Don't panic. Bill Murray broke the day-after-day cycle. If Bill Murray can break the cycle, I sure as heck can. Behavioral changes! That's how he did it. Making the choice to live differently than he did every day before. That's what I'll do.

Starting with a walk. Not a forced march, like Jess made me do. A good, old-fashioned walk up town. It's about two miles to Man Street. That will give me time to think. I can grab coffee from Sal's, then head across town.

There's only one person I can talk to about the whole Darrin-wants-me-back situation. I love Jess and all, but she isn't exactly prone to offering helpful advice. She believes strongly in harnessing Fate and Luck, and while I know those things exist, I don't like to count on them. Mostly because in my life, Fate is a paralyzed introvert and Luck is a raging bitch. Jess is more *veni, vidi, vici* and I'm more *holy crap, how the heck did THAT happen?*

The only person who will have the right answer for me is in Section D of the Risen Hill Cemetery, across the street from the IGA.

Mom talked about that part of the cemetery when she was first diagnosed. Lots of folks probably think it's morbid to spend your eternal slumber 100 yards from a frozen pizza aisle. Not Mom. For one thing, she liked frozen pizza. For another, the IGA was where she laid the foundation for her new life. *Our* new life. Yes, she eventually traded night cleaning shifts for working as a customer support specialist at the local bathware manufacturer. It paid more, offered benefits, and didn't give her varicose veins.

But I know the IGA meant a lot more to her than health coverage and holidays off.

Which is why I didn't mind paying two grand for an end plot on slanted ground directly facing the IGA parking lot. Her headstone slopes and her grave will get covered in grass clippings in the summer, but she's content there. I know so.

Walking through the sliding doors of the IGA brings back

the past. Mostly of me when I was little. Holding Mom's hand when she shopped. Playing in the teensy staff breakroom while she worked at night. Running in on Saturday mornings for milk and eggs once I got my driver's license. Dropping change into the red kettle for the Salvation Army during Christmas.

None of those things were earth-shattering events. But they contain some of my most potent core memories.

Standing in the blast zone of the air curtain, staring at the ancient cashier belts, watching folks shop makes me realize that.

Maybe I should buy the burial plot next to Mom's. The IGA was my new beginning, too.

"Is that Mollie Maris?"

I turn toward the voice. Stella Hartnet. Gosh. She's worked for the IGA as long as I can remember and is approximately 109 years old.

Everyone loves her. Mom especially.

My heart wavers a little when Stella stuffs me into a hug, commenting on my hair, asking about my life. Catching up with her feels like catching up with your grandmother.

I assume.

"I didn't know you were back in town, sweetie," she says, peering up at me through her progressive lenses. "Are you staying long?"

"A month, at least." After that, who the heck knows?

"And how's the D.C. job?"

Complicated. "Demanding." Also true.

"And what are you doing while you're in town?"

Eek. "I'm trying to get Mom's house cleaned up." That's my story and I'm sticking to it. "It needs a little love." And *Property Brothers*.

"Have you seen your mom yet?"

That's one of the things about Pitchette. Even after you're

dead and buried, folks still want to hang out with you.

"I'm on my way to see her now," I say. "Just stopped in for a snack."

I need groceries, too. But they can wait. I can't show up to Mom's place empty-handed. Even though her current address is in a pearly-gated community, that woman will find the nearest medium and send me a direct message regarding my manners.

"Try dairy," Stella advises. "The Reddi-Whip whipped cream is buy one, get one half-off."

Um, SCORE!

I wink at Stella. "Thanks for the tip."

"I'm so glad to see you, sweetie." She gives me another hug. "Tell your mom I miss her around here."

Aw.

No. I'm *not* going to end up sobbing in the middle of a grocery store. My life is too depressing for that.

I tug a blue plastic handbasket out of the basket stack and head toward the dairy aisle. Normal folks probably need something like Nilla wafers or ice cream to feel good about eating whipped cream, but what's the point of adding extra calories to an already perfect snack? It's just heavy cream and sugar whipped into a semi-solid form with a little nitrous oxide. If it was in a liquid form, everyone would call it a milkshake. And milkshakes are totally socially acceptable to eat on their own.

Growing up, whipped cream was for special occasions. Birthdays. Christmas hot cocoas. The night I bawled my eyes out because I wasn't invited to Tara Basher's sweet sixteen. It wasn't expensive on its own, but Mom only bought it when we had extra money left over in the grocery budget at the end of the month. Even now, in my thirties, with my own source of income, I only buy it when I'm celebrating. Or making a life-changing decision.

I don't know the cashier operating the checkout conveyor belt when I *thunk* down my basket of whipped cream. Which makes the judgmental look she gives me super inappropriate.

"Are you helping out with the Little League strawberry social?" she asks sweetly.

She knows full well I'm not. The strawberry social has been planned by the same six people since Moses parted the Red Sea.

"Nope."

She drags cans over the scanner. "Ice cream party?"

"No."

"Hot date?"

I wish. "Uh-uh."

She gives up. "That's twenty-four dollars."

I hand over the cash and leave with my loot.

Oh yeah. Walking to the cemetery is the right call. The day is stunning. Plus, I need to get ahead of the eight cans of whip that are almost certainly ending up on my ass and hips.

Ugh. Geez. What am I, back in middle school?

I glance both ways before jogging across the street and cutting through the cemetery. It's only a day into June, but about half of the grass is already yellow and crunchy. I forgot what summer looks like in Western PA. I mean, D.C. is a swamp in the summer. But this part of Northern Appalachia holds its own when it comes to heat index. Blistering days. High humidity. Dead lawns. This isn't the city, so people don't do crazy things like water their lawns or wash their sidewalks. Some towns have water towers or reservoirs. But most folks out in the country get their water from springs or wells sunk on their properties. That's a true blessing, if your water source isn't contaminated by strip mining or agricultural runoff. The water from places like Pitchette supply big-name bottled water companies. That blue label with the white stag you can find in any grocery store or gas station? Sourced from Pennsylvania. When rainfall is adequate, there are even places around here where fresh spring water runs directly onto the road. Folks who don't have access to potable water drive for miles, park in the ditch, and fill up empty jugs to take home. During dry spells, they'll capture the free run-off in empty drums for farm use and property maintenance.

I've seen those run-offs hundreds of times. But after living so long in D.C., they feel...I don't know. *Archaic.* Like a byproduct of a different era.

How is it possible that just five hours northwest of the White House, people drink water running out of pipes onto the dirt road?

The upright headstone facing the IGA is a whole generation brighter than the ones surrounding it. The jagged edge claws at my fingers when I grip the top and sink into the grass. I set aside the grocery bag, pull off my sandals, and fold my legs.

"Hi, Mom."

Hi, sweetie, she'd say. *You look tired.*

"Ha. You don't know the half of it."

Tell me.

The sun feels so nice. Welcoming. Safe. I stretch out on the ground and turn on my side, facing Mom. Like we're on her bed, watching black-and-white movies. A bowl of popcorn between us. Fuzzy socks on our feet. My classmates spent Saturday nights tailgating or partying at the lake, but I spent them with my mother. It definitely wasn't cool. It's probably one of the reasons why I hate trying to make new friends as an adult. But now that she's gone, the only thing I want is to be back in her room. On her bed. Watching movies.

Lying next to her grave feels like a really crappy next best thing.

"Okay, Mom. Let's get into it."

Let me be clear: yes, I'm talking to my mother's headstone. No, I'm not doing it because I actually think she's listening from the corpse buried beneath me. Mom's gone and her spirit is off doing whatever spirits do. I like to think God is rewarding her for all the decent, selfless things she did with her life on Earth. But I don't pretend to understand the next realm of existence.

Ergo me lying in the middle of the cemetery, talking to her headstone.

Okay. Time to break out the whipped cream.

I break the seal on a canister and *clink* it against her headstone. "Cheers."

She totally would've called dibs on the first squirt of whip. Too bad she's dead.

I smile. "Guess there's more for me."

Geez. Glad no one's around to witness my unholy sense of humor.

Grief is a funny thing. I loved Mom more than anything in the world. I *still* love her more than anything. That woman was my best friend, my mentor, my protector. The love of my freaking life. When she died, so did some of me. And when I buried her, I buried that piece of me, too.

And yet, I somehow feel closer to her now that she's gone. As if because she's moved beyond this realm of existence, she's completely free to be with me at all times. She isn't hemmed in by the physical rules of corporeality. It isn't physically impossible anymore for her to be everywhere at any time. We tend to believe there's this sort of curtain between our earthly existence and the afterlife. But what if there isn't? What if one person's mortality is a channel for another person's immortality? What if the only time you can communicate across the great divide is when one person exists in *this* world and the other person exists in the *next?* What if—

Focus.

Gah. Right. "Sorry. No idea how I got started down that rabbit hole." Probably too much whip.

I swallow my current mouthful and set down the canister.

"Alright, Mom. Here's the sitch."

Tell me, sweetie.

"I quit my job."

Silence.

"What, no comment?"

I'm sure you know what you're doing.

"Ha!" Okay. I'm definitely editorializing. There's no flipping way *my mother* would accept me quitting my job. Also, that she'd believe I know what I'm doing.

I *never* know what I'm doing. See also: the last thirty-three years of my life.

Moving on. "The thing is, my old boss, Darrin—"

Is he the one who asked you out last summer?

"What? Oh. No, that was Daniel."

Right. Did you go out with him?

"Um, no. He's way too into bowties."

Mollie! I did not raise you to be so shallow.

"No, you raised me to use my *brain* and trust my *gut*. Daniel sent up a lot of red flags for me." And he talked about ultimate frisbee way too much. As in, at all.

When's the last time you went on a date?

"Geez, I don't know. I guess it's been—hey! Quit distracting me." Holy crap, I have an overactive subconscious. "We're talking about me quitting my job."

Right. Sorry, sweetie, go ahead.

Gah! "Yeah, so I turned in my two-weeks' notice and then

out of the blue, Darrin—"

Oh wait, he's the one with the emotional range of a robot?

"MOM!"

Call me crazy, but I *swear* I hear her laugh. For just a millisecond. Like a breeze blew aside the curtain between here and the beyond and let her voice through.

Maybe I'm going into hypoglycemic shock. That's a thing, right?

Guess I better eat some more whip before my blood sugar gets too low.

"Darrin called me and offered me my job back. Actually, he offered me a *new* job." I lick the whip nozzle. "He thinks I'd be a good fit for a new team the company is creating."

That's great, sweetie!

"Is it?" That's why I'm here. Because I don't know if it is. "I'm not sure that I want to keep working in marketing." There. I said it.

What would you do, instead?

Yeah. That's the problem. "I don't know. I've been on this path since college. I'm not sure what else I'm interested in."

Hm.

Um. "That's it? 'Hm?'"

Did you expect something insightful?

"I mean. Yes?"

Why? I'm not Mom, Mollie. I'm you.

Oh for Pete's sake. Even my subconscious can't roleplay properly. "I'm not asking you for advice, I'm just trying to organize my thoughts."

What would Mom say?

"She'd say—"

I don't know. That she loved me, first. Then something that would manage to be both criticism and encouragement. Mom never yelled, but she was the queen of scolding. One sentence would leave you feeling two inches tall and strangely empowered.

I roll onto my back, bringing a new can of whip with me. The clouds hang lazily without a breeze to move them along. Bird calls fill the air instead of rustling leaves, killdeer and robins and sparrows whistling as they scavenge the cemetery.

I sigh. "It's a good job. And the pay increase isn't nothing."

But it's not everything.

"No. But I don't know what *is* everything." Love? Family? Property? Investments? Philanthropy? Learning how to fly a Cessna? Most little girls dream about all that stuff. But *this* little girl never grew up to experience any of it.

Seventy-seven is the average life expectancy of an American woman. That puts the half-way mark at roughly thirty-eight.

Meaning statistically, in five years my life will be half over.

Holy crap. *Holy crap.*

Five more years and I start the down-hill slide to death.

GAH!

"I don't want to die in my office." Guess that's my biggest reservation here. Marketing is okay, but it isn't my passion.

I've never *had* a passion. I have things I like doing. Eating. Sleeping. Walking.

Wait. Those are just normal life-things. Crap. Okay, um. Reading! I enjoy reading magazines. Not just brain-rot stuff that you can grab in the check-out line. I like *Popular Mechanics* and *Smithsonian* and stuff like that. Sure, I've never actually subscribed to them. But, you know. If I happen to be in a waiting room somewhere and there happens to be a copy, I'll probably stuff it in my bag to read later. Which is *not* theft.

I like shopping. That's a thing I do sometimes. I mean, not a *lot.* Mom raised me frugally and I don't understand the appeal of accumulating credit card debt. Shopping is one of those things I feel like I do all the time, but my monthly statements say I only do when I need food, gas, deodorant, or emotional support clothes.

Seriously? What kind of grown-ass woman can't think of a single thing she enjoys doing, just for the hell of it? How has my life gone from being a kid to being a college student to working full-time and doing nothing else?

Good grief. I'm one of those people old folks warn you not to be. I'm one of those people who puts in eighty hours a week at a meaningless job for forty flipping years and dies the day before retirement.

That's how Mom went. I mean, she definitely didn't make it to retirement. But her job killed her. Or at least breathing in toxic fumes from the bathware plant did. Probably.

A dull ache settles in the area of my tear ducts. I blink and tears gush down my cheeks. Sticky trails arching over my cheekbones and flooding my ears before dripping into the grass beneath my head.

"I miss you, Mom."

Me, too, sweetie.

When I close my eyes, I can see her smiling.

ELEVEN

"M*ollie!"*

I jerk awake. Two guys are inches from my face.

"What the hell!" I sit up fast and they both reel back.

"Take it easy," one of them says.

Gold hair. Blue eyes. Sexy scruff.

Liam.

DAMN IT!

Okay. I don't exactly know what's happening, but I can tell by the firetrucks and the cops and the cluster of folks ogling me that it's probably not great. And probably super embarrassing.

Dear God, if You're listening, please, *please,* just hit me with a bolt of lightning. Now would be great.

I blink a few times. Rub my eyes. Look for storm clouds.

Everyone's still here.

"Um, what's going on?" I ask.

Liam exhales and looks at the other guy hovering over me. "I think she's okay, Tan-Man."

"Tan-Man?" I shield my eyes against the raging sunlight.

"Tanner Manson?"

He grins and flips his brown hair out of his eyes. "Wow, you actually remember me?"

"Yeah." I dig through my memories for proof. "You played basketball with Jess Johnson's little brother Matty. So you were five years behind us in school. Right?"

"Yeah, she's okay," Liam says. "You can go cancel EMS and tell Chief Miller the police can leave. We'll finish up here."

"Got it. Good seeing you, Mollie. Glad you're okay." He gets up and jogs off.

"What does he mean?" I ask Liam.

Liam's wearing boots, blue tactical pants, and a blue t-shirt with the white Pitchette Volunteer Fire Department logo on the breast. On his hands are a pair of nitrile gloves and he has one knee planted in the grass.

He pulls off his gloves, folding them into each other. "He means we were worried this was a lot more serious."

A plastic medical kit sits next to me on the ground. "What's that for?"

"It's naloxone. We use it to reverse—"

"I know what naloxone is." Geez. I wasn't born yesterday. "I mean why the heck do you have it out?"

He stares at me. "Are you serious?"

"Uh...yes?" What kind of question is that?

"Someone called 9-1-1 because they saw you passed out on the ground and thought you overdosed."

"What? That's ridiculous!"

"The call made it sound like an opioid overdose, so we brought out the naloxone." He glances at the whipped cream canister in my hand. "It doesn't do anything for whippets."

"Whippets?"

"That's when people huff the nitrous oxide—"

"*I know what whippets are!*" Seriously, does he think I'm

totally stupid? "I was *not* doing whippets, for Pete's sake!"

He raises an eyebrow.

"What?" I demand.

"Your eyes are pretty red. Sort of bloodshot."

What? "I fell asleep crying." GREAT. Glad I came right out and admitted *that.*

"And you *do* have a lot of canisters."

My face feels too hot. "I like whipped cream."

"Plus you have a plastic bag."

"To carry the whipped cream!" Honestly! "You can't just walk out of the IGA with an armload of whipped cream canisters and carry them to the cemetery! Folks will think you're nuts!"

"Yeah, we wouldn't want folks to think that." His eyes sparkle obnoxiously.

"This isn't funny! I don't do whippets. I've *never* done whippets. I don't even mix ibuprofen and alcohol!" Geez, I'm BORING. "And it's not because I'm *boring,* it's because I'm *responsible.*" There. That clears it up.

"Good to know." He reaches over my legs to retrieve the naloxone kit. "Although you were going to be my first whippet OD."

"You can overdose on whippets?"

"You can overdose on almost anything." He shakes a canister, flips it upside down, and presses the nozzle. Nothing comes out. "Including whipped cream, apparently."

"I did not pass out from eating whipped cream. I fell asleep. In the sunshine." Okay, so maybe I fell asleep because of the sugar crash. Same diff.

"You look like it."

"What's *that* supposed to mean?"

"Your face is all red. From being sunburned."

Or straight-up mortified. "Oh my lord, is that Shack

Wheeler from the newspaper? With the camera?"

Liam glances over his shoulder to where I'm pointing. "Yep. He's got a scanner app on his phone, so he's always like six minutes behind us." He turns around, lips twitching. "I'm guessing he's working you into Page 2. A little human interest article right above the fire calls."

"I can't believe this is happening." Actually, I can. I can 100 percent believe this is happening. Because why not? "Is it too late to get EMS here?"

Liam's eyes sharpen. "Why? Do you feel dizzy? Short of breath? Do you have a headache?"

"I thought an ambulance ride might be a good way to sneak past Shack."

He relaxes. "You can't use emergency vehicles to escape the press, Mollie."

"Why? Jake Gyllenhaal did it in that one movie."

"No, he didn't."

"Well, that's on him. It's a good idea." I sigh and bury my face in my hands. "I can't talk to Shack, Liam."

"So don't. He can't make you."

That's true. He *can't.* He isn't easy to brush off, but I could do it. Probably. I used to live in freaking D.C., didn't I?

I look at Liam. "Any way I could snag a ride in the fire truck with you? I can hang onto the back. I don't mind."

"I didn't come in the truck. I came in the command vehicle."

"Is that the Tahoe over there? So you have an empty front seat, right?"

"I'm worried how serious you sound right now."

"I am serious! Can I get a ride?"

"No! *You cannot use emergency vehicles to escape the press.*"

So much for taxpayer spending. "Fine."

I haul myself to my feet, grab the dumb IGA bag, and start

stuffing it with empty canisters.

Liam bends to help. "The only time I've seen this much whipped cream before was at the Body Barn."

"Gross! I *so* did not need to know that."

The Body Barn is exactly what it sounds like. A 'gentlemen's club' that operates out of an Amish-built horse barn off some backroad somewhere. I can't find it on a county map, but I can probably point to ten people standing in the cemetery who can.

Including Liam, apparently.

"What?" he asks when he sees the look on my face.

"Nothing."

He rolls his eyes. "I wasn't there to *visit*. The fire alarm went off."

"Uh-huh." Probably pulled on purpose. Rumor has it the place is packed to the rafters on First Responder Night. The food's eighty percent off for badges, and so is everything else.

He drops the last few canisters in the bag. "I'll make you a deal. I'll talk to Shack. You hustle over to the IGA and call someone to pick you up over there."

I frown at him. "Why?"

"What do you mean, 'why?' I thought you didn't want to talk to the paper?"

"I don't." Obviously. "But why are you willing to talk to him?"

He shrugs. "Civic duty."

Okay. Whatever that means. "What will you tell him?"

His lips twitch. "That this is a great example of how being proactive in an emergency can help first responders act fast."

"There was no emergency!"

"There was a perceived emergency."

"For Pete's sake. I'm going to end up on Page 2, aren't I?"

He smiles lazily. "There's a good chance."

"Just shoot me."

"I'm wearing the wrong uniform for that."

Just my luck.

"Alright." I pull my phone out of my pocket. Slip my sandals onto my feet. Pick up my grocery bag. Check the ground to make sure I'm not leaving any garbage or self-respect.

Liam watches. "Ready?"

I kiss my fingers and touch Mom's headstone. "Yep."

"Careful crossing the street."

What am I, a toddler? "Yep."

"See you on the other side, Maris."

He heads toward Shack and I take off running, sandals slapping against the grass. The ground dips and I catch my toe in a groundhog hole, but I pull it together and avoid a faceplant. I call Jess as I half-ass checking both ways on the street and jog across the asphalt to the IGA parking lot.

"Omg, you did whippets without me?" she demands as soon as she answers.

"What? How did you—can you just hurry and come pick me up at the IGA, please?" I glance back to the cemetery. Shack is waving in my direction. "I think Liam's losing."

"Liam? Liam Taggert? Omg, what are you doing with Liam Taggert? And what's he losing?"

"I'll tell you everything when you *hurry up and get here!*"

"Okay, okay, I'm coming. Yeesh. You are no fun when you're high."

"I am not—"

She ends the call.

"—high." Gah!

I don't know where Jess is coming from, but she pulls into the IGA seconds before Shack outmaneuvers Liam and heads my way. She keeps the engine running while I dive into the passenger's seat and order her to go.

"Go where?"

"Anywhere!" I peek out the passenger window. "Preferably somewhere Shack Wheeler can't find us."

"Why was Shack Wheeler in the cemetery?"

"He's got a scanner for police calls and heard the 9-1-1 dispatch."

"Uh-huh. And why was Liam in the cemetery?"

"Liam's a volunteer firefighter." Some sort of officer, apparently, if he's driving around in a command car.

"Oh yeah." Jess smiles. "I forgot."

"What do you mean, you forgot? How do you forget Liam Taggert is a volunteer firefighter?"

"I know, right? I mean, he's Mr. July in the department calendar. I have it turned to him all year."

What? Seriously? "They have calendars?"

"Yeah, you know. As a fundraiser. It's cute, actually. Most of them are posed with a dog or a cat. Something they've rescued." She turns from South Street onto Man. "Under the picture, it has the name of the firefighter and the rescued pet written like a cheeky meet-cute. Like, 'It was love at first bite when Tanner Manson rescued Mr. Cuddles from a storm drain during a major flooding event last April.'"

"Is Mr. Cuddles a dog or a cat?"

"Box turtle."

"What's Liam posed with?" Just out of curiosity.

"A Burmese python."

"What? You're making that up."

"Nope." Jess smiles evilly. "He's got a very clever caption about snakes."

Great. Of course. Given his predilection for the Body Barn, that makes *total* sense.

"Whoa, babe." Jess sends me a worried look. "I think that

sigh shifted the atmospheric pressure in here."

"You have the windows open, idiot."

"You are such a nerd." She slows at a stop sign. "So. Did he perform mouth-to-mouth?"

No, thank God. That's the one thing that would make everything worse. "I didn't need to be resuscitated because I didn't pass out. Because I *didn't do whippets!*"

Jess slides me a look. "Maybe you *should* have done a couple."

Yeah. Maybe.

Jess pulls into a spot in front of Foundations. Because unlike me, she's an actual functioning adult with actual adult responsibilities. She gets out of the Subaru and I check my six before I slither out after her and bee-line for the studio.

"Oh my lord." I spin to her as soon as we get inside. "*Did you leave to rescue me in the middle of a class?*"

"Of course."

"Jess!"

"What?"

"For Pete's sake, why didn't you tell me you were *busy?* I could've—"

"It sounded like a real emergency!" She waves her hand dismissively at the grunts and heavy breathing coming from beyond the closed door of the mirror fitness room. "And that's just circuit training. Val took over the timers for me."

On cue, the door opens and Jess' older sister pops her sweaty head out.

She smiles when she sees me. "Mollie! Everything good?"

"All good!" Jess tells her. "Mollz had a whippet incident."

"Jessica!"

Jess rolls her eyes. "*Alleged* whippet incident. As in she *wasn't* doing whippets in the cemetery, even though Carmie Hottsteller told Glo Thomas that Tandy over at the IGA said she was."

Oh. My. LORD!

Wait, is Tandy the cashier?

"It's all a misunderstanding," I tell Val. I mean for Pete's sake, the woman works in the *freaking county courthouse!*

Val's eyebrows can't get much higher. "I'm sure I'll hear all about it. Want me to finish up in here, sis?"

"Sure."

Val disappears.

"Are you *trying* to get me arrested?" I demand. "Jess, she works for the *government!*"

"Mollz, she's a senior finance clerk in the controller's office."

"Financial crimes? Perfect!" GAH!

Jess laughs. "Babe, that is *not* what she does. And anyway, I don't think drug crimes fall under that purview."

That's probably true. "I was *not* doing drugs!"

"I know, babe. I'm just saying."

My phone buzzes in my pocket. A text from an unknown number. "What the hell!"

"What?" Jess asks. "What is it?"

I pass her the phone.

She reads aloud. "'Mollie, this is Shack Wheeler with the PITCHETTE PRESS. I'm looking for comments regarding the emergency call you were involved in at the Risen Hill Cemetery.' Babe! What the heck?"

"How the hell did he get my freaking number?" Who even has it around here except Jess?

She passes back my phone. "Do not respond. No, wait! Write, 'New phone, who dis?'"

"What? No!" I can't do that. He'll probably consider it my official comment and put it in the damn news report! "For Pete's sake, Jess, what the heck do I do?"

"Ignore it?"

My breath hitches. "What if—oh my lord, he just texted me again!"

"What did he say?"

"'I'm free to talk this afternoon.'" Not freaking out. NOT FREAKING OUT!

Jess shakes her head. "Well obviously you can't just—"

"*He's freaking calling me!*"

"Get rid of it get rid of it get rid of it!" Jess screeches.

I yell and toss my phone. It hits the yoga ball in the corner and bounces into a potted ficus as my ring tone reaches deafening volume.

The fitness room door jerks open.

"What the hell's going on?" Val demands. "We heard screaming!"

"Shack Wheeler is stalking Mollz!" Jess cries.

"What?"

"I think he hung up." I retrieve my phone. "Oh *shit.* He left a voicemail."

"Don't listen to it!" Jess whispers.

"Good lord." Val rolls her eyes. "It's like you two are back in middle school." She closes the door again.

"He left a freaking *voicemail!*" I repeat.

"Don't respond to it," Jess tells me. "Just ignore it! It'll go away. I mean, it's not like he can write anything if you don't talk to him. Right?"

"Um. Right. Yeah, I suppose that's true." I mean, this *is* Pitchette, but the terms of journalistic integrity are universal. Right?

I exhale slowly and delete Shack's voicemail without listening to it.

"Feel better?" Jess asks.

"Yeah." Nope. Not at all.

TWELVE

I wake up Monday morning with my sixth sense tingling.

Something isn't right.

And it isn't just that I'm back in Pitchette. It's something else. A disturbance in the Force. Mercury in retrograde or whatever.

I rub my eyes and scrounge around for my phone. Eight o'clock and a message from Jess.

BABE.

An image is attached. A headline in the *Pitchette Press,* it looks like.

Wait a minute, is that—

"Oh shit!"

I bolt out of bed and stumble into the closest pair of shorts, yanking up the zipper while I wait for Jess to pick up her phone.

"Did you see it?" she asks as soon as she answers.

"Are you kidding me? *Everyone's* seen it!" I cry, shifting her to speaker and swapping my sleep shirt for an old tee. "What the hell is wrong with freaking Shack Wheeler?"

"My mom called me the first thing this morning to ask if you were okay."

"Oh my lord."

"I didn't know what she was talking about, so she sent the photo I sent you. My folks don't have a subscription, so her neighbor brought over his copy."

"Oh my *lord!"*

"My landlord popped in right before I was leaving for my run to ask if I knew you."

"OH MY LORD!"

"*I* know the story isn't true, obviously." She doesn't have to finish the thought.

Everyone who subscribes to the *Pitchette Press* is going to see my face splashed on the front page. Under a headline insinuating I was administered naloxone and revived in the Risen Hill Cemetery!

I can't read the rest of the story in the photo. But it probably isn't flattering.

Or even *freaking true!*

"I don't even know how to respond to this, Jess." I swipe on deodorant, then take her off speaker and hold the phone to my ear. "What do I do?"

She takes a deep breath. "Okay, my brother had a similar situation with Shack a couple years ago."

"Matty?"

"Devon. He was on the school board at the time, and Shack got pissed at him for not giving him a scoop on the hiring of the new head basketball coach. Rumors about who it was circulated online and Shack ended up printing this story that was totally inaccurate before the coach even signed a contract. It basically made Devon out to be this underhanded politician who was trying to get his buddy hired as the coach before anyone realized they were friends."

"Was it true?"

"No. I mean, this guy used Dev's siding company once for a building he owned. But they didn't even realize they'd met until they saw each other at the school board meeting." Jess sighs. "Of course, that was just enough of a connection for Shack to spin things the wrong way."

"So he did it maliciously?" Because I sort of have the feeling this is payback for not responding to his texts or many, many voicemails over the weekend.

"Dev always thought so, but Shack only said he had to use the information he had available. And since the school board wouldn't talk to him, he pursued other sources for information."

Yeah, right. "How did the school board handle it?"

"At first Shack said he was going to print a correction. But the school board solicitor determined that enough of the article was false to warrant a full retraction."

"That's when the newspaper actually withdraws the story, right?"

"Yeah. I mean, I don't know how much good it does in the end. The story's already out there and it's not like the *Pitchette Press* has an online edition it can take down."

That's true, isn't it? The damage is done. All of Pitchette will think I overdosed on opioids. In public. In the middle of the day.

I mean. I *assume* that's what the article says.

Guess I'll have to find that out for sure. Before I take action.

DAMN IT!

Why, God? Seriously?

Wait, is this about that movie I streamed around Valentine's Day? Because I *swear* I thought it was supposed to be about William Bligh! How was I to know *Mutiny IN the Bounty* was different from *Mutiny ON the Bounty?* And that movie description was so misleading! 'Exotic' could totally mean it was filmed on location in Fiji. The only reason I kept watching it was because the freaking thing was $6.99 to rent. I mean, it cost me a whole Starbucks latte! I had to get *something* out of it!

GAH! "Where the heck did Shack get this photo of me, by the way?" Because it's *definitely* outdated. My hair hasn't been that short in years.

"I think that might be your college graduation picture. You know how the paper usually runs a tab on local kids who earn degrees each year?"

"Holy crap, you're right." What the actual hell? He couldn't even use an accurate photo of me?

"And, um, Mom just texted me to say there might be another picture inside. From the cemetery."

Oh, come ON. Really? An article and *two* photos? Is there a freaking timeline of events, too? "I need to get a copy of the paper before I rain hellfire down on Shack Wheeler."

"I'm sorry I don't have one to give you. The gas station should have some. Or the IGA." She pauses. "If they aren't sold out."

GREAT. They're sold out, aren't they? AREN'T THEY?

"I'll find one." Doesn't matter how far I have to go.

"Are you okay? Do you need me to come with? Because I can cancel my class—"

"Don't do that. It's not a big deal, honestly." People get wrongly accused of overdosing all the time, right? In print? In their hometown paper? "I'm going to find a copy of the article, read it, and then decide what to do." And how violent I should be.

"Okay." She exhales into the phone. "I'm so sorry this happened to you, babe. Honestly, Shack Wheeler needs to be fired."

Hard to do that when you're a mostly one-man show.

"Don't even worry about it. Seriously, Jess. I'm good." Sort of.

"Call me when you find a copy. And send me a picture of the article, so I can read it."

"Okay."

She hangs up and I go downstairs, decide I don't have the stomach for breakfast, and slip on a pair of sandals.

The problem is, I don't really want to *buy* a paper. Why should I dish out my own money just to read a story about me that shouldn't have been published? And why the heck should I support a media outlet that propagates lies and spreads misinformation?

The library. The library always has a copy of the paper. I don't have a library card here, but I could at least see how bad the article is and then decide if I need to apply for a loan to buy up and burn every copy in the county.

Of course my luck, someone will call the freaking fire department on me.

And Liam Freaking Taggert will respond to the call.

GAH!

Eight-thirty. The library opens at nine o'clock. It's just across Man Street, so it will take me about forty-five seconds to drive there. I could walk. That would eat up some of the time. It might also help relieve some of the anxiety in the pit of my stomach. Maybe the fresh air will stop me from throwing up.

I grab my purse, lock the house, and start down the sidewalk. Terry Bauer is on his front porch. Reading the newspaper. Hm, maybe I can see if he'll let me—

Oh. Nope. Nope, he definitely sees me coming and is fleeing into his house.

Great. Just great.

I follow the sidewalk uptown, then cut across Man Street

without any confrontations. I can tell who's seen the story by the number of people who see me and quickly glance away. It's sort of heartbreaking, actually. What if I *did* have an opioid dependency? All these people don't even care if I'm okay. If I need help or recovery resources.

The even sadder truth is that most folks around here *do* personally know someone struggling with addiction. The opioid epidemic has hit hard in rural America, even harder in Appalachia. If the number of people who can't look at me right now is any indication of the stigma faced by victims of addiction, no *wonder* it's an uphill battle.

I get to the library at eight fifty-nine, sweaty and anxious. Holy crap. Is that Mrs. Barker standing on the other side of the door? Geez, she was the librarian here when I was in high school. Wonder if she recognizes me?

Judging by the scowl she sends through the glass door, she recognizes me. Hard to tell if it's from high school or the newspaper, though.

At nine on the dot, she unlocks the door. "Yes?"

Um. "I'd like to come in?"

"For what purpose?"

UM. "To browse?"

She huffs and eases the door open. "We have a strict zero tolerance policy regarding drug use."

So the newspaper, then. "Congratulations?"

Her mouth pinches. "If I see any evidence of drug use, Ms. Maris, I won't hesitate to call Chief Miller at the Pitchette Police Department."

For Pete's sake. "Good to know. Can I please come in?"

She rolls her eyes and lets me through the door. The air conditioning is on full blast and it feels amazing.

The library dragon trails me into the fiction section. "Please be advised we have security cameras installed throughout the building—"

"Got it, thanks!" I nod at the little old man who just wandered in. "I think you have another visitor who needs assistance."

Mrs. Barker's attention wavers. I seize the opportunity to duck around a rotating display of Clive Cussler novels and walk around until I locate the periodicals in a corner. *Wall Street Journal. New York Times. Pittsburgh Post-Gazette.* Ah. *Pitchette Press.*

I pull today's edition off the display rack. Geez, what an awful photo. The pressure of graduating college and moving into the work force had given me a terrible acne flare-up back then. And since the front page is printed in color, you can see every little red eruption on my face.

No wonder people think I'm an addict.

Mrs. Barker's voice is loud and heading my way, so I pull out my phone and snap photos of the article. *Continued on Page 2* it says at the bottom of the Page 1 column. Great. Love that.

I flip the page.

Oh damn.

There's a second photo alright. Of me sprawled out on top of Mom's grave and Liam Taggert kneeling at my side. Shack managed not to get Tanner Manson in the frame. Too bad. *Two* firefighters would look *so* much more dramatic.

Fucking Shack Wheeler.

I take photos of the Page 2 spread and slide the paper back onto its display rod. It's actually sort of impressive how big the periodicals section is. There are shelves of the current editions of about twenty different magazines. Plus another rotating display of miscellaneous publications, like the *Old Farmer's Almanac* and holy crap, a gazetteer? They still print those? Geez.

Ooh. Firefighters. Must be the department calendar Jess

was talking about.

Wait a second. Is that—

Holy hell. Liam Taggert with the stupid snake.

I pull the calendar off the rack. Angle it toward the light, inspecting Mr. July. Liam is facing the camera without a shirt, the suspenders of his firefighter pants hanging down by his hips. Every muscle in his torso looks chipped from granite. Traps, delts, pecs, abs. Even those weird ones on the side that have a name I never bothered learning. His skin is smooth and tan and dusted with the perfect amount of sun-bleached hair. Cripes. His pants are slung *low*.

The V of his hips cuts so deep I feel it my pelvic floor.

And draped across his shoulders is a black and brown Burmese freaking python. Its head curls around his left arm, smugly eyeing the camera. Its tail swirls artistically over the rippling edge of his right hip. The tip drops suggestively over the flap of his firefighter pants. Just north of the damn Grand Prize.

And Liam knows it. Which is why he's biting his lower lip, looking you straight in the eye. Promising you. *Daring* you.

Like he's Adam in the flipping Garden of Eden.

The caption: *'It wasn't Assistant Chief Liam Taggert's snake that caused an evacuation of the Calvary Presbyterian Church Hall during last summer's church picnic.'*

"Sweet Jesus."

"Shhh!"

I jump and drop the calendar. It slides under the magazine display.

Great.

Mrs. Barker glares at me from the circulation desk. I send her a little wave, then get down on my hands and knees and use the flashlight on my phone to look under the display case. The calendar is way in the back. Because obviously *that* makes sense.

I sigh and lay flat on the floor. So much for my sort of white t-shirt.

"Gross," I mutter as I wedge my left arm under the display, sliding my hand through grime and dust bunnies.

My fingers brush the edge of the glossy pages. I make miniscule nudges until I can actually grab it between my thumb and forefinger. Then I pull. It sticks fast. Hm. Looks like the spiral binding is caught between the wall and the back of the display. Cool.

I move a little closer, grip the calendar, and yank.

Crip!

The cover of the calendar comes back in pieces. Torn right through Lenny Discot's crotch.

I've severed Mr. January in two and decapitated the teacup poodle in his arms.

Mrs. Barker scowls when I bring my handiwork to the circulation counter, cradled in my hands like an ancient offering.

"I, um, am so sorry," I begin.

"This calendar is ripped."

"I know. I'm really, *really* sorry." I set the poor thing down on the counter. "I can fix it. Do you have tape?"

"We can't *tape* an item that's in circulation!"

"You can check out a calendar?"

"You can check out *this* calendar."

Good grief. I do *not* want to know why folks are checking out this calendar.

"You know what? I might have tape." I start rifling through my bag.

"No tape! You can't tape this. It's a limited edition."

"It's a calendar!"

"It *was* a calendar," Mrs. Barker corrects. "Now it's trash."

"You can't be serious."

"You'll have to pay for it to be replaced."

"I thought you said it was a limited edition?"

"It is. That's why you have to pay for it."

"But if it's a limited edition, how are you going to replace it?"

"The replacement fee you pay will go into a discretionary fund."

I stare at her. "A discretionary fund?"

"It's an account we have for—"

"I know what a discretionary fund is!" Seriously, does everyone in Pitchette think I'm a blathering idiot? "What do you mean, the fee will go into it?"

"I mean the library will use the fee as needed."

"So me paying to replace this stupid thing won't actually replace it?"

"No."

"Then what the hell's the point?"

"You damaged it. You have to pay for it."

"Oh for—this is a shakedown."

"No, it's restitution."

GAH. "Fine. How much is it?"

"Thirty dollars."

"For a *calendar?* Seriously?"

"This calendar was acquired in an effort to raise funds for the Pitchette Volunteer Fire Department." Mrs. Barker taps Mr. January. "These fine young men risk their lives every single day keeping our community safe. I believe the least you can do, Ms. Maris, is offer them a little financial support."

"They've already received the financial support for this particular calendar because you already bought it from them. *You* just want me to make a matching donation to the library."

"Which also provides an important service to the

community."

"Be honest. You use the discretionary fund for coffee runs, don't you?"

Mrs. Barker's Parasol Pink lips flatten.

"Thought so." Geez. How bad is funding for public libraries that librarians need to leverage emotional blackmail just to get a cup of coffee?

I dig out my wallet and empty my cash right there on the counter, change and all.

"There. Thirty pieces of silver." I grab the calendar. "And I'm taking *this* with me!" It's the principal of the thing. *Obviously*.

I stomp out of the library and try to slam the door, but it has one of those door closer things at the top to slow it down and make me look like a real idiot.

"Gah!" I shake the calendar at Mrs. Barker, who's eyeing me through the door and probably ready to call Chief Miller at the Pitchette Police Department.

"Omg. Mollipop?"

Oh shit.

Tara Basher.

Maybe it isn't her. Maybe it's someone who just *sounds* exactly like her. And happens to know that dumb nickname. Maybe it's—

Nope. It's her.

Damn it!

"Tara. Hey."

GREAT. She's in a cute pink sports bra and yoga pants and I'm covered in library floor. Because why not, God? WHY NOT?

I clear my throat. "Were you at one of Jess' classes over at Foundations?"

"Oh yeah. *Such* a great burn. I go with a couple of the girls from work. My Gym Girlies. We love it. So." She does that thing girls do when they size you up and are secretly pleased to find you falling apart. "You're looking...comfortable."

Oh. My. LORD! 'Comfortable?' Why doesn't she just call me a cow and get it over with?

I clench my teeth so hard my jaw hurts. "Thanks."

She leans closer. "So how are you doing, Mollipop?"

"Doing?"

"You know. With the...." She lifts a hand to her mouth, like someone might eavesdrop. "*Drug situation?*"

My vision tunnels. "What drug situation?"

"In the cemetery."

DAMN IT. Shack Wheeler upgraded my alleged whippet episode into a full-blown drug incident, didn't he? GAH! "There was no situation."

"The paper said someone called 9-1-1."

"It was a butt dial!" Okay, I'm grasping. But everyone else is spreading rumors, so why can't I? "Once the fire department showed up, they cancelled the EMS response."

"Omg, they sent the whole fire department?"

"Of course not," I shoot back. "Just a truck and a command vehicle."

"So Liam Taggert *was* there."

I don't like the way she said that.

I also don't like the way she's eyeing the calendar clutched in my hand.

I stuff it in my purse. "Well, I gotta be going. See you, Tara."

I turn around and my purse slips off my shoulder, sending an avalanche of my crap down the sidewalk.

Seriously, God? You can't just let me have the exit? You have to go and make this like high school? GAH!

Holy crap, did Tara just freaking *snicker* at me? Screw her!

"I'm praying for you, Mollipop!" she hollers after me as I

scoop my shit back into my bag and hustle down the sidewalk. “Remember, addiction is a disease!”

Oh. My. LORD! Did she really just yell that in the middle of Man Street, in front of God and everyone? *Really?*

Unreal! This is freaking unreal! We aren’t in high school anymore. She isn’t spying on me in the locker room showers. We are grown-ass women with grown-ass emotions. Who the heck does she think she is, trying to make me feel bad about myself? I do a great job doing that all on my own, thanks. I mean, I’m very average-looking. I know it. One time in D.C., I got pissed off at a dude for whistling at me and then found out the whistle was aimed at the guy *next* to me. So yeah. I’m not under any illusions. And yes, I totally compensate for my insecurities by sinking oodles of dollars into clothes that make me feel like I belong on the set of *Suits.*

Too bad I’m not wearing any of those clothes right now. Because it would be a heck of a lot easier to stomp off confidently in a pair of Kate Spades than it is in a pair of flipflops I impulse-bought at Dollar General.

Okay, I can admit it. I’m a freaking mess.

But I am *not* using drugs!

So Tara Basher can *suck it.*

Also, *so can everyone else!*

THIRTEEN

The article is bad.

BUT it could be a lot worse. I mean, Shack didn't run a fake obituary or anything for me. So that's good.

Still. The story is filled with false information and I need to address that.

I'm just not sure how.

I mean, sticking my foot up his ass doesn't seem like a viable long-term solution.

"What do you think?" I ask Jess when she sets down my phone.

She stopped by Mom's house as soon as she finished her afternoon classes. Her timing was great, because I was seriously considering getting wine-drunk at two o'clock in the afternoon when she pounded on the side door.

"I think it's a load of shit!" she declares. "He practically indicated you overdosed right on top of Daphne's grave! What a freaking jag!"

Yeah, that's bad. "But he doesn't come right out and *say* any of that. It's all supposition. I mean, he uses 'allegedly' in every sentence. And he doesn't officially claim I overdosed, he just says the firefighters who were on the scene brought out naloxone and naloxone is used to reverse the effects of opioid overdose."

"Yeah. And then he says Liam Taggert allegedly administered it. To *you*."

I wilt in my seat at Mom's kitchen table. "Yeah." He does say that.

Has Liam seen the article? Probably, right? Yeah. Probably.

I didn't expect to have a triumphant return to Pitchette.

But damn it, I also didn't expect *this*.

"I need to ask for a formal retraction, don't I?"

"At the very least, babe. Honestly, you need to sue his ass."

Probably she's right. But I don't have the money or interest in a long, drawn-out public battle.

Jess sees the look on my face. "Want me to come with you to the *Pitchette Press* office?"

Yes. But Jess has her own stuff to worry about. "No. I'll be fine."

"Really?"

"Yes." No. Probably not.

"Okay." Jess gets up and gives me a hug. "Listen, I know this is really, *really* awful of me to ask right now. But would you come with me to the community bonfire tonight?"

"What bonfire?"

"In the park. For the baseball team. You know, as sort of a sendoff for their game Wednesday?"

A sendoff for the game? Oh. Well, at least there's something good happening around here. "I don't know, Jess. I'm not sure I should show my face for a while." At least until my face is no longer plastered on the front page of the newspaper.

"I wouldn't ask." She wouldn't, not unless she really needed my help. "But I'll have a table for Foundations in the park pavilion and I could use an extra person there to talk up the studio."

Damn it. She's trying to market her business and here I am, hiding out in Mom's house. Like a COWARD.

"Okay. I'll come. But you might want me to wear a mask or something. I have a feeling being associated with me will not be good for the studio."

"That's ridiculous." Her eyes flash. "I don't care what folks are saying, Mollz! And I *certainly* don't give a damn what freaking Shack Wheeler says. Anyone who thinks any part of that story is true is not welcome in my studio."

Geez. She's more upset about this than I am. "Can you do that? I mean, not let people in the studio just like that?"

"Babe, of course I can." She grins. "I'm the freaking boss."

I go on my Shack Attack with a quart of iced coffee in my veins and my hottest lip stain on my face. Actually, I do the whole war paint thing. Eyebrows, eyelashes, eyeliner. Which looks weird with my baggy shorts and a crummy tee, so I throw on a slick little olive green tailored-shorts-and-vest-top number and step into a pair of platform sandals. I even wash and dry my hair with leftover product from my corporate days.

Which, if this shit keeps up, I might soon be returning to.

The *Pitchette Press* runs three days a week. Monday, Thursday, Saturday. I don't know where it prints. Just based on logistics, I assume it's somewhere in Allegheny County.

I *do* know where the *Pitchette Press* office is. Although 'office' is a loose term. 'Room' is actually accurate. The paper is privately owned by some family that hasn't lived in

Pitchette for generations, but has a hard time passing the quickly dying torch. I can't remember their name, but I know they rent out space in the bottom of an express care clinic a few miles outside of town.

Shack Wheeler is the chief editor slash hatchet man. Whatever news he can't personally cover is generally picked up by freelancers. Years ago, I probably would've recognized some of the names. Today, I probably wouldn't. From what I know of the paper, the assignments don't pay well and there's a lot of turnover. Except Shack Wheeler. I'm sure he'll die at his desk. Right after he hits 'send' on his obituary.

The man himself sits behind a chunky desktop computer, sort of like the one Mom used when I was growing up. It hides most of him. Not because he's slouching. Because he's about five-foot-five, counting the inch of strangely spry gray hair poking out of his scalp. He's always reminded me of a Caucasian fire plug. Stout, boxy, with a pressure cap of about 100 psi.

Which folks feel every time he opens his mouth.

I bypass the desks that are clearly usually occupied but sitting vacant right now. Is that good or bad? I mean, I could probably use a witness for this.

On the other hand, having no witnesses makes hiding the body easier.

Although there are probably security cameras in here, right? Damn it.

"Mollie Maris!" Shack Wheeler has a sweet and slimy smile. "At last we meet."

"That's funny." Also untrue, since we've talked like eight times over the course of my life. "Considering you just printed a huge story about me on your front page."

"Ah." He swivels in his chair, reaching for a copy of today's edition. "Big news, Pitchette VFD responding to an emergency in the Risen Hill Cemetery."

"There was no emergency." I narrow my eyes. "Which you know. Since you were there."

The sonovabitch shrugs. "Hard to tell, since no one wanted to comment on the situation."

"Really? That's it? That's your excuse? Too bad." I plant my hands on his desk and lean across. "Because that shit *definitely* won't hold up in court."

"Court. Hm." He crosses his arms. Not bothered *whatsoever!* "Court seems like a lot."

"Court seems appropriate, considering the fact you printed a false story about my alleged drug use and overdose. Retract it. Or I *will* find a lawyer." Please, God, don't make me find a lawyer. I want this to go *away,* not get bigger!

Shack sighs. And still doesn't remove his ass from his chair. "See, retractions are a tricky thing, Mollie. They can give the wrong impression."

"*What* wrong impression? The whole damn story is fake news, Shack!"

"But it *isn't,* is it?" He looks up at me like *I'm* ridiculous and *he's* of sound mind. The jagoff ticks off the 'facts' on his freaking fingers. "A 9-1-1 call was placed—"

"Who placed it?" Seems like a good place to start.

"You can try to obtain that information by placing an open records request with the county."

I—what?

"The caller said they thought someone had overdosed in the cemetery," Shack continues. "Pitchette police and VFD were dispatched. EMS was called. A naloxone kit was seen at the scene of the incident. By me, as well as onlookers. And *you* were passed out. Coincidentally next to your mother's grave. Who passed away not too long ago. My condolences, by the way."

"Are you *kidding me?*" I'm probably melting my war paint

right off, but I'm too jacked to even care.

"Of course, this isn't accounting for eyewitness reports that your vehicle was left outside Jerry's on Man Street last Tuesday."

"You *know* you're intentionally misconstruing what happened! What the hell is your problem?"

"My *problem* is that if I retract the full story, readers will assume none of it actually happened." He smiles and it isn't nice. "And as we both know, *some* of it did happen."

"This is ridiculous! You're insane!"

"No, I'm in news. And this is news, Mollie. Readers have a right to know how their tax dollars are being used."

"Yeah, but *you* don't have a right to make up whatever the hell you want!"

"I didn't make anything up." Shack taps today's edition with his knuckle. "I think you'll find my report is filled with *alleged* details."

Can he do that? Just slap that word on everything and get away with it? What exactly are the rules here?

I step back from his desk and cross my arms. "What do you want, Shack?" There *has* to be something. This is clearly a targeted attack.

"To give my readers a good story, of course."

"Aren't you supposed to be promoting the truth here?"

"What is truth?"

Oh-kay. This isn't a case of appealing to the man's moral compass. Clearly, he doesn't have one. "Take back the story, Shack. I'm not asking." I'm *begging*.

But hopefully, he isn't smart enough to realize that.

"I'll consider printing some...adjustments." He leans his elbows on his desk and steeples his hands. "But you'll have to work with me, Mollie."

The *hell* I will! "What do you mean?" DAMN IT. I have

the spine of a worm, don't I?

"If I'm taking back a good story, you'll have to give me a better one."

How? *How* is he getting away with this? Folks aren't stupid. They have to know this is how Shack does business. So why the hell do they put up with it?

Because it's freaking *Pitchette.* And Shack Wheeler has been running things since God rained down manna in the desert.

GAAAH!

A police scanner goes off and just like that, Shack moves on to the next breaking story. Poor people. He's going to turn that smoking vehicle into a five-alarm brush fire, isn't he?

"I'll be back!" I warn him when he pulls out his camera and shoves me out the door. "This isn't over!"

For Pete's sake, did he just freaking *wave me off?* Like I'm at the bottom of his damn list of things to worry about? Is he *serious* right now?

I get in my Honda. I could follow him to the call. I could follow him everywhere. Hound him until he retracts the story.

But that might make me look sort of crazy, right? Like maybe there's some truth to his dumb story?

Yeah. Yeah, that might make things worse.

DAMN IT!

My phone vibrates in my purse. I dig it out to find another message from Jess.

With a screenshot of the online Pitchette community group page, which is apparently run by organized assassins.

Judging by the photo of me from the damn paper and the hundreds of comments speculating how my addiction recovery is going, anyway.

This isn't real. This isn't my life. This is a horrible dream

I'm having because I went too hard at Jerry's my first night back in town. Right, God? *Right?*

My hand trembles as I toss my phone in the passenger's seat and go looking for ice cream.

FOURTEEN

By the time I get to the Pitchette community park, I've stopped shaking and am calmly crunching the last of the dipped Dairy Queen cone that I drove about twenty miles out of the way for.

Jess has her Foundations table ready to go. A few other local businesses are also in the pavilion under a sign identifying them as Coyote Pride sponsors. Nice. Contributing to the Pitchette High School boosters club is a really smart idea on Jess' part, because sponsors always get space in event programs and signs hooked up to the chain-link fence around the football field during the season.

I pull into the parking lot, take a deep breath, then get out and cross to the pavilion. The Pitchette VFD is setting up pallets in the gravel lot across from the park maintenance shed. Wonder if Liam Taggert is going to be Assistant Chief Liam Taggert tonight or Coach Liam Taggert? Also, wonder if it's possible to *not* run into him. At all. EVER.

"Babe!" Jess waves to me.

She doesn't seem to notice the other sponsors rubbernecking when I walk through the tables to get to her.

Smiling widely at each of them, of course. Just so they know they don't scare me. Much.

"How'd it go?" she asks as soon as I get to the table.

"As expected. I'll tell you later." I eye her booth. "Babe, this is awesome! Magnetic fridge calendars? Love it!"

"I had pens at first when I started coming to stuff like this, but everyone has pens. I was going for different. And look!" She holds up one of the calendars. "Each month has different important nutritional information for specific diets."

"So you can put it on your fridge and keep it in mind. Genuis!" I look around. "Okay, what's the drill?"

"I've just been hanging out here and chatting to folks as they come by. Give them one of these." She hands me a stack of June calendars for weekly classes. "And a business card. Those are right here. And that's basically it."

Easy enough. "I'll also mention your new socials. We should get those on your business cards."

"Ooh, yes! I'll do that tomorrow."

I sink into one of the two camp chairs she has behind the table. "You should go mingle, babe. Talk to people. I'll stay here to watch the table." And stay out of trouble. Hopefully.

"Okay. That's a good plan." She looks down at me. "You good?"

"I'm good."

I want to tell her again that me being here representing her business probably isn't a good idea.

But I know Jess. She'd have no problem loudly telling me she doesn't give a damn and to sit my ass down.

Which I'd find hilarious most days. Today, I'm too drained to stir her up.

She walks off and I sink lower in my chair. This is fine. A good spot. No one is going to bother me if I don't bother them. And I have a decent view of the bonfire from here, so once that's lit I can just melt into the background. Besides, it's already dusk. Soon it will be dark and I won't need to worry about people looking at me.

Although, shit. The pavilion is lit, isn't it? Gah.

Can't worry about that. I'm here for Jess, and that's all that matters.

Oh damn. There's Liam. In his coaching uniform. Guess he's officially Coach Liam tonight. For Pete's sake, how many uniforms does the man have? At least he's occupied with parents, because I definitely DO NOT want—

Oh *crap*. He saw me.

And he's coming my way.

Um, hello up there, God. Where's the lightning?

People aren't exactly congregating around the Foundations table, thanks to yours truly. I don't mind not socializing, obviously.

I *do* mind that Liam is able to walk right up. I'm about to die from embarrassment and I do *not* want him to be the one administering CPR. That just seems extra cruel. You hear me, God? YOU HEAR ME?

He looks at me from under the brim of his Coyotes baseball cap. "Hey."

"Hey." Is this going to be a long conversation? Because I sort of want to bolt into the nearest lane of traffic.

"I saw the article Shack Wheeler wrote."

Geez, right into it! He doesn't play games, does he? He's a rip-off-the-bandage-quickly sort of guy.

Honestly, it was too much to hope he *hadn't* seen the article. I mean, nearly everyone in Pitchette has by now.

What makes it worse is Liam actually knows what happened. So it just seems extra humiliating.

"Entertaining, wasn't it?" I quip and look away.

"It was bullshit, and he knows it." Liam's words are clipped in anger. "I stopped by his office this morning."

I shoot him a look. "What? You did? Why?" Also, how did we miss each other?

"Because he shouldn't have printed it, Mollie." Liam's voice has an edge to it that's new to me and also sort of sexy. "*Any* of it."

"I mean. *You're right,* considering it was mostly untrue." I tilt my head at him. "But you didn't need to say anything to him. He didn't quote you or anything. He just said you responded to the call."

"That's not the point."

It isn't? "Are you upset about the photo caption? I know he—"

"That *photo* was the worst part." Liam's beautiful eyes glint under the pavilion lights. "That idiot knows better than to run a photo of a medical emergency like that."

"For Pete's sake, there was *no medical emergency!*"

"I know there wasn't, but Shack didn't know it when he took that damn shot. He should've respected your privacy." Liam shakes his head. "And he *definitely* shouldn't have run something like that in the newspaper for everybody to see. It's nobody's damn business."

"He'd probably argue that taxpayers deserve to know how their tax dollars are being put to work." I shrug. "In this case, of course, he completely fabricated how they're being used."

Liam stares down at me.

"What?"

"Why the hell aren't you more upset about this?"

"I *am* upset about it." I sigh and close my eyes. "But at the moment, I'm also *really* sick of talking about it." And thinking about it. And hearing about it.

The chair Jess left next to me screeches across the concrete. I open my eyes as Liam collapses into it with a sigh.

"You're right," he says. "I'm sorry. The last thing you probably want to do is listen to me get all worked up about it."

For some dumb reason, that makes me smile. "It's okay. You're kind of cute when you're worked up." OH MY LORD DID THOSE WORDS JUST LEAVE MY MOUTH? NO! GO BACK, WORDS! GO BACK!

GAAAAAH!

Liam smiles lazily as color floods my face.

His voice drops an octave. "Am I?"

Oh geez. Not answering that. NOT ANSWERING THAT!

I look away, trying to get the heat out of my face by sheer force of will. "Um, so, anyway. I did talk to Shack about it and requested that he retract the whole thing."

"Good." Liam leans forward, planting his elbows on his knees. "What did he say?"

I roll my eyes. "A lot of stuff."

"How about 'I'm sorry?'"

"No. That's the one thing he *didn't* say, actually."

"Jackass." His eyes tighten at the corners. "That moron needs to be sued. He's done this sort of thing before."

"Yeah, how *hasn't* he been sued? Jess told me what happened to her brother Devon when he was on the school board. Seems like that's a case for libel there."

"I don't know, to be honest." Liam frowns, like this is something he's tried working out before. "My gut says the family who owns the paper has the sort of connections that make legal action difficult to pursue."

"What the heck does *that* mean?" Because putting it like that makes it sound like Pitchette is the Chicago of Northern Appalachia.

"It means the small town politics in Pitchette run deep, Mollie." His eyes snag on me. Steady and serious. "And unfortunately, it doesn't seem like you're protected by them."

Big surprise there. I don't belong to generations of family or land or business, like most people in this region. I belong to Mom. And Mom is dead.

"Story of my life," I sigh. "Guess it's a good thing I don't have to worry about impressing anyone around here."

"Oh?" Liam sits back in his chair, crossing his arms over his chest, watching me. "Do you have to impress someone somewhere else?"

Darrin Schwartz, maybe. Or maybe not. Considering I've already quit his company once and he still wants me to work for him.

"Hm. Guess I don't." I frown. "That's sad, right? Yeah, that's sad."

"Or liberating."

He must not have seen the damn Pitchette community group comments.

"Oh yeah." I snort. "It's *so* liberating having people think I have an opioid dependency."

Liam's mouth twitches. "I don't know. It could explain you selling your socks in a Sheetz parking lot."

I throw my hands up. "For Pete's sake, Liam Taggert, you have *got* to let that go! It was a very successful *business negotiation* that I regret *nothing about whatsoever!*"

PLEASE, God, make him move on! Because I can*not* go through life knowing Liam Taggert watched me peddle potential foot smut. That's WAY WORSE than the false opioid story.

Humor lingers on his face for a few seconds. Then it's replaced by something a lot more serious. "What if he doesn't print a retraction?"

Yeah. What if he doesn't? "Honestly? I don't know. I

can't afford to take him to court." Even if I sold Mom's house, I still have student debt and bills, not to mention whatever my cost of living will be whenever I make an actual decision about my future. And I don't know. It just seems so *wrong* to sell Mom's house just so I can sue someone. "I guess I just need to believe that he'll do it. And if he doesn't, I guess I'll just need to figure out a way to live with it."

A crease forms on Liam's forehead. Not an unattractive crease, of course. There's probably nothing he can do to make his face unattractive.

"You're not reacting to any of this the way I expected, Maris."

What the heck am I supposed to say to that. "Oops?"

He doesn't laugh. "I'm sorry this happened to you. Shack Wheeler is an asshole. He was way out of line and that's not okay." He leans forward again, looking me in the eyes. "But I'm also sorry if I overstepped by getting involved. I just...I thought since I was actually there, I might be able to help. And I didn't want you to feel like you had to clap back at him alone."

Okay, Liam Taggert is a war hero and a first responder and standing up to a bully totally falls in line with all that. So there's no need whatsoever for me to get all swoony and flustered over the thought of him yelling at Shack on *my* behalf. I mean, that's just what he *does*. That's just who he *is*.

And eventually, once I've removed myself from his presence and taken a cold shower or three, my lady parts are going to accept that.

In the meantime, they're sort of going a little haywire.

I cross my legs. Because good grief, this is *not* the place to get turned on by Liam Freaking Taggert! "Um. I do appreciate that you said something, Liam. I mean, even though you definitely didn't need to, it's nice to know that someone wanted to help."

The ridges around his eyes soften. "I wish I could *actually* help."

I smile. "Well, according to the paper you straight-up saved my life by *allegedly* administering naloxone 'swiftly within the alleged crucial response window of time.'"

"Geezus. What an idiot."

"By the way, what did you say to him when you stopped him from following me to the IGA lot?"

"That I couldn't comment."

"Oh see? That right there just gave him all the creative license he needed."

That gets a little laugh out of him. Finally.

"You're really not going to worry about the article." He stares at me, eyebrows bunching. "Are you?"

"No."

"But *why?*"

"I'm lazy?"

"You're not lazy."

I am. I am lazy.

But that doesn't happen to be the reason in this particular case. "What's the point, Liam? Worrying about it's only going to make *me* miserable, not Shack."

He shakes his head. "Damn it, Maris. You're just proving my point."

"What point?"

"You're definitely too good for the Army. And for the record." He leans closer, flooding my space with the scent of tea tree and woodsmoke. "You're also too good for Pitchette."

That probably isn't true.

But damn. I kind of like that Liam Taggert seems to think it is.

FIFTEEN

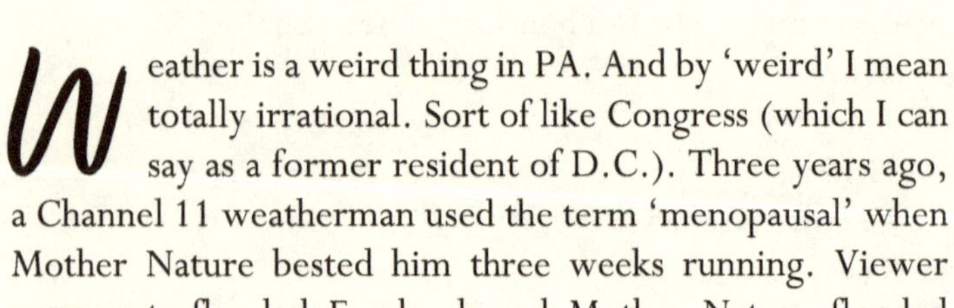

Weather is a weird thing in PA. And by 'weird' I mean totally irrational. Sort of like Congress (which I can say as a former resident of D.C.). Three years ago, a Channel 11 weatherman used the term 'menopausal' when Mother Nature bested him three weeks running. Viewer comments flooded Facebook and Mother Nature flooded Pittsburgh.

I think we all know who got the last laugh.

But seriously, Mother Nature needs some salt tablets. Because this temperamental downpour is unreal and completely irresponsible! Township and borough roads aren't great on a good day. A deluge like this can blow out creeks and wash out roads before folks have a chance to get home safely. Folks like, I don't know. ME, for instance.

Because God forbid I thought I could get away for a Tuesday hike through the state game lands to clear my head over the yet-to-be-retracted overdose story. And simultaneously break in my new hiking boots.

Freaking Mother Nature put the kibosh on that pretty quick.

Twenty-four hours. The story has been out there for twenty-four hours.

Guess there *is* something that can force me to take up hiking after all.

Gah!

Alright. The second setting on my windshield wipers is *not* enough. Guess it's time to break out the Glass Shuddering Ultra Turbo Speed setting. The rapid-fire wiping usually gives me a headache, but it's either a headache or drive right off the road. Okay. So I'm a little out of practice navigating backroads during a storm. I can admit it. Thank God there isn't anyone else out here, though. No use endangering perfectly good taxpayers.

I'm approaching the bridge that runs over Little Drop Run, right before Little Drop Hill. Okay, so Little Drop Hill is the local nickname for the inclining copse right before you cross into the borough from Pitchette Township. We don't *actually* name our hills around here. Usually.

The bridge is little. One-and-a-half cars wide, to be exact, which is useless for everyone. The township has an eight-ton weight limit on it, which is probably one ton more than it can reasonably handle. The bridge railings are iron, the base is concrete, and drain grates are installed on both sides to accommodate stormwater runoff. Mom told me the drainage system had ended up being a two-hour discussion when the Pitchette Township supervisors were opening the bridge renovation project up to bids during their monthly meeting. Who knows why. I mean, what the heck is there to discuss? The grates are there to let stormwater drain off the bridge through the culvert-type thing below into Little Drop Run.

Although right now it looks a lot more like Big Drop Run. Hm. Wonder if the township realizes how badly the ditches are flooding and draining into the creek?

That's dumb. *Obviously* they know. This probably happens every time it storms.

I hold my breath like an idiot and ease over the bridge. What the heck do I think is going to happen? That my Honda will be the straw that breaks the camel's back and I'll plunge engine-first into Little Drop Run?

I'd laugh if Luck wasn't a raging bitch.

Okay. Over the bridge. GOOD.

Now for Little Drop Hill.

I press the gas pedal down in relation to the incline and adjust my wiper speed. At least with the tree cover, the rain isn't so blinding. My visibility is a lot—

Holy crap! Is that Ida Boyko's gold Saturn ditched to the left of the road? It is! How long has she been stuck there? And how is she even allowed to drive? She's practically a century old!

Okay, I can see her moving around in the driver's seat. Good sign. She can't be too hurt. Oh my lord. Oh crap. I have to rescue her, don't I? Gah!

Of course, there isn't a great place to park. She ditched herself going down the hill coming out of the blind curve. If anyone comes down the hill right now, they won't see her or me until it's too late.

Please God, *do not* let anyone come down the hill.

I pull as far to the right of the road as I dare and park. Thank goodness I wore my hiking boots today. Glad to see they're good for something. Woohoo.

I leave my keys in the car. My luck, I'd drop them in the flooded ditch. And I am *not* going to crawl around in this muck to find them.

Ida is flapping her scrawny chicken arms at me when I pull up the hood of my jacket and cross the road. The jacket keeps my torso dry, of course, but my shorts are soaked by the time I reach the top of the embankment. Damn it!

Ida cranks down her window and looks up at me.

"You okay?" I holler.

"No!"

Uh-oh. "Are you hurt?"

"Yes!"

Oh boy. I know exactly zero first aid. "Where?"

"My checkbook!"

Um. "What?"

"I just spent sixty dollars on a color and set," Ida shouts. "And now look at my hair!"

I can't really see it, because it's tucked into a plastic rain cap that's tied under her chin. But considering the rain cap is soaked and mud-splattered, her hair probably isn't much better. Right?

"Any broken bones?" I can handle ruined hair. Ruined bones, not so much.

"Not as far as I can tell," she hollers back.

Phew. Good. "I'm coming down to you, Ida."

"Good luck!"

Thankfully, the embankment isn't steepest where she ran off the road. The problem is it's muddy, and the mud is super slippy. Plus the ditch is starting to fill with water. It's all headed down-hill toward the creek, but I have to cross it to get over the crest of the bank down to her car. Water rushes over the tops of my boots and soaks my socks.

Great. Just perfect. GAH!

I cross out of the ditch and start down the bank. Taking teensy steps and planting my boots strategically on spots that look like they'll give me more traction.

My luck, I'll fall and break *my* bones and *Ida* will need to rescue *me*.

She has a massive scowl on her face when I finally reach her car. It gives her twice as many wrinkles.

"You're that girl, ain't you?" she demands. "In the paper. The one from the city who's on the drugs."

For Pete's sake! "Yep. That's me."

"You on drugs now?"

I wish. "Nope."

"Huh." She sums up the situation before I have a chance to ask about it. "My door's stuck and my seatbelt's locked. Get me outta here."

"I'll try."

I eye the front fender of her car, which is crumpled. The nose of the Saturn is caught between some trees and bushes. In a truck or my Honda, it wouldn't be a big deal. But the Saturn has a .75-inch road clearance and the angle she hit the trees at tilted her car just enough to wedge the bottom of her door against the ground. Damn.

"Ida, how the heck did you do this?" Because it looks like something you'd have to purposefully try to do.

"Damn chipmunk ran in front of me and I tried to hit it."

Oh crap. She may have a concussion. *Great.* "You mean you tried *not* to hit it."

"No." She glares at me. "I tried *to* hit it."

"What? Ida! That's horrible!" And also one of the red flags for a potential serial killer, right?

Holy crap, what if I'm rescuing a freaking *serial killer* right now? Seriously, God? Does it even count as being a Good Samaritan if the person you're helping turns out to be a psychopath?

"It was a stand-your-ground situation," Ida explains. "It was population control. Damn chipmunks steal right out of my birdfeeders! We don't need 'em around here. They should go back where they come from."

For Pete's sake. There's such a thing as an animaphobe? Freaking Pitchette!

I look around. "Ida, we're in the *country!* Where the hell

else are chipmunks supposed to go?"

"No need to swear at me, missy. I got enough damn problems without you swearing at me."

For Pete's sake. "Did you actually hit him?"

"Hit who?"

"The chipmunk!"

"No, damn it." Her eyes turn to slits. "The bastards are crafty. Real strategic. He knew I'd go for him, which was why he ran off on this side. So I'd hit the trees and get stuck."

I guess I can see that happening. Sort of. "How did your rain cap get so muddy?" I mean, it's not like she's trying to walk home in the rain or anything. Her seatbelt is locked!

"I dropped it leaving the beauty parlor." Because apparently, that makes sense. "I was carrying it and it started to rain, so I was trying to put it on and I dropped it in a giant puddle in the parking lot."

"Then why did you put it on at all?"

"I told you! I had a color and a set and I couldn't get my hair wet!"

Why am I trying to rationalize this? Nothing about this situation is rational. This isn't real. *None* of this is real. I'm having a super-specific and totally out-of-pocket nightmare. Probably when I wake up, I'll be able to link all these crazy details back to conversations I had the day before. The rain, for instance. Jess was just saying how much we need it.

"Are you going to stand there getting soaked or are you going to help me?" Ida demands.

Geez.

I *hope* this is a dream.

"Your driver's door is wedged into the ground," I tell her. "I'm going to have to pull you out the window."

"I don't want to go through the window."

Of course. Because why would she want to do the easy

thing? "Well, I could try to wrestle you out the passenger's door."

She grunts.

"Of course, I'd have to haul you over the console."

Ida rolls her eyes. "Never simple, is it?"

I mean. The window solution seems pretty simple to me. "What's it going to be, Ida?"

She thinks about it. "Well, if you can get my seatbelt unlocked, I'll try the window."

Great. Just peachy. "Alright, lean back in your seat."

"Why?"

"So I can try your seatbelt."

"I already told you it's stuck!"

She did. But seeing that she ditched herself trying to smear a chipmunk, I'm willing to take a chance on User Error here.

"Did you try the secret switch?" I ask.

Her ancient eyebrows wobble. "Secret switch?"

Ha. Got her. "Yeah, some of these older cars have them." Liar, liar, pants on fire. "The switch is usually on the bottom of the buckle so you don't accidentally hit it."

"If it's a switch to release the seatbelt, who cares if ya hit it?"

For Pete's sake, I am *not* being outwitted by a rodent killer. "So you don't accidentally hit it when you click your seatbelt," I amend. "Now lean back, Ida. Or do you want to be stuck here for the whole storm?"

She scowls and wags her finger at me. "No manners! Just like the rest of 'em!"

I don't know who "'em" is, but it's probably true. I'm probably like the rest. At least when it comes to rescuing a fussy old lady with a taste for chipmunk blood.

Ida mutters a bunch of old lady nonsense, then clamps her arms across her chest and leans back in her seat.

There's about three inches between her and the steering wheel.

Which will obviously accommodate me, as I'm Gisele's body double.

"Can you move your seat back?"

"This ain't a La-Z-Boy," Ida snaps.

Geez. She's not going to be rescued without a fight, is she? "Alright, well, I'm reaching across you and you're going to get a face-full of boob."

"Been a while since I've had some fun," she cackles.

For Pete's sake. Welcome home, Mollie Maris.

I hold my breath and lean in. Ida says something that doesn't make it past my chest, so I focus on reaching her buckle. Doesn't look damaged. Hopefully she just didn't push the button hard enough. Because if her seatbelt is stuck and her chair doesn't move back, I'm not exactly sure how to get her out of here.

I press my thumb into the red button and pull on her belt. It pops free and slings past my face.

"Look at that," Ida says once I get my boobs out of her face. "The secret switch."

"Yep." I pull the belt off her. "Are you ready to get pulled out the window?"

"Let me get my handbag. Don't want no one to take it."

Oh yeah. I'm sure the criminal element in Pitchette is *super* interested in Ida Boyko's handbag.

"Here." She shoves a gigantic Gucci lookalike out the window at me. "Hold this."

I take it and almost drop it. "Holy crap, Ida. What's in this thing?"

"The usual." Her veiny hands work to tighten her rain cap. "Wallet. Cellphone. Glasses. Metamucil. Colt .45."

Oh good lord. "Please tell me it's not loaded."

"'Course she's loaded. Why the hell would I carry an unloaded gun?"

Yeah, what do I expect? That all little old ladies are sweet people who don't run down chipmunks and conceal carry? Wake up, Mollie Maris! This is *Pitchette.*

Which is why I'm standing on a bank, soaked to my underwear, trying not to throttle a great-great-grandmother.

Instead of hyperventilating, I shoulder the bag and grasp Ida's arms. Between the two of us, we drop five F-bombs getting her through the Saturn's window. I don't know why. I mean, she's as big around as a walking stick and four feet tall.

"You never done this before, have you?" Ida asks as we make a slug trail back up the bank toward the road.

"Rescued someone in the ditch?" I pant.

"Climbed a hill." She snickers at my red face and overworked sweat glands. "Too used to the city, looks like. No fancy underground trains around here, though."

Anyone who calls the Metro 'fancy' is clearly certifiable. What the hell is wrong with the folks around here that they let Ida Boyko out without a handler?

She grunts when she sees my Honda.

"What?" It's a *Honda.* What does she expect?

"Fancy."

"Ida, it's a nine-year-old SUV."

"Exactly." She scowls and shakes her head. "Fancy."

For Pete's sake.

I take my empty sunflower Stanley out of the passenger's seat and stick it in the cupholder. Then I boot Ida up into my car and breathe deeply while I drop her bag in her lap and ignore all her snark. It isn't easy, because she seems to think my not responding means I've gone temporarily deaf and she adjusts her volume accordingly.

Between the rain and the bitching, I kind of feel like

driving into a tree, myself.

Ida screeches and clings to the grab handle over her head. "What the hell are you doing?"

"Making a U-turn." Obviously. "I'm taking you home." Because the only way Ida is ending up in Mom's house is if I'm dragging her body through it to bury it in the backyard.

"What about my car?"

I get my Honda pointing back toward the bridge. "Someone will tow it later."

"I live over on Teeter Furnace, you know."

"I know." Everyone knows. Ida Boyko is older than dirt and has lived in the same house since the day she was born.

"Hope the chickens are smart enough to get in the coop."

"Uh-huh." If they are, they're smarter than both of us.

"Boy, this rain is biblical."

"Uh-huh."

"Bet you don't get rain like this down there in Washington, D.C."

"Uh-huh."

"Not much of a talker, are you? Don't matter. Talking isn't all that great. Most folks don't have something to say, anyway, they just sort of *there's that motherfucker!*"

I stomp on the brakes when Ida throws open her door and somersaults out of the vehicle onto the bridge.

"Holy freaking crap!" What the hell is happening? Omigod, is she dead? Oh shit oh shit oh shit!

I throw the car into park, jump out, and run around to the passenger's side to see Ida pitching my Stanley at something dark and wet darting through the rain off the edge of the bridge. The dark streak disappears and my Stanley rolls off the bridge into Little Drop Run.

"Damn it! What the actual *hell,* Ida!"

"It's that fucker!" she screams. "The one who made me

crash! He ran right in front of us!"

"You jumped out of a moving car *for a damn chipmunk?*"

"Don't swear at me, missy!"

"You threw *my* expensive-ass Stanley into the creek!"

"Get that little bastard!"

"You're freaking insane, Ida Boyko!" She is! I've rescued a madwoman and she's pitched my limited-edition Stanley into the creek trying to kill a chipmunk in the middle of a monsoon!

ARE YOU SEEING THIS, GOD?

"Where do you think you're going?" Ida demands when I swear loudly and stomp off the bridge.

"TO GET MY FREAKING STANLEY!"

"That don't seem smart." She cups her mouth and leans against the bridge railing as I carefully foot my way down the bank toward the creek. "The water's rising here!"

No shit, Sherlock! But my favorite Stanley is caught in a mass of grass and branches and leaves stuck on the lip of the culvert-thing supporting the bridge. I can totally get to it without getting in the creek.

Not that getting in the creek matters all that much. I'm so waterlogged, my fingers are pruney.

The bank is steepest closest to the water, so I grab onto the steel edge of the culvert, crouch, and carefully stretch as far as I can toward the debris pile.

It's just out of reach. Of freaking course.

"Damn it!" This is my fault. Why did I think helping out an old lady would be a nice, easy thing to do? No good deed goes unpunished. I *know* that!

Okay. Alright. I can get a little closer if I just—

"Oh shit!" My feet slide out from under me and I plummet into the creek.

DAMN IT!

"Told ya!" For an old lady, Ida has no problem yelling

through the rain.

I sit up, shaking with anger. Water swirls around my chest and I'm wet and cold in places that should *not* be exposed to the elements. My new hiking boots are probably ruined, aren't they? Because that water guard spray definitely does not protect the interiors.

Ida cackles above me.

Good Samaritan be damned. I am *definitely* throwing a rock at her. Just as soon as I find one.

I pull myself together enough to get to my feet. Which involves a lot of splashing and dislodges the stupid clump of forest litter.

"No!" I lunge as my Stanley bobs merrily downstream, cartoon-style. I splash after it like Godzilla in slow motion. "Come back!"

Turning back is not a thing now. I'm too emotionally invested. I'm getting my *freaking Stanley back* if it's the last thing I do!

We both disappear into the culvert as the skies darken a little more and the rainfall goes from steady to urgent. Damn it, I can't see *anything* in here! Just my luck that I'd end up—

"Ouch!" I stagger to a stop when my left foot sinks into the creek bed.

Deep into the creek bed.

Stuck. I'm *stuck*. There's a freaking hole or a rock moved or something because I certainly can't.

Oh boy. Okay. Yeah, this is probably not great for me. Ida is a spitfire, but she isn't exactly Ironman. If I can't free myself, she definitely can't. Which means I might need to call someone for help. But my phone is in my car. Not that it would've done me much good after I dunked it in the creek. What are the chances Ida won't just drive off with my car and will actually get help if I don't come out of the culvert soon?

"How's it goin' down there?"

Oh for Pete's sake. Now her voice is in my head.

"Missy!"

Wait, is she hollering at me through the drain grate thing on the bridge? Around the water? How is that even possible?

You know what, doesn't matter. I can hear her. Maybe she can hear me.

"Can you hear me, Ida?" I shout as loud as I can, head tilted back.

"'Course I can hear you. I'm looking right at you. What the hell are you doing?"

Okay. Good. This is good. "My foot's stuck. It must be trapped under a rock." Or a blackhole or quicksand.

"No kidding?"

No, I'm *totally* hanging out down here because I want to. "I need your help!"

"What do you expect me to do? I'm just an old lady."

Yeah. Right. "Um."

"Don't you have anything you can use in your big fancy car?"

"For Pete's sake, Ida, it's a freaking Hon—no. Not getting into this." Alright. Let's think. I don't have anything in my car because I'm used to city conveniences like paved roads and tow trucks. My bad. "I think we may need to call someone."

"Like who?"

My instincts say Jess, but I know she won't have her phone on because her guided meditation class is going on right now.

Plan B is just *so* much worse. "Maybe the fire department?"

"Won't matter," Ida calls back. "There's a big crash outside town and the Pitchette trucks are assisting."

Now how the hell can she know that? The woman drove

a freaking *Saturn*. Into a *ditch*.

"How about someone at the township office?" I holler back.

The township has crews that go out to clear roads. If the fire department is tied up, they might have someone available to help. The storm drains and runoff are their responsibility, anyway.

And while they're dealing with the runoff, they might as well go ahead and excavate my foot.

"You want me to walk to the township office?" Ida demands.

For Pete's sake. "Don't walk to the township office! *Call* the township office!"

I'd tell her to call 9-1-1, but I can just imagine what she'd tell them. And I do *not* want that made public record. Especially since it will probably be entered into evidence when I stand trial for geronticide.

Plus, I cannot be the reason for *two* 9-1-1 calls in four days.

"That could work," Ida yells. "I have a cellphone somewhere, I think."

Please, God, let her have a cellphone. Or cyanide pills. "Check your bag!"

"Might take a while for the township to get here," she hollers. "Everyone calls to complain in bad weather."

Great. I'm not going anywhere, am I?

Okay, new plan. I have to cut off my foot. Which will totally ruin sandal season, but it's that or—

Holy crap, is that a log or an alligator? Shit! It's too dark to tell. I mean, *yeah*. This is Pennsylvania, so log is more likely. But alligator isn't *impossible*. It's raining buckets. Who the hell knows what's getting washed down Little Drop Run? And that log has fucking glowing eyes, I *swear!* I mean, I think. Because, hello! *Too dark to see clearly*.

I look up at the grate. "Ida Boyko, get some freaking help *NOW!*"

"Don't worry," Liam Taggert hollers back. "She did."

SIXTEEN

I stare up at the drain grate.

Of *course.* Of *course* Liam Taggert would pop up now!

"Seriously?" I yell up to him. "What do you do, run the whole town on your own?"

"Feels like it sometimes." Liam isn't anything but a dark outline and an annoying voice. "What the hell are you doing down there?"

"Online shopping. Thought I'd have a better signal."

"You know, I don't remember you being such a smartass in high school."

"And I don't remember you being a freaking superhero," I mutter.

"It's the Army training," he hollers down.

Damn echoes. "Would you just hurry up? I'm pretty sure there's an alligator down here."

"So dramatic." Then he's gone.

Wonderful. The Great Liam Taggert bolts from female hysteria. Good to know he isn't Mr. Perfect after all.

I scowl down at my foot, take a couple lion breaths, then

pull with everything in me.

I tilt so far back I end up in a reverse Michael Jackson antigravity lean.

Nothing.

Well, shit!

I'm panicking now, and it's only partly because I'm trapped in a rising creek.

Mostly it's because Liam is going to *find me* trapped in a rising creek.

Okay, God. I get it. You're punishing me for bad behavior. It's the socks, right? Shouldn't have pimped out my socks. Because, yes, I'll admit Twister's intentions might not have been on the up-and-up. He didn't *seem* like that type of rando. But, I mean. We all know that socks are multi-purpose tools.

But, come on, God! DONUTS. You know about donuts. Plus, I didn't even *get* any. I gave that money away.

To Liam.

Wait. Is *that* why I'm cursed? Because I was a smartass to Mr. Hometown Hero? Seriously? He called my brain a weapon of mass destruction and insinuated I'm a smut supplier! How does *that* go unpunished?

No way I'm letting Liam Taggert rescue me right now. He doesn't get to do that. He gets to watch *me* rescue *myself,* thank you very much.

Okay! Great. Feminist Outlook re-established. Hey, what if I loosen my boot laces? Maybe it's the laces that are caught, not the boot itself. And it's not like laces are easy to snap. I mean, that's why prisons take them away from inmates, right? So they don't hang themselves? Which would imply laces are strong as heck.

Of course, I can't see my boot, let alone the laces. It wouldn't be so bad, except my fingers are numb with cold and I can't really feel anything. Stupid double knots. Why the heck did I tie them like this? What did I think would happen, my boot would go flying off somewhere while I'm driving around backroads? Ha! More like *the exact opposite.*

"Gah!"

"Need some help?"

I jump, even though a small part of me knew Liam would be back.

I just hoped he wouldn't be back until I was hauling myself out of the creek.

Damn it.

He clicks on a Maglite, rendering me legally blind.

I blink past the retina spots. "What are you doing down here?"

"Online shopping."

"Funny." It isn't. It isn't funny. AT ALL. "Didn't happen to bring an excavator, did you?"

"Sorry. Couldn't get it down here." Liam carefully moves through the creek toward me. "There's a tree fallen across the hill."

"There is?" Damn. Missed it by *that much.*

"Yep. I got out to take a look at it and I saw Ida down on the bridge, looking through the drain grate. Next to your Honda." The flashlight doesn't illuminate much of his face, but his lips definitely twitch. "Figured that couldn't be good."

Great. Glad to hear I have a reputation.

At least this particular incident probably won't show up as Page 1 news.

"Where's Ida now?" Probably polishing her Colt .45 in my passenger's seat, right?

Please, God, don't let her be skinning a chipmunk.

"Jack Walters was behind me when I stopped to look at the tree, so I walked her up the hill and had him take her home. He can get to Teeter Furnace using Collier Run

Road."

Geez. Poor Jack Walters. He works at a sawmill just outside of town. I bet he'd rather listen to bandsaws than Ida. I sure would.

"So it's pretty bad out there, huh?" I can tell the rain is picking up. The thunder feels a lot closer. Not to mention the lightning. Can you get electrocuted in a creek if lightning strikes it? I bet you can. And if you can't, I bet *I* can.

"Yeah. It's pretty bad." Liam stops next to me and angles the flashlight at my leg. "Not as bad as in here, though."

I frown. "Are you talking about me or the creek?"

"Both. Mostly the creek." He swings the flashlight back down the tunnel in the direction we both came. "See that pile of debris? It's been washed here from upstream and it's getting stuck on the edge of the culvert."

"Yeah, I noticed that earlier."

"At the rate it's collecting, it's going to be difficult to get back out that way." Liam redirects the light back at my foot.

That isn't good. "Maybe we can holler up to someone to bring down some shovels or picks or something to break it up."

"No one to holler to. It's just us."

Ida and Jack. Right.

"The storm's bad and the unpaved part of the township road is partially washed out." Liam crouches to analyze my situation. "All the department trucks are out on call, so I told Jack to tell anyone he passed on the road to turn around. The bigger problem is that on the other side of the bridge is a giant floodplain. If the downpour continues, I'm worried everyone on this road will need to evacuate."

Geez. 'Evacuate' is a term they use in places like Florida and California and New York City. Not Pitchette.

"Why aren't you out on a call?"

"I was headed to one when I saw Ida."

"Oh." Oops.

Liam reaches into the water and feels around my boot. "So why are you really down here?"

Yeah. About that. "Ida was ditched, so I stopped to help her."

"Yeah, I saw her car," Liam says. "But that's up the hill. Why are you down *here?*"

"Well, I was driving her home and this dumb chipmunk ran out in front of us."

"Oh, I know where this is headed."

"You do?" I frown. "So you know about her chipmunk thing?"

"Everyone knows about her chipmunk thing."

"*Seriously?* And you people still let that psychopath run around town on her own?"

"I don't know that she's doing a lot of *running.*" Liam is elbow-deep in the water, nudging around my foot. "More like shuffling. She's eighty-eight, you know."

"Yeah, well, she's a bloodthirsty eighty-eight. She saw that poor little chipmunk and launched herself out of my car!"

"That's why you stopped on the bridge?"

"Hell, no." I shift my free foot, trying to get more comfortable. "Ida Boyko is nuts. I wanted her out of my car anyway. I probably would've left her here, except she chucked my limited-edition Stanley at the chipmunk and it rolled off the bridge and into the creek."

Liam stares up at me. "You got out to get your Stanley?"

"Well, yeah. It's a *Stanley.*" I mean, *yes.* It's just an insulated water bottle. Technically. "It seemed like a smart idea at the time."

He shakes his head.

Yeah. I bet he hears that excuse a lot as a first responder.

"What's the verdict?" I ask.

"Well, Maris. You're stuck."

I roll my eyes. "Geez. Thanks a lot, professor. What the heck would I do without you?"

He might have laughed, but I can't tell over the sound of the creek.

"Hold this." He thrusts the Maglite into my hand. "Point it straight down."

"You know, you're kind of bossy."

"It's the Army training."

"Hey, what's that?" I swing the light toward a dark, mossy, bumpy mass moving our direction. *Holy crap, are those eyeballs?*

Liam looks over his shoulder. "It's a log."

"It's an alligator."

"It's not an alligator."

"Well, it's got claws and a tail and green skin. What would *you* call that?"

"I don't know. A turtle?"

"Please. Like I'd be afraid of a *turtle.*" I would. I would be afraid of a turtle. If the turtle was big and nasty and lived in the sewers. The Teenage Mutant Ninja Turtles are all fun and games until they come after you with their ninjutsu and their nunchakus or whatever. "How can you be sure it's not an alligator?"

"For one thing, the state doesn't stock this creek with trout. So I imagine there's not a lot for an alligator to eat."

Yeah, except us. "What's that thing right there?"

"It's a stick."

"Are you sure?"

"*Yes.* Now quit waving the light around. I need to see what I'm doing or else we—"

A roar drowns out the rest of that sentence.

I flash the light back down the tunnel. "That didn't sound

good, right?"

Liam takes the light from me and angles it toward my foot. "It's the water."

"What?"

"That was the sound of the water. This whole area is in a flood warning because of the storm."

"Shit."

"We're going to be fine. I just need you to stay calm. We're going to get your foot out and then we're going to get out of here."

"Let me guess. More Army training?"

"Boy Scouts."

Right. "You know what? We can leave the foot here."

"Mollie, I'm not amputating your foot."

"Don't know how to do it, huh?"

"I know how to do it. I'm just not going to."

I drop my head back and heave a sigh. "I can't believe I'm going to drown in stormwater."

"At least it's stormwater and not wastewater."

"Oh yeah, that's a total win." I fold my hands behind my head and use my thumbs to rub at the sore muscles in my neck. "On the bright side, I guess I don't have to worry about paying back my college loans. Or getting that damn story retracted."

"That's the spirit. Take this." He hands back the flashlight. "I think I loosened a couple of the rocks around your foot. We're going to try to wriggle you out together, okay? Try not to just twist yourself free with a yank because I don't want to end up dragging you out of here with a torn meniscus. Got it?"

"Ten-four, soldier."

"Cute."

He plants one hand around my shinbone and slides the

other up the back of my calf. I start trembling and having hot flashes and breaking out in hives. Probably from hypothermia.

He looks up at me. The angle of the flashlight makes his blue eyes glow.

"Hold onto me," he orders.

Um, yes, please. I curl my fingers into his jacket, trying not to drool on him.

"Deep breath, Mollie."

I take three.

"Ready?"

I nod.

He grips my leg as we pull together, wiggling my foot back and forth, trying to create space in the crevice. I feel like it's working until he gives a grunt of frustration.

"I'm guessing that's not good."

"No." He wipes water off his face with the back of his hand. The other still cups my calf, but that's probably just a coincidence. "The water's rising, so every time we make a little space, the hole gets filled in with more sediment."

Crap. The water *is* rising. Quickly, too, because it's already mostly up to my thigh. Which means it's either washed out the debris clogging up the end of the culvert, or it's rushing right over it.

"Liam?"

"Don't. Do not say something stupid right now." He stands, glaring around the culvert. "I'm not in the mood."

"Maybe you should go—"

"What did I just say, Mollie?"

"But maybe you have something in the command vehicle that can help."

"I didn't come in the command vehicle. I came in my truck."

"Alright. How about a crowbar or a tire iron or something

to pry me loose?"

"There's a tree across the road. I parked like a quarter mile away. Then there's the debris that's gumming up the culvert."

"You can move it, though." I fist my shaking hands. "You can walk to your truck."

"I can't." He looks at me and I understand what he means.

"This culvert is big, Liam." My voice sounds a lot calmer than I feel. "Even with the water rising so quickly, it won't fill the whole way up. I'll be okay." Probably.

"It doesn't have to fill up. It just has to fill enough to carry something big from upstream that knocks you over and hits you in the head." He wades across the flow of water. "Then when you're unconscious, you'll slip beneath the waterline and drown."

Geez. What a Debbie Downer. "What the heck are you doing?"

He's bent at the waist, reaching deep into the water. "Looking for a crowbar."

"Very funny. Watch out for the alligator."

He mutters something I don't hear over the roar of water. But he comes up with a stick that might have been part of a much larger stick, once upon a time.

"Yeah, that'll do the trick." Sarcasm is one of my defense mechanisms, okay?

He tosses the stick aside and does another deep-dive.

"Liam."

"Forget it, Mollie."

"You don't even know what I was going to say!"

"Yes, I do. So let's just move past it and focus on solutions instead of bickering. Okay?"

"Wow. Guess you really *aren't* in the mood, huh?"

He fishes through the flooding with both hands and

doesn't answer.

The water is officially up to my hips. "Alright, this is ridiculous. I know you're a war hero and everything, but I cannot be responsible for you dying in stormwater. That's just way more than my reputation can handle, okay?"

Liam stands and wades back toward me.

"I mean, between the whippets and the library and that thing with Shack Wheeler, I'm on the fast-track to being tarred and feathered, you know?"

He snakes an arm around my waist and grips behind my knee with his other hand.

"And okay, maybe I'm not exactly Pitchette's favorite daughter—"

"Wrap your arms around me."

I reach around his neck. "But Mom loved this town and it was her *home.* And I—"

"Lift your free leg."

"—*cannot* be the reason people stop thinking nice things about her," I say, hooking my leg over his hip. "The only thing she ever did was—"

"Hold tight."

"—try to give me everything she could and I—*gah!*"

He yanks me up against him so hard my foot pops out of my boot and we topple into the filthy creek. It's so full of crap, I completely stop worrying about the alligator. Because let's face it, I'm definitely going to be crushed by a log or clipped by a tire or contract hepatitis way before I get eaten. I thrash through the murkiness and finally find air.

About twenty feet downstream from the bridge. Shit!

"Liam!" I don't see him anywhere, but that doesn't mean anything. He's a soldier and a Boy Scout and a firefighter and holy crap, is that him clinging to the side of the freaking culvert? What is he, Spider Man?

He hollers at me.

"What?" I yell back.

He might've answered, but I'm too focused on trying to get some footing. Every time I start to stand, my legs wash out from under me. It doesn't seem like a lot of water, but it knocks me around like the shore waves at Lake Erie. And this is really pathetic, but each knock-down zaps my energy until I just give up.

I used to think I was the sort of person who could find her way out of a flooding creek. Apparently, that isn't the case.

"So long, Pitchette," I gurgle as I go down one last time.

Water fills my ears and gushes up my nose and I briefly try holding my breath before I remember I'm giving up. Inhaling is a lot harder. I can't get past the mental block of not breathing water. Weird.

I gasp when air touches my face. The water thins and spreads across the ground, rushing over the floodplain instead of just barreling down the creek bed. I wash out of the flow on my back and stay there. Sure, it probably isn't smart to lay in the middle of an active floodplain. But my boot and my car and Liam are back at the bridge. It's not like I have anything else left to lose.

"Maris!"

Ugh. Maybe if I lay still enough, he won't see me.

Big hands grip my face. "Look at me, Mollie!"

"Can't," I mumble. "Dead."

"Geezus, woman. I thought you died."

I did. I did die. About three seconds ago, when Liam Taggert called me 'woman.'

I crack open my eyes, trying not to cry or throw up. "How come you stayed in the culvert and I got washed away?"

His lips turn up at the corners, shifting the mud on his face. "It's the Army training."

"That's annoying."

"Can you sit up?"

"Do I have to?"

"Yes."

He lets go of my face and pulls my arms until I'm sitting. Ish. Okay, I'm hunched over like an alcoholic waking up on the sidewalk outside Jerry's.

Liam crouches next to me. "Does anything hurt?"

"Yeah."

"What?"

"Everything."

"How about your leg? I pulled pretty hard to get you out of there."

I move it a little and wince. "It's sort of sore around the knee. Not broken. Just a little hyperextended, I think. My foot's sore, but that just feels more like a bruise." Not that anyone can tell. I'm straight mud from head to toes.

"Okay. Can you stand?"

"Yes, but you'll probably have to help me up."

He gets me to my feet and we stand there, sinking into the wet ground while I figure out how much weight I can put on my knee. Enough I can hobble up to the road, I figure. Because there's no way in hell I'm asking Liam to carry me. My Humiliation Meter hit its cap Saturday.

Liam grips my arm as we slowly wade through the floodplain and head for the road. The incline from the ditch is the worst part. I don't ask for help, but Liam pulls me up, anyway, showing me where to plant my sore leg so I won't slip and fall. Again.

By the time I reach the road, I'm panting and seeing double.

"Good thing my car's not far." Okay, it's sort of far. Considering it's parked back at the bridge. But I can see it from here, so that's something.

"Your car's useless right now." Liam nods down the road,

which is completely underwater. "Down there's flooded, which means the road's washed out."

"Oh. What about the other end?"

"There's a fallen tree, remember?"

Right. Crap.

Okay, so the thing is I was lying to myself before. We're pretty far from the bridge. Liam said he parked about a quarter mile away. From the *bridge.* I'm cold and tired and sore and experiencing some sort of post-traumatic shock that has me numb from the waist down and hallucinating that Liam's looking at me like he's really worried.

In reality, that's just me projecting. Because there's a good chance I won't make it to his truck by the Fourth of July, let alone nightfall.

"Go on without me," I say. "Tell Jess I love her."

"Stop being so dramatic."

"I'm not being dramatic. I'm being realistic."

"It is not that far."

"It's pretty far."

"It's just over the hill."

"The hill! Damn it, I forgot about the hill." It'll probably take me three hours to get up that thing. Especially since I'll be crawling. "I appreciate you getting me out of that hole, but I'll take it from here. Why don't you get back to your truck and head to that call you were on before Ida stopped you?"

Liam rolls his eyes.

"I'm serious!" Sort of. Okay, I'm secretly a big baby and just don't want to cry in front of him. "Clearly the situation here is under control. I'm sure you're needed elsewhere."

"Probably." He comes toward me.

"The thing is, I've got nowhere to be. I can just sit here until the storm clears up and the flood drains away."

"Somehow, I have a hard time believing you can just sit down and stay there until it's safe to move."

Oof. That's some harsh truth. I bet I can, though. Especially since my knee really—

"Hey!" I yelp when he does some ninja move that pitches me across his shoulders.

He hooks an arm around my uninjured leg, reaches around and grips my forearm to hold me steady, then starts walking.

I spit wet hair out of my mouth. "What the hell are you *doing?*"

"Fireman's carry. I've never done one this far before. We'll see how it goes."

"For Pete's sake, put me *down!*"

"No. I'm tired and hungry and pissed off, and I don't want to be standing out here anymore arguing."

GAH! I had him until the 'pissed off' part. Now I just feel super guilty and obnoxious.

Mollie Maris, Pitchette's pride and joy. Waterlogged and slung over the shoulder of Mr. July.

At least nobody is here to see it.

"Do you really know how to amputate a foot?"

"Yes."

"How?"

"I could tell you, but then I'd probably want to kill you."

That's fair. "How did you know a full-body yank would get me out of that hole?"

"I didn't."

"Then what made you try it?"

"Physics and desperation, mostly."

Yeah, that's how most of my choices happen.

I sigh.

"Too uncomfortable?" he asks.

"No." It is, kind of. My hipbone is grinding against his

shoulder joint and my boobs are squished. Plus there's the whole agonizing-death-by-embarrassment thing happening. "I can't believe I lost my boot."

"Are you serious?"

"It cost like seventy bucks!"

"For one boot?"

"Well, the pair was one-forty."

"Wow. That D.C. inflation is stupid."

"I bought them at Sonny's."

"Then Sonny was overcharging you big-time." He shifts me on his shoulders, breathing a little harder as the road starts to incline. "He probably saw your little skirt and knew he had a sucker."

I frown. "How would he know how much my skirt cost?"

"It's not about how much it cost. It's about how you look when you wear it."

"What? What does *that* mean? How do I look?"

"Like you belong in the city."

That isn't fair. Sure, I lived in D.C. for a few years. Okay, twelve. But most of my life happened in Pitchette. My first steps. My first words. My first teeth. My first period. My first break-up. Okay, maybe not my first break-up. I didn't really date until I got to college. But my first *heartbreak*. That did happen here. When Mom died.

"You're scary when you're quiet, Maris."

"Sorry."

I don't know how long it takes to cross the bridge, but it seems like it takes forever to get to Liam's truck. By the time we pass my Honda, he's breathing hard and slick with sweat. Well, slick*er*. I try to squirm free when we get to the hill, but he won't let me down. Not even when he edges around the downed tree. Which makes me feel *super* pathetic and ridiculous.

It's just as well. At least he can't see my face.

I feel him relax as soon as he sees his truck.

Then I'm sliding down his body and standing upright.

I avoid his eyes. "Um. Thanks."

"Are you crying?"

"*No.*" I wipe my snotty nose on the back of my hand.

Chest heaving, he opens the cab door and starts the truck. The keys are already in the ignition because you can do stuff like that in Pitchette. The radio comes on, tuned to a Pittsburgh sports station. Liam punches it off. He also turns down the volume of his on-call emergency radio for the fire department, which is going crazy. I watch him crank the heat before he slams the door and moves to the bed, flipping down the tailgate and reaching under the hardshell cover for a plastic tote. The thing pops open like a Pillsbury tube with a zillion spring-operated shelves of emergency supplies.

"Holy crap. What is this, the Batmobile?"

"Better." He extracts a Mylar thermal blanket. "Wrap up in this and get in the cab."

That's a good idea. I definitely don't want to get his seats wet.

Plus now that I'm not worried about imminent death, I can worry about dumb female stuff. Like how my nipples are pushing right through my drenched jacket. So that's fun.

I sound like a giant chip bag when I climb into the cab.

Great. Now I'm thinking about chips. And burgers. And cookies.

Liam lines his seat with blankets from his zombie apocalypse kit and climbs in at the exact moment my stomach decides to curse me out. Loudly.

He tosses a chocolate protein bar in my lap.

Let me guess. "Army?"

"Boy Scouts."

Damn. Wrong again. "The, um, Stanley was a birthday

gift. From my mom."

He looks at me, but I look out the window.

The Glass Shuddering Ultra Turbo Speed of his windshield wipers drowns out the sob in my throat.

SEVENTEEN

I was going to ask him what the plan is, but I must've fallen asleep.

"Gah!" I shout and jerk awake, barely catching myself when the passenger door opens and I start to fall out of my seat. "Holy crap. What?" What's happening?

"Brought you home," Liam says. He glances overhead at the shifting clouds. "Hurry up, before it starts raining again."

"It stopped?" I slide out of his truck, wincing a little. Sore knee. Bruised foot. No boot. Right.

"Barely." Liam helps me hobble out of the way and swings the truck door shut. "It's been coming in bands."

"Any end in sight?"

"The radar still has a bunch of red and violet headed our way."

Violet. That's like tornado stuff, right? Geez.

"Oh crap."

"What?" Liam frowns at my leg. "Do you think something's broken?"

"Mom's housekey is in my car. Shit!"

"You locked the house?"

"Of course!"

"Why?"

I roll my eyes. "Because I'm used to living in the city and doing crazy stuff like that."

Lightning splinters overhead, followed by a clap of thunder I feel in my chest.

"We can't stand out here." Liam hustles me toward the front porch. "We'll have to break in."

Perfect. "Well, Mom painted the front door shut years ago. It's probably easiest to try breaking in through the side door." I mean, maybe. What do I know?

"Got it. Stay here." He helps me up the front steps and hurries around the house.

I should've stayed in the truck. Liam Taggert is breaking into Mom's house because I fell into a flooding stream and left my house key in my car. Great. Just peachy. Mollie Maris, in complete control of her life. As always.

I sigh and lean against the porch rail as the rain picks up and pelts the roof. Visibility is officially zero. I can't even see Terry Bauer's place. Geez. Okay, so it's a good thing I stopped to help Ida. Not that I don't think she wouldn't survive a tornado or anything. I'd just feel really bad for the folks who would have to deal with her when she landed in another county.

A drenched chipmunk scurries onto the porch and up the railing. It twitches its nose and stares at me.

"You got to be kidding," I tell him. "No offense, but this is all sort of your fault."

He sits up on his hind legs.

"No! You may *not* come inside!"

Other people might not think that nose-whisker twitch is him asking to come out of the rain, but *I* know better. I don't condone the slaughter of innocent chipmunks. Obviously.

But Ida was right about one thing: they know *exactly* what they're doing. I can see it in his eyes.

Liam emerges in the downpour. His hair and clothes are plastered to his body and he has to shout over the rain. "Got it open! Come on!"

Into the deluge again. Fun.

"Good luck," I tell Chipmunk.

"What?" Liam shouts.

"Nothing!"

I grab onto his arm to keep from slipping. The lawn between the front porch and the side door isn't slanted, thankfully. Still, it's slick and the water draining from the downspout is already flooding Mom's front flowerbeds. Liam pushes me up the concrete steps of the miniature side porch and follows me inside before slamming the storm door behind us.

We drip in silence for about twenty seconds on the mudroom floor.

Liam pulls the Mylar blanket off me and drapes it over the moving boxes I stacked in the corner.

"I don't want to invade your space," he says. "But I think I'm stuck here until the visibility gets better."

"Oh. Yeah." That makes sense. I mean, a dead first responder isn't much good.

"We should get dried off."

"Yeah. Um." I blink down at the small lake we're creating. The mudroom floor is vinyl, so it isn't such a big deal. Which is good, because my brain sort of isn't working, anyway.

Liam's must be. "Where are your towels?"

I watch him strip off his rain jacket and carefully drape it next to the Mylar blanket. Holy shit, he *is* built like a statue. His soaked shirt clings to like every freaking muscle and tendon in his torso. I mean, *damn.* There are muscles in that little nook right under the bicep? Who even *has* those?

"Mollie?"

"Hm?"

"Towels?"

"Towels!" Good grief. What am I, sixteen? "We need some towels."

"You might not want to track mud and water everywhere," Liam says when I step foot into the living room.

Good point. The floor is wood. Mom loved the floor.

I pull off my jacket, then I lean my ass against the door frame and carefully take off my boot and socks. My knee is actually starting to really bother me, now. That probably isn't great.

"There's a bathroom through the living room." I straighten and gingerly put some weight on my leg. "Towels are in the closet behind the door. It's a full bath, so you can use it to get cleaned up."

Wait. Does that sound like I'm inviting him to take a shower? I mean, not that he *can't* take a shower! I mean, should I explicitly tell him it's shower-optional? Or does that just make things more awkward? I mean, more awkward than him just going ahead and taking a shower?

And GREAT. Now I'm picturing Liam Taggert naked. Naked and in the shower.

Gah!

"Noted." Liam's eyes drift down to my knee. "That looks bruised."

"It's fine! I'm fine." Aside from having a mini panic attack regarding the shower sitch. "I'll, um, just, um…look for something." Like some DIGNITY!

I hobble upstairs and lock myself in the bathroom. I need a game plan here. I really need a shower and dry clothes, but is that too weird with Liam downstairs? I mean, would he hear the shower and then just assume it's okay to get all naked? Not that it isn't! I mean, not like *that,* obviously. Not that I'm opposed to *like that,* I just, you know. Don't want to assume anything.

For Pete's sake. This is ridiculous. We're grown-ass adults.

I flick on the light and glance in the bathroom mirror.

"Oh *shit.*"

That's not Mollie Maris. That's something from the Black Lagoon. Covered in mud and leaves and probably alligator scat. And holy crap, is that a dreadlock starting?

Yeah. SHOWERING. Definitely.

I do it at warp speed, of course. Partly because the lights are flickering. Partly because I'm worried Liam is going to come looking for me.

I mean. I'm 'worried.'

I unlock the bathroom door and listen for a few seconds. No Liam movement. Just rain pounding the house. Too bad. I hold my towel closed, tiptoe into my bedroom, and pull on joggers, a long-sleeved Henley, and fuzzy socks. And it's *glorious.* Like being wrapped in a cozy cloud.

Although, maybe it's a little insensitive to get so comfortable. Liam only has drenched clothes. And it isn't like I have any male clothing to lend him. A flannel, maybe? I probably have one somewhere. Not that it would fit. I like to think my boobs are decent-sized, but Liam's chest is just bigger. I have an old zippered Penn sweatshirt. It's a little roomy on me. Maybe that will work, if he leaves it unzipped. And he can probably fit into my longer gym shorts. His ass is definitely in better shape, but mine is bigger. Sadly.

Liam isn't in sight when I go downstairs, but the bathroom door is closed and the light is on.

No shower sounds. Dang.

I knock. "I have some dry shorts and a sweatshirt for you."

"You do?" Liam sounds surprised, even through the door. "Will they fit?"

"Only one way to find out."

I hear some movement on the other side. I hook the sweatshirt and shorts on the doorknob and scurry for the kitchen as fast as I can on my sore knee. I don't want to be there when he opens the door. Just in case he's naked.

No point in being tempted if you can't give into it, right?

Besides. I'm hungry.

The kitchen faucet *plinks* steadily. Have to get that fixed at some point. I open the fridge door and the power goes out. PERFECT.

My stomach rumbles.

"Hey, I know already! I'm looking, okay?" Ooh. Whipped cream. Convenient. Maybe not entirely nutritious, but it's mostly air, right? Yeah. So, you know. Filling without a ton of carbs. AND it's a dairy product. Which means it could totally go bad, since the power is out.

So that leaves one option.

"Power's out, I see," Liam says from the living room. "You know, I don't know if I should be proud or worried that your clothes—"

He stops in the door of the kitchen as I put the nozzle in my mouth.

My cheeks flame.

Correction: *all of* me flames. Top to bottom. Front to back. I'm not Mollie Maris right now. I'm one giant, molten ball of creamy sweet embarrassment. Slightly damp and sucking whipped cream out of a canister like a middle school bulimic.

Shouldn't say that. Eating disorders aren't funny.

Neither is *Liam Freaking Taggert* walking in on me guzzling whipped cream straight from the can.

GAH!

Mayday, mayday, God! Commence Operation Lightning Bolt!

Liam stares. I stare. There's a lot of staring.

Then he's walking toward me. Slowly. Okay, maybe it's the fact I just got back from drowning, but I *swear* he licks his lips.

He stops close enough that I can see the gold sprinkle of hair across his chest. Even without the kitchen lights.

"Swallow, Mollie."

Right. Yep. Okay. Didn't imagine that. Or that he's breathing sort of raggedly. Looking at my lips. Wrapped around the whipped cream nozzle.

I carefully extract the nozzle. Swallow audibly. "You see, I was sort of hungry—"

He brushes a finger against the corner of my mouth.

It comes away with a large dollop of whipped cream.

His finger hovers between us. The whipped cream glows on the tip like the Eye of Sauron. Consuming my vision. Pinching the air from my lungs. Blotting out everything else in the room.

"Lick it," he whispers.

Okay, God, I guess we have our wires crossed here. That's on me. I speak English and You probably speak Aramaic, right? Probably need to dig up a translator for this because I requested a lightning BOLT not a lightning JOLT.

I'm having a stroke. Because I'm dry drowning. Because Liam Taggert is *not* asking me to lick whipped cream off his finger.

Because I am *not* wrapping my lips around his finger and sucking that whipped cream off.

His eyes dilate. He takes a sharp breath and pulls his hand back. His finger slips out of my mouth with a moist *pop*.

"It's whipped cream," I say. "Can't waste it."

He blinks and stares at me from under creased eyebrows. Like he can't believe I just did what I did.

"You told me to." What? He *did.* "It seemed rude to say no." And also, like it was a once-in-a-lifetime opportunity.

"I said 'lick.'" His voice comes out sort of hoarse. "Not 'suck.'"

"Licking. Sucking. Same diff." It's not. It's not same diff.

But now I'm getting self-conscious and confidence is everything, right? *Right?*

Liam's blue eyes glow in the gray light streaming through the kitchen windows. "You're a nut, Mollie Maris."

"So you've said." Great. The *one time* I try to be flirty and I end up sounding like a lunatic. "Any chance we can never see each other again in a town of twelve hundred people?"

"I seriously doubt it." He doesn't look all that amused now. "I really hope not, anyway."

What the heck is *that* supposed to mean? Probably nothing good, considering I sort of—

"*Eep!*" I squeak when Liam pushes me against the counter, pinning me with his hips.

Holy crap, this isn't real. Liam Taggert isn't grabbing my hips and I'm not fisting his hair and *holy crap oh good lord we are FREAKING KISSING.*

SYSTEM FAILURE.

BRAIN OVERLOAD.

RESTART NEEDED.

RESTARTING.

Holy crap. Holy crap holy crap holy—

Liam Taggert *is* kissing me. I'm kissing him. We're kissing each other. At the same time. TOGETHER.

And oh. My. LORD. He's good at this. Because *of course* he is. He's a war hero and Mr. July and Liam Freaking

Taggert and he's good at *everything.* Even with him wearing my clothes and my sore leg and my through-the-roof humiliation level, this is *still* the best damn kiss I'VE EVER HAD. GAH!

"You're good," I rasp when he finally lets me up for air.

"Baby, you have no idea."

"Hmm." No. I do not. But I'm getting one. FAST.

Liam sucks in a sharp breath when my hand starts to explore that idea all on its own.

And oh, *hello!* Guess I'm not the only one having this thought.

This *great big* thought.

Liam has that you're-a-nut smile on his face. "Hey there, cowgirl." His fingers circle my wrist. Gently, but firmly. "It's been a crazy couple hours. Maybe we should slow down."

"Maybe you should *shhhh.*" I'll be honest, my communication faculties are still offline.

He chuckles and kisses my forehead.

Then my nose.

Then my *mouth.*

Oh sure, he *says* we should slow down, but that is *not* the message he's sending. From *any* area.

Hm. Shouldn't be complaining. I can use that for leverage. Literally.

He groans when I test my theory. Oh *heck* yes, it's working! Pretty well, too. I'm making some important progress.

Until he plants his hands on my shoulders and steps back.

Gah! Damn it! Seriously? I'm *this close* to getting where I want to go and I lose him?

WHY, God?

Liam brushes his knuckles down my cheek. "Let's reassess when you haven't had a near-death experience."

Great. Because Liam Taggert is *definitely* going to want to pick things up where we left off after he's had time to remember what I looked like flopping around in dirty ditch water.

He tucks a piece of damp hair behind my ear. "I'm really glad you didn't die today, Maris."

"Hmm," I purr. Damn it! I meant to say, 'Me, too.'

Pathetic.

Gah!

EIGHTEEN

The storm causes a ton of damage. And not all of it is to property and land. I mean, yes. Lots of folks are going to be filing insurance claims and the power is still off for half the county.

But mostly, the storm wrecks the hell out of my self-confidence.

Because let's review. In the twenty-two hours it took for the storm to pass through Pitchette, I failed to rescue an old lady; got stuck in a creek; destroyed my brand new hiking boots; required rescuing; and failed to romantically entice the guy who rescued me. A guy who kissed me one-and-a-half times, let me feel him up, and then decided, *Meh. Rain check.*

And I lost my freaking Stanley! The very last present Mom ever gave me.

Not cool, God! NOT COOL.

The worst part is I don't even feel like telling the one person I can tell. I mean, I love Jess. But she has the sort of self-confidence that makes it hard for her to empathize with us weirder, nuttier girls who sort of freeze up when we get hit on.

Or in my case, kissed within an inch of our freaking lives and then gently but firmly pushed away.

Can we say PATHETIC?

"Babe, are you sure you're okay?" Jess pushes back her ballcap and frowns in my direction. Again. "That's the third atmospheric sigh you've heaved since you got here."

Three sighs in three hours? Honestly, that isn't all that bad. Considering.

"I'm fine."

Jess gives me a look.

"Okay, I'm not fine. But I don't want to talk about it, alright?"

She holds up her hands. "Alright. I get it. I'll quit bugging you. But I'm here if or when you *do* want to talk about it."

"Thanks, babe." I rock back on my heels and look up at the Foundations storefront. Probably shouldn't be kneeling when my leg is still sore from getting yanked out of a hole. At least I'm using one of those foam gardening pad things. "Are we actually making progress?"

"Yes. Is it a lot? No."

Yeah. That's what I thought. "I know I should be grateful that your place didn't get the worst of the damage, but I'm too grossed out by the rancid tomato sauce to see the silver lining."

Jess laughs. I don't know why. I mean, if the sauce Sal threw in the diner dumpster three days ago got splattered across the front of *my* business during a storm, I'd be Googling how to get my insurance to cover the cost of renovating the storefront.

Jess seems fine chipping off the gunk with a paint scraper and chemical stripper Handy Dandy Andy at the hardware store talked her into buying. After a ridiculous conversation filled with stripping double entendres I was forced to witness. I'll be honest, I initially thought Jess was too much woman for young Andy to handle. Because, you know. She's Jess and he's about ten minutes into adulthood. But he seems to be doing a pretty good job of manipulating her inner cougar into buying pricey products. These stupid paint scrapers were like twenty bucks each.

I flex my sore hand and get back to chipping goop off the pressure-treated wood under the front window of Foundations. "I hope you weren't too blinded by Andy's geeky glasses to see he totally ripped you off with these things."

"Oh, I don't mind." Jess takes another step up on her stepladder to reach above the door frame. "He's just here for the summer, earning some money before he goes back to college in the fall. He's sort of quiet and awkward, but he's sweet. I figured each sale he makes is probably a boost to his ego."

That's a little presumptuous of her. Maybe his ego is totally fine. "For Pete's sake, Jess. Is that why you flirt with him every time you're in there?"

She grins down at me, sweat dripping off her face. "I mean, I figured it can't hurt. Give him a little self-confidence."

"Geez, Jess! He's just a kid!"

"He's a senior in college, Mollz."

"Yeah, which makes you what? Eleven, twelve years older?"

"So?" She gets back to scrapping. "It's just a little flirting. And he goes back to school in August."

Oh good lord. "Holy crap. You actually *like* that kid, don't you?"

Her shrug is far from a denial. "Andy's really sweet. I like talking to him."

I roll my eyes. "Well, just remember how *you* used to feel when guys in their thirties came onto *you* when *you* were in college."

"Wow. Could you have wedged any more emphasis into that sentence?"

"Yes. I could've put some on the word *'thirties.'*"

"Ouch. I get it, okay? I'm too old to be crushing on a twenty-two-year-old."

Crushing! Oh boy. That's way worse than a little harmless flirting. That means she actually has some emotional attachment to Handy Dandy Andy.

Okay, so maybe my current pathetic state isn't so bad. I mean, it isn't *great*. But at least my recent romantic foil was because of an actual grown man. Not some man-child who still has a year to go on his bachelor's degree.

Jess sighs.

Uh-oh. It's catching. Time for a subject change.

"I don't know what the heck Sal puts in her sauce, but it's bleaching the wood." The energetic blue is all speckled where we're scraping off the caked tomato. "I'm guessing the chemical stripper is going to make it worse, right?" I know zero things about chemical stripping. Or wood.

Well. Most wood.

"Yeah." Jess wipes some sweat off her face. "I'm going to have to repaint."

"I'll help." Since I have absolutely nothing else to do with my life. "Do you have paint left over or do we need to get some?"

"You're going to think I'm crazy." She leans her elbow on the ladder and sizes up the whole storefront. "I actually wasn't super thrilled with the blue. I just thought it was really dumb to spend more money on paint after I'd just painted everything."

"Well, now's the time to change it. What color were you thinking?"

"Like a yellowy-orange."

I look at her. "So gold?"

"Yes! Goldish. But like goldenrod goldish. I don't know, something really vibrant and inspiring. Something that catches the eye when you look at Man Street."

That isn't a bad idea. I mean, fitting in with the businesses on Man Street isn't exactly a good thing. And goldenrod goldish will definitely pop next to Gino's brown barbershop.

"It would work with your sign." I nod toward the door. "And not to be that sort of Western Pennsylvanian, but black-and-gold has almost a spiritual draw around here." Probably because it's linked to generations of professional athletic despair.

Hm. Maybe that isn't great for a fitness studio.

"I mean, I don't want to make it *too* black-and-gold," Jess says. "But my instinct is that gold might resonate better with folks looking to get into shape. I think." She sighs. "I don't know, maybe not. What do you think?"

Yeah. What do I think? "Babe, I think you have instincts about your business. If gold feels better than blue, paint the damn place gold."

She smiles. "You think?"

"It's only paint, Jess. You can always redo it." Not that changing her storefront again and again is a good practice from a marketing standpoint. But Foundations is her business. If she wants to change the paint, it's her God-given right to do it. Right, God?

"So we get to go paint shopping?" Not that I'm geeking out over paint or anything. Just seems like a great reason to not focus on my own life.

"Yes."

I look up at her. "Which just means another trip to the

hardware store, right?"

She doesn't look at me. "I figured we can definitely start there."

"Uh-huh."

"But probably there will be better options at Sherman-Willaims over in Lower Burrell."

Yeah. Probably. "Sounds like a road trip to me." Which is good. I need to get out of Pitchette for a while.

Or, you know. EVER.

"Is that Tanner and Liam coming out of Sal's?"

I drop my scraper. "What? No. What?"

"Hey guys!" Jess waves from the top of the ladder.

Oh crap, it is them. And they're coming this way. And I'm STILL HERE!

I stand up so fast, my knee joint cracks. "I just gotta—that thing, you know?"

I duck into Foundations and hide behind the screened windows. I can see Liam. Liam can't see me. Thank You, God, for privacy screens.

Jess' laugh filters through the front door of the studio. She shakes her head and leans her forearms on the ladder to say something to the guys as they approach. Probably making excuses for my wacky departure. I think I left skid marks behind on the sidewalk.

Liam nods at something Jess says.

Then turns and LOOKS RIGHT AT ME.

I mean. Not *right* at me. Obviously. That's crazy, right? He can't see me. You know, because of the whole adhesive privacy screen thing on the window.

He just happens to look at the exact spot on the window I happen to be standing behind.

Liam raises an eyebrow under the bill of his ballcap.

Oh crap.

He smiles lazily.

Oh *crap!*

I'm not stupid. I'm going to have to face him sometime. Because, hello! Welcome to Pitchette, population twelve hundred.

But come *on!* The day after he hauled me out of a creek? And subsequently brushed me off in Mom's kitchen? Can't I have a little more time to partially recover my dignity? I mean, Liam practically bolted out of the house after he shut me down. Just balled up his soaked clothes, stuck his feet in his boots, and tromped through the rain in my shorts and sweatshirt to his truck. Because *that* strategic exit was obviously preferable to spending one more second around Nutty Mollie Maris. I mean, he didn't even knock on the door to tell me when he and Tanner brought my Honda back this morning. He just parked it in the driveway, got out, and left in Tanner's truck.

And here he is. Less than four hours later. Smirking at me through the window of a fitness studio.

GAH!

That's it. I don't have to put up with this. I'm a former marketing associate. I'm perfectly capable of doing damage control.

I pull my phone out of my pocket and hit 'call' on the last number I dialed.

Jess feels around in her shorts, pulls out her phone, and frowns at the screen. She says something to Liam and Tanner before she answers.

"Don't talk, just listen!" I whisper fiercely when she opens her mouth. "Get rid of them and get your butt in here *now!*"

I hang up before she responds. She rolls her eyes and says something that makes Liam duck his head.

I want to believe it's in embarrassment.

But his shoulders are definitely shaking from laughter.

Okay, God. If I stand really still, think You can zap me with a lightning bolt from a million yards away? Stupid question. You can do anything. Count of three, right? One. Two—

Oh great! Now *both* Liam and Tanner are laughing at whatever Jess said.

So much for FRIENDSHIP.

The laughing will obviously be going on for a while, so I roll out Jess' dumb yoga ball. Might as well get some stretching in. Between yesterday's 'rescue' and today's renovations, I'm sore in places I definitely can't reach without medical assistance.

The tea party outside finally breaks up. Tanner socks Liam's shoulder before crossing the street. Jess climbs down from the stepladder. About freaking time.

Although, she's standing there quite a while, just bullshitting with Liam. What the heck do they even have to talk about? I mean, they live like eight miles apart. They probably run into each other all the time. And it isn't like there's a lot of breaking news happening around here. Nothing ever changes in Pitchette.

Except for yours truly.

But they wouldn't be talking about me. Right? Jess doesn't know about the socks or the creek or Liam freaking *kissing me* last night. And Liam isn't the kind of guy who shares his private life with people. It's not that he's standoffish. It's that he's standbackish. He's a lot more likely to watch and listen than show and tell.

So, yeah. They probably aren't talking about me.

They're probably talking about Ida Boyko and her addiction to rodenticide. Maybe they're coming up with a plan to make her surrender her driver's license and Colt .45. I mean, *someone* has to come up with a plan. Before Ida kills somebody.

Yeah. That's probably what they're doing.

Liam turns, catches me arching over the yoga ball, and bites his freaking lip.

Okay, he's probably trying not to laugh at me. But Liam biting his lip is sexy as hell.

DAMN IT!

He says something to Jess, then crosses the street as she pulls open the studio door.

"About freaking time!" I grumble upside down, trying to work at the knots in my back.

Jess looks down at me. "Babe, what the heck is going on with you and Liam?"

"What? Nothing. What do you mean?" I roll the ball until I'm sitting up.

"I mean why did Liam ask me how your leg is? What's wrong with your leg? And why does Liam know about it?"

"My leg's fine." Mostly. I mean, icing it seems to help. Really it's just bruised.

Jess waves her hand expectantly. "And?"

"What?"

"What happened and why does Liam know about it?"

Geez. I do *not* want to answer that.

But I also know Jess. If I don't answer, she'll find out anyway. Somehow. In this case, probably through Ida Boyko.

Good grief. Who knows what sort of rumors that crackpot will spread.

I clear my throat. "Ida Boyko was ditched on Little Drop Hill yesterday during the storm, so I stopped to help her."

Jess raises her eyebrows. "And?"

"Well, when I stopped to help her, I sort of...hurt my leg." TRUE! "Liam happened to be passing and saw it." Also SEMI-TRUE! "And that's everything that happened." FALSE!

She crosses her arms. "That's not what Liam said."

Oh good lord. Surely he didn't. "He told you?"

"Hell yes, he told me!"

That sonovabitch! "I can't believe that jagoff blabbed to you about kissing me after—"

"You kissed Liam Taggert?" Jess gasps.

"I—what?" Oh crap. No! "You said he told you!"

"I was *bluffing!*" Jess cries. "This is *Liam* we're talking about! That man doesn't spill the beans about anything! Omigod, you *kissed Liam Taggert?*"

"*He* kissed *me.*" Mostly. "And he basically ran away after, so he clearly regrets it." Great. Saying that out loud is definitely the booster shot my ego needs.

"Where did he kiss you?"

"In Mom's kitchen."

"I don't mean geographically, you idiot, I mean anatomically!"

"Ew! For Pete's sake, on my *mouth!*" Geez!

To be clear, the 'ew' is directed at Jess. Not at the thought of Liam kissing me *not* on the mouth. I'd use a different sound for that.

"Was Ida there?"

"No!" Thank God.

"Did you leave her in the ditch?"

"Of course not!"

"Okay, so I'm missing a big part of this timeline."

"There's no timeline!" Holy crap, she's worse than Mom. "I got Ida out of the ditch and I was taking her home and got stuck in the creek—"

"You were in the creek?"

"Yeah, she threw my Stanley into Little Drop Run. But I got stuck trying to get it and Liam happened to be driving by and helped me out and he sent Ida home with Jack Walters and then he took me home and it was raining so hard that he stayed for a few minutes to dry off and the power went out and that's when he kissed me."

Jess blinks. "Whoa."

"Yeah."

"No wonder he ran away."

"*Excuse* me?"

"Babe, that one-paragraph synopsis gave *me* emotional whiplash. Poor Liam's head was probably spinning."

'Poor Liam?' He isn't 'Poor Liam.' He's Liam Freaking Taggert. And he left *my* head spinning.

Gah!

"You need to get a refund on these dumb window clings." I scowl at the screens. "Because they definitely *do not* work."

"What?" Jess frowns at the windows. "How can you tell?"

"Because Liam was looking right at me." And based on that dumb smile on his face, he could see everything.

Jess smiles.

"What?"

"You kissed Liam Taggert," she sings.

"Shut up." I did. I did kiss Liam Taggert.

GAH!

NINETEEN

I want a shower. Actually, I want ice cream. But I figure the shower is healthier. And cheaper. Not that I need to be too concerned with money. The first thing I did when my power flicked back on after the storm yesterday was wait for Mom's router to come back online so I could check my bank account.

A nice, fat paycheck from Schwartz Marketing and Media. As promised. Enough to cover my whipped cream expenses. *Not* enough to sue Shack Wheeler.

For the record, I could definitely get used to the whole earning-money-while-not-working thing. I totally get gold diggers now. Too bad I'm not cuter.

What *is* cute is Handy Dandy Andy blushing as Jess leans over the hardware store counter to adjust his glasses. To be fair, they *are* crooked. Mostly because Jess took them off his face to polish them on her shirt.

"Thanks." Andy flashes a one-dimple smile and readjusts Jess' adjustments.

Jess is right about him being sweet. But the poor guy is totally out of his element with her.

Of course, most guys are out of their element with Jess. Hell, I can barely keep up with her a lot of the time.

"So, paint!" I have to say *something,* because the goofy look on Jess' face means she's about ten seconds away from climbing over Andy's counter and tearing off his glasses again. "What have you got for us, Andy?"

Jess blinks a few times as Andy snaps to attention. He moves around the counter toward a paint chip display in the corner of the store. Jess trails him like a puppy.

"Hey!" I snag her arm to hold her back. "What the heck is wrong with you?"

She looks at me with wide eyes. "I don't know! It's like I take one look at him and my brain turns to mush!"

What? That's not Jess. Jess is smart and bubbly and one hundred percent immune to pheromones.

"Well, pull it together!" My whispers can probably be heard across the store. "You're a badass entrepreneur and you're here to buy freaking paint! So snap out of it!"

"Right. Yes." She bites her lip, eyes straying in the direction Andy disappeared. "Um, you may have to help me."

Oh, come on, God! I don't have enough of my own issues in the romance department? I have to be responsible for Jess, too?

"Alright, fine." I look her up and down. "You're covered in flecks of rotten pizza sauce, you hair needs to be washed, and you have a hole in the seam of your yoga pants right over your ass crack. Nice purple undies, by the way."

"Geez! I asked for help, not incentive to hang myself!"

"So don't tell you about the pit stains?"

"Omg, you are *such* a pain in the ass!"

"I bet you can really feel stuff like that with that hole in your pants." Okay. That's funny. "Feel focused now?"

"More like totally humiliated," she grumbles.

"Whatever it takes." I push her toward the paint corner. "Let's go."

"Hey," Andy says when we approach. He holds up a paint chip book. "Unfortunately, we don't have a lot of options in the store. But I can make a special order under Uncle Hank's account if you find something you like."

"I didn't know Hank Tucker was your uncle!" Jess declares.

I elbow her.

Andy ducks his head, looking embarrassed. "Uh. Yeah. Hank's paying me to cover the store while he and Aunt Tammy are on their cruise."

"Aw!" Jess coos. "I heard they were taking one. The Caribbean, right?"

Hank and Tammy Tucker are on a Caribbean cruise? Geez. Maybe I should get into the hardware business instead of going back to Schwartz.

Although, that would definitely give Jess a lot more incentive to hang around the hardware store. And she does not need any more incentives.

I take the paint chip book and flip through colors. "You were thinking something gold. Right, Jess?"

"Uh, yep." She clears her throat. "Yes! A bright yellowy-orange color."

"Marigold," Andy says.

"Omg, *yes!* Marigold. That's it. That's what I want." Jess gazes at him. "You get me, Andy."

Oh boy. "Okay, Jess, let's take a look. Andy, we'll see you later."

He smiles and goes back to the counter.

Jess closes her eyes. "That was humiliating."

Yes. Yes, it was. "Try being the person watching it." Because THAT was way worse.

"Do you think he noticed the hole in my pants?"

"Oh yeah." The problem is, I don't think the hole bothers him. I don't think *Jess* bothers him. I think Andy blushes so hard around her because he actually likes her, too.

Which isn't great. For either of them. I mean, the kid still has a year of college! And Jess is just getting her business up and running. The last thing they need is a summer fling to distract them. What is this, high school?

And how exactly did this end up in my lap again? Because last I checked, I was pretty focused on the whole Liam-Taggert-kissed-me-and-ran-away situation. Now all I can think about is trying to make sure Jess and Andy don't end up alone in a storage closet somewhere.

Or is this God distracting *me?* Trying to keep me from going nuts, wondering what exactly happened last night? Well, TOO LATE, GOD! TOO LATE! I'm back to having the self-confidence and emotionally confused best friend of a teenager.

Freaking Pitchette.

Gah!

Okay. I'm not regressing. I'm helping Jess find her perfect paint chip.

"How about this?" I flip the book around.

"Burning Dawn?" She tilts her head. "Too orange."

"Okay. What about Warm Butter?"

"Too yellow."

For Pete's sake! "Summer Finch? Harvest Grain? Real Gold?"

Jess shakes her head. "No. I'm not feeling these."

I'd leave her here with the dumb book, except I don't trust her with Andy. "Fine. Let's go."

"Where?"

"To the studio. Andy!"

He looks up from the counter.

"We're going to borrow this for a few minutes. We'll bring it back."

He nods. I push through the door of the hardware store.

"Mollz!" Jess darts after me. "What was that about?"

Hormones, hopefully. "Handy Dandy Andy had you totally distracted. Besides, you really need to be looking at your studio front when you're comparing colors."

She doesn't say anything on the walk to Foundations. Weird, right? Maybe she's just worried about the hole in her pants.

"You're right," she tells me twenty minutes later, when we're holding up the chip book in front of the studio. "I did need to look at these colors in natural light. They're all like three shades too bright. I want folks to be drawn in, not overpowered."

I close the book. "So what are you thinking?"

"I'm thinking maybe I don't want Marigold after all."

Aha! So Handy Dandy Andy *doesn't* get her. "Okay. Are we back to blue?"

"No. The blue wasn't right, either."

I know what she's doing. I know, because I've been doing the same thing. Except with my life, not my business. "You need to commit to something, Jess."

"I know." She doesn't look like she knows. She looks like she wants to walk into Foundations and lock the door behind her.

"Babe, what's going on?" Because something is really bothering her. And it isn't just Handy Dandy Andy.

Her shoulders slump as she sighs. Which just seems extra sad, because Jess has great arm tone and amazing posture. Anything that changes that has to be super bad.

"There's this community Facebook group Tara Basher and her friends run," she says. "It's all about Pitchette and events and stuff like that. It's the same group that posted stuff about the overdose article."

"Okay." Not okay. I don't like where this is heading.

"We went to school with a lot of them. Now most of them have kids and—actually, a lot of them are the moms I was telling you about." She gestures toward the studio. "You know, with the family fitness room."

"Oh yeah. The people who want to start working out here, but don't have anyone to watch their kids."

"Right. Well, remember how I talked to Nikki Marchand the other night? At Jerry's?"

"Yeah. About personal training, right?"

"Yeah. Well, she also asked about the family fitness stuff. I told her I hadn't forgotten about our conversation and after I got all of this marketing business stuff off the ground with you, that was the next big thing I'd be focusing on. Just that it wasn't a priority right now for me." Her forehead creases.

"So what happened?"

Jess sighs. "Well, she must've talked to Tara or one of her friends. Because one of them has been posting in the community Facebook group that Foundations isn't kid-friendly."

"*What?*"

"And that families shouldn't support the studio."

"No!"

"And listing alternative fitness locations in Allegheny and Westmoreland counties."

"That's insane! For Pete's sake, what's *wrong* with people?"

"I don't know." Jess doesn't look at me.

Oh crap. "This is really about me, isn't it? About us being friends?"

"Mollz, I don't give two fucks what they say!" Jess bursts out. "Even if it costs me Foundations, I—"

"For Pete's sake, Jess, don't even say that!"

"I mean it, though! Let them drive people away! I'll make it work! *We'll* make it work!"

"Babe, this sucks! Geez, Tara Basher is such a bitch."

"To be fair, I don't know if it's her or one of her Gym Girlies."

"No! Don't cut her slack! You *know* what women like that are like. If it's one of them, it's all of them!" Okay, maybe I'm being unfair. But come on! What is this, high school? Stepford? "You need to show me the comments."

"Mollz, I don't want you to get dragged into it."

"Babe, I'm already in it!" But I'm *not* engaging with them on social media. That's just a lose-lose situation. "I want to see exactly what's being said." So I can figure out how many body bags to buy.

"I want to respond, but I don't know how. I feel like anything I do now with family fitness programming is just going to look like I'm doing it in response to what's being said online."

So what? Who *cares* how people perceive the conception of her fitness programming, as long as they're participating in it?

But Foundations isn't my business. The studio isn't my baby. And Jess the woman might be immune to gossip, but Jess the entrepreneur isn't. It sucks to admit, but what people are saying about her has a major impact on her business.

Even if it isn't true.

"We need something that's going to spin the story," I tell her. "Something that's going to share your side of the situation without directly referencing what folks in the community group are saying."

Public relations isn't the same as marketing, but I know a

few things about framing the narrative. Minimizing fallout. We need to send a clear message here. The problem is Jess is right. Anything she does now to establish and promote her family fitness programing is going to look like a response to the online call-out. Even though she was working on things before Tara Basher's dumb group starting posting. Facts are irrelevant. Perception is everything. You can't negotiate with terrorists.

"Mollz, *please* tell me you have something in mind. I could use a win."

"Not yet. But I will." God, back me up here. "We'll take the paint chip book back to Handy Dandy Andy and then we'll figure this out. Okay?"

"Okay." Jess bites her lip. "Um. Maybe *you* should bring the book back, Mollz. I think I might get a little…distracted."

For Pete's sake. "Babe, you need to figure this out. Because you don't have time for a crush on the college kid who's here for the summer. You have some grown-ass adult problems that need your attention."

"Ugh, I *know!*" She shoves me toward the hardware store. "Just get that back to Andy already."

Geez. Touchy.

Andy looks up when I walk through the door. He doesn't say anything, but his smile droops a little when he realizes it's just me. I'd be offended, except he's like half my age. Okay, two-thirds my age. Ish.

"Did she find something?" He takes the book from me and adjusts his glasses.

"No. I don't think she's in the right mindset to be thinking about paint colors."

A look crosses his face.

Uh-oh. "You know about the Facebook thing, don't you?"

"I saw it. Those people are just stupid. The whole group is more toxic than helpful."

Mm. Interesting perspective for a young person to have.

He takes the book back to the paint corner and I follow.

"I haven't seen the posts yet. Do you think Jess should be worried? I mean, about the impact they may have on the studio?"

He slides the book back into place on the display. "Honestly, I don't think she should listen to them. She's smart and personable. Anyone who really knows her loves her. She shouldn't doubt herself just because a group of women have nothing better to do than go after her for trying to build her business." He looks at me. "Same goes for you. They're all idiots."

Whoa. Handy Dandy Andy has some big feelings about all of this. "You're not at all what you seem. Are you?"

He smiles.

Okay. I can see why Jess thinks he's cute. In a nerdy sort of way.

"If she does decide on a paint, let me know." He heads back toward the counter. "Even if it's something niche. Like textured or reflective or chalkboard or something weird. I can probably order it."

"Did you say 'chalkboard?'"

"Oh yeah. Super popular around here. As you can tell." His hazel eyes are the only thing that gives away his sense of humor.

"You're an interesting guy, Andy."

He almost laughs. Almost.

Jess is working on her computer when I pull open the door to Foundations.

Oh crap! "Jessica Johnson, get off that community group page right now!"

She groans. "What's wrong with me? It's like I'm picking at a scab and I can't stop!"

"Yes! That's exactly what you're doing. So get off."

"There are more comments." She looks at me over her computer. "Some of these folks are people I'm close with, Mollz! People I've known for years! I would've said we're friends. Why are they doing this?"

"We know why. It's because of me."

"That's ridiculous, Mollz! It's Shack's damn story that caused all this, not you!"

"Jess, we both know there's no logic to mob mentality. And social media is mob mentality. It's a coward's crusade."

She looks miserable. Not at all like the Jess I love and admire.

"Handy Dandy Andy says those folks are stupid." Probably shouldn't have told her that.

"Really? He's a sweet guy." Her mouth curves into a small smile. "Which is why I like him so much, of course. That and the fact he doesn't make me feel like a thirty-something going on forty-something."

"Babe, that's so sad." Holy crap, is that what's happening to me?

No, that doesn't make sense. Liam is older, not younger. Phew.

"Yeah. It's pretty sad." She sighs and pulls out a container of sanitizing wipes. "Clearly, I have some stuff I need to work out. I cannot wait for my martial arts class this week."

I snort. "Since when have *you* been into martial arts? I thought you were a yoga girlie?"

"I was up until recently," Jess says, wiping down her counter. "Then I went to a cage fight and sort of got converted."

"Seriously?"

"It's sick, right? All the blood and the violence?" She shakes her head. "It must've flipped a switch in my caveman brain or something. My mom says it runs in the family. I guess my cousin Nico is some sort of master martial artist or combatant or whatever."

"You have a cousin Nico?" How do I not know this?

"Yeah. He's about ten years older than us. I'm not surprised you don't remember him."

"Wait, are you saying he's from Pitchette?" There's someone from Pitchette in our generation and I don't know him? What? What's happening right now?

"He's from here, but he hasn't been home since he joined the military."

Whoa. Someone who got out of Pitchette and stayed out. There aren't many.

Jess finishes cleaning the counter and puts away the wipes. "My dad thinks he's involved in some high-level government stuff, but he won't say what. Or *can't* say what. You know my dad."

Yeah. Some guys golf in their free time. Some guys pilot drones. Tim Johnson listens to podcasts about how Big Ag secretly infuses contrails with chemical compounds that control things like crop yields and water sources.

I mean. It doesn't sound *altogether* impossible when it's put like that. I've seen *Food, Inc.* and *Soylent Green.* Hard to tell which is a documentary and which is scifi.

"You should try a class sometime. It's amazing how much stress relief comes with punching something."

I sigh. "I don't know, Jess. I have a feeling martial arts isn't for me." And also, that I'll end up maiming someone accidentally. Probably myself.

"At least give it a try. I have an all-female beginners class tomorrow night." She glances at the computer. "If anyone shows up, anyway. Everyone is still new at it, so you'll fit in. And it's MMA, so you'll get a little taste of everything."

"Define 'everything.'"

"Kickboxing, jiu jitsu, judo."

Geez. "Any emphasis on the 'arts' part?"

She laughs. "Wow, you really are an old lady."

Yeah. That's what I'm afraid of. I sigh. "How much is the class?"

"Babe, I am not going to make you pay for one of my classes! You're helping me with my marketing, remember?"

"Come on, Jess. How are you going to keep the lights on?"

"By over-charging Tara Basher and her Gym Girlies, of course."

I laugh. "That's evil and genius."

"Yeah." She winks at me. "It's the Jess Johnson Business Model. Tiered service charges based on how much a pain in the ass you are."

"I think that's illegal, but I wish it wasn't." I tilt my head. "So does this mean I'm not actually a pain in your ass?"

"Yeah." She grins. "Usually."

TWENTY

I've officially been back in Pitchette a week.

Well, a week and two days.

It feels like longer. *Years* longer.

If the opioid story and the creek rescue and the kissing Liam and the Pitchette community group disasters weren't enough, I identified three new wiry white hairs on the crown of my head in the mirror this morning. So that's just great. I didn't have a lot of looks to begin with and Pitchette is clearly ravishing what's left.

This is it. Thirty-three is as good as it gets for me, isn't it?

GAH.

I really want to lock myself in Mom's house, hoard my paychecks from Schwartz, and wallow in self-pity. But Jess is taking the brunt of the hate on my behalf, and that is *not* okay. It's one thing for folks to gossip and malign me online. Despite growing up here and calling Pitchette home for the majority my life, I'm still an outsider. Liam said it himself. I don't *look* like Pitchette. I don't *act* like Pitchette. So even though I definitely don't like being publicly accused of erroneous behavior, I understand why it's happening to me.

I *don't* understand why it's happening to Jess. Her family has lived here for generations. She volunteers and serves and loves the community. She has family members in important positions and friends across the county.

Or at least, she did. Until I showed up.

I don't know what I want out of life, but I know I want to help Jess make Foundations work. Any way I can.

Which is why I can't ignore Shack Wheeler's lack of action anymore. The sonovabitch is going to retract that damn story. Because I'm going to give him a better one.

In exchange for something, of course.

"Mollie Maris," he declares when I walk into his office.

No war paint today. No city outfits. Because let's be honest, I'm *way* scarier with a plain face and ratty clothes. A real bruiser.

"Slow news day?" I only ask because again, it's just the two of us. Other people do work here, right? I mean, it isn't just Shack taking up all three desks?

Although it's kind of funny to think of him scurrying around, sitting at each one to fill a role. Like a slapstick cartoon character.

"Comes and goes." Shack hauls himself up from his chair, shuffling around the desk with a notepad, a pen, and a—

Oh geez. A box of donuts.

"Want one?" Shack holds the box out.

Yes. *Obviously*. Of course I want a freaking donut.

Except every time I look at a donut these days, I see Liam Freaking Taggert and his stupid freaking smirk.

"No, thanks." DAMN IT.

Shack tosses the box back onto a table cluttered with used newspapers and media paraphernalia.

"So." Alright. Might as well get into it. "Thank you for meeting w—"

"Hang on a second," he orders when his cellphone rings.

"Mind standing in the hallway while I get this?"

"Um. Okay." Geez, who does he think he is? Bob Woodward?

I walk out and he closes the door behind me.

Not that it does much good. I mean, the door is practically plywood. I can definitely hear what he's saying without even standing that close. The question is why doesn't he want me to hear him talking cutesy talk to someone who's obviously his wife?

Unless it *isn't* his wife.

Hm.

The door whisks open. "Thanks for waiting!"

Is it just me or does he look a little flushed?

Yuck. I do *not* want to know why he looks flushed after his phone call.

"So." He slides back into his desk chair instead of offering me a seat. "I'm guessing you've come back about Monday's lead story."

Geez. 'Lead story.' Like it's even a freaking *story*. "I have."

"I have no intention of changing my terms," Shack says. "I'll print adjustments if you have something else to give me."

Deep breath. Okay. This is just a hostage negotiation. They do it all the time in the movies.

"My friend Jess Johnson is the owner of Foundations Fit—"

"Ah. Stop right there." Shack wags his finger. "Not going to do a story on a new business. That's not what I mean when I say I want you to give me something, Mollie."

EW! Does he know how that sounds? Or is he too dense to look at things through a post-#MeToo lens?

"I'm not suggesting the story be about Jess' business." The words barely get past my clenched teeth. "I'm suggesting it be about *why* she opened Foundations. She has some incredible thing—"

"No."

Okay, this guy is REALLY pissing me off. "Why not?"

"There's no drama there." He taps his nose. "I can smell drama, Mollie Maris, and there's none there."

"Is that why you made up the overdose story? For the damn drama?"

"Ivy League graduate leaves her job in Washington, D.C., returns to Pitchette, and ends up passed out on the grave of her deceased mother." He says it without any emotion whatsoever. Like he's just giving me cold, hard facts. "Drama."

My stomach twists. "That's despicable." And totally out of context! I mean, those things *happened,* but not the way *he says* they happened.

"Drama makes news, Mollie. Readers eat it up. It helps them swallow all the boring stuff. The veggies. Audits and meeting minutes and fluff pieces about summer lemonade stands. Too many veggies and they stop buying the paper." He taps the newspapers stacked on his desk. "My readers need a mixed diet. They need some real meat, something to sink their teeth into before they flip to the obituaries."

He's milking that dumb analogy for all it's worth

But I understand his point. "You want me to feed you something juicy." GAH! Now *I'm* milking the damn analogy!

Shack has the oily smile of a salesman, not a journalist. "I want you to give me a *real* story."

"And if I do, you'll give Jess a story? About Foundations, I mean? About what she's trying to do?" I *hate* that I'm asking. I shouldn't have to *ask* for something like this. I mean, Jess' story *is* flipping news.

And also, I shouldn't have to freaking ask him to TAKE BACK A FAKE STORY!

But that's the problem, isn't it? I *would* ask. I would *plead.*

For Jess' sake.

Shack plants his elbows on his desk. "What do you have, Mollie?"

I bite my lip.

Am I really going to do this? Am I really going to play into Shack Wheeler's dirty hands? Give him what he asks for? Even if it isn't the truth?

Yes. Yes to all of that. I mean, this is *Jess* we're talking about.

I exhale slowly. "I'll tell you what *really* happened at the cemetery. *If* you do a formal, sit-down interview with Jess about the fitness studio."

His beady little eyes crackle with excitement. "What happened at the cemetery?"

What, does he think I'm stupid? "Do the story with Jess. Then I'll give you the scoop."

He cracks a smile. "I don't think so. I know that game. I do the story for your friend and then *you* refuse to talk to me."

Crap. He got me. "What do you suggest, then?"

"First, you need to tell me something about the cemetery incident. So I know there's *actually* a story there."

Great. Just great. "Then?"

"Then, I'll sit down and do the interview with your friend. But I won't run it until *you* sit down with me and give me *your* full story. After I have your story, I'll put in the piece about the studio." He tilts his head. "Veggies after meat."

For Pete's sake. Doesn't he know that's *not* how you're supposed to consume a balanced meal?

I'm not going to get a better deal, though. He holds the whole deck of cards.

"Fine." I'll lie. I'll lie if it stops Tara Basher and her damn Gym Girlies from tanking Jess' chances of making

Foundations the place Pitchette needs it to be. "I *was* doing something illegal in the cemetery. But it wasn't opioids."

Sorry, God. I have to do it. I have to do it for Jess.

Shack narrows his eyes and doesn't say anything for about thirty seconds.

"Okay." He nods, once. "I believe it. Tell your friend to give me a call and we'll talk."

I want to tell Jess right away about my deal with Shack, but I'm honestly not sure she'll be happy about it. I mean, she'll appreciate that I'm trying to help her. But she won't like that my help is coming at the expense of my reputation.

I don't mind. My reputation is shot to hell anyway. Might as well put it to good use.

So until I figure out how to frame the situation so Jess will go through with the interview, I'm keeping my mouth shut.

And letting her throw me around the studio mat, MMA-style. Which wouldn't be so bad, if any one of the other women Jess said would be here had shown up tonight. But since the Gym Girlies are actively discouraging people from coming to Foundations, I'm the proud recipient of Jess' undivided attention.

I *love* Jess' undivided attention. In a bar or a mall or a coffee shop.

In a martial arts class, it's freaking terrifying. Judoka Jess is a beast I've never met before.

Which is good, because Judoka Jess scares the living shit out of me.

"This is the *beginner's* class?" Because that last flip over her shoulder did *not* feel like a 'beginner' flip.

And the bruise developing on my ass is *not* a 'beginner' bruise.

"Yes. I'm still working through my own belts, so

everything I'm learning, I'm passing on to the women taking this class."

Really? "You don't need to be specially certified or something to do that?"

"Martial arts is a strange beast." She helps me up from the mat. "You don't need to have a special certificate or degree or anything to be an instructor. Of course, having official qualifications is preferable. Which is why I'm working on mine."

Geez. If this is uncertified Jess, I am *not* going to survive certified Jess.

Which she must realize, based on the look she gives me.

"You know what?" She points at me. "Let's do some floor work."

Is it just me, or does that sound sort of violent? "What's floor work?"

"Omg, it's *not* something that should put you on the brink of tears."

"I am not on the brink of tears!" I am. I am on the brink of tears. Because for Pete's sake, my ass *really hurts* from getting tossed over her shoulder! And also, I *still* want one of Shack's freaking donuts. Gah! "What's floor work?"

She drops to her knees and motions me onto the mat. "In this case, it's me showing you what to do if you get pinned on your back."

"Ooh. Kinky."

"Yeah, kinky. Except if you're being pinned by a giant dude who trapped you in a shed somewhere in the woods so he can molest you."

"GEEZ, Jessica! What the heck is *wrong* with you? That scenario combines like three of my worst fears!"

"Three?"

"Abduction, rape, and the middle of nowhere!"

"Well, then you better pay attention." She turns onto her back. "Because this is an escape method. Now mount me."

"What?"

"Mount me. Get on top."

Okay, how is she not hearing this? "And you just do this class with women?" I straddle her hips, my butt resting against her drawn-up thighs.

"Yep. I want to bring in a male instructor before I open it up to men." She shifts under me, adjusting her hips. "Grappling does a lot to even the playing field when it comes to opponent size, because it's based more on technique than brute strength. But my gut tells me guys would be more likely to listen to a man than a woman for something like this."

That's probably true. And also sort of sad. "Okay. What now?"

"Now I'm going to roll you. Ready?"

Um. "Yeah?"

Abracadabra and I'm on the bottom and Jess is on the top.

"What? Holy crap!"

She grins down at me. "Go again?"

"How did you do that?"

"Bridge and roll." It's SO UNFAIR how gracefully she goes from straddling me to standing. No one should be able to move like that. "We'll go again and I'll break it down for you."

"Can I take notes?" Because athletic instructions only go in one ear and out the other for me.

Okay, fine. *All* instructions.

"It's simple, Mollz. I'm going to talk us through it. You just pay attention."

I knew there was a catch.

Jess gets down onto her back and I straddle her hips. She draws her knees up behind me.

"Okay. The first step is trapping your arm and leg on the side I'm planning to roll you to."

"Why?"

"Because if I don't trap them, you can just stop the roll by kicking your arm or leg out."

Okay. I guess that makes sense.

"Okay, so I'm going to grab near your elbow and pull your arm in between our chests." She demonstrates. "See? Now your arm is caught because it's tucked under mine. I'm hugging you in so you can't get out."

"Okay."

"Next step is I'm going to trap your leg by walking my foot around yours and hooking it. So I have you boxed in." She shows me. "See?"

"Yeah."

"Now I bridge. Like in yoga."

She lifts her hips and abracadabra, I'm on the bottom and she's on the top

"What? How did you *do* that?" Because I *swear*, I was watching the whole time and NEVER SAW IT HAPPEN!

"Your turn."

We switch start positions and I blank.

"Um. I kind of don't remember what comes first."

"Mollz, I just showed you!"

"Something about hugging?"

She sighs and slides off, collapsing on her back next to me on the mat. Totally defeated.

Oops. Forgot I'm supposed to be distracting her. "Babe, I'm sorry. My retention with this stuff isn't great. Want to show me again?"

"No. It's okay. I know this isn't really your thing."

I could *pretend* to be into it, but she'd see right through me.

It's time. "I setup an interview with Shack Wheeler for you."

"What?" She turns her head to look at me. "When?"

"This morning."

"Omg, you *talked* to that creep? Babe, he still hasn't retracted that story!"

"I know." I can't tell her that's exactly the leverage I needed to get her the interview. "He said he'll talk to you. A formal, sit-down interview. You just need to call him." I sit up and cross my legs. "You should do the interview here, so he can get photos of Foundations. Maybe before or after a class, so you can show folks who are doing your programs."

"If there *are* any folks still doing my programs."

"There are, Jess. Tonight's just weird." Please, God, let that be true. "Just call Shack tomorrow morning and get something scheduled. We'll figure everything else out after that."

"He isn't doing a story about the online posts, is he?"

Yeah. About that. "I don't know what he's planning to ask you. But if he does ask about the community group, just tell him the truth."

"You mean that I've been planning the family programming for a while?"

"Yes. And even though you're focusing on other parts of your business right now, it's still something you're working on."

"Address the community group without addressing the community group."

"Yep." And also. "You should, um, try to distance yourself from me during the interview."

"What?"

"I think that might help to clear up some of the—"

"Absolutely not!" Jess cries. "Mollz, do you understand how much you've helped me since you've been back?"

Ha. "Jess, I can confidently say I'm pretty sure that overdose story undid anything I've done to try to help."

"No! Not true." She moves onto her knees and grabs my shoulders. "What you're doing for this place *so* outweighs what all those jags out there are saying, Mollie. And I am *not* cutting you out of this picture. EVER. I'm not even going to ask if you understand what I'm saying, because it doesn't matter if you do or not. I'm going to tell fucking Shack Wheeler everything you've done for me and Foundations. And when folks find a way to dig their heads out of their asses, they'll see what you've done for them, too."

"I haven't done anything." For real. All I've done is open some social media accounts and upload content. That's it. "*Please* don't make this about me. This needs to be about the studio." The last thing I need is more column inches in the local rag.

Jess exhales and lets go of my shoulders. "Wow. I have an *interview* with Shack about Foundations."

"Yeah."

"I'm going to need to get all this aggression out *now*. Because if I see him and I have any energy whatsoever, I'm probably definitely going to clock him."

I grin. "Well, you can always say you're just demonstrating how fitness has improved *your* quality of life."

"Ooh," she says. "I'm using that."

TWENTY-ONE

"How did it go?"

Jess' excitement bubbles over the phone even before she opens her mouth. "Actually, babe? *So well*. He asked all these questions about Foundations and why I opened it. I started talking about some of the chronic health conditions I told you about, remember? And *he* actually shared some things he's learned over the years from reporting in this region! Honestly, it couldn't have gone better."

"Jess, I'm so glad." I am, really. People need to know about the studio. They need to know about Jess. "Did he say anything about when the story will run?"

"No. He mentioned something about waiting for another piece to go first. I don't know, he wasn't super clear."

Yes, he is. He's holding Jess' article hostage until I come in and talk to him.

Which means the sooner I do that, the sooner her story will print.

There's a special circle in Hell for Shack Wheeler. There has to be.

"Anyway!" Jess chirps. "Where are you?"

Sitting in my car outside the hardware store. The damn kitchen sink drip is driving me *nuts,* and I need it to stop. NOW.

"Just running errands." Okay, so I don't want to tell her I'm seeing Handy Dandy Andy. She's channeling her energy into Foundations, and we need her to stay focused. "I'll check in with you later, okay? Update you on the social media front."

"Okay. Love ya!"

I exhale and crawl out of my car. Next stop is the *Pitchette Press,* so might as well take my time browsing plumbing stuff I know exactly zero things about.

Andy glances up from the display he's installing and smiles when he sees me. "How's it going?"

"About as expected." I nod at the slate-gray board in his hands. "What's that?"

"A promotional display this company sent for that chalkboard paint I told you about." He knocks the board with his knuckle, then reaches for his water bottle and takes a sip. "Honestly, it works better than I expected. And it's weatherproof, so it can be used outdoors. Not that there's a big call for outdoor chalkboards."

Hm. "Really?" I join him at the counter, running my hand over the board. Smooth. And surprisingly realistic. "Don't happen to have any chalk, do you?"

He looks at me, eyebrows raised over the rim of his glasses. Then he crouches behind the counter and scuffles around. He pops back up with lump of white carpenter chalk.

I swirl the piece over the board, drawing a design.

"Do you think it will work?" Andy asks.

Seriously, the kid is way more perceptive than his appearance suggests. "How fast does it go on?"

"It's a fast-set formula. I haven't used it personally, but the display says each coat dries in under six hours."

"Damn. That is fast." I rub my design. "How well does the chalk come off?"

"Says it comes off with water." He grabs his water bottle and dribbles it over the design. The chalk rubs right off on his fingertips.

"So rainfall—"

"Would take it right off. A clean slate." He pushes his glasses back up his face and looks at me. "Do you think she'll go for it?"

"I don't know. But I think it's different. And I think 'different' is what she needs."

Andy nods. "If you're able to figure out how many cans you need by the end of the day, I can get the order in tonight. They'll probably ship tomorrow and get here Monday."

Really? "That fast?"

He blushes when he shrugs. "If I put a rush on it."

Okay. Maybe this weird crush going on between them isn't *all* bad.

My phone vibrates in my pocket. "I'll talk to her and let you know ASAP."

A text from Shack. Saying he's free to talk today. Anytime.

What a jag.

"I'll call you," I tell Andy over my shoulder as I head for the door. Guess I'll have to get my drip fixed another time.

I turn on my Bluetooth and pop in an earbud as I pull away from the hardware store and call Jess.

"Didn't we just talk?" she asks when she picks up.

"I have an idea and it's a little out there. But I think it might be fun."

"Okaaaay."

"What if we use chalkboard paint on the front of the

studio?"

"What?"

"Handy Dandy Andy has this paint at the hardware store that turns wood into chalkboard. Or you know, a chalkboard surface. So what if we redo the front of the studio with that? And then what if we invite families in the community to come hang out one day and decorate the studio?"

She doesn't answer.

"I mean, I know it's super different and maybe it's not the vibe you're going for," I say. "But it could be fun! And even better, we could tie it into your family fitness programming—"

"And make it sort of like a soft opening event!"

"That way if you don't have all the programming lined up yet, you can at least be getting the word out there about it. You know, drumming up anticipation."

"Do you think folks would do this?"

"Honestly? I don't know. But I think if we start putting it out there on social media and if we have something like complimentary Popsicles or snow cones or whatever, we can make into a sort of sidewalk event. That way, we're getting people into the studio who maybe haven't been in it yet."

"I might be able to get Sal to donate hot dogs!" Jess is *super* into the idea. "And my folks may know a couple business owners who might like to co-sponsor, which would help cut down on the expense on our end. But...crap. We may need a borough permit for a sidewalk event like this."

Damn. That's probably true, isn't it? "Can Val look into that? I mean, *I* would but I might not be the best face for the event right now."

"I'll ask her," Jess says. "She knows everyone in the borough office."

Good. Hopefully. "We'd have to get the studio front

painted ourselves. Andy said he thinks he can get the paint here Monday if we let him know how much we need today."

"I'll call him!"

Big surprise there. "Between the two of us, we should be able to get it painted Monday after your last class. And if we start promoting the event now, we can maybe pull it off like next Wednesday? Thursday?"

"Yes! Omg, I'm so in love with this idea right now!"

"Really?"

"*Yes,* babe! It's so different and just...fun!"

I smile. "Okay. Figure out what you need and tell Andy. I gotta go. Talk later."

One problem down.

One to go.

There isn't any real reason to be nervous, but I am. Pulling into the parking lot and walking back into the one-room *Pitchette Press* media center has my body buzzing with adrenaline and panic.

For Pete's sake! This is just a dumb interview fabricated on a *lie.* It's only going to be seen by a few hundred people. And it doesn't even matter who sees it, anyway, because I'm doing it for Jess.

This time, there's a woman at the first desk inside the door. She looks up and smiles. Hm. I should know her, right? She looks familiar. Super pretty. Like a fairy tale princess with long blonde waves and iridescent eyes and high cheekbones. Although the only mystical thing about her perfect complexion is probably that she achieved it with the help of e.l.f. Cosmetics.

"How you doing today?" she asks.

"Okay, thanks." So far. "I'm here to see Shack Wheeler. My name's Mollie—"

"Maris," she concludes. "Shack mentioned you'd be stopping in."

Of course he did.

"He just went on a coffee run, but he'll be back soon." She stretches her hand over the desk. "I'm Arla, by the way. I work the classifieds."

I shake her hand. "Nice to meet you. Is it just the two of you in here?"

She spins around in her chair to gesture toward the room. "The circulation director slash customer service guy Dean is usually here, but he's on vacation this week. And when we have an intern, they usually take that little desk in the back." She spins back to me. "And yes, it does get cramped."

I bet. Especially with Shack taking up space. "Probably nice to have some alone time."

She grins. "You have *no* idea."

Shack walks in. "Ah. Mollie Maris. The person I hoped to see."

Oh boy. "Are we talking here or—"

"Let's go to the conference room."

Um. Okay.

I follow him down the hall. Yeah, this isn't what I'd call a conference room. More like a break room with a folding table and two chairs.

We sit and I try not to throw up. Seriously, why am I nervous? I mean, the story I'm going to tell definitely isn't worse than the one he already printed.

Of course, *that* story isn't my fault. *This* story is.

He pulls out a notebook and pen. "Alright. What have you got for me?"

A strong desire to kick his ass, mostly.

But I don't kick his ass.

I lie through my teeth.

And I don't regret any of it.

When I get done lying, Shack sits back in his chair and

stares at me. "I'll be honest, Mollie. Your candor is commendable."

"Thanks." Jackass.

"Not many folks would be so open about their problems."

I shrug. "Well, maybe this will help them realize they're not alone." I'm sorry, God, *please* don't think I take addiction lightly. I don't! "So, how are you planning to run this?"

Shack bounces his pen off his notebook. "It's not an entirely different story from the original incident, so I don't want to take up extra column inches by running a whole new article. I think it makes the most sense to have this be a follow-up. Providing more details on the call—"

"Correcting the inaccuracies."

He smiles. "Making adjustments."

Whatever. I am *so* done with this. "When will it run?"

"Sometime next week."

Great. *Love* the vagueness.

"And Jess' story?"

"Next edition."

Monday, then. Well, that's good. "What's your drop deadline for that?"

He lifts his eyebrows. "Why?"

"Foundations is planning a community event. We'd love to be able to get the info out in that article, if possible."

"I finish layout Sunday evening." He gathers his shit and stands. "Can't take anything past ten o'clock Sunday morning."

"Alright." I stand, too. "Can I text you the details or do you prefer email?"

"Email." He reaches into his shirt pocket and pulls out a business card. "Thanks for the meat, Mollie."

Gross.

TWENTY-TWO

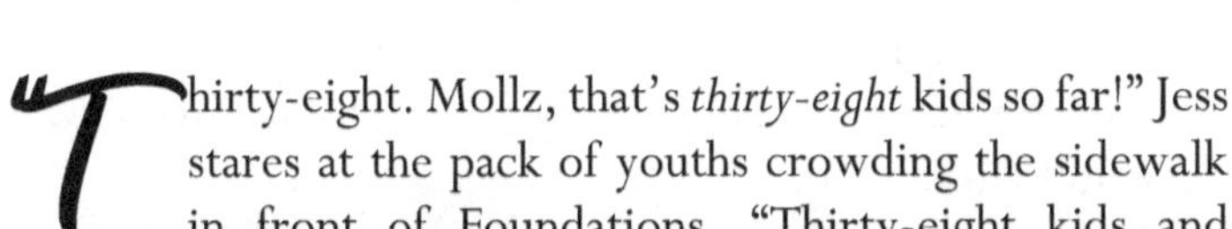

"Thirty-eight. Mollz, that's *thirty-eight* kids so far!" Jess stares at the pack of youths crowding the sidewalk in front of Foundations. "Thirty-eight kids and twenty-three parents. Babe, you're a freaking genius."

I wouldn't go that far. But Man Street is looking pretty crowded. Not bad for a Wednesday in June. After we pulled this together in less than a week. Thank God the borough permit process can be expedited if your event qualifies as a 'pop-up' event.

I look at Jess. "We have to keep the kids interested and occupied, okay? Because if they get bored, their parents will get bored. And then they'll leave."

"Well, I think the hotdogs and chips will help."

"Are you sure we're not sending the wrong message with those? I mean, as a fitness studio?" I'm all for meat byproducts slathered in ketchup and mustard, but there's such a thing as consistent branding.

"Probably. But hey!" She grins. Clearly, she doesn't mind a little brand inconsistency. "We've got to meet people where they're at, right? I mean, hot dogs are getting people *outside* the studio. Maybe working them off will get them *inside*."

Maybe. "Alright. So the kids are going to be chalking the studio front until about eleven-thirty. I talked to Sal this morning, and she said I can run over and grab the food around then. She's going to have everything boxed up, so it shouldn't be too hard to carry."

"Maybe Andy can help you."

Ah. Yes. Handy Dandy Andy. Who nonchalantly mentioned to Jess a couple days ago that he's free during the chalking event and could help out. If she needed.

Oh, she needed.

Problem for another day. Today is about correcting the Tara Basher-Gym Girlies hater vibes still out there.

None of the online community group admins have shown up with their kids. Funny.

I take out my phone and get some photos to get the buzz started on the Foundations' social media accounts. The plan is to post periodically throughout the event to hype things up and maybe attract folks who didn't hear about it beforehand.

"You got things under control out here?" I ask Jess when I circle back a few minutes later. "If so, I'm going to pop inside and get these posted." Because let's face it, I'm totally going to get distracted by the growing number of dinosaur drawings on Jess' building if I stay out here to do it.

"I'm good, babe."

Sweet.

Oh, thank God the building is cool. And quiet. It won't take too long to get things up. I should get some recordings, too. Maybe of parents talking to Jess. Wonder if any of them would be willing to tag Foundations if they're featured in mini talking-head moments?

Maybe that's too ambitious for today. I don't want to be in people's faces. I want people to actually enjoy what's happening here. And to understand what Jess is trying to do. How she's trying to help the community. Yes, the social media aspect is important. But Jess made it clear that she gets the most out of genuine, real-life interactions. I have to stay true to what she wants Foundations to be.

The door opens. Probably someone looking for the restroom.

I turn and smile at— "Oh."

"Wow. Sorry to disappoint," Liam says.

"What are you doing here?"

He lifts an eyebrow. "What, I can't check out Pitchette's one and only fitness studio?"

Of course he *can*. It just seems unlikely he *is*.

Okay, maybe I'm being rude. But I haven't seen or heard from him in like a week. What exactly is the right way to address the guy I felt up who obviously wants nothing to do with me? I mean, romantically speaking. Because clearly he gets a kick out of bugging the hell out of me.

What's he even doing here? Returning my clothes? No, no bag. That's not it. "Do you want something?"

Liam shrugs, a lazy smile settling on his lips. "No. I was just at Sal's and saw the kids outside and thought I'd see what's going on."

Right. "Jess is launching her new family fitness program soon, so we thought we'd do something fun to kick it off."

"Like draw on the building." His teeth flash through his scruff when he smiles. "I like it. Your idea?"

Um. "I mean, we mostly worked it out together." I can't take over Jess' spotlight. That defeats the purpose here. "I just, um, got the chalkboard paint from Hand—the hardware store. I thought it might be fun to get kids together to decorate the storefront." I shrug. "The idea's a little weird, I know."

The corners of his eyes crinkle when he watches the kids chalk. "It's good weird."

Really?

I mean, not that I expect him to have an opinion about it. Not that I *need* him to have an opinion about it!

Still. It's nice to hear the approval in his voice. Liam Taggert is about as tapped into the local pulse as you can be. If he thinks this will work, so will others. Hopefully.

Okay, so I don't know a lot about the local consumer market. But I *do* know that different opinions carry different weights in a place like Pitchette. A Boy Scout slash firefighter slash war hero slash Mr. July showing up at Jess' event has to be good for business.

I mean, not to reduce Liam to a stereotype.

"So." He crosses his arms. "I hear you talked to Shack Wheeler. Again."

What? "Where did you hear that?" Does that mean the story is already out?

No, that doesn't make sense. Jess hasn't murdered me.

"My sister Arla handles classifieds for the paper," Liam says.

Arla. Right. No wonder she looked familiar. She went to school with Tanner Manson and Matty Johnson. I sort of forgot Liam has siblings sprinkled in with Jess'. Between the Taggerts and the Johnsons, you could field a football team.

Wait a minute. "Your sister works for Shack? I thought you sort of hated him?"

"Arla works for the *newspaper,* not Shack." He pauses. "And yes, I'm not a fan of it. But my sister does what she wants."

"Must be frustrating to be around someone like that."

His eyes narrow. "You have no idea. What did Shack want to talk about?"

Should I be worried that Liam asked that? Does that mean

Arla overheard us and told him about my lies? I mean, not that it matters. Everyone is going to find out, anyway. It's a news article, for Pete's sake!

But Liam looks kind of pissed off right now. I mean, that has to be at me, right? Is he worried I said something about him responding to the call? Why? He *did* respond to the call. Shack *saw* him there. I mean, that's the whole reason I was able to escape to the IGA parking lot.

Hm. "Are you worried I said something bad about you?"

"What? No." He frowns. "Why? Did you?"

"Of course not. What bad thing would I have said?" That he didn't perform mouth-to-mouth? That's a *personal* critique, not a professional one. "Why do you look so annoyed?" Why do I care? I did what I had to do. It doesn't matter what folks think about me as long as it helps Jess get on the right footing with Pitchette again.

"I'm not annoyed."

Yeah. Right. "Well, you definitely don't look happy that I had an interview with Shack."

"An *interview?* You did an interview with that asshole? Geezus, Mollie! He printed a *false story about you overdosing!*" The skin around his eyes tightens. "What did you say to him? What could possibly be *left* to say?"

"Why?" I cross my arms. "What do you care?"

"I—"

"Mollz, can you grab some wipes?" Jess hollers through the front door. "Oh hey, Liam. Mollz, I should have some in the storage closet next to the family fitness room."

"Sure thing!" I turn back to Mr. July. "You can relax, Liam. I didn't say anything that would tarnish that pretty Silver Star of yours." Shouldn't mock his Silver Star. For Pete's sake, it's a *military distinction.* Gah! IDIOT.

"I don't have a Silver Star, Mollie."

Oh. Good.

"And I'm not worried about *myself.*" His voice comes out tight and cold.

Oh. That makes a little more sense. I mean, that definitely fits with the whole Boy Scout-firefighter-war-hero vibe.

Geez, I'm such a *jag*.

My face heats. "He just wanted to ask me some questions about what happened at the cemetery." Also known as the Whippet Episode and Number 2 on my list of Top Ten Most Humiliating Incidents.

Feeling up Liam Taggert in Mom's kitchen tops the chart.

Sheetz is Number 3.

Little Drop Run is Number 4.

Geez, how have so many of my most humiliating incidents happened in the last two weeks?

"Right." Liam tilts his head at me. "And in exchange for *your* interview, Shack agreed to do an interview with Jess."

Is it that obvious? Or does Shack do this to everyone? "Yeah. It's called 'framing the narrative.'" Or something like that.

"That's clever, Maris."

My cheeks get hot when I shrug uncomfortably. "It's just business."

Some of the tension in his body disappears. The corners of his mouth twitch.

"What?"

"You conduct a lot of 'business' around here."

For Pete's sake! "Don't say it like that. It *was* business! Both times!"

"Shack had donuts, didn't he?"

"*No.*" DAMN IT! "I didn't even *have* any!"

He laughs. "Glad to see your weapon of mass destruction is still firing on all cylinders."

Now I'm overheating everywhere. "It's not—stop

saying—gah, you are so *aggravating!*"

"I am?"

"*Yes!*"

"Good."

"Not good! Very, very annoying!" And distracting. *Too* distracting.

What the heck does Jess need again? Paper towels, right? Or is it wipes? Something in the storage closet. I'd go ask her, but she's fielding a bunch of moms right now. No, thank you! Besides, the closet isn't super big. I'm smart. I can probably figure it ou—

"Geez!" I yelp as Liam pushes me into the closet and closes the door behind us. "What the heck are you doing?"

"Tell me what it is, Maris."

"Tell you what *what* is?"

"Whatever's bothering you. I can tell something is."

"Yeah! *You're* bothering me!"

"Me?" He lifts an eyebrow. "What did *I* do?"

For Pete's sake! "You kissed me and then didn't speak to me for a week! So message received loud and clear, thanks!"

"What message?"

"*Your* message!"

"What the hell are you talking about?"

Really, God? How many times do I have to relive this? "I'm talking about how you pulled me out of the creek and took me home and took off your *wet* clothes and put on my *dry* clothes and then kissed me and then I got a little handsy and when I offered you more you were not at all interested and bolted, instead!"

His eyes narrow. "I did not *bolt.*"

"Your truck peeled out so quickly I heard the tires squeal over the rain. And then you didn't even bother to talk to me when you dropped off my car the next morning!"

"It was *early*. I assumed you were sleeping."

Uh-huh. "I wasn't *sleeping* when you ran out into a thunderstorm to get away from me."

"Geezus, Maris, that wasn't me saying *never*. That was me saying *not yet*."

"I—what? Wait. Go back." What?

"Mollie, you almost *drowned*."

"That's dramatic." It isn't. I almost sort of died in Little Drop Run.

"And you didn't because I rescued you."

I roll my eyes. "*Okay,* Mr. Superhero." DAMN IT! That's true, too.

"And then you told me about the Stanley being a gift from your mom—"

"A birthday gift," I whisper.

He traces a finger along my jaw. "I didn't want you to jump into bed with me because of all that, Maris. I want you to jump into bed with me because of *me*."

'Want' as in present tense. 'Want' as in *prez-unt tense*.

As in Liam Taggert is talking *now*. Or the *very near future*.

I lick my lips. "Um."

He loosely fists my hair. "'Um?'"

"Um." TALK SOMETHING, BRAIN! IDIOT NO WORDS SOUND DUMMY.

"Well, while you're thinking." He pulls my head back and KISSES ME.

SLOWLY.

Like NOTHING ELSE IS HAPPENING and we aren't HIDING IN JESS' STORAGE CLOSET and we have ALL THE TIME IN THE FREAKING WORLD!

I do not have all the time in the world I have ovaries that are on a deadline and holy crap Liam Taggert has me in a closet with his tongue down my throat and I swear to goodness if anyone opens that freaking door—

"UM!" I cry when his erection drives into my hip.

He moves his mouth down my throat, tugging at the straps of my tank top. Then bra. "No words yet?" He kisses the swell of my breast. "Weird."

Oh, I have *words.*

Okay, I have *onomatopoeias.* Like *Oh!* and *Ah!* and *Ohyesyesyes!*

"Here, Liam!" Aha! WORDS. "Right now!" Holy crap, who the heck made his *freaking clothes?* What are they, glued on?

He groans and jerks against me. "We can't."

"Can!" Is that a zipper? Yes!

"We'd be too loud." He catches my hands and traps them against his chest. "And there's not enough space."

"There's space. I'm flexible!" I mean, I'm not *super* flexible. But I'm highly motivated!

His lips curve up. "Mollie."

I bite my lip. I will not beg. I will NOT BEG! "*Liam.*" Gah! Pathetic.

He brushes his thumb over my lower lip. "I want to do this right, baby. Thoroughly. The way we deserve. Not quickly in the closet of a fitness studio."

"Jess won't mind."

"*I* mind."

Gah! Of course he does.

The problem is, I actually mind, too. I mean, under my raging libido and wobbly knees and whiney vagina and everything. Because this is *not* me. I don't climb guys in closets. I hardly climb guys at all. I mean, when was the last time exactly?

Whenever it was, it wasn't like this. I've never lost my grip on the English language. EVER.

"Okay." I shouldn't be disappointed. This is a good thing.

A good sign about Liam.

"Good girl." He kisses my nose.

Geez. Can he make this any more difficult?

I sigh. "So you leave first and I wait five minutes and follow?"

"Uh. You should leave first." He looks down at his erection.

Oh yeah. "Have fun taking care of that."

"Thanks."

"But not *too* much fun!" I don't want to miss out.

His lips twitch. "Okay."

"I mean, I can stay and help—"

"Geezus, Maris! You're killing me here!"

"Good! At least I'm not the only one suffering."

He smiles like he sort of wants to strangle me.

I sort of think that's sexy.

Uh-oh. What am I, a closeted sadist? I have to get the heck out of here!

Jess doesn't seem to notice I've been missing. Good. Because there's no way I'm going to explain slinking out of her storage closet while I'm hauling up the straps of my top.

I find her behind the front counter. "How's it going?"

"Busy! Can you take these outside?" She drops a pack of chilled water bottles into my arms. "What, no wipes?"

"Um—"

"And tell Killian I can't find any more purple chalk."

"Okay." Who the heck is Killian?

The kids flock to the water as soon as I push through the studio door.

"Killian?"

A red-haired little kid looks up.

"Miss Jess is out of purple chalk," I tell him.

"Aw, man! Now my wolverine will look dumb."

"Sorry, bud." It's the end of the world. I get it.

I mean, I could be having the time of my life in a storage closet with Liam Taggert instead of trying to convince a kid named Killian that blue and red actually make purple.

I feel Liam when he emerges from the studio and passes through the sidewalk crowd, but I don't look at him. I *can't* look at him. Not if I don't want to pass out in front of a group of elementary kids.

Seriously, what is happening to me? I mean, this is *Liam Taggert* we're talking about. This is *Pitchette!* There aren't any happily-ever-afters here, just day-by-days. And I'll tell you one thing for free: Mollie Maris does not end up with the hot guy. Never has. Never will.

So what. Is. HAPPENING.

You know what? Fuck it. I'm going to look. Who knows when this beautiful little bubble is going to pop, right? At least I'll get to enjoy an extra glimpse of Liam's ass.

Except I'm not looking at Liam's ass. I'm looking at his face. Into his eyes. He watches me from across the street and he doesn't look away. My brain tells me there are dozens of people between us right now, laughing and chalking and taking over Man Street, but I'm not seeing any of them. I'm only seeing *him*. Like the light of a train at the end of a tunnel.

I know it's barreling toward me. Hundreds of tons of steel and fiberglass and God-knows-what racing in my direction, promising absolute death.

But it's the brightest light in my world and I don't want to step out of the way.

Shit.

I'm so screwed, aren't I?

Ha. No pun intended.

TWENTY-THREE

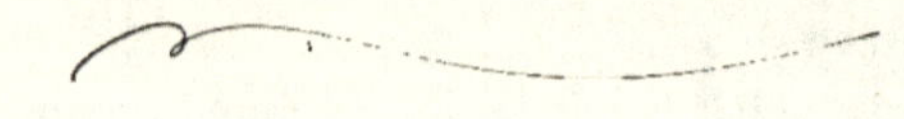

I don't usually go to bars alone, but Jerry's isn't really a bar. Okay, it *is.* But it isn't a dive or a tourist trap or anything. It's just the local watering hole. Which means I can sit in the corner and nurse a beer and work on Jess' marketing stuff without worrying about having to socialize.

Or. I could if Liam didn't spot me.

Okay, he's coming over with the basket of pretzel bites I ordered. That's fine. Totally fine. I mean, it's not like I can't control myself around him. I can. Really. It's only been like thirty hours since his mouth was on mine.

"Hey."

Damn it. One word in and I'm already sweating. "Um. Hey."

He raises an eyebrow at my beer.

"What?"

"Drinking alone?"

"I don't know. Are you going to join me?" *Oh*-kay. I definitely saw that in a movie or a TV show somewhere because *I* do not have game. *I* usually have a bad case of verbal diarrhea.

Liam smiles lazily.

And slides into the seat across from me.

Right. So much for working on marketing stuff.

He nods at my planner and assorted crap. "Homework?"

"I'm helping Jess make some marketing plans for her studio."

"Like the article in the paper." He turns my notepad to read my scratching. "Is this a billboard?"

"Road signs, actually. They're cheaper than renting a billboard, plus reusable. And you can move them, so you can target different areas."

"Hm." He slides my notebook back. "I saw the article this morning."

Oh geez. He isn't talking about Foundations, is he? "Everyone's seen the article." *Again.* Including Jess. Who's not happy. Which is why I'm drinking alone in Jerry's.

Well. Alone-ish

"When you said you gave Shack an interview, I didn't realize you meant a *fake* interview." He watches me closely. "Did you really feed him clickbait just to get him to run a good story on Jess?"

"I don't know if it counts as 'clickbait' if it's in print."

"You know what I mean."

I don't meet his eyes. "He retracted the overdose story." Sort of.

"No, he didn't. He replaced it with a whole new story about how you actually got high doing whippets on your mom's grave. Which was why someone called 9-1-1."

Okay, so it isn't flattering. I know that.

But I also know how people like Shack Wheeler work. And it isn't fair for Jess to suffer just because the world is full of jagoffs. "I don't know what you want me to say, Liam."

"Mollie, you intentionally let him run a negative story

about you just to get space for the studio. A *false* negative story. For the second time." He says it in a neutral tone, like he's trying not to show too much of his opinion on the issue.

Probably because he thinks I'm being really dumb, right?

Maybe I am. I just don't particularly care. "It's Jess. I'd do anything for Jess."

"That's it? That's your reason?"

"Liam, it's my *only* reason."

Liam's eyes glow under the lights. "That's one hell of a loyal streak, Maris."

"It's not loyalty. It's friendship. It's love." I sigh and tear apart a pretzel bite. "Besides. It's not like I don't have a bad enough reputation, anyway. What's another article on alleged drug use going to do?"

I mean, the *Pitchette Press* is hardly the *Washington Post*. It prints three times a week. It's distribution is like eight hundred. And most of the people who get it already hear the news through the grapevine. It's not like there's police reports or anything official backing up Shack's story. For all intents and purposes, he's running a glorified gossip column.

"Something like this would bother most normal people," Liam says.

I snort. "I think we've established I'm far from normal."

"No kidding." Liam glances around the bar. "The gossip mill is bad enough. But to have things like that said in print? Especially when they're not even true?" He looks back at me. "Folks around here still take the newspaper as Gospel, Mollie. I don't think I know anyone who'd intentionally do something like this just to help someone out."

"Jess isn't just someone. She's my best friend." No. That isn't quite it. "Actually, she's more like my sister. We've been close since we were in school, but since Mom died she's been the only person I really think of as family."

His forehead creases. "Mollie, I've been meaning to tell

you that I'm sorry about Daphne. My mom went to her funeral." His face flushes a little. "Not that that matters. I mean, it does *matter,* but that isn't the point. The point is I was sorry to hear she'd passed. And I'm sorry I didn't say something earlier."

"Oh. That's okay." Wow, now I sound like a total monster. "I mean, it's a good thing she died."

He raises his eyebrows. "A good thing?"

"We caught her cancer so late. She was in so much pain. And she recognized that her mind was changing because of the treatments." I think that bothered her more than anything. The idea that the woman she was might die before her body did. And that I'd have to see that happen. "She wanted to go, in the end. She didn't want to linger." I smile. "And she did *not* want me to get all mopey over her."

The corners of his eyes do this thing that makes my stomach flip.

"What?"

"Nothing." He shakes his head. "I don't know anyone like you."

"You mean someone who's not related to you and lives in the tri-county area?"

"I'm glad you're not related to me. And I'm glad you don't care what folks think about you."

"I mean, I care a *little.* It's not like I want people to actively hate me."

"No one actively hates you."

"I'm sure I can think of a few people." Tara Basher. One. Mrs. Barker. Two. Shack Wheeler. Three.

"Then those people better not say anything to me."

"Why?"

He plants his elbows on the table and leans in. "Because I actively *like* you, Mollie Maris."

"Well, that's good. Considering we've made out like three times." Although, we haven't moved beyond that.

I'm trying not to worry about it.

Liam's mouth twitches. "You want to get dinner?"

Um. "Aren't we doing that now?" Because I totally scarfed that whole basket of pretzel bites. Not that I won't eat more food. Obviously.

"I mean an actual meal," Liam says. "Not bar food."

"Oh." Um. "Like go for dinner? Like as a date?"

"Yeah." His eyes glitter. "As a date."

Okay. Okay. This is totally normal. The natural escalation of the storage closet episode.

Liam Taggert is asking me out on a date.

And I'm NOT FREAKING OUT WHATSOEVER.

"Cool." Not 'cool.' Very, very hot. Gah!

I gather my paraphernalia and he takes care of the tab. Which I don't feel at all guilty about. Since he works here. Sort of. Then he follows me outside.

"What sounds good?"

Liam. Duh. "Ice cream." Oops. That slipped out.

Isn't untrue, though.

Liam shakes his head. "Yeah, that was a dumb question. Let's go."

"Where?" Not that it really matters. I'm already trailing him toward his truck.

"To get ice cream."

"Really?" Geez. Do I *have* to sound like a little kid, getting all excited like that? "I mean, that's cool." Perfect. Nailed it.

We climb into his truck and he pulls away from the curb. My Honda watches us head east on Man Street. Past Sal's. Out of Pitchette.

"Murray's?" Yes! I haven't been to Murray's in a long time.

He gives me a look.

"Yeah, that was a dumb question," I say.

Murray's has been an ice cream place off Graphite Road since before the sign for Graphite Road was even installed. The original owners opened it in the fifties, and it's traded hands eight times since then. The name and the sign and the menu have stayed the same. The only thing that's changed is the customers.

And honestly, some of the customers are from the fifties, too.

Liam pulls off the road into Murray's gravel lot. Like a lot of ice cream stands in the area, the place is only open seasonally and doesn't have any indoor seating. Just a ragtag collection of weathered picnic tables and an ancient cement slab for bocce ball. When I was growing up, the local Elks Lodge used the bocce court every Sunday night for their ongoing summer tournament. You don't mess with the Elks. If they're playing, you either go to the IGA for a quart of Turkey Hill or you go home.

The last time I had ice cream here was right before Mom's diagnosis. I drove up from D.C. to visit her for the Fourth of July. We spent the weekend drinking coffee and talking and I'd noticed that she seemed tired. More tired than usual. When I'd asked her about her cough, she told me it was allergies.

Two weeks later, she told me it was cancer.

"Is this okay?"

I blink and look at Liam.

He watches me, eyes serious, hand on the wheel. "We can go somewhere else, if you want."

That's sweet. Too sweet. What have I done to deserve a date with Liam, exactly?

"No." I reach for the door handle. "This is fine."

Mom of all people wouldn't want me to turn down ice

cream because of a sad memory.

I mean, for that one sad memory I have a lot of happy ones here. Mostly with Mom. But also Jess and her family. We used to sit on top of that picnic table, because it was cooler than using the benches. And one time we tossed a bocce ball back and forth, taking a step back after each catch until we were throwing the whole way across the parking lot.

"Why are you smiling like that?" Liam asks as we crunch over the gravel toward Murray's.

"It's just been a while since I've been here."

He studies me for a second, then reaches for my hand. We walk that way up to the order window. The woman standing behind it has a helmet of purple-tinted permed hair and a pair of red-framed cheaters.

Holy crap. Is that— "Margie?" Damn! She's been serving ice cream since I was in eighth grade.

She looks up and gasps so widely, her pink lipstick cracks. "Oh my goodness! Mollie Maris!"

Holy crap. "I can't believe you remember me."

"Sweetie! Of course I do!" She wags her finger at me. "How could I ever forget the Mollipop Special?"

Oh no.

"What's the Mollipop Special?" Liam asks.

"Nothing! I'll take a—"

"Waffle cone filled with whipped cream and topped with rainbow sprinkles and a maraschino cherry," Margie says.

No, God, please, why? WHY? "Actually, just a banana split."

Margie raises an eyebrow.

"With extra whipped cream," I mumble.

"You got it, sweetie. What about you, hon?"

Liam's grin is dangerously close to laughter. "Also a split. She can have my whipped cream."

Oh. My. LORD. I have to leave Pennsylvania for good,

don't I?

"The Mollipop Special wasn't my idea," I tell him after we find a picnic table.

"Really? Because it definitely sounds like you."

Yeah. That's the problem. "I ordered that one time in high school. ONE TIME. After play practice. And some of the girls thought it was hilarious. They called me 'Mollipop' back then, so that's what ended up on the menu."

"You're on Murray's *menu?*"

"Secret menu." Barely. Barley secret menu. "Everyone in there knows how to make it in case someone orders it."

He ducks his head. Since he isn't wearing a ballcap, I can totally see him laughing. He doesn't even try hiding it.

"It's not funny!"

"Come on." He grins as he looks at me. "It's kind of funny."

I scowl. "It's a lasting testament to my humiliating high school existence."

"You did not have a humiliating high school existence."

"The girls in my grade called me 'Mollipop,' Liam."

"So?"

"So it—" Oh wait. Oh no no no. Crap. I can't tell him why they called me that. I'll have to leave Pennsylvania *for real* if I do.

But oh shit, he's giving me that look. The one that says he's onto me. Because I don't know when to shut up and I piqued his interest. IDIOT!

Liam sets his arms on the table and leans toward me. "Why did they call you that, Mollie?"

I shake my head. Because this isn't happening. I'm not on my first date with Liam Taggert having *this* conversation.

Because that wouldn't be a date. That would be a nightmare.

His voice drops. "Tell me, Maris."

I bite my lip.

His eyes gleam. Intense. Focused. "I want to know. Tell me. Please."

Oh boy. Liam begging is a special kind of trouble.

No! I mean, it doesn't matter anyway, right, because I'm a grown-ass woman and this is the twenty-first century and I shouldn't be embarrassed about— "They called me Mollipop because I was the only one who didn't pop in high school!"

SHIT!

GAAAAAAH!

I'm sweating. My face is so hot I can feel my mascara getting dewy.

Liam frowns. "'Pop?' I don't understand."

"You know. *Pop*."

He shakes his head.

OH FOR PETE'S SAKE. "The cherry, Liam! The freaking cherry!"

"Cherries?" Margie appears from nowhere and sets down the sundaes. "I'll bring you a few more."

Do You think this is funny, God? Because *news flash!* IT ISN'T.

"I think I need to die now." I say it to Liam, but I don't look at him. For obvious reasons.

"Hey." He touches my wrist, his warm fingers settling over my pulse. "Why are you embarrassed that you didn't have sex in high school?"

"I'm not."

It's true. I'm not embarrassed that I graduated high school a virgin. I wasn't ready for something like that then, and I definitely hadn't been surrounded by boys who were worth it. Teenagers think they're all that, but they're still kids. Their hormones are out of control and their brains are barely formed. Thirty-three-year-old me definitely doesn't think teens are mature enough for sex. Heck, I know *adults* who aren't mature enough for it. So no, I'm not embarrassed to admit I never had sex in high school.

I *am* embarrassed to admit that my virginity got a nickname.

And that Murray's has a menu item named after it.

And that Liam Taggert now knows that.

I exhale and meet his eyes. "I'm not embarrassed about not having sex. I chose to wait until college, and that was the right call. It wasn't right for me back then, so I didn't do it."

He waits, watching me closely. "But?"

"But it stung to be singled out. It still stings." Pathetic. "Guess I do care about what people think of me."

"Don't. It's not worth it."

I try not to frown when he pulls his hand away and reaches for his spoon. "Easy for you to say. You were Mr. Popularity."

Liam shrugs. "Maybe, but I also never had sex in high school."

"What? How? No way. Impossible. You're lying." I mean, he's Liam Freaking Taggert. If he didn't have sex in high school, who the heck did?

"It's true." He spoons up some ice cream. "I was too focused on school and sports. They took up a lot of my time."

"But you *dated.*" A lot. At least, that's how it seemed to teenager me.

"I went on some dates, but nothing serious. Which turned out to be good. I enlisted when I graduated and it was easy to leave for basic because I didn't have to go through all the messiness of leaving behind a girlfriend."

Does that mean he's never done it with Tara Basher?

How can I ask something like that without coming off all *Fatal Attraction*-ish?

Easy. I can't. GAH!

I carefully pick off the maraschino cherry on my sundae and hold it by the stem. "For the record, I don't normally consider sex a first-date topic."

"Yeah?" Liam's eyes glimmer. "What do you consider a first-date topic?"

"Politics. Religion. Income. You know. The usual."

"I'm disappointed, Maris."

"You are?" Already?

"Yeah."

"Why?"

"Because politics and religion and income are boring and safe topics."

Yeah. Right. "What do *you* want to talk about?" What's left? STDs? The War on Drugs? That one might be touchy. Considering my recent track record around here.

"Easy." He licks fudge sauce off his finger, then reaches for my maraschino. "I want to talk more about your cherry."

My jaw drops open.

He smiles lazily and pops my cherry in his mouth.

OH. MY. LORD!

TWENTY-FOUR

"Show it to me again," Jess demands.

For Pete's sake. It isn't *that* big a deal.

Okay, fine. It is. It is a big deal.

But I *definitely* do not need to be smiling like an idiot when I flip my phone around to show Jess the screen.

She squeals. "Babe! I can't believe you got his freaking number!"

I roll my eyes so she doesn't know I'm secretly squealing inside, too. "Calm down. It's just Liam. Lots of people have his number." And probably more than half of them are women.

Not that I've been obsessing about that or anything.

"And he *gave* it to you. I mean, you didn't have to ask for it. He typed it in himself."

"Yeah." Stop smiling. STOP SMILING! "Not that he made a big deal out of it or anything. I mean, we were eating ice cream and he just—"

"He took you on an *ice cream date?*"

"Sort of." I bite my lip. "Last night."

"*After* he saw the whippet story." A grin bursts across her face. "Oh babe, he's *serious!*"

I don't know about that. I mean, he definitely *seems* interested in me. And yeah, he checked in this morning and we've been texting ever since. Up until about two hours ago, anyway.

I mean. It's after six and still no reply to my last message. It's cool. It's all cool. I mean, I'm not worrying or anything. Didn't he mention last night he's out-of-town this weekend? Yeah, he did, right? So totally understandable that he hasn't gotten back to me. He's busy. I mean, he has a *life.*

Unlike me, who's spending Friday night helping Jess clean and sanitize the studio. Beats being at home, I guess. At least the studio is air conditioned.

"I'm still mad at you for letting Shack write that ridiculous whippet story," Jess declares from under the front counter. "But I really think the studio article he ran Monday did the trick for us. I can't tell you how many folks who came to the event Wednesday have called here asking about classes."

"You should see the people DMing on the Foundations socials," I yell back, spraying glass cleaner on the wall mirrors. "Some of them are definitely spam or bots, but a lot of them aren't. A lot of them are asking about pricing and scheduling."

"Are the majority of them asking about the family fitness programming?" Jess appears in the doorway. "Because that's been most of the phone calls. I'm actually really surprised. I mean, obviously the families with little kids make some sense, just because there's not a lot of options for them to get into sports. But I had three parents ask about classes for their pre-teens."

"Yeah, there are some people with older kids also DMing for info." I crouch to wipe down the bottom half of the mirror. "I was telling Liam I'm surprised about that, and he actually said that a lot of school athletic programs around here are dissolving because they either don't have the funding or the volunteer support to stay active. That plus the population is in decline, so there just aren't as many kids enrolled in school."

"You know the high school didn't have a play this year?"

"What? No way!"

"Yep. There weren't enough students involved, which meant there weren't enough parents. So instead of spending money on the show licensing fees, the school board just decided to skip it."

That is *so* heartbreaking! I mean, I'd never been part of the productions when I was in high school, but I'd been part of the stage crew a couple years. For someone who wasn't athletically inclined and wasn't super popular, stage crew was an extracurricular opportunity well within my comfort zone.

Sad to think there are kids like me who are missing out on an experience like that.

"What did Liam say about the studio trying to get into family fitness?" Jess asks.

I knew it. I knew Liam's opinion made a difference around here.

Although, geez. That's sort of scary, right? I mean, his opinion of me is definitely too good for Pitchette. And I can't really blame Pitchette for that. You know, considering there's been *two* drug-related news stories about me in the two weeks I've been back.

GAH.

"He thinks you might have to open your programming up to accommodate kids in several age groups," I report. "As group opportunities decline because of enrollment numbers, he thinks families will naturally gravitate toward individualized sports. Where kids can compete on their own without having to field a team."

"Martial arts."

"Yeah, actually. That's a good one. Or things like running or track or gymnastics. Not that Foundations can offer those." I tilt my head and look at her in the mirror. "But you could start marketing the studio as a place where kids can go to stay fit in the off season."

"Hm."

"Is that a good 'hm' or a bad 'hm?'"

"It's an 'I-didn't-think-about-any-of-this-before-hm.'"

I get that. "This is a lot, babe. But it's stuff to consider. The more you're able to put Foundations into a long-term context, the better your chances are of being successful here."

"Yeah. See, I *know* that and I *want* that." She heaves a sigh. "But damn, it's just so daunting."

She looks drained. Circles under her eyes. Hair piled up so she doesn't have to mess with it. She still looks good, obviously, because this is Jess we're talking about. But it's been a long week and it's showing.

"Do you want to call it a night?" I gesture around the room. "I can come by in the morning and help you clean whatever else you want." There can't be a lot left, right? We've been wiping and spraying and sweeping for hours. My back and hamstrings are screaming at me. Plus I'm about forty seconds away from passing out due to starvation.

She shakes her head. "No. I want to get this done tonight so I don't have to worry about it tomorrow. Because I want to go home, shower, and sleep."

"Okay." I stand up. "What's left?"

"Nothing. You go."

I wish. "It'll be faster with both of us working."

"All I'm going to do is run a spray mop to clean the floors and then I'm out of here. Honestly, Mollz, there's really nothing else you can do right now."

"You sure?" Only because my stomach is grumbling.

"Yes."

"Because—"

"Babe, you've done so much for me this week. Go home and freaking rest!"

Alright. Twist my arm. "Okay. Holler if you need something. I am literally doing nothing with my life tomorrow."

She laughs. "Okay."

It's still light out when I angle my Honda toward Mom's house. Plenty of folks are enjoying the summer evening, taking walks, sitting on lawn chairs in their front yards. Terry Bauer doesn't wave back when I pull into Mom's driveway, but he also doesn't scuttle into his house to hide. Progress. I guess.

The whippet story hasn't made me any more popular around town. I didn't expect it to, obviously. But *yes,* maybe a small part of me hoped folks would look past Shack's dumb story and see *me*. Mollie Maris. Daughter of Daphne Maris. Friend of Jess Johnson. And possibly Liam Taggert.

It doesn't matter. Honestly. It did what it was supposed to do; give Foundations a step up and cut down on Jess' online haters. The Foundations article is a solid start for turning things around and the chalking event turned out *way* better than Jess and I expected it to. The studio is getting excellent buzz and no one seems to be linking it too closely to me. Jess said she mentioned some of the things I've been doing to help promote the studio, but Shack didn't include any of those quotes in the article. Thankfully. I'm not the man's biggest fan, but he made the right call about that.

So those are all wins. And those wins outweigh any negativity coming my way.

Besides, who knows how long I'm going to be around here? The way things are going, D.C. is offering a better future for me than Pitchette. Maybe not forever, but definitely in the meantime. If there's one thing I've learned since getting back, it's that I actually still enjoy marketing. Even in this small town, single business, entrepreneurial setting. I *love* working for Jess. I *love* building the studio's following. I *love* watching someone's dream root and expand and reach new people.

I *don't* love being a constant source of gossip and the town's fake personal tragedy. Who the hell would?

So while I want to do this for Jess right now, I can't do this forever. I mean, I *said* it didn't matter what people think of me. And it doesn't, not really.

But come on. A person can only take so much public resentment before they lose it. I don't want to stick around and let that happen to me. Yes, there are folks around here who still like me. The Johnson family. Stella at the IGA. Margie at Murray's. Liam. I think. I mean, you know. Just based off our storage closet interaction and little ice cream date.

But a lot of people look at me differently, now. And I can't blame them for that. If one of *my* classmates came back to Pitchette after living in the city for twelve years and ended up in the newspaper twice like I have, I'm sure I'd look at her differently, too.

I don't know, God. You have things under control, right?

Because I don't.

I walk through Mom's house, past my moving boxes, past my temporary business center. My phone buzzes when I drop my purse on the kitchen counter and I scuffle around for it.

An email notification from Darrin. Checking in. Which is annoying, but not unexpected. My month LOA is half over and I haven't indicated one way or another what I want to do.

Because, you know. I've been busy being Pitchette's worst nightmare and letting my life fall apart. And also because I'm sort of maybe seeing this guy who's totally out of my league and whose life is *not* falling apart.

Still no response from Liam.

That's cool. Really. I mean, I didn't even *have* his number before last night. So it's not like there's any established expectations or anything here. *I* have other stuff to worry about. *He* has other stuff to worry about. We both have other stuff to worry about! And we're both adults. We don't need to be in constant contact. I don't need to freak out just because I'm the last one to text and that was hours ago.

He'll reply when he's free.

TWENTY-FIVE

I probably shouldn't start down the entrepreneurial marketing rabbit hole at ten-thirty on a Sunday night. Not that I have to worry about getting up early for anything.

Still. Probably not the best idea to be chugging down coffee so late. Not that caffeine has any lasting effects on me. Just that coffee leads to cookies, and cookies lead to me wondering if I should just be honest with myself and reheat a plate of leftover noodle casserole. I mean, I'm working on my laptop in the kitchen. The casserole is literally two feet to my right in the fridge. Seems kind of serendipitous. Not that I plan—

Is that someone pounding on the side door?

Um. Who the heck is knocking on Mom's door in the middle of the freaking night? And should I have a weapon? Probably, right? Great. Adding *get weapon* to my to-do list.

I peek out the mudroom window, but I can't see much. Just the outline of a guy standing on the cement pad, hands in his pockets. He doesn't *look* menacing. And this *is* Pitchette.

I blow out a breath, then unlock the inside door and pull it open.

Gold hair. Blue eyes. Sexy scruff.

Oh boy.

"Hey," he says.

I push open the storm door. What else am I going to do? Talk to him through the screen?

I mean. I guess I could do that. "Um, what are you doing here?" Because I haven't heard from him since Friday.

"I just got back."

"Yeah? From where?" It better be somewhere that doesn't have cell service. You know, like the bottom of a lake.

"From Drill." He steps inside and closes the door.

"Make yourself at home." I'm being sarcastic. Obviously. "Where the heck is Drill?"

"Not where. What." He takes off his ballcap and slings it on the coat rack. "It was Drill weekend for my unit."

Unit? What—oh. Right. Army Reserve. Duh. "Isn't that all weekend?"

"Saturday morning through Sunday evening. I'm sorry. I tried calling and texting you a few times, but I don't get a good signal where we train."

"So you just got back to town?"

"Couple minutes ago."

"And you came here?" I'm having a hard time wrapping my head around this, okay?

"Yeah." He looks at me, eyes glowing in the weird angle of the light coming from the kitchen. "Is that alright?"

"I mean. Yes?"

He lifts an eyebrow. "Is it not alright?"

I bite my lip.

The edges of his face soften. "Mollie, tell me to leave if you want me to leave. It's your place. You have a right to not want—"

"I want you to stay!" Good grief. Glad I shouted *that* at the top of my lungs. Just in case Terry Bauer across the street needed to hear it. "I mean. It's okay. You know. If you stay."

Liam's mouth pulls up on one side. He trails his knuckles down my cheek. "You sure, Maris?"

I swallow. "Yes." Oh *hell,* yes. Yes yes yes yes yes. My vagina is totally driving the bus right now, and my brain doesn't even mind. Actually my brain is also totally on board, for once. So that's a good sign, right?

I lead him into the living room. "Are you hungry?"

"Yes."

Makes sense. It's almost eleven o'clock. "I have some leftover—"

He catches my arm and pulls me around until we're nose to nose.

"Not for food," he whispers.

Oh.

Oh!

Oh, holy crap. Um. Okay. Alright. It's happening. IT'S HAPPENING!

"Are you sure?" My voice trembles with anticipation and sheer surprise.

Liam's beautiful eyes hold steady. He tucks a strand of hair behind my ear and his finger traces down my jaw.

"I've never been more sure of anything," he says.

If he was any other guy and this was any other time, I'd probably do something totally normal and expected right now. Like kiss him or pull him up the stairs to my bedroom.

Instead I'm doing my best deer-in-the-headlights impression. And growing up in Pitchette, I've seen enough deer in the headlights to know.

Liam frowns. "Are you okay?"

"Yes," I wheeze.

I took my birth control today, right? Because I definitely don't have any condoms. I'm not living a condom lifestyle, if you know what I mean. And everything is closed this time of night, so no point in running out to get anything. I can call Jess, but that's just super weird. Not that she won't be prepared and want to help a sister out, but I sort of don't feel like getting into that conversation when Liam is standing in my house. *Mom's* house. Geez, is it weird to do it with Liam in Mom's house? Not that I have anywhere else to go. I mean, we could go to Liam's place, but he's probably really tired from—

"Hey." He tilts back my head until our eyes met. "Tell me what's going on in your head."

"You mean my weapon of mass destruction?" I breathe.

He smiles his you're-a-nut smile. "Yeah."

"Condom!" I blurt.

His smile dies.

Oh crap. "You don't, um, happen to have one. Do you?" Because not to panic or anything, but it's looking like he doesn't.

He stares at me. Speechless.

"Liam?"

"Condom." His eyebrows furrow. "We don't have a condom."

"You don't have one on you? In your truck?"

"Geezus, Mollie, I don't just *carry* condoms on me." He seems sort of offended at the suggestion.

"Really?" I'm sort of under the impression most guys do. Plus this is Mr. Prepared we're talking about.

"Yes, really!" His tanned face flushes. "Geezus, Mollie. That's not…I'm not that kind of guy."

Wait. Is he actually embarrassed right now? "I'm not crazy, right? I mean, you *did* come over here for this, didn't you?"

"Yes."

"So Drill ended, you got in your car, and you drove straight here."

"Yes."

"Did you stop for gas? To pee? Anything?"

He swallows. "Yes."

"And you didn't think to get any?"

"No."

Um. "Did you think *I* would have some?"

"What? Of course not!"

I lift my eyebrows.

His eyes widen. "No! Not like that. Not that you *shouldn't* have any. And not that you should! I mean, that's totally your right to have whatever you want to have for whatever reason. I shouldn't be—that's not—I just mean—"

"Liam—"

"I was too excited to see you!" Liam's face is fire engine red.

I've seen him amused. I've seen him annoyed. I've never seen him awkward.

But he is. He's totally awkward right now.

And it's totally adorable.

"You were too excited to see me?" I'm smiling sweetly. Okay, *smugly*. Who wouldn't be?

"Of course I was." He shakes his head and grinds the heels of his hands into his eyes. "I'm so stupid. I can't believe I forgot condoms."

'Condoms' plural. 'Condoms' *pluh-ral*. As in, he has big plans tonight. For us.

"They aren't necessary," I whisper. "I'm on birth control."

Liam drops his hands. His eyes are red-rimmed. Tired, but intense. "Mollie."

"I mean it. They aren't." I hesitate. "Unless there's a reason they are?"

We both know what I'm asking.

"No." He leans his forehead against mine, brushing his knuckles against my cheek. The softness in his voice makes my heart pound. "Are you sure, Maris?"

I take his hand, pulling him through the house. "I've never been more sure of anything."

It's true. Something buried in me is looking at Liam and screaming *'IT'S TIME.'* And it isn't my lady parts. Okay fine, it isn't *just* my lady parts. I mean, they're involved. Obviously. But this draw I feel, this pull isn't coming from them. I'm a grown woman. I know what lust feels like. I've experienced it enough times. But compared to *this,* those times feel…shallow. Almost superficial.

The thing that has me leading Liam upstairs into my bedroom runs so deep it's nearly tangible. Concrete. An instinctive knowledge built into my DNA.

Like Jess and her business.

I *wish* I felt this way about a business. Because feeling it about a person makes my knees buckle.

Or maybe that's Liam's lips on my neck.

I flip on the lamp in my room. It floods us in a warm glow.

Liam pulls back just enough to look around.

Geez. Liam Taggert is in my bedroom. Which hasn't changed in decades. Not that he knows that, but what's he thinking? That I'm boring, right? I mean, I don't even have any art on the walls! Just my terracotta bedspread and a couple bookcases and a lamp on my dresser.

Liam smiles lazily.

"What?" I demand.

"It's not what I was expecting."

"What? Why? What were you expecting?" Crap. I'm

right, aren't I? He thinks I'm boring.

"A lot more color, for one thing." He pulls me closer. "You know, since you have all that foot fetish money. This looks like something out of *Amish Monthly*."

"Not funny." I'd be more offended if I wasn't helping him get my shirt off.

"It's kind of funny."

"It's not. It's embarrassing." Okay, seriously, how hard is it to get off a freaking t-shirt? It doesn't even have *buttons*.

"No, it's not. It's beautiful."

"*Beautiful?*"

"Yeah." Liam kisses me as we struggle. "You know who you are. And you're comfortable enough to share that with me."

'Comfortable?' Tara Basher called me 'comfortable.' Except when *she* said, she didn't make it sound so—

Great! Now my shirt is ripped. And not in a sexy, done-by-Liam sort of way. In a Tara-Basher-makes-me-mad sort of way.

"Freaking Tara Basher."

"Who?"

"Tara Basher. From high school." Whom Liam used to date.

"Why are we talking about Tara Basher right now?" He fists my hair and tilts my head back.

"I don't know," I pant. "She saw me the other day and said I looked 'comfortable' and I guess it got into my head."

He kisses my throat. "Were you comfortable?"

"No." Not around Tara. I'm never comfortable around Tara. "I was actually pretty *un*comfortable at the time." There goes my bra.

Liam rolls my left nipple between his thumb and forefinger. It's *delicious* pressure. I sob.

"How about now?" he growls.

"Not thinking about Tara Basher." Mostly.

"Good." He bites my neck. "Neither am I."

The next few moments are a blur of striping and kissing and fondling and then I find myself tossed on the bed.

Liam follows after me, climbing between my thighs, priming the missile for launch.

"Are you still sure, baby?" His voice is rough. Charged with emotion. "Because we can wait."

Wait? And not have him inside me with nothing between us? I've never gone bare before.

I've never *wanted* to go bare before.

"No." I look up at him. "I want this, Liam. I want *you.*"

He rocks back on his heels and gazes at my body, lips parted, eyes hooded. I'd be more self-conscious about him looking at me like that if I wasn't so busy looking at him. Geez. God is a Master Craftsman and Liam Taggert is the proof. The chiseled wall of his torso. The sun-bleached sprinkle of chest hair.

The angry, rosy headed erection that makes me wonder if I'm finally going to get to use a safe word.

"Damn it, Mollie."

I cringe. "That bad, huh? It's probably all the whipped cream."

"No, baby." He settles over me, one hand cradling my head, the other gripping my hip. "It's not the whipped cream. It's you. It's all you. I know you're beautiful. I just didn't know you're *this* beautiful."

He's beautiful. Like a statue of Adonis, lover of both Aphrodite and Persephone.

GREAT. Now *that's* in my head. How the heck is a girl supposed to compete with two freaking goddesses?

That fire department calendar shot is pretty great, but it does *not* compare to the in-person experience. Liam still looks like he's carved marble, but he feels like silk. The curve of his ass. The dip of his V-cut abs. The crest of his shoulders. Running my hands over him is like running my hands over glass, or between satin sheets, or through water. He's smooth and warm and perfect. The epitome of a male specimen.

Like that snake. That freaking snake. Sliding over Liam's taut, tan skin. Winding over his hard body. Slow and sensual. Sultry. A symbol of temptation going back to the dawn of humanity.

I don't like snakes. At all. *Ever.* Not in nature or at the zoo. Not even in books. But something about Liam naked and glistening and *handling* one just makes me so—

"Are you laughing right now?"

His body shakes against mine. "Yes."

"Why?"

"Because you're so eager."

"*Excuse me?*"

"You're making all these little noises just from touching me." He pushes himself up and looks down at me. Smiling and way too satisfied with himself. "I haven't even started the fun part yet."

"Oh." Good grief, I'm that noisy? That's embarrassing. "I was, um. Thinking about something."

"You were?" His eyes narrow. "Then I'm not doing a very good job."

"It was about you."

"Now that changes things." He rolls his hips and his cock nudges through my slit. Not hitting me where I need him to, but *so* fucking close. "What were you thinking about me?"

"I saw it," I blurt.

He lifts an eyebrow. "Saw what?"

"The calendar. Mr. July. You with your dumb snake."

He blinks. "You mean Selena?"

"Oh, of *course* it's a girl snake." No wonder she looks so smug in the picture.

He frowns. "I'm confused. The sounds you were making made me think you were enjoying yourself."

"I was. I am."

"So you're turned on by the snake?"

"What? No!" For Pete's sake, God, what's the ETA on the lightning bolt? "It wasn't the stupid snake I was enjoying, it was...."

"What?"

GAH. "You *with* the snake."

He stares at me.

Crap.

I'm blowing it, aren't I? I finally have Liam Taggert naked and in bed and I'm TOTALLY BLOWING IT! What an idiot! I'm thirty-three years old and I *still* can't figure out how to close with the hot guy.

Jess is going to freaking kill me when she hears about this. And Tara! Shit. She'll find out somehow. And then she'll probably post all about it in that stupid community group. Good thing I'm probably going back to D.C. because between the socks and the whippets and the calendar and the telling Liam Taggert I think he's sexy when he's covered in snakes, I won't be able to show my face around here EVER AGAIN.

I start to sit up.

Liam plants his palm on my sternum. "Where do you think you're going?"

"Um." I look at his hand. "I figured the snake thing probably freaked you out so—"

"You were going to run away?"

"I mean. Sort of."

"I don't think so." He pushes me down.

I bounce lightly on the bed. "I'm not freaking you out?"

"No."

He lowers his head, rubbing his scruff over my breasts. *Marking* me. My nipples ache from the harsh friction. And *damn,* I want his mouth to soothe them. But his mouth isn't on me. *Why* isn't his mouth on me?

I groan. "R-really?"

"Yes." He shifts, letting his cock burrow through my wet folds. Hitting my clitoris. *Teasing* me.

I gasp and arch, trying to figure out which fire to put out first. "I mean, I'd g-get it if you did. Who wants to hear about pythons at a time like this?"

He reaches a hand down to my mound. Squeezing. His fingers rubbing me around his cock. Using my slickness. Which is so freaking *hot.* Then he slides down my body, kissing and licking. His beard scrapes an exquisite trail all the way to my honeypot.

He pushes my legs wide.

Looking at my swollen clit. My wetness.

Holy shit, what are the rules for breathing again? Something about in-out, right? And am I supposed to do something with my lungs or do they take care of things on their own?

"I want to hear about pythons," he answers.

"You do?" I choke.

"Yeah."

"*Why?*"

"I want to hear about everything going on in your head." He kisses the inside of my thigh. "About snakes." Another kiss. The other thigh. "About whipped cream." And *gah,* this time the tip of his tongue! *Barely* flicking my throbbing clit! "About me. You're a nut, Mollie Maris." His blue eyes burn into mine over the crest of my stomach. The little smile on his beautiful lips sends butterflies through me. "And baby, I like that. A lot."

He opens his mouth and lowers his head. Engulfing me. *Watching* me as he moves his tongue.

OH GOOD LORD I LIKE THAT—

"LIAM!"

A LOT.

TWENTY-SIX

There's a naked man in my bed.

Not just any naked man.

Liam Freaking Taggert.

Holy crap.

Holy crap holy crap holy crap.

Alright. Okay. Don't panic.

God, hear me out. I did not abduct him, I *swear*. He crawled into bed with me all on his own! *Willingly*. And not to brag or anything, but he was sort of excited about it, I think. I don't know. He probably told You, right? I mean, he yelled your name a lot last night.

Oh wait. Maybe that was me.

Gah!

Okay. Not panicking. NOT PANICKING!

Liam shifts on his back. Inhales deeply. One hand rests on his abs. The other grazes my hip under the sheets.

Oh boy.

I've had a few fun nights before, but I've never awaken feeling like *this*. 'Afterglow' isn't the right term. This isn't just physical contentment. It's more like...like *fulfillment*.

Like everything that happened to me over the last year happened just to lead me to last night. Like God maybe knows exactly where I need to be, and it isn't in any of the places I typically look. Mom. Jess. Work. Pitchette. Or maybe it's in all of those places combined. And those combined places exist in Liam?

Geez. What the heck is wrong to me? I'm *not* philosophical. Especially not this time of day. I rarely even *see* this time of day. I barely function before ten o'clock, most of the time.

I'm functioning now. On *all* levels.

Geez, he's beautiful. Even dead asleep. His hair all messy like that. His face softened. The corners of his lips a little slack. From this distance, I can see the fine lines around his eyes. Around his mouth. The strands of silver in his blonde beard. Tender signs of aging. I hate seeing those signs in my own reflection, but on Liam, they're stunning. They're sweet and vulnerable and lovable.

Oh. My. LORD.

"Mollie," he mumbles in his sleep.

Holy crap. He's dreaming. About *me.*

Okay, yes. Maybe it's pathetic to get all tingly and pleased over a guy dreaming about me. But come on! He's dreaming about *me!* He, Liam Taggert!

"Mhm." The corners of his mouth flicker sporadically. "Mhmsocksss."

Oh no. Oh *hell* no. He is *not* dreaming about me and Twister and my stupid sweaty socks! NO! Not today, Satan!

I lean over and kiss his jaw, moving my lips over his face.

He murmurs something unintelligible. *Not* 'socks.'

Progress.

I trail my mouth over his. Coax him open with my tongue. He groans.

Then his eyes drift open. Slowly. A little disoriented and still very sleepy. "Baby."

I smile down at him. "Good morning, Mr. July."

"Mmm." He slips his hand into my hair. "'Mornin'."

I move my mouth down his throat to his chest. My raw nipples brush his sternum.

He groans. "I like waking up this way."

That makes two of us.

"Mmm." He shudders under my lips. "What time is it?"

"You talk too much," I say against his navel.

He sucks in a breath. "I do?"

"Especially in your sleep."

"Sleep? Did I—" He makes a noise in his throat and his hips move restlessly. "Uh. Say something bad?"

"Very."

"Good-bad or—" He grunts and grips the sheets near his hips. "Bad-bad?"

My eyes cut up to his as I kiss below his bellybutton. Following the fuzzy path to his Grand Prize.

Oh, he's *wide* awake now. His blue eyes are dilated and his mouth opens with a strangled breath.

"Good-bad?" he guesses.

I sweep my hair over my shoulder, gripping him at the root.

I open my mouth and lower my head. Swallowing as much of his big cock as I can. And holy *crap,* it's not easy.

"Mollie, baby," he moans. "*Geezus!*"

He cradles my head as I slide up and down on him.

Words turning into desperate grunts.

Grunts turning into cries.

We don't do a lot of talking until we're both showered, dressed, and in my kitchen eating. I'd call it breakfast, but I sort of don't know what time it is.

The shower took a while, okay?

Liam sips his coffee and studies the steady drip *plinking* in Mom's kitchen sink. "Have you already called someone to fix this?"

"It's on my list." As is *buy more groceries* and *see if Hell had a late frost.*

"I could do it, if you want."

"Do what?"

"Fix your faucet."

I pause in the middle of biting my toast.

Liam looks over at me. "I'm getting the feeling that freaks you out. Why?"

"Um." It's alright. This isn't panic, this is…um. Thinking. "You don't have to fix my plumbing, Liam."

He smiles lazily.

"What?"

"I like it when you talk about your plumbing."

I roll my eyes.

Okay, fine. *Yes.* I secretly like that he likes it.

"I don't mind fixing it, Mollie. It's something I can do." Liam joins me at the kitchen table. "And you won't have to pay me seventy-five bucks an hour for it."

"What *would* I have to pay you?"

"I think you have a good grip on what my services are worth." He sips his coffee.

A little heat creeps into my face, but it isn't anything I can't manage. "I don't think my mother would approve of me paying to fix her kitchen sink with sex."

"I don't know. Daphne was pretty understanding. She was awesome."

I grip my coffee mug. "She was. She was awesome." The best person I've ever known, in fact. "I didn't know you really knew her."

"I'd run into her every now and then. Usually at the

grocery store." He scoops up a fork of scrambled eggs. "She was always smiling. And she'd always ask me about work and my family."

Mom knew Liam's family?

"When I moved back to Pitchette after separating from the Army to go into the Reserve, I ran into Daphne at Sal's." Liam shakes his head. "She paid for my meal, then sat with me at the counter for like forty minutes, just listening to me talk. I'm not even sure I had anything to *say,* really. I just needed someone to listen to me while all these Army stories came spilling out. I love my folks, but I wasn't really in a place to talk to them then about stuff. And she just felt…I don't know. Safe."

My throat closes so suddenly, I almost choke swallowing my toast.

Mom *was* safe. My whole life, she'd been my safety net. When we were poor. When I was scared. When we didn't have anyone to celebrate birthdays with, except each other. She was always there. Always. Just her and me.

I don't even realize I'm crying until Liam kneels next to my chair and pulls me into his chest. He says something I don't hear and strokes my back, which makes me sob like twice as hard. Huge, ugly sobs with lots of snot and wailing and stuff. The works.

Geez, Mom would be so mad at me! She *told* me not to cry over her after she was gone, and I didn't! Not during her funeral, not during her burial. For *months!*

Which is probably why everything is coming out right now. In the middle of her kitchen. All over Liam.

Why, God? GAAAH!

I choke and pull back. I'm okay, really. Everything is fine. I don't need to be clinging to Liam's shirt right now.

"I'm s-sorry," I hiccup.

He tucks my shower-damp hair behind my ear. "For

what, baby?"

"For c-crying."

"Mollie, why are you apologizing for *crying?*"

"My m-mother told me n-not to!" And I've done it *twice* since being back.

His lips shift. I have the feeling he's trying not to smile, but I can't prove it.

He kisses my temple. "I think Daphne would understand."

For Pete's sake. Half of his freaking shirt is soaked and snot-covered. "I'm s-such a m-mess!"

"You're not a mess."

Tears drip down my cheeks. "L-look at your sh-shirt!"

"It's just a shirt."

"It's all w-wet!"

"And it's going to dry." Liam tilts my chin up. "It's okay, Mollie. You can cry. I want you to feel safe enough to cry on me."

For some reason, that makes me stop.

Because *of course* it does. Gah!

Liam kisses my forehead and moves back to his seat.

"I have something to ask you." He picks up his fork. "It's going to sound super high school, though."

I blow my nose into my napkin. "Um. Okay." I mean, he already knows I was a virgin when I graduated. How bad can it be?

"Will you come to my game Wednesday?"

"What game?"

His lips twitch. "We've qualified for the PIAA championships."

"You have?" Heat floods my face. "Oh geez. That's a big deal, right? I mean, I should've known about it—"

"Relax, Maris." His eyes crinkle at the corners. "I know it's not your thing."

But it *should* be, shouldn't it? I mean, I should care about Liam's interests. For Pete's sake, he's the freaking Pitchette High School head coach! And little old Pitchette qualifying for the PIAA championships is *huge.* I mean, even *I* know that.

"You want me to come?" My voice comes out all croaky, and it isn't from crying.

"Yeah." His gaze catches mine. "I want you to come."

The damn dripping faucet fills the silence. Which is loaded with all the things my coming to Liam's game would imply. I mean, folks aren't stupid. Probably everyone knows we're sort of seeing each other. Between getting ice cream at Murray's and Liam's truck spending the night in Mom's driveway, I'm sure the word is already out.

Going to Liam's game will just be backing it up.

In a very real, very public setting.

Am I ready for that?

Butterflies burst in my stomach when I bite my lip. "Okay. I'll come."

Liam smiles lazily and leans toward me, slipping his hand into my hair, tilting my head.

"Just for that, baby. Yes," he whispers in my ear. "You will *definitely* come."

My vagina groans as loudly as I do.

TWENTY-SEVEN

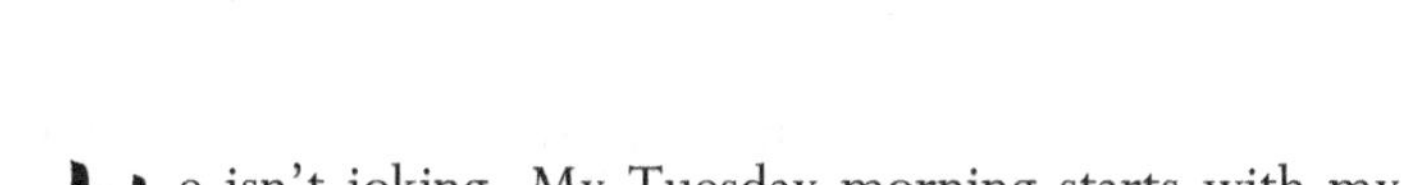

He isn't joking. My Tuesday morning starts with my headboard slamming into the wall and an orgasm that makes my eyes roll back in my head.

By the time I find my way back to this plane of existence, Liam is breathing normally and staring at my pussy.

"Oh crap, what's wrong?" I try sitting up, but my muscles can't coordinate their efforts.

Oh well. I'm naked and in bed with Liam Taggert. There are worse ways to go.

"I think I may have gotten the coordinates for your weapon of mass destruction wrong."

"Um, please don't associate my vagina with volume and ruin. Thanks."

"What did it cost you?"

"What?"

"It's enchanted, right? What did it cost you?" He looks up at me, sweat curling his golden hair, running down his face. "Blood? Immortality? The name of our firstborn?"

I swallow. "Did you just say 'our?'" Did Liam Taggert just say 'our?'

"I hope it's that one. My family likes to name firstborns after ancestors. So we could end up with a Talbot or a Moira."

Uh-oh. "Talbot Taggert or Moira Maris?"

"You want a boy to be named after me and a girl to be named after you?"

"What? Yes. I mean, no! I mean, I haven't thought about it." But now I can't *stop* thinking about it.

Seriously, what is my life right now?

"You look freaked out. Are you freaking out?"

"No," I wheeze.

"It's okay, baby." Liam runs his hands up my legs. "I'm mostly kidding. Just breathe."

I'm trying to but I can't stop worrying about sending Talbot and Moira through the D.C. public school system. There's no way I can afford private tuition for two kids on my marketing salary and Liam is probably going to be deployed any day, being in the Army Reserve. Is there a Starbucks in Kaiserslautern?

I lift my hand to my heart and try to stop it from beating out of my ribcage, à la Looney Tunes. "I think I'm having a heart attack."

"Then let me kiss it and make it better." Liam drops his mouth between my legs.

Which basically restarts the whole headboard-slamming-eyes-rolling-spinning-through-space-and-time cycle.

"Don't go," I mumble when he lifts his head off my sweaty chest a while later.

"I have to." He brushes my hair off my face. "I have a shift."

"After?"

"Ball practice."

"For Pete's sake. I'm already coming second to stupid baseball?"

He laughs and kisses my forehead. "This isn't me choosing baseball over you. This is me making sure I have enough recovery time before I encounter your enchanted honeypot again."

"Hey! That's what I call it, too."

"Because that's what it is, baby. A pot of honey." He presses a kiss to my lips, giving me a taste. "And I'm already hooked."

The high Liam leaves me with carries me through most of the morning. Right up until my phone rings.

"I think I screwed up!" Jess gasps in my ear.

Oh boy. "Where did you leave it and how much bleach do you have?"

"I accidentally sort of maybe told Shack Wheeler that Foundations is having a hard launch for my family fitness programming and he printed that in the *fucking newspaper yesterday!*"

He did? I'll be honest, I'm sort of boycotting the damn *Pitchette Press*. You know, because of the whole fake news thing. Since the whippet story made it in, I've been successfully keeping my head buried in the sand.

And okay, yes. *Also* in Liam Taggert. GAH!

"Babe, why the hell would you say something like that? You *know* what he's like!" I yank open Mom's fridge and grab the iced tea Liam left. Raspberry mint. Mm.

"Because I'm an idiot!" she cries. "He popped up at the chalking event last week asking about the dang community page comments and I panicked and told him that I was finalizing kid-friendly fitness classes and I wanted to sound smart and professional and words just kept coming out of my mouth!"

Well, I totally get that. Happens to me all the time. "Okay. Just breathe."

"Mollz, I didn't even think he was listening! He didn't even seem to care, and I didn't think he'd just go ahead and put it out there! I mean, he didn't even verify any details or plans or *anything!*"

Yeah, because Shack Wheeler doesn't 'verify.' He fills in the blanks himself. "When did you say you were doing this launch event?"

She mumbles something.

"What?"

"Saturday. Omigod, I'm *such an idiot!*"

"Saturday? *This* Saturday?"

"Omigod."

Oh shit. Yeah, that isn't great.

Actually, it's kind of terrible.

And we have to do it. The news is already out there. And with everything that's been happening and all the things folks have said, Jess not following through on this will look bad. REALLY bad. Like Foundations doesn't know what it's doing.

I mean, it's already going to look like that because we have exactly zero information out there about this alleged hard launch. People are going to wonder why we didn't say anything about it during last week's pop-up event. Why we chose just to announce it in the dumb newspaper.

FOR PETE'S SAKE!

I am *so* over this shit. I lived in freaking Washington, D.C. for TWELVE YEARS.

THREE WEEKS in Pitchette and I'm ready to call it quits.

And no offense God, but how the heck am I supposed to be considering my future with Schwartz when I'm too busy running around dousing fires like this?

So much for my beautiful, wonderful, orgasmic morning! Glad to know things still aren't coming together in my life! *Love* that for me.

GAAAAH!

"Mollz? You still there?"

Alright. We can do this. We can figure this out.

Oh boy. Hopefully we can figure this out.

"Text me exactly what the damn paper said about it." I sit at the table with Liam's tea and open my laptop. "I'm going to pull together some visuals and start getting the word out about this. Do a full-on media blitz. I'll send what I have to you, so maybe you can ask your family to help spread the info."

"It's so last minute, Mollz." Jess is flat-out panicking. "I mean, it was one thing to do the chalking event, but something like this? Something more formal? I mean, I haven't even worked out all the programming details—"

"Just focus on a few core concepts." I pull up my web browser, opening tabs for everything I need. "People will understand that you're still developing things."

I *hope* they will understand.

"How are we going to get this done?" Jess asks.

"A lot at a time." Funny. That right there sort of describes my whole return tour to Pitchette. "I'm sitting down right now to make a list of everything we need to do for this. We have four days." Well, like three days and twelve hours. "We can pull this off."

Hopefully.

I have no idea what time it is when Liam walks through the side door in shorts, a t-shirt, and a dusty Coyotes ballcap. Carrying a pizza box from Sal's.

"I thought you had practice?" I ask over the top of my laptop. Damn, the pizza smells AMAZING.

He raises an eyebrow. "I did. At five o'clock."

Oh geez. It's eight? Since *when?*

"Have you been here since I left?" He stares at the mess on the table.

Notebooks, folders, pens, coffee mugs, water glasses, plates with grape stems and cracker crumbs.

"Um." Holy crap, my eyes feel like sandpaper. "Jess accidentally announced a real launch event for the family fitness programming at the studio."

"How?"

"She sort of said something to Shack in passing. And he sort of printed it in the newspaper yesterday for real."

"Why the hell would she do something like that?" Liam demands. "She *knows* what he's like!"

I smile.

"What?" he asks.

"That's exactly what I said to her." Man, are we in sync or what?

Liam sighs and sets the pizza box on the counter. "So you've been sitting here all day, working on launch event stuff?"

"Yep. I—oh damn!" I grip the back of my chair mid-stand as pins and needles cascade down my legs. "Oof. Guess I've been sitting too long."

Liam frowns at me as he pulls down plates from Mom's cabinet. "You need to stop for the night."

"Can't."

"Mollie, your eyes are bloodshot."

Really? Well, that's great. "I need to finish up sending some emails to folks who might be interested in co-sponsoring a last-minute launch."

"No, you need to eat and you need to rest."

"Why?"

Liam shoves a plate of pizza into my hands. "So you have energy later."

So I—

Oh! *OH!*

Oh.

"Geez, you know, I'd really love to," I say. "But I can't tonight."

"What do you mean?" He pauses in the middle of dishing his own slices. "Are you okay? Are you too sore? I can—"

"Not that. I mean, I *am* sore. A little." More than a little, honestly. Not that I really mind. "It's just that I've got a lot of work—"

"Excuse me?" He closes the pizza lid. Slowly.

"Well, you know." I clear my throat. "Because Jess sort of put us on a tight schedule if we want to get everything done—"

"Let me get this straight." He sets his plate on top of the box. "You're telling me you can't have sex with me tonight because you have to *work*."

"Um. Yep. That's...that's what I'm telling you." I mean, it isn't *un*tr—

WHY IS HE WALKING TOWARD ME WITH THAT LOOK ON HIS FACE, GOD?

"What are you doing?" I rasp. Damn it, Legs, wake up! MOVE!

"Just clarifying. You want *this*." He picks up my pen. Holds it in front of my nose. "*Not* this."

He touches the cool metal cap to my lips, trailing it down my chin.

My neck.

My chest.

Across my clavicle. To my shoulder.

He uses the tip to slide down my straps.

"Yep," I croak.

"Okay." His eyes glimmer. "So just to check, you *don't*

want this?"

My planner? What the heck is he doing with my spiralbound planner? Dragging the hard edge up the back of my thigh like that? Why is he—

"*Oh!*" I yelp when he smacks my ass with it. HARD.

"You *don't* want that. Right?"

"No!" I sob as my knees wobble.

"Hm. Okay." He raises his eyebrows. "Or this?"

WHAT IS HE DOING TAKING THAT MINI CLOTHESPIN OF THAT STACK OF PAPERS?

Oh holy crap, why is he pinching it open? Where—

OH MY LORD, HE'S CLAMPING IT TO MY FREAKING NIPPLE!

"*NO!*" I moan. "I *don't!*" I do, I do, I DO!

"Oh. Okay." He unclamps the clip from my shirt and tosses it onto the table with the pen and the planner. "Just checking. You want ice water or tea with the pizza?"

"I want to get all the stuff on my list done tonight so I don't have to worry about it tomorrow because I don't want to miss your game!" For Pete's sake, THERE! I SAID IT!

Liam stares at me. "What?"

"I want to make sure all of this *mess* is out of the way, because I *really* want to not worry about it tomorrow, okay? About any of it! I want to go to your game and cheer the team and just *be* there without this crazy stupid launch hanging over my head. *That's* why we can't do it tonight, because if we do we'll be up forever and I'll be dragging tomorrow and behind on all this planning and I'll be miserable and end up not going. I'm *sorry* we can't have sex tonight!"

"Geezus, Mollie." He traces his knuckles down my cheek. "Don't ever apologize for something like that. You don't need to apologize for not sleeping with me. I want you to be there tomorrow. But even if you weren't coming, I want you to be with me only if *you* want to be." His eyes soften at the corners. "Never because you think *I* want you to be."

"Oh. Right." I bite my lip. "But just to clarify, you *do* want to be with me. Right?"

His lips twitch. "Yeah, baby. I want that. *Very* much."

"Okay. Good to know."

"And I don't need to have sex with you to be with you." He pulls out my chair and pushes back my work debris. "I like just hanging out with you. Talking."

"You do?" Because honestly, I'm sort of all over the place in the communication department. I mean, the last few weeks have *not* been my finest hour.

"Yeah. I do." He retrieves his pizza and sits. "So tell me what I can do to help with work."

Geez, the mini clothespin is right *there*. It came in a pack of fifty from Walmart. Who the heck knew such a tiny little thing could be so intense?

"Maris?"

I mean, and that's even *through* my tank top and bra. What the hell would it be like without wearing anyth—

"Mollie?"

"Hm?"

"How can I help?"

Um. "Out of curiosity, how do you use a ruler?"

Liam glances at the clothespin. Then my face.

He smiles lazily. "Tell me what I can do to help and maybe I'll show you."

TWENTY-EIGHT

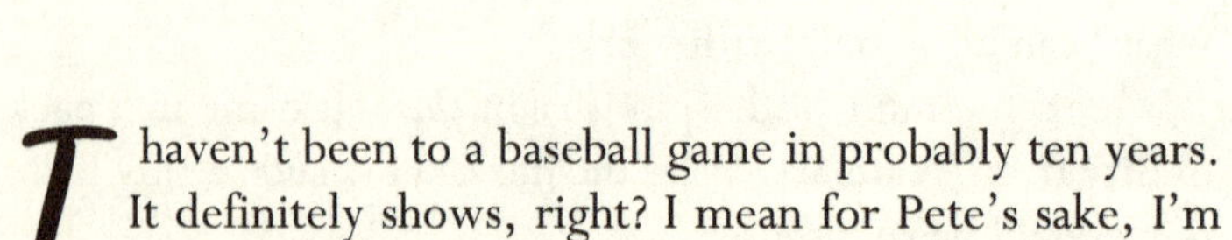

I haven't been to a baseball game in probably ten years. It definitely shows, right? I mean for Pete's sake, I'm not even wearing the right colors! Why did I think I could just wear shorts and a shirt and look like I belong in the bleachers with everyone else? IDIOT!

Although, my clothes probably don't really matter as much as I think they do. The folks from Pitchette are staying far away from me, anyway. Yes, a few of them smiled at me when I first walked up the steps with my corndog. But they haven't engaged beyond that. Not that I blame them, of course. Because, you know. The whole drug abuse allegations thing.

I should be glad they don't have the event officials drug testing me or something.

I sigh and stick to my corndog. Too bad Jess isn't here. She'd sit right next to me and talk the whole time. I didn't ask her to come, of course, because she has classes to hold and a studio to run and I'm a grown-ass woman. I don't need a *buddy* just to go to a ballgame. I'm not *that* pathetic.

Okay, I am. I am that pathetic.

But I don't *want* to be. I want to be someone who doesn't care what people say about her *for real.* Who can go to a sporting event to support the guy she really, really likes. Who can shrug off the gossip and laugh off the stupidity and just *enjoy* being back in Pitchette. With Jess and Liam. I mean, I can do that. I'm *capable* of doing that.

And despite the number of times I roll my eyes at what passes for life in Pitchette, there are parts of it that really *are* special. Like right now. All these people here, taking time out of a weekday to drive an hour out of town just to watch the high school baseball team play. These people *love* these boys. This team. Liam. They show it every time the Coyotes get a runner on base. Every time Baxley makes an out at first. Every time the kid on the mound strikes out the opposing team.

This is the Pitchette Mom tried raising me in.

Thirty-three years of trying, and I still feel like I'm on the outside looking in.

Right now, the only thing that makes it bearable is the six-foot-three firefighter standing next to the dugout, arms crossed, talking to his catcher.

Glancing up at me every inning, making sure I'm still here.

I am. I am still here.

I'm here when the shortstop has a bad collision at second and needs to be helped off the field.

When the game goes into extra innings.

When Pitchette ends up losing.

When the crowd still stands at the end of the game, applauding both teams, hollering for all the players.

I wait for the families to filter down from the bleachers before I grab my purse and empty corndog plate and follow. Liam is talking to the team in the dugout, so I scoot behind everyone waiting to see the kids and head for the bathroom. There isn't much of a line, thankfully. My bladder isn't happy about the iced coffee I downed earlier.

I come out of the bathroom, cut around the back of the building, and groan when Shack Wheeler comes around the corner, toting a camera. A woman is with him. Probably his wife.

Except. Hm. It's been a few years since I've seen her, but I could swear his wife is shorter than he is. That woman is definitely taller. I mean, not even counting her shoes. Maybe she's a relative. Or a friend. Could be a friend. It's sort of hard to imagine Shack with friends, but—

Oh, *hello! That* is definitely not a friend thing.

I mean. *Yes,* Liam and I have done…similar things. And yes, I'd call us friends.

Which tells us everything we need to know about Shack and his lady companion, doesn't it? *Doesn't it?* Wonder if that's the person who called him when he made me stand outside the office? Or is that a different wo—

Oh *crap,* he sees me watching him! Oh crap oh crap oh crap—

"Mollie!" he hollers.

SHIT!

Actually…no. *Not* shit. Why should *I* be embarrassed? *I* didn't do anything! PER USUAL!

I turn around when he hustles up to me, red-faced and out of breath.

"What the hell do you want, Shack?" Because I don't have a damn thing more to give him.

"I think you may have gotten the wrong impression just now."

"I doubt it. Pretty hard to misinterpret a woman sticking her hand down your pants."

"Shh!" The sonovabitch flushes as his eyes dart toward the

crowd near the dugout.

"Oh, sorry." I raise my voice. "Is that a secret? I'd hate for folks to misun—"

"Alright! Keep your voice down!" He passes a meaty hand over his face, wiping away the sweat. "I can see how this might become…difficult to contain."

What the hell does that mean?

He looks me in the eye. "So what can I do?"

"Do?"

"To make sure this doesn't go any farther."

I don't—

Wait a minute.

Holy crap.

Shack Wheeler thinks I'm going to blackmail him.

Ha!

What?

Okay, okay. Be cool, be cool. *He* doesn't know I really don't give a damn who he fucks. Right now, he's just desperate and confused and *super* guilty.

He'll do whatever I ask, probably. If he thinks I'll never, ever tell anyone about what I saw.

I smile. Evilly.

The color drains from his face.

Then it slowly returns. "I'll run it in the Saturday edition."

Hell yes, he will. "I'm sorry. What will you run?" I need to hear him say it.

"A full retraction." He nods, resigned to the inevitable. "I'll take it back. All of it. The alleged overdosing and the whippets and the naloxone. It was just a misunderstanding."

The hell it was. He knows the whippet thing is false, too, doesn't he? And the jagoff wrote about it, anyway. Because it's freaking *drama.*

Funny how he doesn't like drama when it involves *his* life.

"I'd be happy to provide you with some quotes clearing up any misinformation." I sling my purse over my shoulder. "Later. Right now, I'm meeting someone."

Shack dissolves from my attention as the crowd thickens, the ball players coming out of the dugout to see their families and friends. It's really sweet how many folks turned out for this, honestly. It *is* a big deal that little old Pitchette made it this far.

Although, I'm not that surprised. Not with Mr. July leading the team.

"Hey, Maris."

I turn around and he's right there, watching me with his beautiful eyes.

And yes, looking fine as *hell* in his ballcap and coaching uniform.

"Hey, Coach." I nod toward the field. "Good job out there. I mean, you know. Even though you lost."

He smiles lazily.

"What?" I check my shirt. Nope. No mustard.

"I like it when you call me 'Coach.'" He traces his fingertip down my nose. "It's hot."

"For Pete's sake, not *here!*"

"Yeah, you're right. Probably should set a good example."

"Exactly." DAMN IT.

His eyes cut over my shoulder and he frowns. "Was Shack talking to you?"

"Oh. Um. Yeah. But don't worry, it wasn't anything bad."

His eyebrows bunch. "What was it?"

Um. "A surprise." Hopefully a good one.

"Mollie—"

"Really, Liam. It's alright."

He studies me. "Really?"

I smile. "Yes. So, you're going back on the bus, right?"

"Yeah. My truck is parked at the school."

"Makes sense. Um. Are you guys celebrating or anything?"

He shakes his head. "Some of the parents bought hoagies for the ride back, so the kids will eat. A few are just going home with their folks now."

"Uh-huh." I clear my throat. "Does that mean you're not coming over tonight?"

"Actually. I was thinking about that."

"You were?" It was last night, right? That's what did it? He's worried if he comes over tonight, I'll ask him to schedule more social media posts while I check in with the folks Jess thinks might help sponsor the launch. "Oh sure. It makes sense, I don't—"

"Have dinner at my place tonight."

I—what?

I mean. What?

Liam's place? I mean, I know where he lives. Obviously. It's Pitchette. I know where almost everyone lives.

I just...I don't know. Never really thought I'd get to see his house. His *home.* I guess it makes sense, though, right? That I'd eventually spend the night at his place instead of him crashing at mine. For Pete's sake, it isn't even *mine.* It's Mom's.

And let's be honest, Mom. You've been watching us, right? I mean, not to be creepy or anything. *I'd* be watching us. This is Liam Freaking Taggert we're talking about! So probably time to take the party elsewhere, huh?

Like to Liam's.

Okay, so *that's* sending butterflies all through me.

I grip the hem of his shirt. Mostly because if I don't, I'm probably going to collapse. "Yeah. Your place."

He breaks into a grin.

Then he kisses me. Completely oblivious to the team and half of Pitchette gawking at us behind his back.

"See you at home," he whispers in my ear.

Home.

I'm not going to lie. My knees actually wobble when he saunters off, giving me a great view of his ass and a wink over his shoulder.

TWENTY-NINE

Liam's property used to be a farm, judging by the ancient barn foundation still partially buried across the yard. The garage looks a lot newer than the house, with a single car bay and what looks like an upstairs storage loft. Liam's truck is parked outside, so I pull up next to it in the gravel. My Honda fits right next to his charcoal gray F-150. Not that that means anything, of course.

Alright, God. Let's not freak out, okay? I'm here for *dinner*. Because Liam *invited me*. That's all. No need to get all weird about it, right?

Right.

I grab my purse and get out, locking my car as I cross his trimmed yard. Okay, yes. I don't really need to lock my car. Liam's closest neighbor is three miles down the road and this is Pitchette, so his neighbor probably takes personal property rights very seriously. And it's not like the road gets a lot of traffic. It's just that my city habits are super ingrained. They aren't going to die just because I happen to sort of be in a relationship with a hometown hero. I mean, I have to stay in practice, right? Just in case I decide to go back to Schwartz.

Because that's still on the table.

Although, the table feels like it's getting a lot smaller these days. Especially if Shack really does print that retraction.

Not that I'm holding my breath.

I climb the steps of Liam's wrap-around porch and pause, leaning against the porch railing to look over the field. The house sits roughly in the middle of what I estimate to be about twenty acres of rolling land, surrounded by woods on three sides and the road at the bottom of the property. The barn foundation sits back off the road about sixty yards. It was probably built before the road was put in. Liam has two sets of raised beds behind the garage, probably filled with vegetables. And it looks like over there against the tree line are fruit trees and berry bushes. A bird of prey screams above. A hawk, circling the field, clearly zeroing in on its next meal. My breath catches as it cries and dives, snatching up a little squirming animal with a precision humans can't possibly achieve.

Footsteps thump against the wooden planks of the porch and stop just behind me.

"This place is beautiful," I say without turning around.

"It is." Liam folds his arms and leans against the porch post next to me. He's showered and changed into a white t-shirt and a pair of worn jeans. "It's nice to come here after getting off a shift. At the station or at Jerry's."

"I bet." I mean, *I* wouldn't mind coming here at the end of the day. Not because I have a high-pressure life or anything. Just because it feels so peaceful.

And okay fine, *yes. Also* because the hottest guy in Pitchette happens to live here.

"Why are you smiling?" There's a hint of humor in his voice.

I shrug, meeting his eyes. "Just looking forward to

dinner."

"Uh-huh." He doesn't believe me, clearly. "I have steaks marinating. I've been trying to recreate the flavors of this machboos dish I loved when I was stationed in Kuwait. I haven't quite gotten it yet. Mostly because I haven't found a place to get dried black limes."

Um. Liam Taggert likes to tinker with recipes? And has a taste for international food?

Okay. We're still in Pitchette, right?

"Delicious." I mean it, too. And not just about the steaks. I'm not typically a steak person, but I'd eat cardboard if I got to watch Liam cook it for me.

He pushes off the post. "Would you like a tour of the house before I gas up the grill?"

"Gas!" I dig my phone out of my purse. "Holy crap, I totally forgot to get gas on the way back from the game. I *knew* I was going to forget!" Idiot!

Liam peers down at my phone. "Are you texting yourself a note to get gas?"

"It's my system." Maybe it doesn't make a lot of sense, but it works. I usually ignore alarms and I lose sticky notes, but an unopened text message from myself can't be ignored. For whatever reason. "I know it's weird."

Liam's mouth twitches. "If it works, it works."

He takes me into the house through the back door. The circular porch lets me see most of the outside and the property at the back, including a small outdoor covered patio with a poured cement floor and a stone firepit. Everything's so simple. Almost elegant. Way different than Mom's house of juxtaposed patterns and pieces.

I slip my sandals off when I get inside. Liam doesn't ask me to, but I want to. There's something strangely intimate about walking through his home barefoot. I mean, I do it all the time in Mom's place, but here? On Liam's hardwood? I don't know. It feels personal. And I like that.

He leads me to the kitchen where he pulls out two beers from the fridge. We sip them as we walk through the house, exploring each room.

"Geez." I stare as he shows me a massive living space outfitted with floor to ceiling bookcases and brown leather furniture. "Liam, this place is *huge*."

"It's an old farmhouse. A lot of them are surprisingly big. Families had more kids back then, which was good when it came to needing extra hands to help with harvests or livestock. The earliest deed we found on this property was dated 1809." A smile tugs at his mouth when he looks at me. "So back in the day, this place was probably packed to the rafters with kids."

My smartass comes out. "But you're the only kid who lives here now, right?"

"Yeah. For now."

Damn. Okay. That's a loaded answer. I *definitely* hear the implication. He didn't end that sentence with a period, he left it *dot dot dot*. As in, he's open to *sharing* this place with someone. Like kids. Or, I don't know. ME.

Okay, I'm getting ahead of things. This is just a visit. Liam is just showing me where he sleeps on the nights he doesn't sleep next to me. That's all.

"How long have you lived here?" Really? *That's* what I want to know? Not the size of his mattress or what books are on his shelves or where he keeps his coffee or does he hang or fold his shirts?

"I bought the property off my uncle about four years ago, but I've been living here for six. My aunt and uncle lived here until they got divorced. That was about nine years ago, so the place was vacant for a while." He points at some spots around the living room. "I renovated a few areas. Knocked out that wall to join these two front rooms. Added a half bath down here because I wasn't crazy about visitors walking around upstairs just to use the bathroom."

He likes his space. Makes sense. I like my space, too.

"You, um, did all the renovations yourself?" Not that I'm picturing Liam sweaty and shirtless with a tool belt hanging off his hips or anything.

"My brothers helped with a lot of it." Liam's mouth tilts up in a partial smile. "Simon is a contractor and Drew likes to butt in."

Simon and Drew. Right. They're several years older than me, so I only really know them by reputation.

"Is that a freaking *fig tree* over there?" Wait a minute. This place is covered in plants! Floppy plants, spiky plants, plants in pots and jars and good grief, is that a coffee mug? "Geez, Liam. Are you a botanist or something?" Do I find that hot?

Liam laughs. "No. Just really bad at walking through the garden section at stores." He lovingly strokes the spider plant that I swear to goodness is *leaning* toward him like he's the freaking sun.

Oh. My. LORD!

I need to get out of this plant infested room before my panties melt right off.

The kitchen seems like a safe bet. All cool granite countertops and sleek cabinets and a wide farmhouse sink and FOR PETE'S SAKE, IS THAT AN AFRICAN VIOLET ON THE FLIPPING WINDOWSILL?

Okay, I need to get it together. Liam already knows about my dumb snake kink. He can*not* know I'm getting all hot over the idea of him being a plant dad. I mean, they're *plants.* Keeping a plant alive isn't like keeping a dog or a cat or a kid alive. Plants don't experience emotional turmoil or puberty or bullying or stuff like that. They just sort of exist. Quietly.

A person basically just has to water them. And, you know. Pay attention to them. Be aware to their needs. Adjust their sunlight and soil.

My mouth goes dry.

Geez! What the heck is wrong with me? Do I have freaking jungle fever or something?

I lean my ass against his kitchen island, crossing my arms over my chest. Liam stands, hands in his pockets. Watching me closely.

"What?"

He glances around. "What do you think?"

He wants to know what I think of his home? That's sort of sweet.

And sort of terrifying.

Warmth spreads through my chest. Don't bring up the plants. DO NOT BRING UP THE PLANTS. "I didn't realize the Fortress of Solitude had so many houseplants." DAMN IT!

"My mom gave me a couple when I first got out of the Army. She said they're good for boosting mental health, but I think she just really wanted to get rid of some of hers. And she knew I wouldn't just let them die, so...." He shrugs sheepishly, running his hand down the back of his neck. "It turns out I have sort of a green thumb."

"'Green' isn't how I'd describe your thumb."

"Oh yeah?" He raises an eyebrow. "How *would* you describe it?"

Intuitive. Talented. Thick. Surprisingly informed regarding female anatomy. "Average."

He smiles lazily. "Such a liar."

I am. I am such a liar. "Why don't you have a pet?" Not that he needs to have one. It just seems like someone who has their life together *would* have one.

Liam shrugs. "I'm gone too often to give a dog proper

attention and I'm allergic to cats."

Interesting. "What if I had a cat?"

"I'd take medicine."

What is that word for the condition where a person gets swoony and anxious? Because I have that. Right now. "You'd commit to a lifestyle change? Just like that?"

"Of course."

'Of course?' What the heck does he mean, 'of course?' How can he commit to changing his *life* like he doesn't have to think twice about it?

Liam's eyes soften. "Don't panic, Mollie. Please."

"Not panicking," I rasp.

"Hey. Look at me, baby."

I'm trying to, honest, but my sight is mostly black spots right now. Which is silly because I don't even *have* a cat and this is all HYPOTHETICAL NONSENSE.

"I don't want you to be worried. I don't want you to feel scared."

"Scared of what?" I pant.

"The next step. What happens now." He plants his hands on the island, trapping me between his arms. "We have the whole future."

"Right. Um." Holy crap! Okay. That means something BIG, right? "What exactly does that mean? You know, um, in your own words?"

"It means I don't want to rush any of it. I don't want to *waste* any of it." He tips my chin back with his knuckle, peering into my eyes. "I want to experience every moment with you, Mollie Maris. The good, the bad, and the nuts."

"Are you sure?" Because there's definitely going to be emphasis on the 'nuts' part. I can't help it, okay? I know who I am. Who I am usually sends people running *away* from me, not toward me! "Why?"

"Because, Maris." His eyes don't waver. "I love you."

Those words. They settle heavily in my chest. Right in the middle, where I have a heart. Supposedly.

If I have a heart, why can't I say the words back to him? Why can't I tell him what I'm feeling, what I want him to know? Why am I melting and drowning at the same time, both desperate for and afraid of him? Of his attention and touch and devotion?

Okay, I'm panicking *for real* this time. I'm flat out freaking because he's looking at me with his beautiful eyes and my heart is somersaulting in my chest and I *want* it to calm down but I don't know how to MAKE IT CALM DOWN!

I lurch up and bury my tongue in his mouth. He moans around me and the sound makes my nipples tighten.

Okay, *yes.* It started out as a panic kiss.

But now it's getting *super* hot and interesting and *oh!*

Holy crap, I'm flat on my back across Liam Taggert's KITCHEN ISLAND!

"Mollie," he rasps when our mouths break apart.

"Shh." I know we should talk, but I can't right now on account of I'm trying to get out of my shorts. Damn it! Should've worn a skirt.

He starts to say something. Something *serious.*

So I do the only reasonable thing I can do; whip off my shirt and tug down my bra to show him my boobs.

His Adam's apple bobs. "Please, Maris. We need to talk."

"We do?" I run my hands over my breasts. Pinching my nipples. *Playing* for him. Hm, does he have any mini cloth—

"You won't distract me." His voice thickens. "I'm not going to cave on this."

"You're not?" Okay, I'll be honest. That's going to be a problem for me. *I'm* turned on. So if he isn't going to help me out here, I'll have to—

He groans and cups my breasts. "I know what you're

doing."

FINALLY! "You?"

"Not that. You're—"

He sucks in air when I pluck open the button on his jeans and slide my hand inside his briefs. I think he may have said something else, but I'm too busy stroking his cock and getting him distracted and okay maybe not just distracting *him* because *holy crap* I need him inside me. RIGHT NOW.

"Help me," I grunt, pulling back my hand to struggle with my shorts.

Liam has them off in seconds flat. And my underwear. And my bra, because let's be honest, it definitely isn't supporting anything right now.

"This isn't what I expected to happen," he pants when I pull his shirt over his head and fling it away.

"It isn't?" Because we've been doing this *a lot* lately.

"Not like this." He bites my neck. "In my kitchen."

"Then where?"

"Don't know. Couch. Or bed. Or truck."

I have a few alternative ideas, too. Involving me on my knees or bent over the counter or across Liam's lap or pushed against a wall. "We can—"

"No. This is good. This works." He thumbs my clitoris, driving a thick finger inside me. "I like this."

I gasp and tilt my pelvis into the pressure, already panting, already widening for him. "I like this, too." Really? I can say *that* but I can't tell the man I like *him?* That I lo—

"*GAH!*" I cry out when he adds a second finger. "*LIAM!*"

"Right here, baby," he groans against my lips, cupping my neck with his free hand, sinking deeper with the other. Swirling his big green thumb around and around and *oh holy crap YEEEES!*

He's going to realize I'm not worth it. That this whole

fling between us is just an isolated bubble of happiness. That I don't fit Pitchette and Pitchette doesn't fit me, so we'll never fit, either.

But right *now* we fit. So damn well. And when he replaces his fingers with his cock and plants himself in one single, blunt thrust, when I curl off the smooth countertop and lock my legs around his waist, digging my heels into his ass as he plunges into me over and over, gripping my hips, sucking my neck, I push the future away.

I push it so far away that I completely lose sight of it when he pulls me off the island and turns me around, bending me over the counter *exactly* like I want. When my fingernails scrape the pretty granite desperately. When we finally stumble out of the kitchen and through the house. When we collapse on the stairs. When we eventually, miraculously somehow find his room.

I refuse to give the future any space in my head until it barrels back to me in Liam's bed, when he's seated the deepest anyone has ever been inside me, cradling my head in his hands, crying out the words that started this sequence to begin with.

And as we come, so does It. The Unknown. The Unknowable.

Lots of elements in my life are unclear right now, but the only one that scares the shit out of me is the man rolling onto his back, bringing me with him, tucking my head under his chin as his heartbeat booms in my ear. I can handle myself. I always have. Even though I don't know what my future holds, I know I'll find a way to make it work. I'm Mollie Maris and I always make it out okay.

But *this.* I don't know if I can make it out of *this* okay. I don't know if I can find a way to make this work.

And worse than that, I don't know how to tell Liam.

THIRTY

Mom always told me if you're in a relationship with a man who pressures you to say 'I love you' before you're ready, it's a giant red flag.

Which makes it worse that Liam *doesn't* pressure me to return the words. He lets them lay between us, like a gift given out of the blue with no expectations of returned favor. He *wants* to say them again. I can tell by the way he drops a lingering kiss on my lips the next morning before he pulls out of me and rolls out of bed for his shift.

"Dinner at your place or mine tonight?" he asks.

Yeah, we never actually made it to dinner last night, did we? "Um. My place. I can cook." If I can get my head straightened out by then. And can remember how to walk.

He glances down at me, and I see them there. The words. Teetering on his lips, pooling in his eyes. But he must know that I'll bolt if I hear them again, so he kisses my forehead and leaves the words behind in the bedroom. With me. Naked and raw and still spinning.

It's pathetic how badly I want to call him back to bed. To selfishly beg him to blow off the day and stay with me. But how fair is it to request that when I can't even tell him how I feel? It isn't fair. At all. If I can't say the words, how can I ask the question? I mean, I've *shown* him my feelings. I've been showing him my feelings for a while.

But that isn't the same as saying the words out loud. Liam deserves to hear them. From me, specifically.

And please, *please,* God, help me find the courage to say them. Because even the thought of him hearing them from another woman has me looking for the nearest sharpest object, ready to cut a bitch.

Jealous fits of rage are *so* not my thing. Not because I'm highly evolved or self-assured or anything honorable like that. Mostly because I'm just lazy.

And because I've never really been in love with a guy before.

THERE. I said it. Or, you know. THOUGHT IT.

Okay, so I haven't said it to Liam's face like I should have. But come on! I'm working on it. *Hard.* Because everyone needs to be told they're loved, even if they aren't used to hearing the words. Even if they're scary to say. Why am I afraid? This is *Liam.* He isn't going anywhere, right? Pitchette is his whole life! And he's already told *me* how he feels, so it's not like I have anything to lose.

This connection between us gets bigger every day.

That's scary, but also true.

This is the big time. The real deal.

And I'm all too capable of screwing up the real deal. I mean, I detonated my whole career just because I wasn't feeling it anymore. I still have one foot in the door only because Darrin Schwartz himself stopped it right before it slammed shut.

I bolted from D.C. just like I bolted from Pitchette after graduating.

Just like I bolted from Philly after Penn.

Oh good lord. Holy crap. I *am* a runner. Just not the healthy kind, like Jess. The *un*healthy kind, like Julia Roberts in that one movie with Richard Gere.

Julia Roberts changes in the end, right? I mean, she doesn't spend her whole life hopping from one failed relationship to another, does she? For Pete's sake, that movie came out in the 1990s! Happy endings existed back then. The script writers wouldn't tank the happily-ever-after for the sake of art or realism or whatever. *Right?*

I mean…there's hope for me, too, isn't there? I can learn to settle down. To call Pitchette home. I can!

What if I can't?

I sit up in Liam's bed and reach for the medium-sized potted plant on his dresser. A peace lily, according to the tag wedged into the soil. The white blooms sprouting up from among the rich green leaves are simple. Elegant. Understated. Deceptively shaped like tongues of fire.

Liam has a tongue of fire. Liam has an *everything* of fire. That's part of the problem. I want to be mature enough to have the feelings talk with him, but it's hard to think about that when I'm crawling out of his bed and into his shower. Swapping my scent for his delicious tea tree body wash. Wrapping my wet hair in his fluffy blue towel.

His life is just so *clear*. He's settled. He has things figured out. That's so evident when I walk through his home in yesterday's clothes, my hair damp and a mug of coffee that he brewed before he left clutched in my hand. Everything in his house breathes masculine balance. His walls are shades of brown and green. His furniture is simple and comfortable. His bookcases are organized. His kitchen faucet doesn't drip. His fridge has milk and eggs and his cabinet has three types of heart-healthy cereal. And we all know the houseplant situation. I mean, between the two of us *he's* the old maid and *I'm* the bachelor. For Pete's sake, I've been living out of cardboard boxes for close to a month.

How the heck is this supposed to work between us?

Ringing. I hear ringing. It's definitely my cellphone. Where the heck did I leave it? I'll be honest, I sort of lost track of everything last night after Orgasm Number 3.

Yep, there it is. Under the couch, for some reason. Geez, if my phone is under Liam's furniture, where the heck is my purse?

I crouch and hold my coffee aloft while I stretch for the phone. The name flashing on the screen makes my stomach plummet.

Darrin Schwartz.

Shit.

It's a sign, right? I start considering alternative futures and my past comes hurtling back.

You know what? No. Not right now. I'm not going to take a call from Darrin in Liam's house. I don't need to disrupt the peacefulness he has here with my inner turmoil.

Besides. His plants would probably tattle on me. And I definitely don't want him hearing that I'm maybe probably going back to D.C. from his freaking aloe vera.

I have to get out of here. Before I go entirely bonkers and start accusing Liam's plant babies of assassination plots or something.

The man *said* he's ready to handle my nuttiness, but he really probably isn't. *I'm* not, most of the time.

Darrin's call goes to voicemail. Great. I'll have to listen to that later.

Right now, I have to get home and change before I meet up with Jess. I'm probably already late. I don't want to have to explain the whole sleeping-at-Liam's-place thing to her. Not until I've processed it myself.

I find most of the junk I came with, shove everything back

into my purse, and leave through the back door. Liam didn't say anything about locking up, so he must leave his house unlocked most of the time. Or he has an electronic system he can use remotely. Probably that. I mean, Liam's chill but he isn't stupid. He probably makes sure his plants are tucked in safe and sound when he isn't here.

Okay, I meant for that to be snarky. But it's sort of adorable.

I unlock my car and check my phone. Seven o'clock! Geez. Barely enough time to get home and get ready to meet Jess at seven-thirty. And damn it! Gas. I forgot I need gas. I probably have en—is that a pastry bag on my dash?

I pull open the door and reach for the bag.

Holy crap. A donut. A plump, chocolate covered, cream-filled donut.

Keep your socks on today, baby.

I stare at the words on the bag. Scrawled through the center of a big heart drawn in marker.

Liam got me a donut.

A *cream filled* donut. Which is like the sexiest donut there is. Second only to the long john, for obvious reasons.

When the heck did he even have time to run out and get a donut? He spent the whole night making me come! And most of the morning. Wait, is that what he was doing when I woke up this morning? I thought he just took a shower and went downstairs, but maybe I fell asleep between rounds? Maybe he was gone longer than that? Come to think of it, he *did* have clothes on that last time. I remember the zipper of his jeans digging into my ass.

That would explain why I had to coax him to get back into bed. He must've been about ready to leave for his shift and I sort of distracted him.

But wait. Why did he come back upstairs? Is that why my

keys were on his nightstand? I had to unlock my car just now, which means he locked it after putting the donut on the dash. If he went out early to get me a donut, does that mean....

I get in and start the car.

Oh geez. He filled my tank. Fourteen gallons of unleaded love.

My eyes prick.

Before I can stop them, tears drop down my cheeks.

I don't deserve Liam Taggert.

Even as I savor my donut and drive past the gas station, I know I don't deserve him. Mr. July puts everyone before himself.

And I usually put myself before everyone.

"Omigod, *there* you are!" Jess cries when I walk into Foundations. "Babe, I was starting to think you ditched me."

"Of course not." I'm not at all feeling pressured to get away from Pitchette. Not at all. "What's, um. What's on the agenda this morning?"

Because whatever it is, it looks important. Jess has stuff *everywhere.* The front desk. The floor. The walls. It's a good thing she closed the studio today, because anyone who walked in on this mess would turn right around and walk out.

"I've lined up food for our launch Saturday, so we can cross that off the list. Oh, can we do a sort of sponsorship post for Mertz Farms? That's who's providing the fresh snacks and since they're local, I thought it would be good to splash them up on social media. You know, show that we're collaborating with other area businesses. Here." Jess digs through a pile of papers on the counter. "I have their farm flyer somewhere and you can pull info off of that, if you want. Also, I talked to—"

"Babe! Take a breath!" I need to take a few, myself.

Jess skips her breaths and dives for a pen. “Sorry, my brain’s been on fire since like five o’clock. I woke up with all these ideas for the launch and I wanted to get them out before I forgot everything. Here’s my list.”

Oh boy. That isn’t a list. That’s a military operation plan. “We need to get all of this done today and tomorrow?”

“That’s my plan.” Jess scoops her short hair up into a really messy bun.

“Jess, we’re going to need help with this.” A LOT of help. We’re capable, not superhuman.

“I know. My sisters are going to be coming by to grab the yard signs and run them around to the folks who agreed to let us plant them in their yards.”

“Okay, that’s one thing off the list. What’s this thing that says ‘Dec—Fri eve’?”

“Two of the moms who are coming to the launch event volunteered to decorate.”

“Decorate what? You’re launching a fitness program, not an events venue.”

“So they had this idea about the Wall of Winners,” she says, dragging a storage box into the family fitness room. “They think people might want to have a place to take photos. Sort of like one of those photo booth things at weddings and baby showers and stuff.”

What? What’s happening? “Is that something *you* want? Because it sounds like the Gym Girlies talking, babe.” Which is *not* okay. Jess is in charge here, not that damn community group.

“I mean, it’s not a *terrible* idea.” She emerges from the fitness room with a wrinkled forehead. “I don’t know, Mollz. I didn’t even think that folks might want something like that at this thing. What do you think?”

“I think you shouldn’t be trying so hard to please other

people, Jess. All this?" I fling my arm around the room. "All this isn't you. I mean, come on! Freaking *streamers?* Are you kidding me? And *please* tell me 'balloon arch' is the name of a new yoga pose you're going to have the kids try."

"Omigod." She stares around the studio, like she's seeing the mess for the first time. "You're right, aren't you?" Her shoulders sag. "This isn't...*none* of this was what I...this isn't what Foundations is about. What the hell am I even *doing* right now?"

I've been asking myself the same thing since last night.

Can't worry about my thing now. Jess' thing has an actual deadline, and this situation with Liam...well, the man has a house full of *plants.* That means he's pretty patient, right? Yeah. He's patient.

I mean, not counting that one time he threw me over his shoulder to carry me up a hill because I was taking too long.

Hm.

"Mollz?"

"Sorry. Right. You." I shake my head. "Okay, give me that mega list and let's re-evaluate."

Jess chews her lip. "Re-evaluate?"

"Yep." There's the list. "I'm going to say the things on here and you're going to just answer 'yes' or 'no,' straight up gut reactions. Got it?"

"Okay." She doesn't sound like she means it.

"Hey!" I clap loud enough to make her jump. "I need Jess Johnson right now! I need Badass Jess! I need that girl who wants to open a freaking fitness center in the middle of freaking Pitchette because she wants to serve her community! Any idea where she is?"

"Here."

"Pardon? What was that? I had a hard time hearing you over the giant lack of enthusiasm."

Jess rolls her eyes. "Omg, you're a pain in the ass."

"One of us has to be if we want to make this thing work." I settle onto a yoga ball.

"You okay?" Jess raises her eyebrows. "Why are you moving like you're sore?"

Because Liam Taggert is working me harder than I've ever been worked in my *life*. Seriously. He's given me more orgasms in the last three weeks than I've had in the last three years. "No reason."

She grins.

"What?"

"You're getting it good, aren't you?"

Heat races into my cheeks. "I'm crossing off 'balloon arch.' We definitely don't need one."

"For the record, I did *not* see Liam coming," she says, ignoring me. "But I guess that's something you're seeing all the time now, huh?"

Oh for— "Can we please focus? You're seriously not setting up an ice cream bar, right? Because that totally defeats the whole healthy-lifestyle message we're trying to send."

"Did he come over last night?"

"No."

"Liar!"

"I'm not lying!"

"You are, because you're *definitely* moving like you spent the night—" She gasps. "Mollie Maris! *You* went to *his* place! Didn't you? *Didn't* you?"

Geez! "So?"

Her eyes widen and she covers her mouth. "Oh my goodness! He must be *really* serious about you, babe."

"What? Why do you say that?" Great! Focus completely shattered! We are never getting through this list.

"Liam Taggert doesn't bring anyone home, Mollie! I'm not just talking about women. I'm talking about *anyone*." She shakes her head, a smug smile on her face. "I mean, the man is as close to a hermit as you can get without actually living in a cave. He likes his privacy and he likes his space. So if he opened up his cave to *you*...."

My pulse thunders. "What?"

She shrugs. "Well, I'd say you've been claimed."

"*'Claimed?'* I'm not a freaking piece of luggage, Jessica! I can*not* be 'claimed.'" Even if that's *exactly* how it feels when Liam's inside me.

When he kisses me.

When he buys me donuts and fills my car.

Oh shit. He's claimed me. Not like 'claimed' in a sexual way. Although he's for sure done that. 'Claimed' as in spiritually. *Emotionally.* As in we're partners. For real.

When the hell did that happen? And where the hell was *I* when it did? I'm supposed to pay attention to stuff like that!

"Whoa, babe. Are you okay?" Jess peers at me. "You just got super pale."

"I'm fine." I am. I am fine. Nothing wrong whatsoever. "Let's, um. We need to adjust this to-do list."

So Liam is serious about me. I already knew that. I knew that last night, when he told me he loves me. And I mean, I'm serious about him, too, so....

Jess isn't saying anything I don't already know. I don't have any real reason to be freaking out. None whatsoever.

That's the problem, though, isn't it? I don't need a reason to freak out.

I mean, we all know I'm totally capable of freaking out over nothing.

THIRTY-ONE

Considering we had zero intention of hosting a family fitness program launch before Monday, we're doing pretty damn good on the event-planning front. I mean, after I cut down on the crazy stuff Jess has on her to-do list. Sure, a bounce house would be AWESOME. But Foundations doesn't have the money for that. Also, we don't have a permit from the borough to inflate one on Man Street.

"Next time," I tell Jess.

She blows out a big breath. "I'm glad you're here, babe. Honestly, I wouldn't be pulling this off without you.

"Yeah, you would." It's true. She would.

Because Jess Johnson is a freaking badass who pulls off damn near anything she gets involved with.

"It's a good thing Hail Mary plays seem to be our thing." She looks at me over the top of her computer. "You're good at this, you know."

"Moral support?"

"Event promotion and marketing."

I laugh. "Well, *that's* good. Considering that's basically what the last twelve years of my life has been about."

"And you definitely don't want to keep doing this?"

"I don't know. I *thought* I didn't." I sigh. "But with Darrin's offer on the table about returning to Schwartz. . . ."

"It's hard to walk away?"

"Yeah. I mean, it's a good job, Jess. With decent benefits. I'd be nuts to walk away for real, right?"

"Well, self-employed Jess who doesn't have a 401(k) and pays out-of-pocket for healthcare is inclined to say yes, you're nuts." She smiles. "But self-employed Jess who loves what she does and wouldn't trade it for the most secure job in the world says screw it. Be nuts. Be whatever you need to be to be the most authentic version of *you*."

Um. Riiiiight. "I think your yoga meditations are making you a little hippie-dippie."

She chuckles. "Actually, I read that on a piece of wall art from T.J. Maxx. But I stand by it! If that job in D.C. doesn't make you sing, it's not worth it. Life is short and everyone is dying, so make the most of the minutes you have."

Yeah. *That* sounds more like the Jess I love.

"Are you opening the studio tomorrow?" I ask when we finally get more than half of the items on our event list done.

"Yes." She stretches behind the front desk, rolling out her neck. "I hated to close it today, to be honest, so I offered the folks who missed their classes a chance to join anything they want to Friday."

I frown. "Geez, babe. Don't wear yourself out. I need you bushy-tailed on Saturday."

"Trust me, I know. I'm hoping my sharp, new, professional Foundations polo will distract folks from the circles under my eyes."

I grab a pen and find my clipboard for Saturday. "I'm adding 'concealer' to the list of stuff I need to bring."

"Good thinking."

I start cleaning up our creative mess. Trashing empty food

containers from Sal's, gathering our notes, hauling out the boxes some of the new equipment came in.

"What's this?" I ask when I move a yoga ball and find some sort of standing machine with wood handlebars and a swiveling plate on the bottom. Like a cross between an elliptical and a hover board.

Jess looks at it and straight up blushes. "Andy made that. For the family fitness room."

"Handy Dandy Andy?" That explains the blush. "What does it do?"

"The kids stand on that plate and hold onto the bars and swivel back and forth." She smiles at her computer screen. "I could say it helps build core strength, but honestly I just think the kids will use it like a giant fidget spinner."

"Aw. It sort of reminds me of a playground carousel. You know, that thing you grab by the handles and run around and jump on once you get it spinning?"

"Yeah." She bites her lips, trying not to let me see her smile.

I cross my arms. "You didn't leverage that boy's crush to get custom-made equipment, did you?"

Her smile disappears when she shoots me a glance. "What? Of course not! He came to *me* with the design and asked if it was something I thought the kids would be able to use." She hesitates. "Do you really think he has a crush on me?"

Oh boy. Not this again. "I think Handy Dandy Andy is a really nice, really shy guy, Jess. And you're way too much woman for him." Not to mention a generation older.

"Yeah." She sighs and visibly deflates. "You're right. I'm being ridiculous. I mean, he's young and cute and I'm not that young and tired all the time."

"Oh, babe, don't be sad." I walk behind the counter,

sliding an arm over her shoulders. "I mean, you've got so much going on here! Do you really want to add a guy to the mix?"

"Guess not," she mumbles. It's not convincing.

Okay, God. This is a switch. Usually *I'm* the one with man-induced ennui and *Jess* is the one giving me a 'there-there.'

I love Jess. But I wouldn't trade places with her right now if doing so was the answer to world peace.

Okay, *maybe* if it was the answer to world peace. But you get my point. The price would need to be very, *very* high. Because being with Liam is light-years better than being on my own. Yes, I'm still getting used to having someone in my space. And yes, there are *definitely* moments when we seem to be on entirely different pages. Or when he flat out disagrees with me, as in the case of the Little Drop Run alligator.

But then there are moments like when I'm driving home from Foundations and don't need to stop at the gas station. Or when I walk into my bedroom to change and inhale the clean, calm scent of tea tree.

God, Liam Taggert smells delicious.

By the time he pulls into Mom's driveway later in the evening, I'm aching to see him. *Hungry* for him, even. Like I haven't just spent the last four days talking to him and the last four nights with him in bed.

Honestly, the flutter in my belly when I watch him step down from his truck is exhilarating. And terrifying.

He comes in the side door without knocking and finds me in the kitchen, frantically rinsing lettuce like I didn't just dart to the window to admire his ass. Silly, right? I mean, Liam knows I like his ass.

"Hey, Maris." He kisses my temple and drops an insulated bag on the table. Inside are the steaks we didn't eat last night.

I didn't want to waste them.

And also, I want to eat something prepared by Liam.

He leans a hip against the counter, watching me arrange the lettuce on a chopping board, snagging a cherry tomato from the bowl near the sink.

"What can I do to help?" He asks like we've done this a thousand times.

We haven't. So why does sharing a kitchen with him feel so natural?

I clear my throat. "Can you check the grill out back? I don't even know the last time it's been used. We might have to broil the steaks."

He smiles lazily. "Okay."

"What?"

"You look nervous."

"I'm not nervous, *you're* nervous!" Great. *Super* convincing. "Why would I be nervous?"

"Don't know." He moves closer, letting our bodies brush, letting his eyes smolder. "You tell me."

"You put gas in my car this morning!" I blurt.

He lifts an eyebrow. "So?"

"So I, um...." Okay, deep breath. I can do this. I can tell him how I feel. "I...that was sweet of you. And I, um, wanted to say thank you." DAMN IT! *Coward.*

His eyes soften. "You're welcome."

He leaves a kiss on my lips and goes out to check the grill. It must be in working order, because he comes back for the steaks, meat forks, and a porcelain platter I found next to Mom's pie plates. Good. That's good. Him cooking outside gives me a chance to focus on chopping the potatoes I boiled for potato salad.

By the time I have the potato salad mixed and the garden salad assembled, he's returned with two slabs of glistening, charred meat. Holy *crap,* they smell good.

"I'll set the table," Liam says.

Seriously, were sexier words ever spoken?

He pulls down plates and my phone *pings* with a message. I wipe my hands on a tea towel and pull it out of my back pocket. Jess, updating me on her to-do list before Saturday.

Ah crap. And a voicemail. I totally forgot about Darrin's dumb voicemail. Damn it! Should've listened to it earlier.

I should just listen to it *now* so it doesn't completely ruin my whole evening.

I sigh and punch my way through the voicemail gauntlet until I reach his new message. From twelve hours ago. Oops.

"Hi, Mollie. This is Darrin Schwartz with Schwartz Marketing and Media."

For Pete's sake. Like I don't have the man's flipping voice tattooed into my brain by now. And also like his number isn't saved in my contacts.

"...together in the next day or so. It will be a good opportunity to talk face-to-face, since I'll be in the area."

Wait, what? Hold up. Go back!

I chew my thumbnail as I wade through the freaking voicemail rigmarole a second time and listen to his whole message, start to finish.

Twice.

Shit.

Darrin wants to meet up. In person. In *Pitchette.*

What the *hell* is he even doing in Pennsylvania? I mean, wasn't the man in a different hemisphere like a week ago? Or...crap. Has it already been two weeks?

It doesn't matter, because that doesn't explain why the heck he's coming *here!*

Darrin Schwartz *cannot* come here. To Pitchette. I mean, that's all there is to it! Because that will pop my happy Liam Taggert bubble. And I am *not* ready to say goodbye to Mr.

July.

"Everything okay?"

I swing around, clutching my phone to my chest. Liam raises his eyebrows, watching me closely. Like he *knows.*

"Yep!" For Pete's sake, can I sound guiltier?

He sets the salad bowl on the table, eyes never leaving my face. "You sure?"

"Um." Damn it! Why can't I flat-out lie to him? Seriously, God, what did You do? Give him some sort of lie-killing superpower? Because I have *no problem* fibbing to everyone else!

See also: Shack Wheeler and All of Pitchette.

But one glance into Liam's hot-as-hell baby blues and I'm ready to hand over my name, rank, and bank account number.

"Mollie?"

"Message from my old boss!" Oh COME ON. Why did I blurt that out like a dirty secret? "I mean. My old boss Darrin Schwartz called me and left a message. Which was what I just listened to."

"Oh." Liam lifts an eyebrow. "I didn't realize you were still talking to your D.C. firm. Is everything okay?"

"Um. Yes! Yes. Just some personnel paperwork he needs me to figure out." See? Even when I try to lie to him, I end up telling him the FREAKING TRUTH.

If this thing between us ever turns into something long-term, I'm going to have to seriously step up my game. Because let's be honest, there's bound to be stuff Liam won't want to know about. Just from a legal perspective.

He doesn't say anything.

What he isn't saying is super loud.

I bite my lip. "What?"

"Nothing."

"For Pete's sake, *what?*"

He smiles lazily. "I just know there's something you're not telling me."

CRAP. "Then why are you smiling like that?"

"Because I know you feel super guilty about whatever it is you're not telling me." He pulls out my chair.

I frown and drop into the seat. "So you're okay with me keeping a secret from you? Hypothetically, I mean?"

"I mean, I don't like it. Obviously." He sits in the chair to my left, putting us adjacent to each other instead of on opposite sides of the table. A frown pulls his face out proportion. "I don't like you feeling like there are things you can't tell me, Mollie. No matter how big or small." His voice changes. Softens. "I love that you're independent. And I never want to take your independence away. But I *do* want to be someone you can be independent *with.* Someone you trust. Someone you want to talk to. About anything." His lips curve up. "Ideally about everything."

Trust. He thinks this is about trust?

I mean, of course he does! I pretty much sort of admitted there's something I'm not telling him and I didn't explain at all *why* I'm not telling him. *Obviously* he assumes it's because I don't trust him. Not because I'm a coward who doesn't want to make an actual, grown-ass decision about my future.

I meet his eyes.

I can do it. Right now. I can tell him about Darrin and the job and the fact that I'm actually considering going back to D.C. Not because I don't like him, because I definitely, *definitely* do. *A lot.* But Pitchette is Pitchette and D.C. is...well, *D.C.*

Telling him is the right thing to do. I mean, the man paid for my freaking gas! That's the twenty-first century equivalent of a knight serenading a damsel. Or whatever knights did to court damsels. Not that I'm a damsel. More like a hedge witch who probably spends most of her time in the stockades.

Although Liam would make one fine as *hell* knight....

Stop it, Brain! Stop thinking about Liam Taggert in chainmail and boots and ooh oh holy crap what if he has a freaking sword? No wait! *A mace.* A big, thick, spiky, heavy mace. Oh, *yes please*—

"Mollie."

I swallow the drool pooling in my mouth. "Hm?"

He watches me with eyes that wrench me right out of my medieval daydream and back to Mom's kitchen.

"You can tell me anything, baby," he says.

I can. I can tell him.

Except I can't.

"I know." I reach for my wine, trying to give him a believable smile. "But it was hypothetical. So there's nothing to tell."

His forehead creases.

But he doesn't press me. "Right. Well. Just as long as you know I'm right here. Whenever you need me."

The words hurt. I can tell by the flash of sadness in his eyes, even though he doesn't say anything. Even though he doesn't belittle me or pressure me. Just like he hasn't belittled me or pressured me to tell him I love him. He just watches and waits and *trusts* me to get there on my own.

I haven't...I've never been with someone that patient before. That generous. That *giving*.

"I know," I tell him.

He nods.

I reach across the table and catch his hand before he picks up the steak plate.

"Thank you," I whisper.

He raises an eyebrow. "For what?"

"For giving me time. And for not letting the alligator in the creek eat me." Did I thank him for that already? Can't remember.

He rolls his eyes. "Mollie, there is no alligator in the creek."

"Agree to disagree." Because there is. "Thank you for not letting me drown, then. And for putting gas in my car. And for the donut. And the many, *many* orgasms. And I don't know, Liam, I guess just everything. My life has…it's been different since I came back to Pitchette. *Better.* Because of you." I curl my fingers around his. "I'm so grateful and I love…I love being with you." DAMN IT! *What the heck is wrong with me? GAAAAAH!*

He doesn't say anything for a few seconds.

Then he lifts his hand and strokes his knuckles down my cheek. "You're welcome, Maris." His lips twitch. "For everything."

My throat closes so sharply, I almost choke. I turn my head and kiss his palm.

His gaze heats when his eyes drop to my mouth. "How hungry are you?"

Not that hungry. Not when he's looking at me like he wants to eat *me* instead of the food on the table. "I think the steaks will be ruined—"

"I don't care." He pulls me out of my chair and across his lap and oh *damn,* he's HARD. *Already?* "They can wait. I can't."

THIRTY-TWO

Sal's diner isn't *really* a diner. Not in the chrome siding, egg cream special, red vinyl seats sort of way. I mean, there's a counter with barstools and laminated menus and an old-fashioned register with actual buttons. But the place is more of a café than a restaurant. A café that serves decent food, of course. Sal wouldn't have lasted long in Pitchette if she couldn't cook. Probably her cabbage pizza is straining her customer relations.

A group of senior citizens opens the place during the week. Literally. They get up so early that years ago, Sal made them a spare key and told them to unlock the doors and start the coffee if they got there before she did. I know that sounds crazy, but it's true. Seniors have come and gone over the years, but that key has stayed hidden and well-guarded. The only people who know how to access it are those who have been carefully vetted for the group. Joining it is a big deal for the folks in town who live to see retirement. It's a status thing. Some people look forward to the day when their Social Security checks clear and their Medicare kicks in. Folks in Pitchette look forward to hitting the 'Brew' button on Sal's

Bunn.

Jess' grandpa Lon Johnson is making the rounds with the regular when I walk in Friday morning. Darrin politely accepts a refill from Lon and pushes it aside when I join him at his table.

"Not the Americano you're used to?" I guess.

"It's adequate." The slight grimace on his lips suggests otherwise.

I wave at Lon, who brings me a clean mug from behind the counter and fills it with coffee.

I smile up at him. "Morning, Lon."

"How you doing, kiddo?" He nods toward Darrin. "And who's this fella?"

"Darrin Schwartz." Darrin sticks out his hand and offers a corporate handshake. "Mollie's boss."

Um, *that's* a little presumptuous. If Darrin thinks he can bully me into taking his offer, he definitely doesn't know I'm more easily swayed by money.

What? I can be sensible about business. Sometimes.

I lift my mug. "Thanks for the coffee, Lon."

Okay, so it isn't Starbucks. But a little cream and a packet of raw sugar and I can't tell the difference. Mostly.

"Are you getting breakfast?" Because I smell bacon and damn it, I want some.

"I ordered a muffin."

Geez. Boring. "Sal's waffles are the best I've ever had, just so you know."

"The muffin hits my breakfast carb target."

"Really?" I snatch up a menu from the condiment holder in the center of our table. "I didn't know Sal had nutritional information on these things."

"She doesn't." Darrin casually looks around the café, eyeing our fellow diners. "I asked her for the recipe and calculated the carbs per muffin per batch."

Um. Okay. Not normal.

Actually, false. Not normal *for Pitchette.*

"Well, I need food. Be right back."

I push back from the table and walk up to the counter. Sal pops out of the kitchen to take my order—bacon and waffles, obviously—and I go back to Darrin.

He's watching Lon top off mugs. "He seems sort of...advanced to be working here."

"You can say 'old' around here." I grin. "Trust me, no one is going to pop out from HR and correct you."

"Of course." Darrin nods stiffly.

"And Lon doesn't technically work here. He just likes to help Sal out."

His eyebrows shift. "You mean he's not being paid?"

"Well, I'm sure he gets coffee comped."

"Why would he wait tables if he's not getting paid?"

"He's not waiting tables, really. Just pouring coffee." I sip mine. "It's not about the money. It's about the company. This is where he and his friends hang out. Sort of."

What, does Darrin not have that? A place he likes to go with his friends?

Wait, does Darrin have friends?

"I'm glad you called me back last night." He adjusts his suit jacket, glancing around the restaurant. "I was beginning to think you were avoiding me."

Now what gave him that idea? "It's been a crazy few days for me. I'm helping one of my friends with a business launch—"

"You're launching a business?" His eyes cut back to me.

"Not exactly. I mean, her business has been open for a few months. I've just been helping her boost her marketing and generate some interest in new programming."

"Interesting. Have you been financially compensated for

your expertise?"

"Excuse me?"

"I'd hate for you to be in violation of your noncompete clause."

Um. What the hell?

His mouth curves up. Barely. "I'm joking, Mollie."

Uh-huh. "Funny."

Handy Dandy Andy walks in, spots me, and comes over to say hey.

"Is Jess ready for tomorrow?" He asks like he isn't super interested, but he is. The way he watches me closely for my answer says so.

"As ready as she's going to be." I smile. "She told me about the swivel machine you built. That was really sweet of you."

He blushes behind his glasses. "Just thought it might be something the kids could use."

"I bet." I grin.

Andy clears his throat. "Well. Got to go."

"See you tomorrow!" I call after him. Because let's be honest. He's going to be there.

"It looks like you've made a few friends since you've been back."

I look at Darrin. "I mean. I'm *from* Pitchette. I've known most of these people for most of my life." Even if I've never been close with them.

Even if a lot of them think I'm battling addiction.

"But you're comfortable here."

My mouth goes dry. "What?"

"You're comfortable in Pitchette. Helping your friend with her business."

'Comfortable?' What the hell made him choose that word? And why does everyone feel the need to tell me I'm *comfortable* being here? I'm not comfortable being anywhere, most of the time! And I'm certainly not comfortable being back in Pitchette. Thanks largely to Shack Wheeler. Although, that particular issue might be going away. We'll see tomorrow, I guess.

Also, since when has 'comfortable' been a trigger word for me? Who *cares* about being comfortable? *I* don't. I haven't since I moved away from this place. I mean, that's *why* I was able to get out. Right? Because I'm not attached to home like so many of my classmates are?

Except here I am. Back in Pitchette. Living at home. Literally.

But that doesn't mean I'm comfortable! That just means I'm figuring out the next step in my life. Right? I mean, I'm not afraid to take risks. Try new things. Learn new skills. Me being back in Pitchette doesn't mean I'm *settling*. It means I'm re-evaluating. Resting. Before I embark on my next life chapter.

Right?

I mean. This isn't 'it.' This isn't all there is to my life. I haven't lost my edge. My city instincts and corporate drive. I still want more than cups of coffee poured by Lon Johnson and getting news from a paper that prefers storytelling to facts. I do!

I lick my lips. "I've enjoyed working with Jess the last few weeks. It's been good to see how well I can apply my skills in an entrepreneurial setting."

"Is that a diplomatic way of saying you're turning down my offer?"

"No, it's—" What? *What* is it? I've spent the last few weeks living two lives. One happening now, in the present, with Jess and Liam. And one happening later, in the future, after I....

After I go back to D.C.

Holy crap. I've been planning to return this whole time,

haven't I? Even when I wasn't thinking about it. Even when I was helping Jess and fighting with Shack and falling for Liam.

I came back to Pitchette ready to turn the car around and drive back to D.C. I needed the break, it's true. A chance to catch my breath after Mom's burial. But this wasn't ever meant to be anything permanent. This isn't who I am! I mean, I lost a freaking overpriced boot after getting stuck in a flooding creek bed while trying to rescue my Stanley, which was thrown into the creek by a little old lady with trucker mouth! Safe to say I am *not* cut out for the Western PA lifestyle.

Sal brings over my plate of bacon and waffles and Darrin's muffin. Neither of us moves to eat. Darrin is probably waiting for me to finish my thought. I mean, *I* am.

"It's not me turning down your offer." Okay. Clarified that. Now what? "But I'm…."

Alright. Enough of this crap. To hell with professional boundaries. I mean, Darrin sort of obliterated those already by dropping into Pitchette.

"I'm not sure that accepting your offer is the direction I need to go right now," I say bluntly. "Going back to D.C. feels like I'm taking a professional step backward, not forward. And I want to be moving forward." Professionally *and* personally.

That's the problem.

I can't have both Schwartz and Liam. People like to say it's possible to have everything, but it just isn't. Not for me, anyway. I don't have that kind of fate. Or luck. I knew that going in.

And I still let myself get tangled with Liam.

Worse than that. I let Liam get tangled with me.

What the hell have I done?

Liam trusts me. Liam *loves* me.

And this whole time, I've had one foot out the door. I *fell for him* with one foot out the door.

What sort of screwed up asshole *does* something like that?

Darrin watches me closely. Geez, he's intense. His face doesn't display any emotion, but his eyes are like peepholes into his inner chaos. Like he's seconds away all the time from completely snapping. I don't remember him being this way before. Was I *that* oblivious?

Or have I just gotten used to Liam's calm gaze? His balance and steadiness?

"What if you didn't move back to D.C.?"

Um. "You mean like I would work remotely from here?" My pulse hammers.

I mean. It would certainly make things easier right now, but it's illogical. It would be a different discussion if I was being hired specifically for *digital* marketing. Traditional marketing is hands-on, and you need to have a firm grasp of both location and client to be successful.

"Not remote. We could set you up in our Pittsburgh office."

UM. "I'm sorry. Schwartz has a *Pittsburgh* office?"

"Yes."

"Since *when?*"

"Since eight years ago. We also have offices in Boston, New York, and Philadelphia. I'm in the area because I just finished visiting our Philly office and am on the way to visit our Pittsburgh location."

"Are you kidding me?" Pittsburgh is *maybe* thirty minutes west of Pitchette. *Maybe.* "All this time, you've been trying to get me back to D.C. and you could just as easily have moved me to Pittsburgh?"

"I don't know that I would say 'just as easily.' There aren't any openings in the Pittsburgh office. Yet." He lets that hang in the air for a second, just to drive home the emphasis. "And the position that I've offered you in our D.C. office doesn't have a counterpart in Pittsburgh, because the clientele need isn't there. So you'd be working for less pay than if you moved to D.C."

Right. Of course. Because no one can have everything.

Darrin shifts in the booth. "Tell me what your reservations are, Mollie. Maybe it's something we can fix."

This is insane. Darrin Schwartz is sitting across from me in Pitchette's only restaurant, offering to give me whatever I want in a job. And I'm *waffling*.

"I'm not worth this much, Darrin." I lean forward. "I *know* I'm not worth this much. Every year, you get a stack of resumes from fresh-faced graduates willing to work their asses off for next-to-nothing pay just for a chance to add their names to the Schwartz employee directory. They all have the same academic credentials I do."

"They don't have your experience."

"Neither did I when I first started for the company. Everyone starts somewhere. I learned a lot on the fly."

"Not everyone can."

"But I'm not the *only one* who can. Why aren't you focusing on finding new blood? On investing in the next generation? You'd get the same amount of work out of a new hire for half the pay. You might even get *more* work out of them." Not that I advocate for wage disparities in the workplace or anything. "Why are you here right now? Why are you chasing me so hard?"

Oh crap! Is this a sexual thing? Am I being stalked by Darrin Schwartz?

Wait, isn't he gay? Pretty sure he brought a guy to the corporate Christmas party last year. Or no. Maybe that was Neil from payroll. Gah, they look sort of similar. And I was so focused on Mom at the time.

"Mollie?"

Oops. Forgot about the stalker. Focus on the stalker. "Sorry, what?"

"I was saying I'm here because so far, you're the only person I've met who's right for this position."

Hm. Okay. If I wasn't looking at him through a Stalker Lens, that would probably sound normal. And wouldn't have an emphasis on 'position.'

I cross my arms and lean back. "So if you met someone else during your Pitchette getaway, you'd offer them the job, instead?"

"Yes." He smiles. A little. "The only thing special about you, Mollie, is I believe you're the best person for this job. And I want the best people working for Schwartz. That's all."

Now I'm both insulted and relieved. Guess that's a step up from thinking my molested corpse is going to surface in the woods somewhere, right?

"So." Darrin folds his hands, like this is his office and I'm his client. "What will it take to help you move forward?"

'Move forward.' Not 'come back.'

When Darrin says it, it doesn't sound like I'm running away. It sounds like I'm making progress. For once.

I really, *really* want to make progress. I don't want to be a candidate for Sal's senior openers group.

"I want to see the revised handbook policies on PTO before I start working." Geez. Okay. Weird place to start.

"Done. And?"

I blink. Just like that? He can just…*do* it?

Of course he can. His name is on the damn company.

"And I don't want to just join this academic marketing team. I want to lead it." Geez! Where the heck did that come from? I don't *lead*. I flop around pretending to know what to do until things start to click.

Darrin's lips twitch. "Fine. And?"

"A gym membership." Guess I'm sort into fitness now. Thanks a lot, Jess.

"And?"

Oh, *now* it's a challenge. I mean, he has to say 'no' to something eventually. Right?

"I want to be able to pick my team. I want the artists to be in direct contact with both sales and clients for better communication. And I want sales to see the creative process and the designers to see the sales process. Everyone should be aware of how everything works, even outside their department. We look like idiots in front of clients whenever we can't answer questions beyond our scope and shuffling clients around to get their questions answered is just unprofessional. And coffee! We need better coffee in the breakroom. And better chairs. Folks will be less likely to run out for Starbucks if they can grab something just as good in the office and feel like they can enjoy it in peace. And get rid of Bella in reception who makes rude comments to every guy who walks in the place. If she was a man, she'd have been slapped with a misconduct charge a long time ago."

"Anything else?"

"Probably. I'll have to get back to you."

Darrin's shoulders visibly ease. Who knew there's a difference between Stiff Darrin and Relaxed Darrin? "Does this mean you're accepting the position?"

"I want to review the new paperwork first."

"Obviously."

I lick my lips. "But I guess, yes. Start processing it."

He breaks out a full-face grin. I almost go blind.

"You're a tough sale to make, Mollie Maris," he says.

Let's just hope the investment is worth it.

I gave Darrin the go-ahead on my new employee contract. Now it's just about the closing.

I *want* to close, of course. I wouldn't have told Darrin to give me the paperwork if I didn't, right? But telling Darrin in the diner is one thing.

Telling Liam afterward is another.

I'm not stupid. I knew from the start a fling with Liam Taggert was too good to last. He's Mr. Hometown Hero, Mr. July, Mr. Everything I'm Not. He has goals and achievements and three different uniforms in his closet. I have an over-priced suitcase and half a pair of over-priced hiking boots in mine. Liam has people in Pitchette. *His* people. Related by blood. That's important around here. It might be the twenty-first century in the rest of the world, but knowing your people still means something in Western PA. In Northern Appalachia. It means honoring your past and having shared history and growing new branches from roots planted long ago. I mean, there's even a freaking sociological term for what happens in this region: boomerang migration. Folks are born here, grow up, move away, move back, and stay until they die.

I think it happens because there's so much familial history in America's Rust Belt. In the mountains and the rivers, in the mines and the mills. Maybe you can't see it until you get out, but once you get out…oh boy. It's all you *can* see. All the folks still at home. All the places that raised you. And remembering those things sucks you back, for better or worse. Because shared identity is more powerful than any job or money or position. It's tribal. It's community. You might run far and you might run fast, but you still have something drawing you home. Blood calls to blood.

That's the problem. Liam has blood here. Lots of it. *Generations* of it. Grandparents and parents, siblings and cousins, aunts and uncles.

All I have is Mom. And Mom is gone.

When I walk away from Pitchette, no one is drawing me back. There isn't any boomeranging. I can leave. I can plant my own roots anywhere I want to, and not have to worry about something yanking them up. Not have to worry about folks who have known me all my life gossiping behind my back or spreading rumors.

I need to tell Liam about the job. Tonight. Right now. The longer I wait, the worse it will be.

It's just that it's sort of difficult to concentrate with Liam slamming into me from behind.

He has one hand gripping my hip and one hand rubbing my clit and the combination has me on the brink of a massive coronary.

"*Liam!*"

"Almost, baby."

I don't need *almost,* I need *now.*

My hands fist the sheets as I buck back against him. My arms burn and my legs quiver and I can't see straight.

Three thrusts and he's bending over me, moaning my name, coming in hot spurts while I clamp hard around him. I see stars. I see life beyond Pitchette. I see everything that was and everything that will be. My legs give out on the last shockwave and we fall forward on his bed, a tangle of sweaty limbs and gasps and the three little words Liam can say so easily and I can't.

Liam kisses my shoulder and my spine and my neck, wrapping his arms around me from behind, his damp thigh locked between mine, nudging my tender flesh as we ride out the aftershocks. Completely spent.

"You're trembling," Liam whispers into my hair.

"So are you."

"Yeah." He pulls me closer, yanking the sheets over our

cooling bodies.

We fall asleep plastered together.

And when the morning comes and he isn't there, I feel a twinge that goes a lot deeper than telling him I'm going back to D.C.

And I'm *so* not ready to face whatever the hell that means.

THIRTY-THREE

Okay, yes. I could've told Liam about D.C. right after I met Darrin Friday morning.

But honestly, the job kind of took a back burner to things with my scurrying to help Jess get Foundations ready for the Saturday launch. And now it *is* Saturday and, well. It's the launch.

So the D.C. conversation just has to wait. That's all. Liam will understand.

Right, God?

"My brother Simon's going to be there."

I look over at Liam, glancing in the mirror from the driver's seat of his truck.

"What?"

"Simon's got two boys. Eight and five. He texted me this morning that Cass, my sister-in-law, has been following Foundations online and wants them to swing by today."

"Really?" Okay. That's cool. No reason to freak out. I mean, I've already met one of his sisters. So I'm going to meet his oldest brother's family.

"My folks might stop by, too." Liam leans his elbow on

the window. "They like seeing what the grandkids are up to. So we might run into them."

So I might be talking to Liam's folks *as well as* his brother and sister-in-law and nephews. Cool. Cool cool cool. No problemo. *Totally* not freaking out over the fact a quarter of Liam's family is going to be at the second-ever community shindig I helped plan. I'm sure they are definitely going to like me and not at all be swayed by the stories in the paper.

At least for the forty-five minutes before they find out I'm going to break Liam's big, beautiful heart.

"Mollie."

"Hm?"

"Look at me."

I don't want to. Because we all know I can't straight up lie to the man. And one glance at the guilt on my face and that's exactly what I'll have to do.

"I'm fine," I say, looking straight ahead.

Because I'm *not* telling Liam about D.C. on the ride from his house to Foundations.

And I'm *not* telling him about it when we walk into the studio to find Jess chatting with Bobby and Karla Taggert. And whoa. Liam's genes must be split right down the middle. He gets his blonde hair from Karla and his blue eyes from Bobby.

And I'm *definitely* not telling him or any other living soul about D.C. when Liam introduces me to his parents as his girlfriend and Karla Taggert pulls me into a hug. Holding me like only a mom can.

"I'm sure folks tell you this all the time," she says when the hug finally loosens. "But honey, you look *just* like your mom. So pretty. And that hair! My daughter would *love* to get her hands on it."

"Oh. Um. Thanks." What the heck am I supposed to say

to that?

"Way to make it weird, Mom." Liam smiles and looks at me. "My sister Macie is a data entry specialist, but she cuts hair on the side."

"And she'd love to cut yours, but don't you dare let her," Karla warns. "This length is beautiful on you."

Liam smiles lazily at me. "I agree."

Oh, big surprise *there.* My long hair gives him plenty of leverage in the bedroom.

And assorted other areas.

Oh great. Now I'm blushing HARD.

And Liam's stupid smile is widening.

In front of his parents, God? Really? GAH!

An older, stockier version of Liam with less hair walks up and hugs Karla.

"This is Simon," Liam tells me as a plump woman with sparkling green eyes and two boys joins us. "And this is Cass, Rhett, and Roman."

"Uncle Lee!" Rhett, the older boy, detaches from his mom's hand and launches at Liam.

My heart melts and drips all over my insides when Liam scoops him up into a bear hug. Roman is quiet and reserved, but he flashes me the sweetest smile when Liam introduces me to his brother's family.

"Maris," Simon tilts his head as he shakes my hand. "I don't think I know any Marises."

"You do now," Liam says.

"There's only one around here, as far as I know," I add. "So this is sort of a rare sighting."

"Funny." Simon's mouth pulls up into a smile. "Liam's girlfriends are usually a rare sighting, too."

Liam crosses his arms. "What the hell is that supposed to mean?"

"Language!" Karla points at the boys.

"Nothing." Simon grins at me. "It's nice to meet you, Mollie."

Liam rolls his eyes at the backs of his family when they stroll away.

I look at him. "They seem nice." More importantly, they seem to be happy to meet me. Which is more than I can say for most of Pitchette.

"They're okay. Most of the time."

I try to keep my voice even. "Have you introduced them to a lot of girlfriends?"

"Nope." The corner of his mouth pulls up. "Just you, Maris."

Oh.

Um. That seems big. Right?

Shack Wheeler walks in and Liam stiffens. Shack bee-lines as soon as he sees me.

He holds up a paper. Today's edition. With my face splashed on the front. *Not* my college graduation photo. This one looks like he cropped it from a shot he got during the chalking event last week.

"What the hell?" Liam snatches the paper from Shack. "What is this?"

"Um. Surprise." Okay, that's weak. Probably something else I should've told him about, right? But I didn't because I'm an IDIOT!

Liam's eyebrows inch up his head as he reads whatever the hell Shack wrote.

Okay, time to run interference. "Glad to see you could make it!" I shuffle Shack away from Liam.

"You drummed up quite a bit of last-minute buzz for this thing," Shack says. "Heard about it from a couple different readers."

"Really?" That means our social media platforms are

reaching the right demographics. And that our marketing is working.

"Yep. I was going to send the intern, but figured it rated my attention." He hefts the camera dangling from his neck. "Could be a Page 1 shot."

Wow, is Shack Wheeler magnanimous or what? "I know Jess will be excited to talk to you. She's got a lot to say about the new programming."

"Uh-huh." He eyes the growing crowd. "I want to talk to a couple visitors, too. See what they have to say."

Nothing but great things, hopefully. Jess put her sweat and tears into this thing. Please, God, let people see that.

Jess isn't cutting the ribbon of the family fitness room until eleven, so we closed the door to build suspense. Right now, she's showing a few parents around the Pilates slash yoga room. Which works out great, because Shack seems enamored with getting a photo of her near the studio mirrors. Probably going for some artistic shot. Not exactly the vibe we're going for here, but hey. A Page 1 shot is a Page 1 shot. Besides, Jess is hella fly with her new black fitted Polo with the Foundations logo on the chest and her black pants. She looks sleek and professional. And her hair is perfectly blown out.

Damn. I should get a couple shots of her myself for the website. This is exactly the sort of image we want for Foundations.

Liam comes up behind me. "How's it going?"

"So far, so good." I nod at Shack, who finally corners Jess. "I'm hoping he'll make a big deal out of this for her."

"I'm sure he will." He shakes his head, scowling. "We both know he likes to make a big deal out of things. Want to tell me about this?" He holds up today's front page.

I bite my lip. "Is it…."

"He took it all back, Mollie. Everything. Except that

Pitchette VFD and police responded to a 9-1-1 call in the cemetery." His eyes burn into mine. "What the hell did you have to do this time, Maris?"

Liam is *super* hot when he's angry. Which is not great. Because that is *definitely* incentive for me to make him angry.

I clear my throat and watch Jess. "The implied terms are I have to keep a secret."

"*Whose* fucking secret, Mollie?"

Oh boy. "Shack's."

Oh, Liam *does not* like that. At ALL. *Damn,* look at that thing pulsing his jaw. YUM.

Better calm him down before my womanly resistance spontaneously combusts in the middle of Jess' studio.

I tap the paper in his hand. "People will read this and forget about the other stories." Probably. "And that will be the end to this whole circus."

"You know that's not the point." His eyes spark. "It shouldn't have happened at all."

The warmth in my chest erupts into a smile. "I don't mind that it did."

"I know." He twirls a piece of my hair around his finger. "*I* mind."

"I know." I kiss his cheek. "I find that very sweet. And *very* sexy."

"Maris." His lips twitch. "Don't make me take you in the storage closet."

"Um. Don't you mean '*into*' the storage closet?"

His eyes burn. "I said what I said."

"Liam!" I smack him. "There are *kids* here! For Pete's sake, your *nephews* are here!"

"And how exactly did those kids get here, Mollie?"

My face flames. "By stork, just like in Disney movies!"

He laughs. He's probably going to kiss me, except a

couple comes up to congratulate him on the baseball season. He pulls away to talk to them, but I feel his eyes follow me as I move through the crowd. Geez, there are a lot of people here. Which is good! I just hope we have enough food for everyone.

Everything comes to a brief pause when Jess steps up to the family fitness room with a pair of scissors. She spends about two minutes talking about Foundations and why she wants to bring family fitness to the studio. Then her cousin Lauren Shire, who's the pastor of the Pitchette Evangelical Church, gives a blessing for the studio and everyone who steps foot inside.

I forget that's how life works around here. Faith and business so entwined. And whole communities that come together and pray like this, regardless of their sect. Because everyone in Pitchette just takes it day-by-day. It's hard to live like that. But it's also sort of beautiful. Especially when you see this side of it. Folks helping Jess build her dream. Supporting and loving her, despite the ugliness people spread about her business. There are a lot of unhappy endings in this town, but that makes the happy endings much more precious.

And I so want Foundations to end happily for Jess. After a long and prosperous run.

Time is just a concept as I flutter around, grabbing photos and video. Posting everything to the Foundations accounts. Tagging the local businesses that helped the day come together last-minute. Most of the parents I talk to can't say enough about the programming Jess has scheduled, but the kids are more enamored with the chalkboard store front. So many of them weren't at her decorating event, and they're making up for the lost time.

"Babe, you're going to have to start buying chalk in bulk," I say when Jess comes over to watch them work.

"Seriously. Do you think that's a Costco thing?"

"I'm thinking it's a find-an-online-distributor-and-schedule-a-regular-order thing."

"They'll get over it after a while, right?" She bites her lip. "I mean, it's just chalk. It'll get old fast."

"The chalk might get old." I nod at a group of girls drawing Rapunzel's tower up the side of one of the windows. "I'm not sure drawing on a building will."

"Good grief, am I really going to have to add a line item for *chalk?*"

"Let's classify that as a problem you *want* to have."

"Yeah. You're right." She shakes off her worrying. *There's* the smiling, peppy Jess we love. "I saw a couple of the photos you took. They're *amazing,* babe. And did you see the Pitchette community group had a livestream running of the ribbon cutting?"

"I did see that." The Gym Girlies are hopping on the Foundations train. Which is good.

Even if they are only doing it because they want to share Jess' spotlight.

"By the way, Jake Karowak's here with his grandkids and he told me he's *super* impressed with us putting together an event like this so quickly and so well."

"Who's Jake Karowak?"

"He's on the board of directors for Prior Federal Credit Union. Actually, he sits on a lot of boards. I told him this all happened thanks to you. Then I gave him your email."

"What? Why?"

"Because you're great at this, babe. There are a lot of businesses around here that need someone like you on their team."

What? What the heck does that mean? "Are you saying I should consult?"

"I'm saying you *could* consult. I know a few people who need the sort of help I did getting off the ground." Jess glances at her watch. "Alright. An hour to go."

"Don't tell me you're actually counting down?" I wave my hand around, pushing aside the consulting thing. I have a job. With Schwartz. "This is prime Jess Johnson action right here! Socialization and kids and fitness!"

"And parents. It's draining, babe. I feel like I've been smiling for hours."

"You probably have. I mean, you're smiling in all the photos I got."

"My cheeks ache." She rubs her jaw. "But it's fine! It's good! Another hour."

Uh-huh. "And then?"

"And then I'm heading home to a hot shower and a bottle of wine."

I grin. "That's my girl."

She sighs. "Normally I'd wish you were a man saying that. Today I don't have the energy to care."

"One day, babe."

"Yeah. Right."

She plasters on a new smile and goes to talk to some kids arguing over drawing space. I sneak back inside and glance around. Liam's standing near the Wall of Winners, talking to Lon Johnson. And he doesn't look happy about it. That's weird. As far as I know, everybody loves Lon. And I definitely know everybody loves Liam. He hasn't been left alone for a second since we got here.

Now he sort of looks like he just wants everyone to go away.

That isn't good. Did Shack say something? Or maybe he said something to Shack?

Twice I try to track him down in the studio and ask what's wrong. Both times he disappears before I get the chance.

And then it's one o'clock and my focus shifts to helping Jess wind things down.

Liam emerges in the thinning crowd. Why the heck does he look so annoyed?

"Why don't you both come over to the farm tonight?" Karla ruffles Roman's hair when he leans his head against her hip. "Simon and Cass are bringing the boys over for a fire. Drew will probably be there, too, and the girls might swing by. We'd love to have you both."

"Sorry, Mom." Liam drops a kiss on her cheek. "Rain check. We're going to help Jess clean things up here and then we're headed out."

We are? I mean, obviously we're leaving at some point. And yes, I'm totally intimidated by the idea of being around *all* of Liam's family for the first time. But it's one thing for *me* to be weird about going. It's another thing for *Liam* to be weird about it.

But he is. He's totally weirded out right now. The corners of his eyes are tight and the tendons in his jaw flutter. And he barely looks at me when he answers Karla.

Actually, he's barely looked at me for like the last hour. Ever since he talked to Lon Johnson.

My stomach twists.

"Oh. Alright. Some other time." Karla turns to me. "It was good to meet you, Mollie. Finally. After everything I've heard about you, I can't believe this is the first time we actually talked."

"I'm just glad that after everything you've heard about me, you still *wanted* to talk."

Karla laughs. "Actually, all the talk made me want to meet you even *more*. I couldn't wait to get the real scoop. Now that I have, I understand." She winks at Liam.

Oh. Um. Is that a good wink or a bad wink?

Liam doesn't confirm either way.

In fact, he barely says a word when his family hugs us goodbye and we start helping Jess get the studio cleaned.

And when he does speak, it isn't exactly what I want to hear. "Ready to go?"

He didn't say 'home.' He's been saying 'home.'

"Yep." It's not a big deal. He could just be tired. We've definitely been burning the candle at both ends recently. I mean, *I'm* exhausted and I'm not the one making fire calls or pulling bar shifts.

Not that he's been pulling a lot of bar shifts lately. Mostly, he's been pulling me.

The knot that's in my stomach when I finish up with Jess and follow Liam out of the studio is saying that might change, though.

Oh lord. Is this…is this the bubble popping?

No. *Please,* no. This is the start of the end, isn't it? This is reality checking in. Luck getting the last fucking laugh.

I didn't even get a chance to fight it, it just…*happened.* When I wasn't even paying attention.

"Liam!"

He pauses next to the grill of his truck. Back to me, head tipped down. I see the tension hunching his shoulders. The only thing I want to do is wrap my arms around him until that tension melts away.

Except *I* put the tension there.

The last thing he wants is to be touched by me.

He slowly turns, looking at me from under hooded lids. Not saying anything, just pinning me with those damn eyes.

"Um." I swallow and scuff my sneaker across the sidewalk. "Where are we going?" Seriously? *That's* what I ask? Like I'm a toddler or something?

"My place. Your car is still there."

That answer is definitive. No punches pulled. He didn't

say 'home' on purpose. And he insinuated the only reason he's taking me to his place is to get my car.

I don't have any right to be bothered about that. I don't. I knew this was all going to end. I propagated the ending by agreeing to return to Schwartz!

Schwartz. D.C.

I still haven't told him about D.C.

Is that why he's silent when we get into the truck? When he turns over the engine? Because he didn't hear about D.C. from me? Please, God, not silence. I can't take the silence. Not if that silence means Liam is done with me. I mean, I expected things to end, just not...not like this. With yelling and crying, yes. Not without a whimper. Not without a sound.

I slam my door shut and Liam pulls away from the curb without a word.

THIRTY-FOUR

Liam is a great driver. He's upset, but you wouldn't know it watching him in the truck. He keeps his hands on the wheel and his eyes on the road. Posture relaxed. Attention alert. Must be the Army training. Or do the Boy Scouts have a merit badge for driving responsibly?

He's killing me with the silence, though. Not that he's super chatty to begin with. But there's a major difference between Liam's happy silence and his unhappy silence. For one thing, his happy silence doesn't include a windshield-melting, face-creasing scowl.

Which actually ratchets his sexiness up a few levels. Damn it.

Alright. Enough of this crap. "What's the matter?"

"You tell me."

"I *would* if I knew!" I think I know. That's the problem.

His jaw flexes, but he keeps his eyes plastered through the windshield.

"Liam, I can tell something's wrong." *Really* wrong. "For Pete's sake, *talk* to me." And make it quick, because my stomach is twisted so tightly, there's a chance I'll vomit all over the truck.

Actually, it might be happening now. For real.

"Pull over."

He looks at me. Finally.

"Pull *over!*" I holler.

Liam hits the brakes as we approach Little Drop Run and pulls off the road near the bridge. I'm already tumbling out of the truck by the time he stops. The fresh air hits me in the face and I suck in a lung-full. Putting distance between me and the truck seems to help. I stop walking about half-way across the bridge. Close my eyes. Just listen to the creek and the birds and the peacefulness. Funny how soothing this place feels. How special.

Funny how I never thought Little Drop Run was special before Liam and I almost died in it.

Liam's boots stop behind me. "You okay?"

No. I'm not okay. I'm being eaten alive with anxiety and guilt. Because I *know* why Liam is so angry right now. And if I wasn't such a chicken, this wouldn't be happening.

I wouldn't be having a conversation with him that's going to break both of our hearts in the prettiest place in Pitchette.

I exhale slowly. Now. I have to do it now. I waited too long. I put this off until I ran out of time altogether.

There isn't any humor in Liam's eyes when I turn around. No amused tilt to his mouth. No shoulders shaking with laughter. He has his hands in his pockets and a look on his face I've never seen before.

A look on his face I never want to see again.

"What happened back there, Liam?" I don't want to know. I *have* to know.

"Lon Johnson told me you had breakfast with Darrin Schwartz." Liam's eyes burn. Not a sexy smoldering burn. An angry burn. "That's your old boss."

"Yes."

"So it's true. Your old boss is in Pitchette."

"Yes. I mean, no. Technically." Oh geez. "He *was* here. He's on his way back to D.C."

"Why didn't you tell me he was here?"

"It happened so last-minute. It didn't occur to me." Okay, maybe it did. Maybe I was just too afraid to let Liam know. To see what would happen when my worlds collided. Maybe I selfishly thought I could keep my little Pitchette bubble safe. Forever. Because I'm an IDIOT!

Liam's face tightens. "Do you have feelings for him?"

What? "Of course not!"

"You had breakfast with him, Mollie. At Sal's."

"So? I had breakfast there with you a few days ago!"

"That's my point."

"Are you serious?" He is! He is serious right now! "Liam, this is ridiculous. Darrin is inconsequential. He's nothing to me." A boss, maybe. That's all.

"He came to Pitchette for you." Liam looks so sober. Like all the humor evaporated out of him and what's left is the wary soldier hiding underneath. "From D.C. That's not inconsequential, Mollie."

I don't have a good reason for it, but now I'm really pissed off. "Darrin didn't come to Pitchette for me. Darrin came to Pitchette for *Darrin*."

"I don't know what the hell that means."

"It means he's in charge of one of D.C.'s top marketing firms," I say. "He does what he wants, whenever he wants."

"He wants you, Mollie. Why else would he come here?"

"He wants me to work for him, Liam! He wants me to move back to D.C. and take over a new position!"

Liam's head snaps back. "You're leaving?"

I *knew* how awful it was to wait, and I still did it. Because I'm a big fat coward. Because it's easier just to say goodbye after I'm already climbing into my car.

Because really, Mollie Maris hasn't grown up whatsoever in thirty-three years.

I swallow. "I should have said something earlier—"

"Damn straight, you should have!"

"I just...Pitchette isn't *home,* Liam." My voice breaks.

"And D.C. is?"

"No." It isn't. "But maybe it could be. One day."

Liam's mouth tightens.

"What?"

His voice comes out calm in a way I've never heard before. "If it could be home one day, then why didn't you ask me to move there with you?"

He'd leave Pitchette? Where generations of his family were born, raised, and dead? Maybe in other places it's easy to walk away from that sort of legacy. To sever your roots and establish new ones. But in Northern Appalachia, roots run deep. *Centuries* deep. And people don't just yank them up and find a new place to bury them.

"Liam, I didn't ask you to move to D.C. because why would you?" My voice shakes, but I can't help it.

"Mollie, I love you. I'm *in love* with you." His eyes glisten. "Why wouldn't I?"

My heart. It's splintering in my chest. Little shards zinging through my body, lodging deep. Everything tingles and tenses. Like I'm getting ready for a fight.

I *know* Liam is in love with me. I'm in love with him.

Love is a strong tether, but stronger than heritage? Than history? Than family ties and sense of place? And if it *is* stronger than those things, is it fair for me to leverage it? To use love to compel Liam to leave everything he chose before I came back to Pitchette? To walk away and start over? Just for me?

I used to roll my eyes at this part of the movie. I always thought it was a lazy way to force love interests to confront their true feelings.

But now I'm standing on a bridge, watching Liam's heart break. Knowing what it means if he trades Pitchette for me. Feeling the weight of that choice resting on my shoulders. I mean, I have okay self-esteem, most of the time. But am I worth *this?* Am I worth a man leaving his family and his home and all the people he loves to serve?

I *see* how people love Liam! I saw it just now at the studio, when he talked to everyone and engaged with all the kids.

Liam Taggert is Pitchette's.

Leaving Pitchette means he's mine.

And how am I supposed to compete with a place like Pitchette?

"Say something, Mollie." Liam stares at me. Eyes steady. Hands fisted.

I shake my head.

"Yes," Liam insists. "Say something. I'm baring my soul here. The least you can do is respond."

Respond? How the hell can I respond? No matter what I say, I will shatter what we have.

"Liam." It comes out like a plea.

His jaw flexes. "Do you love me?"

"*Yes!* For Pete's sake, of course I freaking love you!" GREAT. Glad I'm angry and shouting the first time I tell him that. Gah!

At least he doesn't seem to notice that part. "But not enough."

Oh crap. I'm going to cry, aren't I? "It's not the love part I'm worried about."

He frowns. "What does that mean?"

"It means what if I'm not worth it, Liam?" I shout. "What if I'm not enough and I ask you to move to D.C. and you do and you get there and you realize I'm too much and not worth the hassle?"

His mouth hangs open a little.

"And what if you realize leaving Pitchette was the worst idea you've ever had and you hate me for asking you to do it and it destroys any chance we have at being happy together and not only that but any chance we have at being happy with *anyone* and what if we have kids and we screw them up—"

"Are you *serious* right now?"

What?

Wait. Is he *angry* about what I'm saying? "Um—"

"You think I just blindly fell in love with you?" A deep flush spreads beneath his scruff, taking over his face. "That I don't know exactly who you are? Exactly what being with you means? That I don't want to be with *all* of you? That I just want the easy parts and not the parts that make me work harder? Try more? Be better?"

I mean. He *has* already seen me at my worst. A few times. Actually, *most* of the times. "There are other things to think about. Your family is *here.*"

"You think I'm incapable of leaving my family to start one with you?"

Do not get distracted by that last bit. Do NOT GET DISTRACTED! "I think it's not as simple as you're making it seem, Liam!"

"What's making you say that?" His eyebrows crease, like he's fighting back pain. "What do I need to do to show you how serious I am about us?"

God, please! *Please* help me explain what I'm trying to say! "Liam, you're part of Pitchette and Pitchette's part of you. Your family has been building this community for generations!"

"So?"

"You live and breathe this place! I mean, you're a baseball coach and a firefighter and a bartender and people here love you! They *depend* on you!"

"And they'll depend on someone else when I'm gone." He crosses his arms.

"And what will *you* depend on? Because we both know I'll just screw things up. I'm a giant mess."

"You're not a giant mess. And you won't screw things up." His eyes glint. "And if this is you worrying I need to have a mission to feel *useful* like a shepherd or a cattle dog or something like that, stop it. I know my worth without anyone or anything telling me what to do. And I'm highly employable, in case you don't know. I'm a first responder and my MOS in the Army was military intelligence."

Of course it was.

What does he want me to say? That I'm scared? *Obviously* I'm scared! I've never been in love. I've never had a man want to build his life around me. The only person who's ever loved me like that was Mom and she isn't even here to talk to. I'm trying to figure this out by myself. Which sucks. Because Myself does *not* have things under control.

Which is why I spent the last month living out of moving boxes in Mom's house.

And why I'm going back to a job I'm not crazy about.

And why I angrily shouted 'I love you' at Liam for the first time. On the bridge over the creek where I almost killed him.

That lightning bolt is never coming. Is it, God?

"Tell me what's going on in your head, Maris," Liam says.

What *isn't* going on in my head?

I look over the bridge railing. "I don't know if I'm ready."

"To tell me?"

I wish. "To build a life with you." I shouldn't say this, should I? I should just keep my mouth shut and not say what

I'm about to say. "I'm not used to having someone else in my life. I mean, not like *this.* Not someone who's there when I get home from work and who makes me mad and who shares my bathroom and who runs out to get groceries when I'm out of milk. I'm not used to *being* with someone, Liam! I'm struggling to even *think* like that! I've just—I've lived on my own for so long and I'm—I'm not sure if I can. . . ." I can't even say it.

"If you can what, Mollie?"

I stare at the creek, cheeks hot. "If I can be part of a family."

Geez. How pathetic is *that?* There are billions of people out there with real-world problems, like starvation and homelessness and lack of potable water! And here I am, on the brink of tears because someone wants to build a life with me?

For Pete's sake, how selfish is *that?*

Gravel skips across the bridge as Liam comes closer. "You and your mom were a family."

"It's not the same."

"Why?"

"Because Mom and I never *grew!* She never married. She didn't have other kids. She never introduced me to my grandparents. She never told me if I had cousins. It was just us for thirty-three years!"

"It will be just us starting out."

"But it *won't* be. Because you already have a family, Liam. A big one. For Pete's sake, I just met like six of your immediate family members! And they *all* live right here! In Pitchette! Where everyone's related, except me." My throat throbs. "Like your brother said: I'm the only Maris."

"So no one shares your last name." Liam's voice is hard. "There are people here who love you. Isn't that enough?"

"Spoken like someone with a big family," I whisper.

A look comes over his face. Like he's seeing me differently.

But this is who I've been the whole time.

I swallow. "You have a home *here.* How can I take you away from that?"

His eyes soften, just a little. "Pitchette's not *home,* Mollie. You are."

This is it. This is the big one. I'm in full-on heart failure.

A huge log shifts on the left bank of the creek. Claws. Tail. Green skin.

No. That's just a flashback panic hallucination induced by Liam saying he'll give up everything for me. Because that *definitely* isn't what I think it is.

Or wait.

It IS. It IS what I think it is.

HOLY CRAP. "*Alligator!*"

"What?"

"Right there! Near the bank!" My finger shakes as I point. "Oh my lord holy crap it's a mother-flipping alligator!"

"Stop it, Mollie."

"I'm serious, Liam! It's *right there!*"

"I know what you're doing." Liam sighs and looks over the railing. "You can't run from big feelings forever. One of these days you're g—*holy shit, that's an alligator!*"

"Ha! I *told* you!" I lean over the rail. "I *knew* I saw one down there, but I didn't—"

"Get away from that thing!" Liam yanks me back. "Are you nuts?"

"Yes. *You* said it's one of the things you like about me."

"Geezus, Mollie, now's not the time! There's a fucking alligator down there!"

"Yeah, I know. I tried telling you that before. Wait a minute." I laugh. "Are you *scared?*"

"Yes! Of *course* I'm scared!" Liam's eyes blaze. "There's a prehistoric apex predator sunning himself ten feet away from us!"

"He's just a little guy." I peer over the edge. "I bet he's no more than six feet long."

"Six feet is too many feet!"

"That's snout to tail. Which means he's shorter than you lying down."

"Holy shit!"

"What happened to being a Boy Scout and a soldier and a firefighter?"

"You know what those things have in common? *They don't involve alligators!*"

I roll my eyes.

"Where the hell are you going?" he demands when I start walking off the bridge. "Mollie, come back here!"

"Somebody's got to catch it."

"What? No! Stop!" Liam panics. "Damn it, Mollie Maris, if you go near that fucking dinosaur, we're *done!*"

"Then it's a good thing we're done, anyway!" I yell back, stepping over the guide rail onto the embankment.

THIRTY-FIVE

Okay, I'm not planning to actually catch the alligator. *Obviously*.

But I'm also not planning to stand there and let it disappear into the creek again. Folks come down here all the time to wade in the water. What if some little kid gets chomped? What if folks find out I knew about it? Shack Wheeler will have a freaking field day. It will totally defeat the purpose of the retraction. One more strike against me in Pitchette's little black book.

The alligator doesn't move on the other side of the creek as I approach, which doesn't reassure me whatsoever. I'm probably headed for a major jump scare, right? Not that it matters. As there's no way in hell I'm going to capture the thing, the only reasonable conclusion to this situation is me dying or blacking out in fright. Neither of which I want to do in front of Liam. Hopefully he's cowering in his truck.

"PA Fish and Boat are on the way."

"Geez, Liam!" I clutch my chest. "Don't sneak up on me like that! Are you crazy?"

"*You're tip-toing toward an alligator* and *I'm* crazy? Damn it, woman!"

Gah! "How long until Fish and Boat get here?"

"I don't know. I don't care. We're leaving *now.*" He grabs my wrist.

"We can't just leave! What if Chops—"

"Geezus, you *named* the damn thing?"

"Did you call the police? The township? Does Pitchette have an animal control department? Doesn't the fire department have one of those gigantic parachute things to catch folks jumping out of buildings? Maybe we—"

"Everyone's on their way right now with everything that's needed to catch an alligator!" Liam pulls me back up the embankment. "Now for Pete's sake, Mollie, shut up and—"

"*Liam!*"

The alligator slithers into the water so fast that by the time I yell, he's popped up on our side of the creek. And *oh shit* he's running right for us! Shitshitshit, what's the protocol for an alligator attack? Bear attack is make yourself bigger. Shark attack is push in the eyes. Snake atta—

"*Oof!*"

I fly across the embankment and tumble into the bushes, Liam nothing but a blur in my peripheral.

That freaking moron pushed me and *launched himself* at the flipping alligator and now they're both rolling back down the bank into the creek!

"*No,* Liam, you idiot!"

Doesn't he know alligators roll their prey to kill and drown it right before eating?

I trip and skid my way down to the creek, crashing through the water as they both come up for air, wrapped together like an episode of *Animal Planet* gone very, VERY WRONG!

"Are you fucking insane?" I holler at him as he gasps and

thrashes.

"Get back!" he yells.

"Liam!"

"GET BACK *NOW!*"

GAH! Liam Freaking Taggert is going to freaking die wrestling a stupid freaking alligator!

"Some hero!" I scream as I scramble toward them. "I'm going to tell Shack Wheeler how dumb you were right up until you died and I'm going to make sure he puts it all in your dumb obituary!"

"MOLLIE!"

"And *then* I'm going to rent that billboard next to the football field and plaster your dumb face up there with a message about staying away from dangerous wildlife!"

"DAMN IT!" he sputters, disappearing into the water.

Seriously, God? Just my flipping luck to find the perfect guy just in time for him to get *EATEN BY AN ALLIGATOR!* NOT FUNNY!

Chops' tail splashes a few inches from me and I grab it out of instinct. Is this what it's like to touch a dinosaur? All bony and scaly on top and sort softish underneath and *holy crap,* I'm touching a damn dinosaur!

Liam shouts something the next time he surfaces. I can't hear what he says, but it probably involves a lot of cussing and promises to kill me, anyway. The thing probably weighs in the area of 180 pounds, but the weight kind of evens out between us. Some inherited primal instinct takes over and we half-wrestle, half-haul the beast toward the bank—me lugging the tail, Liam handling the head. We're drenched and muddy and *super* pissed off.

Okay, Liam is pissed off. I'm sort of grinning ear-to-ear.

"Don't," he pants.

"We just caught a freaking *alligator!*"

"Not yet, we haven't." He nods toward the grass. "Aim

for that flat spot."

I gasp. "Is that blood on your arm? Did he bite you? Liam, why didn't you *say* something?"

"Little preoccupied," he grinds out.

"I'll call an ambulance—"

"Don't need an ambulance. Need you to move."

He does, he *does* need an ambulance! And stitches and antibiotics. Also a rabies shot. Do alligators have rabies? Crap, is an alligator bite like a Komodo dragon bite, with the venom and bacteria and paralysis and everything? What if Liam loses his freaking arm because of me? What if I cause Liam Taggert to get an amputation? WHAT IF I MUTILATE A WAR HERO? GREAT! GAAAAAH!

The alligator makes a strange *chuffing* noise when we plop him onto the bank.

Liam moves quickly and drops down, straddling the alligator, breathing heavily. He has his knees pressed behind Chops' arms and is using his full weight to hold him still. Both of his hands wrap around Chops' snout and he's struggling to pull the nose up so his paddle-sized head is perpendicular to his body. It probably *is* sort of hard to move when your spine has a ninety-degree angle in it.

"What's the plan?" I ask. "Hold him like that until Fish and Boat arrive?"

"Do you have a better one?" he answers through clenched teeth.

"Um. Maybe." I survey the situation. "Yes, actually."

I take a step toward him.

"Stop! Do not move. Stay right there. Tell me what you're going to do first."

"I'm going to unbuckle your belt and loop it around Chops' jaw. Then at least you won't have to hold him like that."

He pants and glares at me from under puckered eyebrows. Like we have all the time in the world.

I wave my hands impatiently. "*Well?* Do you approve?"

"Fine." He frowns. "Just move slowly. And if I tell you to stop, for God's sake *stop*."

Geez. What a control freak.

I approach from an angle, trying to keep out of Chops' eyeline. Considering his current situation, maybe he doesn't care about me moving in. Still. Why take chances?

I ease into a crouch next to Liam.

Chops jerks and I jump.

"Easy," Liam soothes.

I can't tell who he's talking to.

"I'm reaching around you," I warn.

"Do it."

I exhale and stretch forward, lifting Liam's torn shirt to access his buckle. His heart pounds rapidly in my ear when I lean into his chest, trying to tug his leather belt through the wet loops of his jeans. It takes a little wriggling before it slips free.

"Alright, big guy." I blow out a breath. "Stay still."

"I'll try."

"Funny."

Chops makes a loud grumbling noise that sort of makes him sound like he has a cold. Do alligators catch colds? It makes sense. I mean, this isn't exactly a tropical climate. Aw. Poor guy. Now I feel bad cinching his snout.

The belt doesn't have a notch where I need it to, so I leave the first loop a little loose and tuck the tail down through it before pulling the belt tight.

Liam eyes the knot. "Will that hold?"

"Well, it held for the fashion influencer I learned it from."

"Geezus."

"Only one way to test it."

He sighs. "Alright. Move back."

"You know, you're really bossy in an emergency."

"Someone has to take charge. At least with me calling the play, we're less likely to end up dead."

"I'm going to remember you said that."

I stand and step back, watching Liam wrap the tail of the belt around his right hand. Pulling the belt taut, he slowly lets go of Chops with his left.

Chops doesn't move.

"Holy crap. I can't believe that worked."

Liam sends me a look.

"I mean, I *hoped* it worked. I just didn't *know* it would."

He shakes his head.

Large engines echo in the distance.

"Sounds like the posse's arrived."

"Great," Liam grumbles. "Glad they made it."

A Fish and Boat truck pulls across the bridge and parks, followed by a state police cruiser, two Pitchette police cars, a Pitchette fire truck, a township truck, and Shack Wheeler's dented Honda Pilot.

"Geez." I stare at the commotion. "Did you make sure to call the mayor?"

"I erred on the side of firepower. I didn't realize you could wrangle a prehistoric reptile with a leather belt."

"Well, we know for next time."

"No, we do not."

We watch duties get divvied up. Once the flares are set and the road is blocked, two conservation officers holding catch poles come down the embankment with Chief Miller and a peach-fuzz townie I don't know. Shack steps over the guide rail and moves along the embankment, camera clicking. The cops stop half-way down. The conservation officers walk right up to Chops. They introduce themselves as Nowak and Sweeney.

"This is a first for us," Nowak says.

"An alligator?" I ask.

She smiles. "Visiting Pitchette."

Great. No wonder we have free-range alligators.

"Hm. Your form is impressive," Nowak tells Liam. "I like it."

Okay, probably she isn't trying to be flirty. Probably it's just some gross female gene that makes me roll my eyes.

"Thanks," Liam says. "If you don't mind, I'd like to get up now."

"Sure." Nowak hefts her pole and moves around Chops. "We got it from here."

She and Sweeney get the poles into position and Liam eases off. He gives Chops a pat on the back and heads for me.

With a look on his face that makes me turn and bolt up the bank.

"That big guy is scary, isn't he?" Chief Miller hollers as I dart past.

"You have *no* idea!"

I crest the bank and stagger onto the road, gasping for breath. Liam is right behind me, but I figure he won't kill me with so many witnesses around. Most of whom are law enforcement.

"MOLLIE MARIS, DO NOT MOVE!"

Okay, maybe he doesn't care about the witnesses. He's the hometown hero. They'd probably all cover for him, anyway.

Alright, time for Plan B: Lightning bolt, God! LIGHTNING BOLT!

"Is that thunder?" I ask as Liam approaches. *Please,* let it be thunder. Or an earthquake. Or a tornado. Or a flock of flying monkeys.

Geez, his blue eyes are straight up deadly when he's *really* angry. Like pools of noxious gas. Is this his soldier face or his I-hate-Mollie-Maris face? Because call me crazy, but I get the feeling this is personal.

I lick my lips. “You see—”

“No! You don’t talk! *I* talk!”

Geez, what a caveman. “Can’t we do this later? You’re sort of—”

“*Stop talking!*”

The state trooper looks over at us and frowns.

“Hey!” I wave him over. “This man needs medical attention! Is EMS coming?”

“Shut up!” Liam seethes. “You’re not getting out of this!”

“What’s the problem?” the trooper asks.

“He’s been bitten,” I explain.

“I didn’t get bitten.”

“He might need stitches.”

“I do not need stitches!”

“See, officer? Right there, he’s got a bite on his arm and it’s bleeding all over the place.”

“It’s a *scratch* and I’m fine!” Liam shouts.

The trooper holds up his hand. “Sir, I need to you stay calm.”

“I am calm! I just wrestled a damn alligator and I’m *calm!*” Liam squeezes his eyes shut and starts some strange deep-breathing routine.

“Boy Scouts?” I guess.

“Army,” he grunts.

Now that he isn’t flapping his arms around, I can see his wound better. It doesn’t *look* like it’s made by teeth, but it still looks bad. And between the dirty creek water and the dirty primordial reptile, it definitely needs to be irrigated.

“He probably doesn’t need an ambulance,” I tell the trooper. “I’ll take him to the hospital.” It will be the first and last trip Liam and I take together.

The trooper asks Liam some questions. I tune out because I'm too busy watching Nowak and Sweeney wrestle Chops into some sort of sliding-door crate. Miller and his sidekick help the conservation officers lug it back up the bank and deposit it in the back of the Fish and Boat truck.

I walk over. "Where's he headed?" Maybe it isn't cool to admit it, but I don't want him to be euthanized.

"There's an exotic animal rescue center in Allegheny County that can accommodate him," Nowak says. "He'll be in good hands."

That's good, right? They probably have other apex predators there. He'll make new friends.

Nowak and Sweeney talk to the cops.

I lean against the back of the truck, peeking into the cage. "So long, Chops. Best of luck."

His slitted eyes glow back, green-gold trackers eyeing me suspiciously. I take the rumbling noise he makes as a farewell.

Miller walks with me back to Liam. He looks miserable sitting on the bumper of the fire truck, wrapped in a silver Mylar blanket.

"How you doing, son?" Miller asks.

"Just great." The clenched teeth suggest otherwise.

The Fish and Boat truck pulls out and the trooper follows. Shack has the township guy cornered and is peppering him with questions.

"Well, guess everything's under control here." I avoid looking at Liam directly. "We should be heading—"

"Hey!" Tanner comes flying down the road on foot, weaving through vehicles, dressed in civilian clothes. "I heard the call! Where is he? Where's the gator? How big was he? Is he okay?"

"He's fine," I say. "On his way to a five-star exotic animal rescue."

"I'm fine, too," Liam mutters. "Thanks for asking."

"Holy cow, this is insane!" Tanner's eyes are popping out of his head. "An actual gator in Little Drop Run! How the heck did he get here?"

"Mostly likely scenario is someone got him when he was real little," Miller declares. "Probably thought he'd make a neat pet. Of course, he was a lot less neat once he got big. So he got illegally dropped off somewhere and ended up in the creek."

"Crazy," Tanner breathes, eyes wide.

"Yep. Crazy," I agree. "Sorry, guys, we got to be getting—"

"How did you get it?" Tanner asks Liam. "Dart gun?"

"Where the hell would I get a damn dart gun?"

"I dunno. Sonny could probably hook you up."

"Our boy didn't need a dart gun," Miller explains. "He wrestled it and then cinched its jaw closed until the game commission got here."

What? "Um, excuse me, but *I*—"

The murder on Liam's face stops me.

I clear my throat. "Yep. That's how it happened."

"For real? C'mon, man!" Tanner gripes. "Why does Liam get all the best calls?"

"What the hell made you decide to use your belt?" Miller asks.

Hair still dripping, chest heaving, Liam glares at me through slitted eyes.

"Physics and desperation, mostly," I say.

THIRTY-SIX

My coffee mug is cooling for the second time next to my computer when Jess' contact photo pops up on my phone. She probably wants to video chat, but I have too much stuff to do. I put her on speaker.

"Hey, babe!"

"Hey."

"How's the CEO of Pitchette's first marketing consulting firm?"

Aw. It sort of sounds almost legit when she says it. Not at all like I'm still struggling to figure out the legal process behind starting a consulting business.

"Busy." It's true. The new business paperwork is straight up killing me. Maybe I should hire an intern. No, no. Focus. No money in the coffers for an intern.

"Good!" Jess croons. "Tell me about it."

The daily check-ins were adorable at first, but I'm starting to feel like Jess has me on suicide watch or something. Like she thinks turning down Darrin's D.C. offer is a sign of mental distress.

I mean. It probably is.

I'd be in more distress if I took his offer.

Because let's be honest. I wasn't agreeing to go back to Schwartz out of *want.* I was agreeing to go back out of *fear.* Because returning to Pitchette without a gameplan is scary and working for Schwartz was comfortable. Ironically.

I was afraid to see what else is out there.

I'm still afraid.

But it's a different sort of fear now. It's an I-helped-wrestle-an-alligator sort of fear. My heart's pounding, but I'm still going to do it. I'm done with Schwartz. I'm done with D.C. I'm done *running.*

D.C. wasn't home. Not that Pitchette is, either. Yet.

Maybe it isn't blood that causes boomerang migration in this place. Maybe it's just this place.

And maybe it isn't bad to feel comfortable *here.* I mean, if I'm going to feel comfortable somewhere, why not where my mother and my best friend built their lives?

"I'm still working on getting the business part off the ground. But I've already lined up a few projects in the meantime." They're all fairly small, but I have to start somewhere.

"Yay! Like what?"

"The library wants me to help get the word out about the evening book club." Not that the library has a ton of money to spend on marketing, but I'm sort of considering it penance. And a good way to get under Mrs. Barker's skin. "And I actually just talked to Jake Karowak over at the credit union about signing a year-long consulting contract." Once I figure out how to first, navigate the PA Department of Community and Economic Development website and second, register my brand-new brain child. That's going to keep me busy for a while.

"Babe! That's amazing! I'm so proud of you right now."

"You'll be very proud of me for this one," I promise. "The fire department asked me to do next year's fundraising calendar." *That* I'm doing for free.

Okay, maybe I'm not doing it entirely for free. I mean, *hello.* Firefighters.

"Ooh! What's Liam say about *that?*"

Gah. Damn it. Walked into that one. "I don't know. I haven't seen him."

"Since when?"

"Since I took him to the hospital for his alligator bite and he spent twenty minutes yelling at me in the emergency room about approaching dangerous wildlife."

"No!" Jess gasps. "Why didn't you tell me all this sooner? I thought you two were just keeping things private! It's been two weeks since you've seen him?"

"Really? That's what bothers you? What happened to the Sisterhood?"

"I mean, not cool that he yelled at you. Obviously. But, you know."

I raise my eyebrows. "I know what?"

"It's *Liam.*"

"And?"

"And he doesn't yell at *anyone.* Even in high school, he was a cool character. Guys would go after him on the football field or on the mat and he'd just shake them off and outperform them. He's always been self-assured and mellow as hell. You have to really, *really* piss him off to get a rise out of him."

"Yeah, well. Mission accomplished." I sigh.

"Ah, babe. I'm sorry. I was really shipping you guys."

"See, that's where we went wrong. We got our hopes up." This is Pitchette. No happily-ever-afters here. Just day-by-days.

A short-lived surprise fling with the hottest guy in town

is as good as it gets.

"Ugh. Great," Jess gripes. "Now I'm all depressed on this glorious summer day. Let's do something fun this weekend, okay? No firefighters or alligators."

"I'll let you know." An email notification pops up on my computer. "I got to go, babe. Work to do."

"Okay. Love ya."

I open the email from Shack Wheeler. The body has one line: *This work?*

Funny how accommodating he is these days.

My cursor hovers over the attachment, but I don't click. It's going to hurt, isn't it? Seeing him. It's hurt every day *not* seeing him. So this is probably going to be ten times worse.

Especially after what happened last week, when Tanner stopped by the house. He handed me a bag with my sunflower Stanley and told me Liam found it in flood debris from Little Drop Run.

The Stanley is ruined. But that's not the point, is it?

The point is Liam cared enough to get it back to me. Not enough to see me.

I don't blame him. I mean, the alligator incident was pretty damning.

Okay. Deep breath.

I click on the attachment.

Liam, wet and beautiful. Damp hair curling. Muscles glistening through the tattered shirt clinging to his body. Mud smeared across some very delicious parts. Beltless jeans riding low on his hips. One hand looped tightly in Chops' makeshift rein. The other flat against Chops' soft throat. And Shack caught him looking down, like he's about to drop a big kiss on Chops' snout. The bloody cut on his arm is hidden from this angle. Too bad. That would've been the cherry on top of the sexy heroic sundae.

Despite the ache in my chest, I grin. "Hel-*lo,* Mr. July."

Actually, Liam isn't just next year's Mr. July. He's next year's cover model.

Good thing we aren't seeing each other anymore. Otherwise, I'd feel super guilty about keeping *that* a secret from him. Or, you know. *Trying* to keep that a secret from him.

Guess he'll find out when he sees it displayed in the library. Oh! Maybe I can convince the library to rent the billboard next to the football field. Slap a message up there about department calendars being available for check-out. No, scratch that. For *purchase.* Mrs. Barker can get over herself and let the fire department sell calendars through the circulation desk.

Liam wrangling Chops will increase library foot traffic for *sure.* And more foot traffic equals more funding, right? If I'm able to help them secure better fun—

Someone bangs on the side door. Loudly.

If this was D.C., I'd be reaching for my phone preparing to call 9-1-1 about an attempted burglary. But this is the middle of the afternoon in Pitchette, so my thoughts are more along the lines of *who the heck is bothering me right now?*

Probably Terry Bauer, wanting to yell at me for leaving my trashcans out overnight instead of putting them out this morning at the asscrack of dawn. I mean, I don't know what he's so angry about. I picked everything up after the coons got into the cans last week.

I push back my desk chair, crack my neck, and I hug the wall until I'm able to peer out the mudroom window to see who's on the side porch.

Gold hair. Blue eyes. Sexy scruff.

DAMN IT.

Okay. I don't *have* to answer the door. As far as Liam knows, I've moved back to D.C., right? He doesn't know I turned Darrin down. Or that I've taken over next year's firefighter calendar. *Right?*

Shit. He probably knows. I mean, this is *Pitchette.*

What if he's here to stop me? Somehow?

He pounds on the door again. "Mollie Maris, I know you're in there. Your car is here."

Gah! My car. Totally forgot I didn't park it in the freaking garage. Geez. Even with Jess' awesome martial arts classes, I would make a *terrible* covert operative.

Alright, God. Stand by RE: the lightning bolt.

And whose brilliant idea was it for me to dress like a swamp monster this morning? I couldn't throw on a pretty sundress and some makeup? I *had* to go with the ratty black tank-top and the old jean shorts and the bare feet? GAH!

I run a hand through my knotted hair, get my fingers stuck, yank them free, and reach for the door.

Liam looks incredible, of course. Hair shiny, skin glowing. And holy *crap,* he smells amazing. The blue shirt really brings out his eyes and the faded jeans really bring out his ass. He's wearing work boots and a tactical watch and has a shopping bag clutched in his hand. Probably holding the Nitrile gloves and bleach he needs to dispose of my mutilated body.

"I'm warning you right now, I won't go down quietly," I tell him. "There will be witnesses and you'll be covered in evidence."

"Hm. Good thing I'll have a jury of my peers."

Great. *That's* probably true. Half of them will probably be related to a Taggert, too.

I surreptitiously move my foot so it blocks the door. Just in case he remembers the whole alligator-wrestling situation and has a fit of sudden violence.

"Your scar is looking good." GREAT. Glad I felt the need

to go ahead and remind him of the alligator-wrestling situation. Idiot!

"The stitches just came out." Liam moves his arm to give me a better look. "Getting bitten by an alligator has made me kind of famous."

"You swore up and down it was a cut, not a bite!" Not that I believed him. Entirely.

He smiles lazily. "Someone once told me it's all about how you frame the narrative."

"Yes. That someone was an idiot." In so many ways. "Why do you want to frame the narrative? I sort of got the impression at the hospital that you never wanted to hear the word 'alligator' again."

Mostly because one of the things he yelled at me was, *"Do not ever say the word 'alligator' to me again!"*

Although. Hm. Maybe he just doesn't want to hear *me* say 'alligator.'

Oops.

Liam shrugs. "I guess I kind of like being a superhero."

I snort. "Okay, Mr. July. I know you're brave and a Boy Scout and war hero and all, but I don't know that I'd classify you as a *superhero*."

"Really?" He lifts an eyebrow. "You did before."

"Yeah, in jest." Sort of. "You can't just *decide* you're a superhero. There are boxes you got to check."

"Yeah?" he challenges. "Like what? Alter ego? X-ray vision? Bodysuit?"

"Sure, those. Plus, you know. *Saving* people."

"I save people all the time."

I roll my eyes. "I'm not talking about *regular* saving people. So you're a freaking first responder! There are *lots* of first responders. I'm talking about *extraordinary* saving people. From asteroids and aliens and stuff."

"How about that time I saved you from that creep who

wanted your socks?"

"Um, excuse me, but Twister and I had a business transaction. I *sold* him my socks." I frown. "You just happened to show up at the weirdest possible time for that."

"How about when I saved you from drowning?"

"There's no evidence I would've drowned."

"There's evidence I saved you from an alligator."

"*I'm* the one who strapped him!"

"*I'm* the one who wrestled the damn thing!"

Okay, that's sort of true. So is the whole saved-me-from-drowning thing.

And yes, I do secretly believe Liam Taggert is a superhero.

But I'm annoyed and embarrassed and he just looks so freaking *good,* damn it! Like he came over here just to show me what I'm missing.

"Like I need any reminders," I snap.

"What?"

"For Pete's sake, *I get it,* okay? You're good and brave and sexy and perfect and *I'm* the idiot who screwed up and will regret losing you for the rest of my life!" I grab the door. "Message received! Thanks for dropping by!"

I swing the door closed.

Liam slaps his hand against it, keeping it open. "Mollie."

Oh good grief. Just hearing him say my name has me tingling. How pathetic is *that?* Gah!

"Look," I tell him. "Just because I'm staying in Pitchette doesn't mean things need to be awkward."

He lifts an eyebrow. "What?"

"I mean, Pitchette's a reasonably sized town—"

"So you're really staying?"

"—and okay, maybe it's not *that* big, but we can map out boundaries!"

"Mollie."

"Like I'll stick to the east end of town and you can have the west end. No wait, that doesn't work. The fire station is on the east end."

"Hey, you!"

"Jess' studio is also on the west end, and I'm sort of working out of there right now. Crap. Okay, new plan. North and south."

"Yo Mark Cuban!"

"Of course, I definitely need access to the cemetery to visit Mom. You have family there, too, right? Maybe we can plan alternating weekends with that."

"Geezus, woman."

"Okay, alternating months, then."

"You're a nut." He pushes inside, slams the door, and drops his bag.

"The *point is* this doesn't have to be weird."

"You're right."

"And if we plan carefully—"

"Shut up."

He kisses me.

As in *full-body* kisses me.

As in head-pulled-back, tongue-down-the-throat, hands-up-the-shirt kisses me.

Like I'm the only thing he's been thinking about for the last two weeks.

"Geezus, Maris, I've missed you," he groans into my neck.

"Really?"

"*Really* really, baby."

"Because I haven't seen you in fourteen days." Which is 336 hours. Or 20,160 minutes.

"I know. But I *knew* you wouldn't just leave."

"You did?" Because *I* didn't. I mean, not at first, anyway.

He tilts my head back to look into my eyes. “I knew you wouldn’t leave *me.* Not after what you said on the bridge.”

Crap. What did I say? “Was it the, um. The ‘I love you’ thing?” Because that’s a pretty big thing for me. And the only time I told him, I was angry, sweaty, and totally freaked out.

“No.” He gives me his you’re-a-nut smile. “It was the family thing.”

I frown. “Um. You mean all the stuff I said about never really being part of a family and being super insecure about being part of one now?”

“Yeah.”

“Well, great. That’s just great.”

“Baby, it *was* great.” He drags his thumb over my lower lip. “It was you trusting me. Wanting to talk to me. About anything.”

Yeah. Like my deepest, darkest, most humiliating fears. “You found my Stanley.”

He cups my cheek. “I’m sorry it’s ruined.”

“You had Tanner drop it by. I thought that meant you didn’t want to see me.”

“The *only* thing I wanted was to see you. But I needed you to come to me.” He leans his forehead against mine. “I *hoped* you’d come to me. I wanted to give you space to figure this out. And I tried to be patient, but I can’t take it anymore. You broke me, Maris. I’m shattered.”

Shattered? “Aw, come on, Taggert. Don’t tell me you *caved.*”

“Yes,” he whispers. “I caved. And I will cave as many times as it takes to have you in my life, Mollie Maris.”

I swallow. “I’m scared, Liam.”

“I know, baby.” His eyes burn into mine. “So am I.”

“And I *want* to figure this out, too. *With* you.” My breath hitches. “I love you.”

I moan when he kisses me, tongues tangling, teeth sinking into flesh.

We come up for air in the middle of my bedroom.

I pant and blink. "How the heck did we get up here?"

"You yelled, 'Take me upstairs, damn it!'"

"Geez. Really? Did I black out?" That's super unsexy.

"I don't think so." Liam's lips twitch. "You were pretty responsive when I hauled you over my shoulder and carried you up the stairs."

"Oh, yeah." I remember that. That was *hot*. "Where's my tank-top?"

"Downstairs." He yanks down my shorts. "Where you ripped it off."

"Geez. What about my bra?"

He smiles lazily. "You weren't wearing one."

For Pete's sake, what am I? A nymphomaniac? All he has to do is show up and kiss me and I jump into bed? How embarrassing.

Of course, I guess I'm not *that* embarrassed, because we're still yanking off clothes and heading for the bed. I'm almost completely over my humiliation when Liam suddenly pulls back.

"What's wrong?" I'm naked and all sprawled out.

"I forgot."

"What?"

He rolls off me and leaves.

"I—what?" What? What's happening?

Did Liam Freaking Taggert just leave mid-coitus? Not even *mid!* More like pre-*pre*-mid! For Pete's sake! Is this some sort of twisted, masterminded retribution for Chops? Get me totally naked and ready and then just walk away, leaving me totally mortified? Is he really still *that* mad? Geez, how long does it take to get over a little alligator bite?

He reappears as I sit up.

"What's the matter with you?" I demand. "You were just going to leave me?"

He frowns. "What? Of course not. What are you talking about?"

Okay. So I'm a little paranoid.

He pushes me back down, then climbs onto the bed and straddles my hips. One hand behind his back, the other resting on his thigh. Beautiful as always. Gloriously naked. Tan everywhere. Well, *almost* everywhere. The area where he isn't tan is mostly dusky reddish purple right now. Which is even better.

I bite my lip and run my eyes all over him. "I don't understand."

"What, baby?"

"Why God gave you so much and others got so little." I meet his gaze. "I don't understand, but I'm still going to appreciate the hell out of His fine work."

"Good. This fine work was made just for you."

That sends so many ripples of pleasure through me, I visibly shiver. "How do you know?"

I'll be honest. It seems really unlikely that I, Mollie Maris, Pitchette High graduate slash former marketing associate slash unemployed thirty-three-year-old, ends up with Liam Taggert, Boy Scout slash war hero slash hot-as-hell Mr. July.

I mean, let's face it. In my life, Fate is a paralyzed introvert and Luck is a raging bitch.

"Because, baby." Liam strokes his hand up my leg. "I know exactly what you want."

"Ha! That's funny." How can he possibly know what I want? *I'm* just now figuring out what I want.

Liam smiles. Not his lazy smile. Not his you're-a-nut smile. Not his I-want-to-strangle-you smile.

This one is new and evil and delicious.

"What?" I demand. "I swear to goodness, if you tell me this is just a quickie because you have to leave for a shift—"

He pulls a can of whipped cream out from behind his back.

"Holy shit." I stare. "You *do* know exactly what I want."

"Yeah." He leans over me, planting a hand next to my head, positioning the nozzle over a *very* interesting spot. "You're a nut, Mollie Maris, but you can't fool me. I know everything that goes on in that wild head of yours."

I smile.

Liam stiffens. "Uh-oh."

Abracadabra and *he's* on the bottom and *I'm* on the top. Thank you, Judoka Jess.

His gapes up at me. "What the hell?"

I catch his ribcage between my knees. His cheeks flush and he groans as I move my hips back and forth, getting comfortable. I lean forward to grab the whip can and the tip of my breast brushes his jaw.

He makes a noise in his throat and flicks his tongue out to catch my nipple. "Okay, baby." He squeezes my ass. "Good call. I like this way a *lot* better."

"You do know I can't be doing this *all* the time, right?" Although I really, really, *REALLY* want to. "I have a new business to get off the ground."

He moans and clutches my hips. "How is the department calendar coming?"

So he *does* know about that.

"I've already got it covered." I bite his neck. "So to speak."

He freezes under me. "No."

"Oh, yes." I sit back on his thighs, shaking the whipped cream canister. "In fact, I've even got your caption written."

His eyes widen. "*No,* Mollie! The snake was bad enough!"

"Oh, babe." I grin and tip the canister upside down. "We can do better."

He sucks in short, sharp breaths as I whip him on some carefully selected areas.

"What's the caption?" His voice comes out strangled.

I toss the canister on the floor and use the tip of my finger to wipe a spot of whip off his rock-solid navel.

"You'll have to wait and buy next year's edition." I hold the dollop to his lips. "Lick it."

Thank you for reading ***Good As It Gets!*** If you're inclined, please consider taking a second to leave a review on Goodreads, Barnes & Noble, or Amazon!

And as a special thank you, here's a sneak peek at Book 3 of *The Directory Series*…

THE KEEPER

Nico Gatti is a man of many names. These days, he's answering to 'Father Dom.' Impersonating a priest is just one of the ex-operative's top secret skills. He'll do anything to take down the Directory. Even if it means posing as a Keeper.

A Keeper is exactly what Celia Cruz needs. Between a family death, a newborn, and a sick mother, she's barely keeping it together. Police detective Alita Perkins promised to help Celia get back on her feet. But it's Alita's brother Syd who ends up facing down the Long Beach gangster who's stalking her.

As a doctor at Beloved Heart Hospital, Syd Perkins is no stranger to playing the hero. But 'hero' gets a new meaning when he finds himself in the middle of Long Beach's evil underbelly.

***

The ridges of the Corten steel shipping container still held heat from the day. Nico felt the warmth through his glove as he planted his left hand on the top of the container and sprawled silently. The feet of the bipod supporting the barrel of his long range rifle fitted into the steel grooves. Beneath the poly-cotton blend of his tactical ware, his muscles welcomed the position. Laying prone with a rifle notched against his shoulder felt familiar. Simple.

Nico brought his cheek against the rifle stock, letting it take the full weight of his head. He released his breath and closed his eyes. Checked for any tension in his neck and shoulders. Any cramping that might pull his shot off its mark.

Enemy fire shattered the night air. Shouts followed, echoing off the stacks of shipping containers.

Nico opened his eyes. The operative appeared in his scope, a little off-center in the scope shadow. He shifted and replanted his head for a better position. The lines of the reticle settled on the figure about 90 meters away.

The shooter's unbraced stance and improper location screamed amateur.

But the Directory didn't deploy sharpshooters to cover up its mistakes.

Nico exhaled slowly.

Then he squeezed off a shot.

The Keeper, coming to shelves soon!
Visit **www.samanthabeal.com** for release dates and details.

FROM THE **AUTHOR**

I turned thirty in September of 2025. In May of 2025, I began having dreams about this book. I'm not talking about cute, I-dream-of-being-a-romcom-author dreams. I mean *actual,* wake-me-up-at-night dreams. Whole scenes came out when I should have been sleeping. For about a week, I'd wake up, shuffle to my computer, and type them out.

I wrote the first draft for GOOD AS IT GETS in roughly twenty-eight days.

Now that I've put distance between myself and that first draft, I can identify most of what inspired this book. My childhood in Western PA. Coming from an out-of-state family. Going to school in Northern Appalachia. Making friends with kids whose last names are on street signs or maps or charters. If you haven't lived a small town life, that may not mean anything to you. If you have, you get it.

I never intended to write a romcom.

Maybe this *isn't* a romcom. Maybe this is a memoir. Maybe this is an autobiography. Maybe this is a testament. Because a lot of this book is truth.

I never intended to write it.

It wanted to be written.

When you wake up seven days in a row and write about 10,000 words, it's not *you* writing. It's the Muse.

This isn't the Great American Novel. This isn't my *magnum opus.* (Although peaking at thirty would be funny as hell. Right, God?) But this book is *something.* It's pivotal. For me.

I won't remind you what they say about villages.

Because that's what it's taken for GOOD AS IT GETS to reach this moment.

I'm grateful. So, so grateful.

For my beta readers: Mom, Dad, Adela Santana, Vicky Harak, Kathleen Welsch, and Annette Rosati.

For my expert contacts: Chuck Bartley and Jennifer Youn.

For everyone who understands what "slippy" means. And "crick" and "jagoff" and "iggle."

For everyone who's loved and supported me along the way. *That* list is far longer than I deserve.

For you, my readers.

Most of all, for you.

xxoo,
S.

P.S. Yes, people do dump alligators and other non-native creatures in rivers in Pennsylvania. During my news days, I one time had the pleasure of reporting about a pacu that washed up on the bank of a local lake.

ABOUT THE AUTHOR

SAMANTHA BEAL was born in Oklahoma and grew up in Western Pennsylvania. After a nearly 10-year career as a reporter, she walked out of the newsroom and refused to look back. A self-diagnosed "recovering journalist," Samm is (probably) hard at work plotting her next novel.

Visit her at: **www.samanthabeal.com**

<u>Let's connect!</u>
Facebook: @sammbauthor
Instagram: @sammbwrites
TikTok: @sammbtok
And find me as a Goodreads author!

www.ingramcontent.com/pod-product-compliance
Lightning Source LLC
LaVergne TN
LVHW100505110826
845146LV00002B/521

* 9 7 9 8 9 9 3 7 8 0 3 1 3 *